ALONE WITH GLORY

It is 1808 and Napoleon commands ma
in the process of conquering Spain and l
Emperor's jigsaw. The British send help.
Napoleon himself, backed by a huge army
bravely decides to head into Spain and face

_..oore

Two of Moore's officers on this campaign are the half-brothers Tom
Herryck and Robert Blunt – the one a Royal Engineer, the other an
experienced light infantry officer. Different kinds of men, but fiercely loyal
to the army and to one another, these two become caught up in the gripping
events that lead to the excitement – and tragedy – of Corunna.

The story is the first in the *Ties of Blood* series which will follow the
adventures of a colourful cast of characters, both real and imagined, through
the gripping drama of the Peninsular War – featuring sieges and battles, love
and death, honour and betrayal – a continuing drama which would take its
final curtain some seven years later, on the bloody fields of Waterloo.

Peter Youds was born in Cheshire and was educated in that county. His
early career involved the law, newspapers and the theatre. He settled into life
on the fringes of the entertainment business, where he remains. From two
generations of professional golfers, he is an enthusiastic amateur tennis
player. He is married and lives in Nottinghamshire.

Hope you enjoy it.
Best Wishes,
Peter Young.

ALONE
WITH
GLORY
Ties of Blood: 1

Peter Youds

BICORN

First published in 2008
Bicorn Books
38 Long Acre
Bingham
Nottinghamshire
NG13 8AH

www.bicorn.co.uk

for Helen

PORTUGAL and SPAIN, 1808

By the spring of 1808 the French were masters of Europe. Napoleon had comprehensively defeated Austria and Prussia and had made a treaty with the Tsar dividing the continent into French and Russian spheres of influence. Only Britain, with its massive sea power but comparatively puny army, stood against him.

Napoleon hoped to undermine his enemy by preventing it from trading with continental Europe and by rapidly building up a powerful navy of his own. He would absorb the fleets of neutral Denmark and Portugal and initiate a massive domestic shipbuilding programme. But the plan didn't work – the Royal Navy seized the Danish fleet at Copenhagen and the Portuguese sailed away from Lisbon, just a day before General Junot's army arrived there.

As part of his plan to subdue Portugal, Napoleon had signed the Treaty of Fontainebleau with Spain, enabling him to push troops over the Pyrenees, supposedly to protect communications with Junot. But soon the border fortresses were occupied and eventually the French took Madrid itself. Napoleon then persuaded the Spanish Royal Family to abdicate in favour of his own brother, Joseph.

But the ordinary Spanish people had other ideas. On the 2nd of May 1808 there was a revolt in Madrid, brutally suppressed, but inspiring popular uprisings all over the country. Regional councils, or Juntas, attempted to co-ordinate the resistance and looked for outside help.

This was the chance the British had been looking for – the opportunity to land an army on the continent to fight a sustained campaign against the French. The Iberian Peninsula was ideal – it had deep-water ports like Cadiz, Lisbon and Corunna for the Royal Navy to supply the expeditionary force, but the interior was mountainous and poor, with few good roads or navigable rivers, making life difficult for the big French armies.

By chance, an army had been assembled at Cork, intended for a South American adventure. Instead, this small force was now to be assigned to the promising young general Sir Arthur Wellesley and sent to Portugal to confront Junot. The drama of the Peninsular War was about to begin.

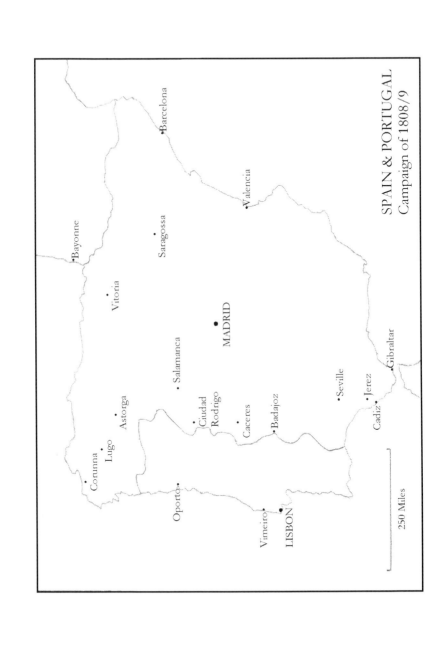

SPAIN & PORTUGAL
Campaign of 1808/9

Barcelona

Valencia

Bayonne

Saragossa

Vitoria

MADRID

Salamanca

Gibraltar

Seville

Jerez

Astorga

Ciudad
Rodrigo

Caceres

Badajoz

Cadiz

Corunna

Lugo

Oporto

Vimeiro

LISBON

250 Miles

Old Castile, Spain, November 1808

There was a sharp, ringing noise as the ball hit the rock in front of him and dropped flattened and harmless into the snow.

'Not bad,' he said to himself.

No, not bad practice at all, to get that close to hitting him at best part of a hundred yards with nothing better than some sort of fancy long-barrelled musket. It was good shooting; but the tiny wisp of smoke had given away the man's position. Now the Englishman looked across for his mate, spotted him crouched in the snow forty yards to his right, completely still, hidden from the enemy by a fallen tree. He had his rifle balanced on the trunk, nice and steady, ready to pick his shot. He glanced back, gave the slightest nod of acknowledgement to his officer and put his eye to the sight.

The Englishman looked to his front again, concentrating. There were still two of the Spaniards left, two of nine who had started out hunting them, but who were now the prey. It had taken days it seemed, scrabbling about there in those bleak, desolate hills in the freezing rain, waiting for them to make their mistakes. But the two redcoat soldiers were trained for this, knew how to out-think and out-manoeuvre an enemy in open ground. And the others weren't real soldiers, not trained fighters, so they didn't know the value of patience and eventually they had made those little errors, one by one paying with their lives. So just two left now – proud and dangerous men turned fugitive – but he knew that only one of this last pair had a musket. That still made him a danger, so he must be dealt with.

It was a strange way to be fighting a war, he thought, stalking your supposed allies, miles from anywhere. He had come to Spain to fight the French, not fools who had nothing better to do than try to kill the friends of their country. But he was there to do his duty, whatever that took; and at present he believed his duty, both to King George and to himself, was to make certain he stayed alive.

Another shot, the ball slapping useless into the churned snow three feet to the right of him. He counted the seconds it would take the man to reload. He was quite quick, this one, for an amateur, a foreigner – bite the cartridge, prime the pan, powder, wadding and ball, ram it down, cock and present – twenty seven or twenty eight seconds he generally managed. Not as fast as the routine speed of a trained British infantryman, of course, but not so bad at all.

At exactly twenty five seconds he made his move; he came to his feet and, crouching low, went left. He saw the musket barrel come jerking up to follow his run – and heard the familiar crack of the rifle to his right. He straightened now and kept going, ignoring the pain from his wound, not bothering with the musket-man, knowing he was dead or certainly taken out of the fight. It was the other one he wanted – the Spanish traitor who had ordered their deaths.

Sure enough, he came out of the cover of the rock – hat long gone, boots split, his elegant white and gold coat torn now and as grubby as the snow at his feet. This was their captain, the one who had led this band of dangerous gentlemen-renegades in their bid to discredit their country. This was the one who had wanted the two redcoats dead. But he was no more than a cornered animal now; he knew he was finished and there was a visceral look of cold fury on his face. He held a pistol, a gentleman's pocket piece, little more than a toy; it would not save him but still he levelled it and fired at the Englishman coming at him – fired and missed. He threw the weapon down with a curse, thought of running.

But where would he run? Where in that barren landscape – with eight of his men dead now on the cold ground – where could he go to escape these English devils? It was hopeless. The man he had tried so hard to kill was walking slowly towards him. He had no wish to dignify the fellow by looking at him, but found he couldn't help but examine this irksome, tenacious enemy: he saw a man whose face was covered with filth and powder stains, who had taken a cut to his arm when they had tried to take them in a desperate night ambush, his faded red coat slashed down the sleeve. The Spaniard cursed his luck that the sabre had not cut more true. His band had still been six then, shouting with triumph as they fell on the enemy camp at dead of night. But the foreigners had been waiting, the two English brutal and grimly efficient in the dark. Weapons fired, they had kept together, working silently with blade and rifle butt, grunting like beasts and fighting for their lives as if they had ten hands each and eyes that saw in the dark. Then the Spaniards were down to four, had needed to run back into the night like whipped dogs and regroup for their next doomed attack...

He realised that the Englishman had stopped, was simply looking at him, unbothered by the bitter wind and frozen rain. An ugly brute, he just stared, as if he had the impertinence somehow to be measuring him, to be trying to fathom his purpose. As if so gross a specimen might understand a fraction of the matters which weighed so heavily for Spain! He saw that the other one, the servant, was also coming out from his cover now. God's blood, he had even lit his pipe – as cool as you like! The Spaniard was beside himself in his impotent rage, but he would not show it. His feelings were his own, but the bitterness of defeat was difficult to contain. He was still finding it hard to credit what had happened. How could his elegant design have been so completely ruined in these barren hills? He swore – swore again to all that was holy – made his sacred oath that he would have his day with this one, this stubborn, interfering Britisher. God would grant him that, would give him his moment with this murderous heretic – and then he would kill him. But not on this day; this day it was the Englishman who had won.

For his part, the redcoat officer was relieved, simply glad that it was over. It had been a hard challenge, this chase, a sideshow he could have done without. He was tired and hungry, his clothes sodden wet; his arm throbbed and ached, his lips were cracked and blistered. Bringing this dangerous Spaniard to heel had pushed him to the limits. But he knew it had been necessary work – and this particular game had finally been brought to a satisfactory conclusion. He had done his job and he had kept himself alive for King George. Now he could go back where he belonged and get on with the real war.

Chapter One

Tom Herryck was proud of his uniform. As a lieutenant of the Royal Engineers serving in the red-coated British army, it was certainly distinctive – short blue jacket, white waistcoat, crimson sash, white breeches, knee boots and black cocked hat – but if it was elegant enough, it was not the most practical wear for the intense heat of late afternoon in the height of the Andalucian summer. Cadiz was reputed to be the oldest living city in Europe and, as Tom explored, he had discovered it to be both exotic and intriguing. But to a young Englishman who had passed his last few months in the gentle warmth of a Kentish summer, above all it was very, very hot.

Tom had wandered along the waterfront, passing open squares and well-tended gardens, admiring the fine churches and handsome public buildings. He hadn't a word of Spanish, so the street-seller's insistent cries of "Hay dulces buenos!" or "Zumo fresco" meant little to him, but he eagerly drew in the sounds, together with the smell of the raw sea and the sweet beguiling scent of bougainvillea and oranges. He could feel the sweat running down his neck and back and he envied the street urchins their loose, baggy shirts and bare feet. Yes, a town fifteen hundred miles south of London that had lizards sporting in the flower beds, as well as a grand theatre playing "School for Scandal", was far too singular an experience for a twenty five year-old with an enquiring mind to fail to enjoy. Yet a leisured examination of this fine old city was the last thing Tom might have imagined when he sailed from England. He had not come to the Mediterranean for sight-seeing.

Tom had landed at Gibraltar three days previously, with orders to join Sir Brent Spencer's expeditionary force of 5,000 men. But he found that General Spencer's command had lately departed for Portugal to join the new army being put together there under Sir Arthur Wellesley and he was told that he must wait for fresh orders. Nobody seemed quite certain what to do with a displaced Royal Engineer lieutenant. Technically Tom Herryck – like all engineers and artillerymen – belonged not to the army command at Horse Guards but to the Master-General of Ordnance. The Ordnance Corps maintained a completely separate establishment from the general army, with its own medical department, paymaster and transport, all of it financed by a parliamentary grant independent from the rest of the military. Wide-ranging responsibilities for the Ordnance included such specifics as supervision of defence works, maintaining barracks and military prisons, mapping and even supervising the Royal Carriage Works!

The Royal Engineers were different...Tom Herryck rather liked that.

At Woolwich Military Academy he had learned everything from chemistry and mathematics to fencing and dancing. They had also laboured to hammer some knowledge of the French tongue into him. He had often thought it ironic that an organisation devoted to confounding France and the French had most of its terminology in the language of that nation. It further amused him that a man such as himself, who struggled horribly with all foreign tongues, should all too readily grasp the essence of demi-lunes, tablettes and orillons. But for all his potential to build or destroy bridges, map fortifications or design siege works, Tom was well aware that his most natural gift was simply for recording what he saw before him on paper. His sketching was a useful professional skill, but it also afforded him an enjoyable pastime. And stuck there on the rock, he had the opportunity to take a good look about him and to draw to his heart's content.

His room at The Three Anchors was perfectly comfortable, the food decent enough, and a compliant, black-eyed young chambermaid called Josefina the perfect antidote to having spent more than a fortnight at sea. Yet two days examining Gibraltar – admittedly exotic, boasting splendid fortifications for the young professional to admire, but undeniably British in its essence – proved more than enough and Tom was ready to see something else. It was, as he reasoned, one of his vocational duties to observe. With no prospect of hearing back from Lisbon for a couple of days at least, he had obtained permission to make the short sea journey up the coast to the Spanish mainland, to see what he could find in the famous port of Cadiz.

The artist-officer was captivated. While there was certainly a share of the black-clad old women and shuffling, sunken-eyed beggars he had been told to expect anywhere in Spain, he found that Cadiz was populated for the most part by healthy, good-looking people. The younger ladies, in particular, looked extraordinary to Tom, who was naturally charmed and fascinated by their pitch-black hair and dark good looks, their ornate and beautiful clothes and extravagantly coiffed hair. One or two of them looked curiously at the tall, blond Englishman, quick glances from dark eyes over their wafting fans, but none returned his smiles. Tom didn't mind. He still found them utterly charming. He wished he might have more time in the city, perhaps finding a way of communicating with one or two of these beauties, but he realised that he must content himself with his drawing. The alluring senoritas would no doubt still be there the next time he visited.

But strangely, if the elegant young ladies of Cadiz were undeniably magnificent of looks and dress, far more numerous and no less extraordinary were the men. The city appeared to be full almost to bursting with young army officers, all of them dressed in different uniforms, each seeming to wish to outdo the next in the richness and outlandishness of his costume. No tall hat was complete without ostrich feathers, no coat could have enough braid or buttons, no boot dare be untasselled. The sound of their conversation and laughter filled every square and garden. Cadiz appeared to be like a cross between Vauxhall Gardens en fête and the most spectacular of military reviews. Tom Herryck thought it quite magnificent.

But now it was most definitely time for him to find a drink: his water bottle was long since empty. He had somehow contrived to find himself thirsty in one of the shabbier, less well-populated areas of the city. But with a simple logic Tom reasoned that everyone needed to drink. He looked down the length of the next narrow street and saw what appeared to be a sign hanging above a doorway. This proved to say nothing more informative than "Casa Raul" but, although he knew no Spanish whatsoever, Tom did recognize the familiar low tones of men talking over their drinks and he went inside, determined to find refreshment.

It was little more than a drinking cave. He found that he was staring into a long, gloomy room, dimly lit by a few candles, with a counter running down one side. The wall behind the counter was lined floor to ceiling with barrels and from the ceiling itself dozens of whole hams hung from the blackened beams, as if they had been there as long as the building had. A stout, red-faced man in a grubby apron, very possibly the Raul of the signboard, was at the far end of the counter, talking lethargically to a couple of grey-bearded old characters who leaned there smoking their pipes, half-listening to what he had to say. Tom saw that a number of tables at the far end were occupied by groups of younger, more active-looking fellows sitting on half-barrels, all of them appearing to be examining him carefully through the smoke and gloom. But Tom had been in too many country inns to be bothered by such a welcome and, besides, he was thirsty. He put his coin on the counter and called for wine, using the English word, as he knew no other.

Without waiting to see if he had been heard, he turned and took possession of a table and stool halfway down the room. It was bliss to take the weight off his feet. As he placed his hat and satchel down and took off his sword belt, he saw the landlord coming around the end of the counter with a pitcher and cup and a small dish of what proved on close, suspicious examination, to be pieces of ham. He nodded his thanks to the man, who in turn eyed him with no great kindness, before shuffling off without a word. Tom didn't care, he was just glad of some kind of refreshment at last. He discovered that the meat was far tastier than promised by the dry-looking joints hanging from the beams, if a little salty, and the harsh, dusty wine was at least wet.

The low hubbub of conversation gradually picked up again. A tavern was, after all, a place to drink and talk. Tom imagined that one more soldier in a city teeming with them would be of no lasting curiosity to the locals. He too began too feel more relaxed after a cup of wine and a bite and was soon looking around the room. The men at the far end could be anything – soldiers, sailors, fishermen, workmen, peasants – but there were certainly some wonderful faces. All of them were much darker of complexion and hair colouring than he was used to at home, of course, but these men were also much different from the dandified officers he had seen elsewhere in the city. They were a rough crew, for sure – dour, rugged and vicious-looking. Many of them had magnificent moustaches or beards and a couple of them had eye patches, while one even wore a hook to replace a lost hand. Their clothing was for the most part rudimentary – tunics, loose-fitting pants and sandals – but there were some tasselled caps and wide brimmed straw hats, some wore colourful sashes or cross belts and one or two wore battered leather boots. A finer band of corsairs he could not hope to find. He was soon busy with the sketch-book.

He was concentrating so intently that he was slow to realise that a man was now standing alongside him – was, if fact, leaning down towards him and hissing a word, presumably a Spanish word, uncomfortably close to his face. He was a big brute, with greasy hair, a pock-marked complexion and eyes pink where the whites should have been. Tom could smell the man's meals of many days previous and he felt his nose wrinkle with distaste, but he looked back at the fellow calmly enough and gave him a little smile and a shrug to let him know he didn't understand. Not budging an inch, the man simply repeated the word, which began with an "F" sound and then tailed off in some angry vowels. The whole room was quiet now and everybody seemed to be observing the scene with undisguised interest. He realised that they were waiting for his move.

This wasn't good; the young officer recognized that he was in something of a fix. It would be unfortunate to get drawn into a tavern brawl in the city of an ally, particularly when the odds were likely to be unsporting, but it looked as if he had little choice. If it was to be a mill, he was confident he could knock the fellow down. If it got truly nasty then he had his boot knife and his sword was to hand. He lay down his sketch-book, his eyes fixed on his opponent, and was thinking about pushing back his seat to give himself room when the big man himself straightened up. He nodded down at Tom, offering an unpleasant gap-toothed smile and snarled the same word again, as he reached slowly behind him to pull out an unpleasant looking long-bladed knife. There was no longer any possibility of misunderstanding, now it was time for action. Tom dropped his hand to the top of his boot and tensed to spring, when a deafeningly loud bang caused everything to stop.

Everyone, Tom included, was looking now towards the street entrance. Sitting at a table just inside the door was a man he hadn't noticed when he came in. He noticed him now, as he was holding a gently smoking pistol pointing up at the ceiling, while its brother was sighted unwaveringly at Tom's large friend.

The man in the corner snapped some kind of command in rapid fire Spanish. The big man, who looked very uncomfortable indeed, shrugged and made to utter a reply but was cut short by another curt volley of words. Tom was soon sitting alone again.

'Now you, sir,' said the man in the corner in good, very slightly accented English. 'Might I suggest that you gather your belongings and do me the goodness of joining me at my table here? I believe I can promise you a cup of wine superior to that you have been tasting.'

'You are very kind,' Tom said, already picking up his things. He was all too happy to keep company with a man who had better wine and a brace of pistols.

'Forgive me if I remain seated and do not greet you correctly, but it will remind those people there that they still have my attention. My name is Carlos Federico Rivero y Castro.'

'I am pleased to meet you, sir.' Tom bowed and said his name. He took the proffered seat, glancing over his shoulder at the men further down the room. 'Are they likely to inconvenience us?' he asked, as he sat.

The man gave a thin smile. 'No, Lieutenant. They are of no consequence, just some of the rabble that has been drawn here by the war. They are mostly brigands and cowards. However, you should perhaps know that the man who accosted you thought that you were a Frenchman, from your blue uniform. Possibly he believed that you were a spy or had escaped from the prison hulks in the harbour.'

Tom failed to hide his surprise that he could be thought to belong to the enemy, there in Cadiz. 'Prison hulks?'

'Just so. Many thousands of French have been brought here as prisoner over the last few weeks,' Rivero explained. 'They were supposed to have been sent home under treaty, but they have instead been placed in confinement in the old ships. Some of the locals are nervous of their possible escape. Please, I beg you will try some wine.'

Tom was happy to oblige, 'Thank you. You're right; this is a precious good tap, infinitely better than the poor stuff I was drinking over yonder. It is quite delicious, but not a flavour I recognize.'

Rivero slowly uncocked the pistol and lay it alongside its brother on the table, clearly judging any immediate danger to be at an end. He took a sip from his own wine cup. 'This? It is fino from Jerez, a few leagues from here. Sherry wine you might call it in your own country. Those who produce it say it is the finest in the world.'

'Are you yourself from Jerez, Senor Rivero Castro?'

Rivero gave a little shake of the head. 'No, I am like you, a long way from my home. I am from Galicia, in the far northwest of this land.'

Tom made a guess at the distance, not all that far short of a thousand miles. 'You certainly are a long way from home. Are you serving in the army?' Tom looked at the man's clothing. He wore a simple brown jacket and trousers, elegantly piped with fine braid, with good quality, if rather worn, riding boots.

Again, the thin smile; Rivero was lighter-skinned than many of the men Tom had seen about Cadiz, but his hair was very black, with just a few flecks of grey above the temples and he had a neatly clipped moustache under a long, tapering nose. Even when he smiled his dark eyes remained solemn. 'Happily not, Lieutenant. It has been my honour to travel to Andalucia with the representatives of the Galician Junta, as an attempt has been made here to unite the regions of Spain against the French.'

'Junta?'

'The governing body, if you will. Each of our large cities or regions, such as my own, say, or Asturias, Seville or Valencia has its junta and each of them thinks itself the most important in all Spain.'

'Were you successful in your mission?' Tom sipped again at the wine, which was cool, sharp and refreshing.

Rivero made a dismissive gesture, a sour look on his face, as if the prospect was absurd. 'Of course not. No, this is Spain, Lieutenant Herryck, a nation whose glory faded two centuries ago, but which remains a great power solely in the imaginations of its rulers. Mine was no more than a fool's errand, I regret to say. There was little real possibility of reaching an accord of any true value. The juntas are selfish and divided, you see, and each looks only to its own local interests. Even now, in the face of Bonaparte's worst outrages, they will not act.'

The young Englishman was interested, if surprised, by the Spaniard's candour. The very reason Tom was there was because of the French occupation of northern and central Spain six months earlier, skilfully concealed by Napoleon as an innocent operation of "allies" of Spain, as both nations had at the time been at war with Portugal. These allies from France had flooded in great numbers across the Pyrenees and had garrisoned several important northern fortresses, then Napoleon's brother Joseph had arrived in Madrid to proclaim himself Spain's new monarch. Only then had the locals at last realised the French plan was to wholly occupy the Peninsula. The British government, long the friend of the Portuguese, but now pleased to find another potential ally right on France's border, was pledged to support the Spanish in removing Napoleon's armies from the Peninsula.

Tom was all too keen to get the full picture, or at least learn as much as he was able, so this Rico was quite a find. 'But surely there have been successes for you against the French invasion? In England, before I sailed, I heard about the Spanish uprisings in May – in Madrid and elsewhere.'

'Dos de mayo? Yes, the people rose against the French occupation of the capital, sure enough – and the result was five hundred Madrillenos killed. They say the French executed men for owning a pair of scissors. It was a bloodbath, but it stirred the nation at last. Then there were riots all over the country. It could, should, have been the beginning. The people here are slow to anger, Lieutenant, but they will not stand for occupation. Dos de mayo gave us an opportunity. But each action in each city was separate and nothing was achieved, nothing but for some sad and useless bloodshed.'

Tom was by now almost desperate to find some good news for Spain. 'But your army, your regular army, has now taken to the field.'

Rivero shook his head gloomily, clearly not to be consoled, even by this. 'Many Spanish armies have taken to the field and almost all of them have already been roundly beaten by Bonaparte's marshals.' He gave an apologetic shrug, a regretful smile. 'Forgive me if I do not sound cheerful, Lieutenant, but these are dark times for my country. It is not because the soldiers are cowards or lack stomach, it is because their generals are fools, their equipment lacking and, most crucially, we have no central command to govern their actions.'

Tom nodded, 'Which is why, I imagine, you and your junta people have been meeting – fruitlessly, as you say – but no doubt working as best they can to try to put that to rights? Surely your leaders must see that the merits of uniting against a formidable enemy such as Napoleon are plain? It is certainly no time to be at odds with your friends. But tell me,' Tom said, brightening, still trying to cheer his glum rescuer, 'I hear everywhere of the mighty Spanish victory of Bailen! Now that was great news, sir. Everyone in Gibraltar was talking of it and here, as I have moved around Cadiz, I have heard the word spoken countless times with great pride and emotion.'

'Ah, Bailen,' Rivero said the word as if it was a joke. He took a sip of wine.

'Was it not a great victory?' Tom pursued. He too took a drink of wine. He was enjoying talking to this intriguing, melancholy Spaniard and yet he was perplexed by Rivero's brutally honest view of his county's position.

He shrugged, 'It was a victory. Yes, yes. It was a blow against the invader. So it was good, yes. But you must forgive me if I say that I believe it may prove to damage Spain more than a dozen defeats.'

Tom was puzzled. 'But to defeat the French in the field – '

Rivero nodded, good-naturedly holding up his hand. 'Forgive me, please. It is clear to me we have much to discuss, Lieutenant Herryck. Finish your wine, if you will. I propose that I give myself the honour of walking back with you to your boat or your lodging and we can talk some more. But believe me, Lieutenant, you might gain little encouragement or satisfaction from my company. Discussing the shortcomings of my country's military and government is a subject that could quite easily occupy a leisurely march to Madrid and back.'

They stood, Tom buckling on his sword and Rivero carefully gathering up his pistols, casting a last dismissive glance down the room. He dropped a coin on the table and gestured politely for Tom to leave, following him out onto the street. 'So, let us take a little *paseo* and talk some more. But forgive me, my friend, I have been most uncivil. With all my prating I have shown the coarseness of my manners by not asking something of your own situation here. So, I must make amends and quiz you a little. Your blue uniform, for instance, that so intrigued those fellows. Are you then an artilleryman?'

'…so, if I have this correctly, Lieutenant, you tell me that you have no soldiers who work directly under your command, but you, as you say, you have to *borrow* some men from the infantry when you need to dig a tunnel or build a defence work?'

'That's quite right – and I promise you sir, that it makes life damn difficult for those of my service. They're lively fellows in the infantry, of course, enthusiastic and so forth, but I fear the ordinary soldier wouldn't know a gabion from a fascine.'

'I'm sure.' The Spaniard said dryly.

Tom smiled. He realised how odd the Royal Engineers' method of working must appear to the outside observer. 'Well, however rum it may be, that's how we go about our business. We are admittedly a rather strange and rare breed. In all of the British armies posted around the world there are presently less than two hundred officers of Royal Engineers, thirty or so of whom are field officers – and I assure you, Senor Rivero Castro, the last place you are likely to see any of those august gentlemen is anywhere near action in the field!'

Rivero shook his head, 'That is truly remarkable. It is such a senseless manner of conducting military affairs it could easily belong to we Spanish.'

Tom smiled again, noting with approval Rivero's dry humour. They were enjoying the cooler early evening air now, walking along the city ramparts, the sea lapping restfully below them. Tom remained impressed by Cadiz, but he was especially glad to have been adopted by this intriguing northerner with his near flawless English. If he had something of a gloomy air to him, a sadness almost, Rivero was excellent company. He was extremely knowledgeable and had a dark, mischievous sense of humour that appealed to Tom. He felt that he had learned more useful background to the political and military situation in Spain in a couple of hour's conversation with the Galician than he could have accomplished with days of studying the accounts in English newspapers.

But Tom, while paying full attention to what Rivero told him, couldn't help but gaze from time to time at the exotic evening life of Cadiz. It was quite a sight. There were even more people out strolling now – locals of all ages and classes and seemingly hundred upon hundred of army officers, all of them still appearing to Tom to be wearing different, if always colourful and elegantly cut, uniforms. These soldiers all seemed wonderfully pleased with themselves. Yet another group passed them, escorting a number of ladies and their chaperones. The Englishman and the civilian, hugging the wall to allow them to pass, were coolly ignored. Tom was intrigued:

'There must be countless regiments in your army to judge by all of these different uniforms?'

9

Rivero snorted derisively, 'If only that was the case! Very few of these peacocks you see strutting safe in the city walls belong to any real army. They are mostly what is called los Voluntarios Disguidos de Cadiz. It is a kind of local militia, more or less useless. Most of them would shit at the sound of a musket going off. In truth they are little more than a battalion of cupids, fit only for the kind of manoeuvres you are witnessing. It is quite laughable. Their rules are careful to forbid service outside of Cadiz, so they are safe to boast and show off their feathers. It is just another part of what I was telling you of, Lieutenant, how Spain has no chance of victory while the juntas remain divided and half of our armies perform their drills for pretty girls and their mamas.'

Tom was amused at his vehemence, 'So tell me then, with such poor clay just how did you fashion a win at Bailen?'

But even this didn't seem to console Rivero. The Spaniard seemed anything but pleased at the mention of the battle. 'Ah, Bailen, Bailen! Everyone talks of nothing but Bailen.'

Tom was surprised. 'But surely it was a great victory for Spain?'

Rivero stopped and turned towards Tom, sighing and holding up his hand in entreaty, 'Enough of Bailen, Lieutenant. Forgive me, I have no wish to be discourteous and I am sensible of your goodwill in this matter, that you should wish to praise my countrymen. That is indeed civil in you. No, it is simply that I find I am weary and also it is getting late for you to return to your inn if you wish to find your dinner.' He gave a little shrug of apology, 'I fear I must make poor company. And yet I have enjoyed our conversation very much. You are plainly a conscientious and energetic young officer who will serve his country diligently and well. So, if it will please you, I am content to place myself at your disposal tomorrow and we will talk more. I am interested in what you tell me of the workings of your British army and, if you can tolerate it, I shall tell you more of my poor country's plight. I will even tell you something of this affair of Bailen. Will that please you?'

Tom nodded, 'Very much.'

'Excellent. In that case I will do myself the honour of waiting on you by the Puerta de Tierra, the large gate down there at the entrance to the city, at nine tomorrow morning. I will arrange for horses, so that we might ride out and look at something of the country here. You English officers of engineers do ride, I take it, Lieutenant?'

*

10

Tom Herryck had, in fact, grown up around horses, enjoying from a tender age the run of his father's well-stocked stable in the good hunting country of south Nottinghamshire. He was therefore pleased to find that Rivero's own horses were fine, healthy animals – so fine that the pair had soon moved well away from the city, cantering gently along the narrow strip that connected Cadiz itself to the mainland and on into the countryside. They were following the main Seville road, in the direction of Jerez. Already, not yet mid-morning, the sun was hot in a cloudless, China-blue sky. They were into the wine country now. Tom was fascinated by the whiteness of the landscape, almost blinding under the remorseless sun, the light seeming to bounce back up from the clean, white surface of the land. His companion gestured to the neatly tended fields of vines all around them, the plants all covered with plump bunches of near-ripe fruit.

'As you see, it is almost the harvest time, the most important phase of the year here. The fields nearer to the sea on the east side of Jerez itself give the best grapes for the Fino. You get something of the salt air in the flavour of the wine. The climate here is unbearably hot for much of the year and the soil is thin, chalky stuff, but the little vine has many yards of roots which seek out what water there is to nourish the fruit. Some even say that the worse the soil, the better the vines. Certainly these fields give us magnificent wine, unlike anything else in Spain or any other vintage I have tasted. Your poet Chaucer talked of sherry wine centuries ago and the great thief Drake liked it so much he once stole three thousand barrels from the quayside at Cadiz! But even that criminality was good for sherry-makers, for El Draco sold the wine and that made it popular in your country, so that English traders were forced to begin buying it legitimately. But that is as it should be. Wine is a civilising force. Even the Moors, who are forbidden strong drink, allowed the Christian and Jew to cultivate these grapes for wine. They were clever men of business and they did well enough because they charged duty on the sale of the wine, the dogs. The sherry trade is and always has been paramount here. Everything of any importance to do with this corner of the world is concerned with wine.'

Tom was impressed by his guide's knowledge and also curious, 'For a northerner, Senor Rivero Castro, you appear to know a great deal about this part of the world.'

The Spaniard glanced back at him. 'Please call me Federico. If you wish, you may call me Rico, as my friends generally do. With the present condition of my family's affairs, I assure you that for myself to own such a name is something of a Spanish joke.'

Not a family blessed with wealth Tom guessed. He felt it wisest not to enquire into the doubtless complicated business of the Rivero Castro clan, not until he knew his new friend a little better. But he was happy they were getting along so well, delighted to have so knowledgeable a guide. 'Very well, Rico. And I would be honoured if in turn you would call me Tom.'

They nodded amiably to one another.

'But you ask of my familiarity with this place,' Rico continued after a pause. 'That is because my aunt was married to what you might call a wine merchant, who had extensive interests here in the country around Cadiz. He was, if fact, an Englishman like many involved in the wine trade here. My English uncle died some years ago, but my cousin continues the business in his father's place. These excellent horses belong to him, in fact. Each of my summers has been spent around these parts at the vendimia, or the harvest, since I was a boy. My cousin's house still buys and ships wine to England, but he also has bodegas that produce his own vintages. That is how I have some understanding of the wine-making of this region. The fact that the family is English has also assisted me to a poor knowledge of your tongue.'

'Well, that explains a lot and I tell you most frankly that I'm grateful both for your wisdom about this land and your excellent English.' Tom looked around him, still quite amazed at how completely different this landscape was to anything he had seen before. There were men working in the fields, quietly and efficiently with the practice of ages, just as they might be seen working at home in a hop field or an apple orchard. But it was so very different to England as far as Tom could tell, it might be the surface of the moon. He believed that he liked that difference, that simple foreign ness to it all. The place had a sense of being as it should be, at ease with its ancient character. The very real prospect of seeing French soldiers moving amongst those white fields, just as they had trudged remorselessly across fields all across Europe, disturbed and depressed him and he could well imagine that such an unwelcome notion must positively enrage Rico and his countrymen.

They rode on, companionably silent for a while. Aware that he must avoid causing offence to the proud Spaniard by hectoring him, Tom knew nonetheless that it was his military duty to find out all that he could about the present, as well as the past. A little more quiet, then: 'You told me yesterday, Rico, that you had travelled here with people from your junta in Galicia? There was some hope of uniting the regions of Spain?'

'A fool's errand,' Rivero snapped, the subject obviously still a sore point.

Tom allowed another pause. Yet he realised that he would be unlikely to have ready access to someone so informed on Spanish affairs once he was absorbed back into the bosom of the British army. 'Are things truly so bad?' he persisted. 'My own government has great hopes that Spain will hold against the French, you know? We are sorely in need of an ally and are more than ready to fight with you.'

Rico nodded, 'An ally that is prepared to fight with us against the French tyrant is what Spain needs above all things, but I believe we must wait a while for that kind of alliance to come about, my friend. Simply having common cause against Bonaparte will not do.'

'But I believe our administration is in earnest,' Tom protested, 'that it is committed to halting Napoleon here.'

'I am sure. Your government is indeed generous with arms and gold for the juntas, but that will not answer, I fear. The gold is put in private purses and the arms are put in citadels to gather rust. And still the juntas call out at each other and ignore the French who grow strong in Bayonne and on the Ebro. Bonaparte is biding his time – building his armies and priming his best marshals. Soon they will come again and this time it won't be the conscripts of Bailen he sends, but the veterans who have conquered all Europe.'

'But an alliance is possible, surely? General Wellesley has probably twenty thousand men in Portugal. We have also offered to land an army right here at Cadiz.'

Rico smiled, 'The memory of El Draco is still too warm in these parts for that and the memory of your new hero Lord Nelson hotter still. The juntas of Cadiz and Seville will certainly not permit an English army to march here. But they will certainly take your money.'

Tom could perfectly understand the distrust of an ally whose navy had sunk the Spanish fleet at Trafalgar less than three years earlier. But it seemed a shame that a chance was being lost to show a united front to Napoleon somewhere in the Peninsula. 'Would your own junta in the north allow an army of my countrymen to land at Corunna or Vigo?'

Rico thought about it for a moment. 'Possibly; but I regret that the Junta of Galicia is no better than the rest – indeed it is as proud, stubborn and selfish as any other. No, it is hopeless. I now realise that there is simply no true will for a united purpose amongst these vain, stupid men. The future of Spain will not be won by its government or by its army.'

'Ah, the army again,' Tom smiled, 'Forgive me Rico, but you are the only Spaniard or Englishman I have heard of who thinks your army is anything but utterly formidable and in magnificent order, quite ready to defeat Bonaparte should he venture south.'

A small smile flitted across Rico's lips. 'Time will prove who is correct, my friend, but the tragedy for Spain is that by then it will be far, far too late.'

By late morning they had reached Jerez itself, entering the walled town through a heavily fortified gate. The Seville road continued through the middle of the town and out the other side, but Rico proposed that they look around then take a meal in the town and eventually return to Cadiz, possibly by a different route, so that Tom could see something more of the country. That plan suited the Englishman well enough. Jerez was much smaller and quieter than Cadiz, but was filled with quaint little streets and squares, as well as fine churches and palaces. There were fountains and orange trees everywhere, but above all there were the bodegas – worshipping places for the sherry wine that made the town its fortune. And all of the while, as they took their leisure around the town, Rico kept up a relaxed commentary on what they were passing, on wine, on Spain and its rich history – and on the bleak prospects of success in the war against the French.

They ate in the cool of a shaded courtyard, at one of half a dozen tables belonging to a small inn, where the ostler was taking care of their fine horses. Early for the rhythm of Spanish stomachs, they had the place to themselves. Tom Herryck was an unusual Englishman in that he was content, curious even, to taste the food foreigners enjoyed in their own country and he was perfectly happy to let Rico order their meal. He was even happier when they were presented with a delicious fish and bread soup, a dish of baked eggs with potatoes and sausage and what Rico eventually convinced him was indeed a bull's tail, braised in red wine and served with local vegetables. This they washed down with the straw-coloured fino wine and finished their meal idly picking at a plate of delicate cinnamon and almond-flavoured biscuits.

'That was magnificent,' Tom said at last, fearful for the well-being of the fastenings on his breeches after such a feast. 'It was like nothing I have ever eaten before and all the more wonderful for that.'

Rico, who had lit a little paper-wrapped cigar, blew smoke and shrugged, 'It is the food of the region. It is well enough for those who live in the hot sunshine all of the year. But in my family's country, which is green and suffers true winter, we Gallegos enjoy heavier dishes, as well as feeding on the finest fruits of the Atlantic fisheries. It is good, strong food, fit to fill a man's belly. And as you, my friend, are a man who clearly enjoys to eat, I hope that I will perhaps be fortunate enough to entertain you to a fiesta, a proper feast, in my own Galicia, *free* Galicia, one day soon.'

Tom nodded his thanks for the sentiment, so handsomely expressed, while at the same time privately wondering how likely it might be that duty and Napoleon's ambitions would allow him to visit the north-west of Spain any time soon. But he wasn't going to risk spoiling the meal with any such pessimistic reflections and said with perfect honesty, 'I heartily look forward to that day, Rico. I have been amazed by what I have seen of the country thus far and long to see more. Your Galicia sounds a noble and interesting place. But for now it will be my pleasure to pay the landlord's bill for such excellent food and drink.'

Rico's expression darkened. 'No my friend, you are my guest – '

Tom held up his hand, determined to have his way. 'And you are my saviour of yesterday, at that less pleasant place in Cadiz where you shared your wine with me; and today you have been my guide and teacher. So it is *your* turn to be *my* guest. Besides, as friends, you will surely have many an opportunity to take your own turn with a bill another day, perhaps even in your own country, as you say.'

For a moment Rico looked as if he might continue the argument, might show that renowned Spanish pride and see it as a point of honour to insist, but then he slowly nodded, accepting his defeat with grace. 'Very well then, under those terms and those alone, I accept. I am pleased that you enjoyed these simple dishes and found them different to your English diet. And I am in turn grateful for the honour of your company and for your generosity.'

'The honour is mine,' Tom said with complete honesty. Besides, he suspected from what had earlier been hinted that Rico's purse was unlikely to be over-heavy. He had no such worries; he had plenty of Spanish dollars in his own pocket, even had twenty English sovereigns sewn into the soles of his boots against emergency. And besides, he had long since learned that a man's true worth could not be measured by his welcome at his banker's.

Rico nodded. 'So then, as I promised I will see it as a duty to show you a true Gallego feast in the green country. But do you know, I have once again been unforgivably discourteous. I have again been so busy telling you of my own lands and our troubles here that I have still asked you nothing of your own circumstances, of your family and of your life in England.'

And that had been exactly as Tom wished it. It had suited him perfectly well to let Rico do the talking. He felt that he had nothing in particular in his own life to hide or be ashamed of, but he truly and unaffectedly felt his own background could offer little of interest to the Galician. In particular, Tom felt he could not possibly compete with all of the drama and exoticism of everything that he was seeing and learning about Spain. But he realised that out of simple good manners some response was called for.

'Oh, as to that, you know, there is very little to tell. My father is fortunate enough to own some little land in our county of Nottinghamshire, which I am sure might rival the green of your Galicia, if not its mountains and fisheries. I had a gentle, comfortable upbringing and as sound an education as a good school could work with poor clay. I fear I was never much of a hand at Latin or Greek.' Tom gestured for the waiter to bring their reckoning. 'I am one of three sons and, with my older brother for the estate books and t'other for the clergy, I was always likely to be marked for a life in the military.' He smiled, 'And as a lad, I used to show a fondness for throwing dams across my father's trout stream or filling his copses with tree houses. So I was packed off to Military College as soon as was decent. My mother, as loving a parent as you could hope for, had formed the entirely understandable notion, you see, that an officer of Engineers might be expected to do no more than encourage the fighting soldiers with an occasional piece of Mister Vauban's elegant theory or some trifle of technical advice and would accordingly be removed from the worst dangers of the battlefield. That isn't quite how the service works, but it was a nice thought on her part. Besides, she liked the sound of the blue jackets, a favourite colour of hers.'

Rico smiled. Though not himself a soldier, he was wise enough in the ways of war to realise that those mining, sapping or laying charges in the presence of the enemy were infinitely more vulnerable to disaster than most. 'We should never underestimate the wisdom of our mothers, who always want what is right for their sons. But I am pleased at least that your father has held on to his land. I only wish that were true of my own family. The towers of our castle once overlooked the country for ten leagues in each direction that made duty to us. But generations of my forefathers have been imprudent or have failed to embrace the changing of the times. Now the towers look down only on their own decay and precious little of the land remains to us.'

'I am sorry for your distress,' Tom said.

Rico shrugged, 'It is a situation completely of our own making. We have lacked vision, failed to adapt. It is similar to the way in which all of Spain now causes its own ills.'

The mood had darkened once again, Rico back to wearing that solemn, brooding scowl. But Tom was at least saved from having to frame some kind of reply by the noise of people outside. They both looked to the archway leading to their courtyard, as the sound of raised voices and laughter preceded a party of diners arriving to join them. About a dozen men and women, all of the men in uniform, followed the waiter into the yard. They were a merry group. The men all appeared to be splendidly dressed army officers, each of their coats a completely different colour, each hat bearing different cockades. Tom was surprised as he watched and listened to them, almost sure that the men were speaking in French, but his grasp of languages was too frail to be certain. Their leader, who even looked like a Frenchman from his features, appeared to be a tall cavalry officer, gorgeously decked out in tasselled boots, heavily braided white uniform and a bicorn hat sporting several tall feathers. He made an impatient gesture for the waiter to pull alongside a couple of tables, so that they could sit together in the shade. The rest of his party waited for this to be accomplished, watching the hard-pressed waiter struggle to drag the tables across the cobbles. The girls – who appeared to Tom to be rather young countrywomen – stood giggling, one or two taking drink from pot jars they carried. A couple of the soldiers snapped at the harassed waiter to hurry as he moved around the yard gathering in chairs.

'We should leave now,' said Rico, who himself looked anything but pleased by these new arrivals. He stubbed out his cigar on the table.

'I haven't paid the bill.'

'Just leave a few coins,' the Galician said curtly.

'But how many?'

'We must go.' Rico stood, his chair scraping on the ground.

As if noticing for the first time that there was anyone else in the compact courtyard, the white-coated officer made a show of examining them, his face transforming from anger at the waiter's performance to apparent delight.

He removed his hat and made a flamboyant bow, smiling broadly. 'Don Federico, buenas tardes. Que sorpresa marivillosa a su encontrarme aqui con usted. Tiene prisionero frances?'

Rico showed no sign of sharing the man's delight at their encounter. 'Good day, Don Julian. My companion is an Englishman.'

'Ingles? Otra sorpresa.' He turned to his companions with a broad smile. 'Caballeros, tenemos aqui uno de los famosos soldados de Inglaterra. Es muy feroz, eh?'

One of the girls smiled and said, 'Es muy guapo, el extranjero,' and her friends giggled charmingly, as they looked at the Englishman. But the man called Julian lost his smile and glared at them, instantly quieting the girls while the rest of the soldiers inspected Tom coolly from under their hats.

'You might care to speak in English, Don Julian,' Rico said. 'The Lieutenant here has no Spanish – nor, I believe, any great command of French – and I know that a felicity with language is one of your many accomplishments.'

The officer, plainly suspecting the tone of voice, gave a frosty bow then turned to Tom. 'I am delighted to meet you, sir. I am Major Julian Rodrigo Duarte Vasquez. These gentlemen with me are representatives of the Spanish forces which, you may know, so recently vanquished the flower of France on the field of Bailen.' At the mention of the name, the various officers smiled and bowed. It wasn't clear whether any of them understood English, which Duarte Vasquez spoke almost as well as Rico, but the magic name of the battle was enough to cheer them. 'I trust that you have heard all about our great triumph, Lieutenant – ?'

'My name is Herryck, sir, Royal Engineers. Yes, I have been fortunate enough to hear many accounts of the Spanish victory. I give you joy of it.' Tom bowed and gestured to include the whole company. Many bows were returned.

'And were all of you gentlemen present on the field each day of the battle, er, *Major*?' Rico asked Duarte, with an arch expression.

Duarte Vasquez gave Rico a cool look, bordering on open dislike, then threw up his arms in a gesture of horrified regret.

'For my own part, it is to my eternal sadness that my duties obliged me to remain in Cadiz, playing my humble role in the defence of the city.'

Rico said nothing, but offered a thin smile.

'However, I rejoice that my esteemed comrade, Teniente Lucena Valdano here,' and a young man in a green uniform gave an expansive bow, 'had the great honour of being present alongside General Castaños himself during every glorious moment of the affair.'

Rico affected to look impressed. 'Indeed? And did you then witness all of the battle, Teniente?' He asked in Spanish.

'That was my good fortune, sir,' the young man nodded.

Rico turned back to Duarte and reverted to English. 'How odd. What Teniente Valdano achieved was most impressive. I realise, of course, that your pressing duties in the city kept you yourself from his side, Major, but it was my understanding of Castaños' dispositions that the good general commanded the conduct of the field of Bailen from the village of Andujar, some several miles from the actual battleground and removed from sight of it by some inconsiderate hills.'

Duarte, clearly used to engaging in such verbal jousting, affected exaggerated surprise. 'How odd, as you say, that you should understand that, Don

Federico, when the Teniente here has just informed us quite clearly that he had the privilege of being present at the fray.'

Rico nodded his head thoughtfully, then looked Duarte in the eye, 'How odd it is indeed, er, Major. How particularly odd this is, when – and did I omit to mention? – when I myself was attached to General Castaños' staff at Bailen and, try as I might, I fail to recollect seeing this young man at the general's side at any time during the long, very long five days of the wretched encounter.'

For the first time Duarte looked uncomfortable for a moment. Indeed Tom thought, just from the man's dark eyes, that he looked icily furious. But he wasn't long in darting back a riposte, 'How very confusing. Do I understand you then to doubt the word of my young comrade? My esteemed comrade here, who is after all a soldier and not a civilian, however exalted a civilian, such as yourself, Don Federico.'

Tom was glad that the conversation was in English because he could quite clearly see danger looming. The two Spaniards were now glaring at each other with almost open contempt. Why had Rico not told him that he had been at the battle? And what was behind this refined, unpleasant sparring? He had no idea what there was between Rico and this Duarte, but clearly there was no love whatsoever.

He spoke up before Rico could answer Duarte's deliberately provocative question, a polite smile on his face. 'And were these other distinguished gentlemen involved in the victory, did you say Major?'

'Eh?'

'Major?'

'I beg you pardon?' Duarte seemed to have to battle to take his gaze, hard and reptilian, from Rico.

'These officers,' Tom continued, as he struggled for words soft enough to diffuse the situation, 'were they too fortunate enough to be involved in your army's great success?'

'Involved? Naturally they were involved. They are my comrades in arms.'

Rico let slip a scornful laugh.

Tom gave him a look; his friend wasn't helping.

Duarte, clearly struggling to keep his composure, himself looked away for a moment to listen to something the young officer in green had said to him. He smiled and turned back to Tom.

'You must forgive my friends' lack of your language – they are, after all, merely warriors in our country's sacred cause and might not be expected to have leisure to study the tongues of distant nations. But I am bidden to ask you, Lieutenant, most humbly, if you will honour us with an opinion as to whether or not you consider that your own English army will now feel it safe to return to the shores of Andalucia?'

'Safe, Major?'

'Why, yes. There was a considerable force of your soldiers at sea, just off our coast. But your General Spencer appeared to have felt it necessary to leave for Portugal as the French arrived here. Teniente Lucena Valdano wonders if the victory of Bailen might now convince your army that it would once more be prudent to board ship in Lisbon and to come back to our protection, here in the Bay of Cadiz.'

Tom glanced over at the young officer, who looked rather pleased with himself. The girls and the other officers were quiet now, watching the exchange with some fascination.

Tom turned back to Duarte, quite understanding how Rico could so plainly dislike the man, but determined that he would remain calm and keep his temper. 'I believe the reason that General Spencer quit Andalucia was that his soldiers were required in Portugal to join a move against the French in that country. That is why he was ordered to leave here. I confess, Major, that I was myself just as disappointed to find the general was no longer here as you yourselves might have been. But, of course, your own forces coped quite admirably at Bailen without need of our assistance.'

Duarte relayed his version of what Tom had said to the young man.

Tom was surprised to feel Rico grasping his wrist. 'Softly, friend,' he whispered.

Duarte turned back, again that unconvincing smile: 'Teniente Lucena Valdano is sensible of your kind words, so valuable from an ally. And he suggests that, should your soldiers indeed now choose to return to our shores, our victorious Spanish armies would be most honoured to escort them safely north to Calais, as we shall presently undertake that trifling journey ourselves in pursuit of the tyrant Bonaparte.'

Tom bowed stiffly, feeling his patience with this tomfoolery ebbing rapidly. But he would play the game a little longer: 'That is kind of the Teniente, kind indeed. I am sure such an escort would be of great comfort to our forces. An alliance with Spain is my government's fondest desire, you know. However our General Wellesley is, as I understand it, presently committed to removing General Junot from Portugal.'

'Ah, Portugal again.'

'Indeed, sir.'

'How charmingly convenient.'

'Convenient, sir?' Any lightness was completely gone from Tom's voice now. Enough was enough.

'For your English soldiers.'

'I must beg you to explain – how so, convenient?'

'Why, for your army to be safely cantoned in Portugal, when plainly the true battle is here in Spain.'

'Do you suggest – '

'Tom!' Rico hissed.

' – do I understand you to suggest that the British are in some way shy, Major?'

'Shy, Lieutenant?'

'Of battle.'

Duarte shrugged expansively, as if the matter was of the tiniest concern to him. 'If that is the suggestion, it is not my opinion, Lieutenant Herryck, but that of my young companion here.'

'Your young companion the noted duellist,' Rico sighed.

But Tom's eyes and ears were only for Duarte. He said, 'Would you be so good as to ask the Teniente to confirm that?'

The exchange of Spanish was brief. Apparently Lucena Valdano was all too content to confirm his words, offering a deep, solemn bow – even though those words had in fact originally been Duarte's.

'Then I regret that I must ask the Teniente to explain himself.' Tom said shortly.

Duarte gave the slightest of bows. 'As you wish, Lieutenant Herryck. You are an honoured guest here, so naturally you must have your wish. As to a discreet location, I believe that the Plaza de Toros will be peaceful this afternoon,' he said, as if the thought had just come to him. 'Shall we conclude our business there?'

Chapter Two

'How on earth did you do that?'

William Truelove looked again at the impassive, tough-featured face of his opponent, then back down at the chess board. It wasn't a pretty sight. He might not like it, but there was no doubting the plain fact that it was mate and that, for the eighth time in a dozen games, he had lost to the soldier. With a couple of stalemates thrown in, Truelove found himself forced to accept that the record was now quite decisive in his opponent's favour. He was relieved that his original offer of a modest wager on their play had been politely declined. The loss of cash would, in fact, be trifling to a man of Truelove's considerable means, but the regular passing over of the coins would serve to emphasise the enormity of his all too regular defeat.

Yet, looking up again into Blunt's face, he found it difficult to imagine the man capable of gloating or making anything of his superiority by showing away in public. It was a singular face; one of Blunt's grey-green eyes was slightly larger than the other and his nose had been broken at least once. His sandy hair was slowly receding above a lined forehead and there were small scars in his left eyebrow and on his jaw line. He would be in his mid to late thirties. There was certainly sadness in those eyes, Truelove thought, and the man had obviously seen plenty of the harder side of life. But it was nonetheless a face that spoke of honesty and when Blunt smiled, which he did only rarely, those odd features somehow managed to transform themselves into a pleasing harmony of warmth and gentle happiness. If Truelove had to lose to someone, he decided there were many who would prove considerably less agreeable than the quiet and gracious Blunt.

The two men were at present sitting in the gunroom of the 74-gun ship of the line *Amethyst*, Captain Flemyng, which was making its way steadily south off Spain's Atlantic coast under orders to join the Mediterranean fleet. A soldier and a civilian, they were united as intruders in the peculiar, highly-regulated world of the sailors. Yet it was something of an odd match. In almost every material respect – breeding, profession, wealth, personality, one quite deeply religious, the other not at all – they were chalk and cheese.

Captain Robert Blunt, a career soldier who belonged to the 52nd Regiment, but who at present was in charge of a small group of soldiers of the 43rd

Infantry being returned to their own regiment after sick leave in England, was a guest of the wardroom, berthing in the second lieutenant's little cabin. But Blunt felt in no way cramped: his worldly possessions fitted neatly into one portmanteau and a haversack. The faded, artfully patched uniform he wore each day, with its buff facings and questionable silver lace, was the only one he possessed. William Truelove, on the other hand, wore a different coat at least three times a day. He was a wealthy merchant acquainted with some of the first families of England, and was for his part lodged in rather more splendour as a guest of Captain Flemyng, the ship's commander. But the two men had quickly formed a friendship, allies in their need to pass their time and to keep out of the way of those running the ship. And once they had discovered a mutual fondness for playing chess, they were set fair. The gunroom table offered the pair of them as near to an oasis of calm as was available and they had enjoyed several sessions of play together, with some gripping battles on the chessboard and some diverting, relaxed conversation, often accompanied in their leisure by off-duty ship's officers playing music, writing letters or sharing the long table to play their games of cards.

Truelove gave the board a last look, then picked up his coffee cup, disgusted to see that it was empty. 'Well, I tell you truly Blunt, I'm utterly confounded if I know how you can spend so long on the defensive, then ruin my dreams with such unexpected haste.'

'Tricks of the trade,' Blunt said in his soft, slightly countrified voice.

Truelove gave him a puzzled look.

'The first rule of war, sir, is not getting killed. Then be patient and wait on your chance. When the chance comes, take it.'

Truelove was intrigued. 'You see this, our game, as war?'

Blunt looked surprised by the question. 'Of course. It's to do with winning and losing, isn't it?'

'I suppose so. But war?'

'Why, yes. Strategy and tactics, working your pieces in harmony with one another like army units, choosing ground, defensive lines, searching out weak spots in your enemy – ' Blunt shrugged apologetically. 'War is all I'm good at, Mr Truelove.'

William held that look for a moment, then smiled. 'Well, I don't for a moment imagine that's the case. But if you're as accomplished on the field of battle as you are over a chess board, then I would suppose our country is blessed, Captain Blunt. You must be a terrible opponent indeed.'

'I'm still alive,' Blunt said gruffly, by way of acknowledging the compliment. He began to set the pieces onto the board again.

William sat back in his chair, 'And, as I see you are getting ready to give me yet another drubbing, it will be something of a relief to my destroyed self-confidence, if not my appreciation of good company, that you'll soon enough be delivered back to your war. Captain Flemyng tells me we should sight the Portuguese coast by morning.'

Blunt looked pleased at this news. 'Good. That's very good. I'm fed up with wooden walls, now. I could do with a stretch on dry land.'

'Understandable, for a soldier; and yet you seem well enough suited to life at sea. No sign of *mal de mer* in you, even in the choppiest waters.'

Blunt gave a little shrug. 'I've been on ships often enough over the years, being transported to one campaign or another, but I reckon my place is marching under the colours, not watching 'em flutter above pretty sails.'

'When the Captain spoke to that frigate we passed yesterday, the news was that General Wellesley had defeated the French down near Lisbon. Two small battles, but for once the French are dished, I believe.'

Blunt nodded with satisfaction. He too had heard the welcome news of the army's Portuguese victories, the talk of the wardroom dinner table at their last meal. 'Wellesley seems to be a good man. He was well thought of in India and it sounds as if he's done well now in Portugal.'

William nodded his agreement. 'I am pleased to hear you say so, although I must confess a personal interest in the general's success, as I am acquainted with the gentleman. The Wellesley family honours my company with their custom. Sir Arthur strikes me as a modest and intelligent man with a thorough knowledge of soldiering. Yet I fear not everyone in England appears to have had faith in him.'

Blunt finished setting the board, then swung it around, to give Truelove the change of pieces. 'I don't know about that. I've little time for politics and I've not myself had the chance to serve with General Wellesley. As I said, he has a good reputation as a fighting general after India and he deserves his chance. But if I'm honest, my own preference would have been for the command to go to Sir John Moore, who is more experienced at European campaigning and who has the absolute confidence of the soldiers. He's done a lot to bring our army into the modern age, almost single-handedly re-training our light troops and bringing in new tactics. He is a good, thinking soldier who would certainly give Boney a real run for his money. But unfortunately I think Sir John ain't particularly popular with the politicians in London. He is no friend of the Tory ministry. He has a habit of telling them the truth about the worth of some of their schemes and they don't always care to hear it.'

William steered wide of politics and moved his first pawn. 'Well, possibly it won't matter who commands. The French are leaving Portugal, so it seems, and the Spanish are getting ready to sweep them out of their own country.'

'Are you an optimist, then, Mr Truelove?' Blunt said, raising an eyebrow, a small smile on his face.

William confessed his guilt. 'I've certainly been accused of it. In which particular respect do you mean?'

'I wonder if you truly believe the Spaniards capable of beating the crapauds – defeating the French, that is?'

William thought about it for a moment, 'In all honesty Captain, I am myself part Spanish – proud of it – and yet I would be either lying or being utterly naïve if I suggested that I truly believed Spain capable of standing alone against the French. That is one reason why I am so pleased that Arthur Wellesley has made such a good start to the Iberian campaign. But if Napoleon decides he will take Spain, then take Spain he likely will. As to keeping it, however, that may be quite a different matter. The Spanish people may not warm to politics or to the whims of the ruling class, but they will become exercised indeed if a foreign power is seen to be in occupation of their country. The Golden Age may be a long way behind Spain, but she is still capable of a spirited response to a genuine slight.'

'A genuine slight is an interesting way of putting – '

'Captain Blunt, sir!'

'Why Captain Beddows,' Blunt looked up smiling at the officer of marines, who had come bustling into the wardroom looking quite unlike his usual, calm and affable self, 'How can I help you?'

As a fellow redcoat, Beddows had done much to make Blunt feel welcome onboard ship, ensuring that he felt comfortable as a temporary member of the *Amethyst*'s wardroom. The marine was of an age with Blunt and was a fellow west-midlander. Beddows shared something of the infantryman's cool demeanour, but at that moment he himself was plainly discomforted.

'Right now it is I who wish to do a service to you, Blunt,' he said, the urgency plain in his voice.

'Indeed?'

'I suggest you go directly to the galley. As quick as ever you can, sir. You might just be able to prevent your man from being flogged.'

The individual Captain Beddows described as Blunt's "man" was in fact his servant, a Derbyshire-born private of the 52nd called Widowson. They had marched together for many years and Widowson, a difficult and impenetrable character, had served his captain loyally and well, occasionally saving his life and more often quietly doing a thousand small things to make that life more tolerable in barracks and on campaign. His more distant past was opaque, even to Blunt, but it was known that he had at times been many things from a tailor to a barber, even an undertaker at one time. His deadly facility with rifle or musket suggested, moreover, that he might easily have spent time as a poacher or even as a gamekeeper in peak or dale; Widowson was a man of accomplishments, a jack of many trades. Indeed it was a brief and inglorious career as a bigamist that had led to his hasty enlistment into the army in the early years of the Revolutionary Wars. Now it appeared that Nathaniel Widowson was to be flogged.

Captain Beddows of the marines, more accustomed to the ship's complicated geography, had led Blunt, accompanied by William Truelove, along the cramped lower decks to the dark, smokey galley at the far end of the vessel. As they approached they could hear raised voices, an unusual thing in a well-disciplined ship of war.

And yet the scene they came upon was anything but disciplined – indeed there was the very real threat of imminent chaos.

'Sergeant Wheel!' Blunt barked, his voice dark with authority, instantly taking in how very dangerously matters stood, 'The men will stand to attention.'

The sergeant looked at his officer, then down at the seventeen inch long triangular bayonet that he, like most of the other redcoats, held at the ready, facing a file of grim-faced marines who stood opposite them with their muskets levelled. The two determined-looking groups of men were ranged but feet apart in the crowded space.

'Marines will ground arms,' Beddows called in turn, doing his share to try and calm the situation.

With barely a pause, each group of men obeyed their officer, however unhappy their facial expressions. Blunt took in the scene, looking coldly at the two sets of redcoats, saw that Widowson was there sure enough, standing between two marines each a foot taller than him.

'Very good.' A blue-coated officer now appeared from behind the rank of marines. He looked the infantrymen up and down, then glanced at Widowson, whose round, inscrutable face showed no sign of emotion. 'Now, Sergeant of Marines, do your duty. Clap that man in irons. He will be flogged at the Captain's pleasure.'

There was a rumble of anger from the soldiers; the marine sergeant looked to his officer.

'Silence for and aft!' barked a ship's petty officer.

'Lieutenant Kingman,' Blunt said, stepping forward to confront the ship's first lieutenant, actually his superior in equivalent rank, 'One moment, if you please. May I ask what has occurred here?'

Kingman looked at him with open distaste, his features set hard under the bicorn hat, as if considering whether he should feel obliged to give the soldier an answer. But a glance at the angry faces of Blunt's men, still holding those potentially lethal bayonets, convinced him that it would be the sensible course. He would indulge the soldier: 'A man, that man there,' and he pointed to the small figure of Widowson, still firmly held by the two burly marines. 'That man is guilty of theft. We do not tolerate theft onboard ship. That is the end of it sir, the man will be punished.'

'And tell me, sir, just what was the nature of this crime?' Blunt asked, standing his ground, trying to keep his tone civil. It wasn't easy: he and Kingman had barely spoken during the *Amethyst*'s voyage, the first lieutenant having early made plain his low opinion of the army in general and in particular of having to tolerate its lubberly representatives on board one of his Majesty's warships. "The shifting ballast" had been his scornful description of the soldiers.

'I told you, theft.'

William Truelove stepped forward now, a polite smile on his handsome face. 'Ah, wicked larceny, is it? That is surely a most terrible thing, gentlemen. Even to the eyes of a mere landsman it is plain that theft in so ordered a community as a ship of war would be most disagreeable. But theft of what, pray, Lieutenant Kingman? May we know what has been taken? I am sure that, much like myself, Captain Blunt here is simply interested in the exact nature of the crime.'

Kingman looked as if it was causing him the greatest pain to continue the conversation. He was the *Amethyst*'s second in command and should not be frittering his time here, still less be having his authority questioned; but against that he knew this man Truelove was the Captain's guest and the mood of Blunt's soldiers was still palpably ugly. So he would favour the civilian, for now. He turned abruptly in the direction of the galley coppers and snapped the name, 'Farrow!'

Farrow was the ship's cook, a huge man with a wooden leg, a pock-marked, crimson face and a long, greasy pigtail. He stepped forward, wiping his hands on a none-too clean cloth. He looked nervously at the first lieutenant.

'Speak,' Kingman told him.

Farrow needed no second bidding. He nodded malevolently at Widowson, then said, 'Which he helped himself to the slush, didn't he?'

'Slush?' Blunt said, looking at Widowson. The soldier stared straight ahead; there was nothing to read on the pale, lined face. But Blunt knew instinctively that it was unlikely that any great crime had been committed. It wasn't the little Derbyshire man's way. He knew Widowson's curious morality tolerably well after so many years together. His servant was not above acquiring a chicken from a farmyard or a pair of less-worn boots from a corpse when they were on service, was certainly adept at relieving dead enemies of their other earthly possessions, but he had never stolen from his countrymen – and nor would he here onboard *Amethyst*, of that he was sure.

'So, just what is this mysterious slush?' Truelove asked, his voice deliberately light, as if he were asking simply by way of making small-talk in a comfortable drawing room or coffee house.

'It's the grease from the cooking,' Beddows explained softly.

'Grease,' Truelove said in surprised tones. 'The man has removed some grease and is to be flogged for it?'

Kingman looked at him as if no other outcome were conceivable. 'Most certainly, sir. Slush is the perquisite of the cook. That is the custom of the service. If it is has been taken without Farrow's consent, then that is theft. And theft is punishable by flogging.'

'Ain't that somewhat extreme?' William said.

Kingman gave him a savage look, 'No by God, it is the law. Now sir, if – '

'You will not flog my man,' Blunt said quietly, his voice steel-cold.

He knew all about the lash, of course. In his time he had seen an enlisted man seized to the triangle and whipped simply for committing a "crime" as trivial as forgetting to doff his hat to an officer in the street. It was a fact of military life, just as it was central to Royal Navy discipline. But the 52nd wasn't a flogging regiment. And Blunt did not himself hold with flogging at all, unless in the last resort for a very great crime.

'I beg your pardon?' Kingman looked as if he genuinely could not believe what he had heard.

'I said you will not flog this man.'

Kingman, his face purpling, looked ready to burst with rage. Leaning towards Blunt, he literally spat out his words. 'By God, sir, I tell you plain that I will do what I damned well like! This is a King's ship under the command of the King's officers. You hear me? I don't give a damn what you lobsters get up to, we live under the rule of law in this service, sir. By the law,

I say! And if I so choose, then damn me if I won't have you yourself flogged for a saucy, impertinent rogue!'

If Blunt was moved by the threat he didn't show it. His own words were softly spoken: 'This man will not be flogged. And if you have an issue with me sir, then I believe you and I may choose to settle it like gentlemen.'

Kingman, face like thunder, clearly struggling to compose himself, regarded Blunt, taking in his glacial stare, his completely relaxed posture. This was a preposterous situation; he could barely credit what he had heard. It was outrageous, but Kingman had been long enough at sea to smell a lee shore. Here was real and imminent danger and he knew that his next words would be of the greatest importance. Whatever he thought about Blunt, however ill-bred and insolent the man might be, he had the cold look of a killer.

But before Kingman could speak, Truelove again intervened. 'I think you said, Lieutenant, if I recollect it right, that if a crime has indeed been perpetrated here, then the Captain must decide punishment for the criminal? That must, of course, be quite right. Captain Flemyng is, as my humble understanding goes, close to the almighty on the vessel. Why do we not cease to trouble ourselves with this vexing matter of, er, *grease*, until we have the opportunity to hear the wisdom of the ultimate authority?'

Kingman looked from Blunt to Truelove, then at the still impassive Widowson, his fury still barely contained. The fifty or so souls gathered in the small space waited silently, with many other pairs of ears about the ship primed for his response. In the end he said nothing at all, simply nodding to the Marines to take Widowson away, while he himself spun around and walked briskly from the galley. The bosun's mates and sergeants rapidly began to get the men about their business and away from mischief.

Truelove turned to look at Blunt. The soldier was standing stock-still, still ashen-faced with anger, yet still managing to look quite calm. William wondered at his coolness. He had been within an ace of calling Kingman out, an unthinkable action. It was unlikely the sailor would have refused and one of those two officers might easily die; certainly they would risk their careers. Madness. He sighed, putting his hand on the soldier's shoulder. 'So, if I remember correctly, Captain Blunt, you were telling me just now that for a soldier to stay alive one patiently waits for one's chance…'

They were to be five at dinner.

Captain Flemyng, almighty or not, had responded handsomely to his cabin-guest Mr Truelove's gentle suggestion by promptly inviting his first lieutenant, his captain of marines and Captain Blunt to join them to dine in the great cabin. The captain of the *Amethyst* was an easygoing man who, although a thorough seaman himself, generally left the day to day running of the ship in the hands of his premier, Mr Kingman, whom he respected as a taut, if occasionally over-zealous disciplinarian. Flemyng was by instinct a fighting captain who transformed almost magically from a relaxed gentleman sailor into a calculating, absolute leader when there was the remotest sniff of battle. At other times he remained detached and content to let his officers do their job of keeping the *Amethyst* in absolute readiness to perform its duty.

Flemyng had positively welcomed William Truelove's company on the short voyage from England. The ship's captain by necessity led a lonely existence, his rank and authority denying him the regular companionship of his inferiors, so he was grateful for the presence for a short while of his wealthy, cultivated civilian guest. The wine trader was not only good company but had shown his gratitude for his "lift" down to Lisbon by offering a generous supply of port to the wardroom and, the holiest of holy, several dozen of good claret for the captain himself. The war with France had been going on long enough to make that country's wines – decent ones at least – difficult to come by for the English. By that gift alone, Truelove was assured of the skipper's good will in anything that did not threaten the well-being of his ship or the good of the service in general. In that very respect, however, the hastily planned dinner patently had its risks.

Each of the officers was wearing his best uniform – although in Blunt's case his best jacket was the one he generally wore – and the civilian William Truelove sported an elegantly cut black coat. The captain's cook – a man of far greater accomplishment than poor Farrow, who had to prepare for six hundred odd mouths, not just for the captain and his guests – had done them well at short notice. They were not long out of Chatham, where the ship had enjoyed a comprehensive refit, and fresh stores were still plentiful. The dinner was as fine as could be expected outside an admiral's great cabin. As well as the many side dishes, they had been given hake with anchovy sauce, roast suckling pig, a sea pie (an extraordinary dish constructed of layers of meat and pastry constructed like the decks of a ship) and a universally well-received jam roly-poly pudding. Now the port had arrived.

And the conversation had gone well, up to a point. There was an almost inevitably sticky moment when the subject of Wellesley's recent victory in Portugal had arisen. While the triumph was universally welcomed, inevitably the ancient rivalry of the two services surfaced. Kingman had spoken little all evening, but Captain Beddows – as a marine more a sea creature than a land animal, despite his fine red coat – while full of praise for the victories at Rolica and Vimeiro, had felt it his duty to compare the success rate of the senior service overwhelmingly favourably with the modest achievements of the army.

'No, the records of the two services scarcely bear comparison in recent times, I fear,' he told the table, his face now almost the same colour as his uniform, 'No comparison at all. There have, I confess, been solid victories for the army in India and there was the great success in Egypt in the year one,' Beddows conceded. 'Now, that was well done.'

'Not accomplished without some little participation from Sir Sydney Smith and, of course, Lord Nelson himself.' Captain Flemyng observed with a smile. Without a word, the five of them solemnly toasted the mere mention of the late hero's name.

'But otherwise, Blunt,' the marine said, with no trace of malice, but more of regret in his voice, 'there has been a sorry trail of disasters and near-disasters for the army for well-nigh fifteen years. It pains me to say it, but the modern army has signally failed to live up to the legacy of Marlborough, Wolfe and Clive. Sure, we can take a nice little sugar island or two from the French, but we appear to have lost the ability to mount a serious land campaign. It is a sorry business, I fear, this way the army conducts itself. There was the Duke of York's folly in the Low Countries in '95, Ostend, the Helder catastrophe, to-ing and fro-ing in Scandinavia and recently the lamentable disasters in South America. Why Colonel Beresford even surrendered to a rabble of Spaniards at Buenos Aires and the unfortunate General Whitelocke compounded the sin by doing the exact same thing a year later!'

Robert Blunt twirled the glass thoughtfully between his fingers, clearly weighing what had been said, then he spoke softly, at first not looking directly at Beddows. 'It is interesting to hear what you have to say, Captain, interesting indeed, I was fortunate enough to have served in several of the campaigns you mention, so I can claim some poor knowledge of how affairs stood. While I would most certainly feel obliged to resent any general criticism of my service, I take your meaning to be that the army has been ill-served by those commanding its movements from London. In that I can only agree with you. Those gentlemen in Parliament seldom seem to have much notion of what it takes to bring brave soldiers up against their enemy in anything like decent condition. They are loath to spend the money and apparently incapable of doing the necessary thinking and planning. So, thus far, I agree with you, sir.' Then Blunt looked up, fixing the marine in the stare of his oddly mismatched eyes. 'As to the matter of the South American campaign, from which I am myself lately returned, I feel that I should and must point out that I believe Colonel, now General Beresford, to be a most able and active commander. Indeed, you should know that it is to be my honour to serve on the general's staff in Portugal once I have delivered my soldiers to their regiment.'

Beddows looked appalled, his face turning even redder. 'Why then sir, I instantly withdraw my remarks.'

Blunt looked at the flustered marine for a moment, then he nodded his satisfaction.

'Oh, gentlemen,' Truelove said, smiling broadly, his voice light, sounding amused even, 'I have heard something of this kind before – all too often, in fact. The mere sight of red and blue coats seems to set perfectly cultivated and rational officers at one another's throats. Captain Beddows,' and he bowed civilly at the marine, 'Might even be forgiven for some confusion, wearing red yet existing here onboard ship amongst so much blue. And presently poor Captain Blunt here, clearly no sea dog, is thoroughly outnumbered. So, you will have your little disagreements.'

'But I confess, gentlemen,' William continued, 'I do think the Royal Navy is at times guilty of being a little hard on its dry-foot brothers. Of course, I personally have the greatest respect and gratitude for the navy, if only from the most selfish of motives. Why, when the French stole into Oporto last year, if the Royal Navy had not secure command of the seas, I would not have been so fortunate as to be able to get my stock away safe to London. Naturally we are all most sensible of the achievements of the service in so zealously keeping the French from British shores and from the shores of friendly nations and possessions abroad,' here he looked pointedly at Blunt, who creditably managed a nod of agreement, tacitly echoing Truelove's praise of the navy. 'But that is surely not the entire picture. For all of the shining achievements of your kind, gentlemen, the army also has a difficult job to accomplish; think only that France alone has twice the population of Britain, as well as a vast empire of conquered nations to call on for its conscripts! All of these campaigns Captain Beddows mentioned, conducted all over the world by our hard-pressed soldiers, are pursued with a fraction of the manpower at work in your fine ships and in the dockyards at home and abroad. You have impressments to fill your ranks, where the army might only accept volunteers or the sweepings of the gaols. To make comparison like with like is surely unworthy. No, for myself, I say a hearty hallelujah for both services, each proficient in its own element. I feel proud and grateful that we are defended by such stout hearts, both at sea and on land. And what's more, I propose to drink their health this very minute, to *your* health, gentlemen, yes, at this very moment. To both services, say I!'

The toast was echoed cheerily enough and William was complimented on his fine sentiments. Then Captain Flemyng steered the table conversation to a discussion of the less martial, but nonetheless impressive operations of Truelove and Dunn in Cadiz, Oporto and London, enquiring solicitously how his guest's business and that of his fellow shippers had been affected by the recent French incursions into Portugal and Spain. Again William was able to take Captain Flemyng's lead and talk them into calmer waters.

And yet, however stiffly polite the company and however skilful were the host and his principal guest at steering away from conversational reefs, the chief cause of the evening's gathering loomed unmoved and dangerous and would finally have to be addressed:

'And so gentlemen,' said Captain Flemyng at last, a further supply of port having arrived, 'I hope it will not interfere either with digestion or with the protocol of the table to invite you to discuss a matter kindly brought to my attention by Mr Truelove and also by my first lieutenant.'

The others said nothing, but all looked attentively at Captain Flemyng. Each knew exactly what the "matter" was. Kingman cleared his throat noisily and Beddows passed the port decanter – an excellent vintage from Truelove and Dunn, of course – to Blunt on his left. The soldier silently moved the wine on to William Truelove, saying nothing and keeping his eyes on the Captain. William allowed himself a half-glass.

Flemyng continued, 'I speak of course, gentlemen, of what I have heard passed in the ship's galley this forenoon. I have made enquiry of my own and I have also had a report of the incident in question from my second – my second lieutenant, that is – who has spoken to those who were present. I am content that I have the full facts. It seems in little doubt, Captain Blunt, that the crime was committed.'

'If I may, sir – '

Flemyng gestured for Blunt to continue.

'I realise sir, that at sea it is unwise, even treasonable, to contradict the captain of a ship and it would also be indecent to do so in his own great cabin, having been so royally entertained.'

'But...' Flemyng said with a smile, granting implicit permission for such a contradiction.

'But I would nonetheless trouble to suggest to you sir, that while I accept offence has been given and received between Widowson and the cook, it arose from a simple ignorance of the ways of the sea and that no slight and certainly no crime was intended.'

'Have you interviewed your man?'

'Yes, sir.'

'And why did he make the thef – why, pray, did he remove the valuable slush from the galley?'

'In innocence, sir, and from duty; he says it was as a commission from the soldiers. They had complained of their metalwork, particularly their precious fire arms, suffering in the salt air. Widowson simply used his intelligence to seek out a source of grease to remedy the situation. The man had no notion that cooking fat might have a value.'

'It does to a sailor,' Kingman said, speaking for the first time.

'Private Widowson is not a sailor.'

'But aboard this vessel, he is subject to the sailor's laws,' Flemyng said mildly.

'And our people have not taken kindly to soldiermen flashing blades 'tween decks.' Kingman said. 'They have taken it very chuff indeed. An example will have to be made.'

'Widowson will not be flogged.'

'Possibly I shall decide that,' Flemyng said, his voice remaining soft, but no sign of a smile now.

Blunt felt a sharp pain as his ankle was kicked under the table. He glanced accusingly at Truelove, then back at the Captain.

'I apologise, sir. Naturally I fully accept your authority. I beg that you will forgive my clumsy words, spoken hastily on a difficult matter. I confess that I feel particularly strongly about the business. Widowson is a valuable man, a seasoned soldier and loyal servant of his country with much creditable service behind him – but he is of late years now, small of stature and I fear that a flogging would certainly break him.'

'And you seek clemency on his behalf?'

'Yes, sir, with all my heart.'

'Hmmm,' Flemyng steepled his fingers, clearly undecided on which course he should take; it was an unusual situation to resolve. He had no scruple in handing out hard punishment when it was merited and his instinct was naturally to back his own man. Kingman plainly felt his dignity and authority had been threatened. If the Captain did not quite love his first lieutenant, he certainly valued and respected him and had no wish to slight him unnecessarily. If it were a purely naval matter he would have no second thought, but the military and civilian worlds had become involved. The army captain struck him as uncultivated and brash, but he was likely a decent fighting soldier and also he appeared to have made a good impression on Truelove.

As if on cue, William spoke up:

'If I might say, Captain, I am much concerned at what Mr Kingman tells us. The incident was clearly most unfortunate. I was myself witness to the shocking sight of Captain Blunt's men at daggers drawn with the marines and sailors. It was most regrettable that there should have been such an occurrence. I can easily imagine there must be some bad feeling.'

'Tempers are running high,' Kingman said stiffly.

William looked suitably concerned. 'On both sides, I am sure. The seamen will be displeased at the perceived slight on their worthy traditions. And then, of course, the soldiers will surely be anything but delighted to see one of their own suffering under the lash. Who knows what mischief might pass before we make our landfall at Lisbon? Why, my civilian heart trembles at the thought of a dreadful bloodbath, as our nation's finest slaughter one another for so little reason as a dollop of dripping! That would surely be a needless calamity. So, if you please, I have a solution to propose.'

'What solution?' Kingman said.

Blunt said nothing, looking enquiringly at his friend.

Captain Flemyng poured himself a glass from the decanter. 'Mr Truelove, I assure you that you have our full attention. A solution to our present troubles would be most welcome. Might I beg that you share it with us?'

'Some bloody solution,' Robert Blunt said testily, looking apprehensively from the ship's side over to the beach, across at the surf breaking vigorously on the vicious rocks that protected the distant sands. The ship's largest boat had been lowered and manned by its crew of rowers. Slowly and with great difficulty the soldiers and their equipment had then been coaxed over the side and loaded into the middle of her. The men of the 43rd, all now safely aboard, looked uncomfortable in the gently bobbing craft, if at least happy enough to be going ashore. Now they waited only for Blunt and for the vessel's commander, Lieutenant Kingman.

His friend affected to look hurt. 'Well, I was rather pleased with my idea. I thought it something neat and tidy. Putting you and your fellows ashore to make your own way gets your man Widowson out of the Navy's clutches and keeps everyone's honour intact.'

Blunt kept his eye on the churning surf, 'Just as long as we manage to stay intact beyond those breakers.'

William Truelove, elegantly turned out as usual, turned his gaze to the remote, unwelcoming shore. 'I believe this is just exactly how General Wellesley's army landed some weeks ago.'

'Yes, I'm sure they did, brave lads; but unlike ourselves they couldn't simply sail gently on down the coast into Lisbon harbour because it was full of Frenchmen at the time.'

'Don't be so fussy, Robert. You got your man back, did you not?'

Blunt glanced down at Widowson, still looking quite unperturbed amongst the other soldiers, his grey hair pulled back in a neat queue under his shako. 'Aye, and for all I know, ready to be turfed over the side into the briny. That damned Kingman will probably tip us into the sea of a purpose.'

'I doubt it. Sailors themselves can seldom swim, you know. Besides,' and he gave his friend a significant look, 'He will want to get you onshore in one piece, I believe.'

Blunt looked back at him, surprised that Truelove should have read the situation so astutely. If there was a tacit understanding between himself and the ship's first lieutenant, he had voiced nothing of it to his friend.

'Mr Kingman, when you're ready,' cried the Captain from his quarterdeck, his tone of voice failing to disguise his impatience. 'I have no wish to be here when the tide turns, I thank you. Handsomely, if you will; let's have our guests ashore now; I've no intention of making the acquaintance of those shoals.'

Kingman saluted and looked icily at Blunt. The naval officer must by the lore of his service be the last one into the boat and so had to wait for the soldier to make his move.

'I hope to see you again, Robert,' William Truelove said as they shook hands, 'God bless you.'

Blunt nodded awkwardly to the civilian, but with genuine liking. 'William. I'm honoured to have met you. And I truly am grateful for your kindness. Yet somehow I doubt that you've seen the last of me, you know. For one thing, I long to taste the very good sherry wine you have told me so much about. And I've never seen Cadiz, nor any other Spanish city. So, I have your addresses and will try my damnedest to write.' It was a long speech for Blunt. 'I hope that will be soon.' Truelove said, as he watched Blunt getting awkwardly over the side. Then, to himself, 'Just so long, God willing, that you are spared – now and later.'

*

Sergeant Wheel had the men standing in line, arms shouldered. Their packs were neatly piled alongside them. The sergeant paced in front of his charges, uttering soft rebukes and commands to the soldiers, who were effectively on parade there under the hot afternoon sunshine. Fifty yards away, across the strand, the sailors stood in an untidy huddle around the beached ship's boat. The two groups eyed one another warily. It was a difficult moment. The truth was that the supposed animosity between the soldiers and the sailors onboard ship had been almost imaginary. There would always be rivalry and good-natured abuse between the two services, but over the matter of Widowson and the cook, there was little disharmony, the first lieutenant having exaggerated any rancour. Farrow was widely loathed among the crew and Kingman himself was generally thought of as a hard-horse premier, too keen on the stopping of grog and the use of the lash. But now things were altered, the atmosphere subtly changed, and Sergeant Wheel was obeying his officer's clearly stated orders, keeping the soldiers well apart from the boat's crew, firmly at attention. The fact that the men of the 43rd were even now forbidden their pipes, after days of shipboard discipline which proscribed smoking anywhere but in the dread galley, did nothing to improve the redcoats' mood.

On the naval side, matters were equally complex. The sailors too were without their officer, though none of them was surprised by Kingman's absence. But it was clear that not everybody back onboard ship had known what must take place once the boat was beached; Captain Flemyng had obviously seen no reason to deny his First Lieutenant's keenly stated request to personally oversee the disembarkation of the soldiers by taking command of the boat – a command far better suited to a midshipman or junior officer. Possibly suspecting some hint of unworthy vindictiveness or even plain gloating in the lieutenant's move, but all along having tried to uphold Kingman's dignity and authority, Flemyng had decided to let him see Blunt and his men ashore. If the premier wanted the satisfaction of seeing off the soldiers at first hand, so be it.

By silent consent, the moment the boat had grounded, Kingman and Blunt had taken the opportunity to march unsteadily off up the beach, each accompanied by two men of his own service, on out of sight of the ship and of the men waiting by the boat. It did not take long. The men heard the pop of a shot, then another. Kingman was the first to come back; he was supported by the two master's mates who had accompanied him. The left arm of his shirt was crimson with blood. Kingman himself was conscious, but ashen-faced and he walked with great difficulty. They got him down the beach as quickly as they could. As the sailors helped their officer into the boat, Blunt then appeared, accompanied by Widowson and the platoon corporal. He had his jacket back on and was obviously unharmed. They made directly for the soldiers. A glare warned his men that a cheer would be unwelcome, but he couldn't prevent them from grinning. The wounded Kingman had by now been settled in the stern-sheets of the boat and already the sailors had shoved off.

'Well then,' Widowson handed his captain his hat.

'Well what?' said Blunt.

Widowson nodded in the direction of the departing boat. 'Ah'd say that's like to teach yon chap t'price of a bit o' grease.'

'Join the men, Private.'

'Aye, sir,' said Widowson, the shadow of a smile on his lips.

'Have you killed the bugger?' Sergeant Wheel asked softly, coming to stand by his officer. He had been as outraged by Kingman's treatment of Widowson as the rest of the men. He had also seen the amount of blood soaking the seaman's shirt.

Blunt shook his head. 'Not if the ship's surgeon is up to his work. Shoulder muscle, I reckon. If he keeps any bits of ball and shirt cotton out of it he'll do well enough.'

Wheel asked, 'Could you have killed him, sir?'

Blunt looked back at him. 'Well, what do you think? He'd had his shot and missed. To his credit he stood firm.'

Sergeant Wheel was an old, experienced soldier who had seen his share of killing. He had also seen something of Captain Blunt in action and also in charge of training men at Shorncliffe Barracks. He nodded, 'I think with pistol, rifle or even an 'orrible musket, you're as good a shot as I've seen in an officer, sir.'

'Well, perhaps it's good thing he didn't chose swords then, isn't it?'

Wheel offered a tight-lipped smile. 'You're good at that as well, sir.'

Blunt sighed, shaking his head, looking over to where Widowson was calmly checking the straps on his officer's pack. 'Well, I didn't kill him, Sergeant, and that's that. There wouldn't be much point in saving a soldier's back to do Boney's work on a sailor, would there?'

'If you say so, sir.'

'I do, Sergeant Wheel, I do. And let's make sure that's an end to the matter, shall we? Now, what I have to say on a far more important matter, is that it's high time we got down to real business and turned ourselves back into soldiers after our pleasure cruise. The men could do with a little work, I believe. Do you concur?'

Wheel snapped to attention. 'Yes, sir.'

'Very well, then. The gentlemen in the wardroom were kind enough to tell me precisely where we are in this place. By my reckoning we are a hundred and twenty odd miles from Lisbon.'

'Lisbon, sir?'

Blunt finished buttoning his short jacket. 'Lisbon is where the army is, as far as I know, so that's where we'll go. It's pretty damned easy, because it's on the coast due south of here and there's that nice big hot sun to tell us just where south is. So, what say we stop gabbing like fishwives, get these packs on and do some hard marching, eh? There's plenty of light left in the day, so let's use it. Open order now, if you please, Sergeant Wheel. Let's see if the men of the 43rd have remembered how to be light infantrymen.'

The days quickly settled into a pattern for Blunt's little troop of foot soldiers. The Portuguese autumn sunshine was still formidably hot in the middle of the day, far too hot for Englishmen unused to the conditions to cover much ground, so they marched in two sessions early and late in the daylight. Each of the men, Blunt included, was carrying equipment weighing around 80 pounds. Unlike all of the other soldiers but Widowson, Blunt had a short rifle slung on his back rather than the muskets the men carried. Like Blunt's own 52nd, the 43rd was a light infantry regiment, but only the designated rifle regiments such as the 60th and 95th were routinely issued with the relatively new Baker rifles. But Blunt and his servant were on detached duty and, both fine shots, they preferred the accuracy of the rifled weapon.

So they marched the hot Portuguese roads at the routine seventy five paces per minute, aiming to accomplish around fifteen miles a day. They had mostly been on sick leave for several months in England, so at first it was tough going. The days were hot, locusts chattering and lizards darting across their path. It was very different to Kent. They kept broadly to the coast, simply because Blunt knew that Lisbon itself was on the coast and that they were less likely to bump into any stray bands of Frenchmen, local bandits or renegades so close to the patrolling grounds of the Royal Navy. As they got fitter, he worked the men hard, often marching them in quick time, which was 120 paces to the minute, and having them make their bivouac in the open air. The soldiers were happy enough with the regime, glad to be away from the ship. With the knowledge of old campaigners, they would happily sleep the cool nights in their greatcoats, their legs through the sleeves and the body buttoned up to their necks, boots stuffed in a haversack to make a pillow. Once they were accustomed to being on active service again, it was easy going compared to what most of them had been through in one place or other through the years.

Blunt wasn't their own officer, not even of the same regiment, but he was determined that they would arrive with the men of the 43rd in proper condition for elite light infantrymen. He didn't have much of a problem with discipline; these were all experienced men. Most of them had heard of Blunt or had even campaigned with him. They knew that, like other Light Brigade officers, he had himself gone through six months of training like the common soldier. More to the point, they knew he had fought in, and survived, more actions than most. He was the sort of man it was easy for a soldier to follow.

If not a formal platoon, they were a comfortable unit. The soldiers divided naturally into two messes, each of ten men. Each mess had a big solid Flanders kettle for cooking, that took a huge amount of wood to heat. Captain Flemyng had allowed them five days' provisions. The army ration was similar to the navy and each man had a daily supply of a pound of salt pork, a pound of ship's biscuit and a third of a pint of rum. The rum was kept in a little barrel, closely watched at all times by Blunt or the sergeant.

On the fourth day, they passed through the village of Vimeiro, where General Wellesley had won his victory against the French in August. As they marched past a small convent, the men were delighted to be hailed in familiar tones by three old comrades of their own regiment who had been sunning themselves in the garden. The men had been wounded in the battle and left in the care of the nuns to recover. Blunt called a halt and the men settled to sharing news. The wounded men were naturally full of the adventures of the 43rd at Vimeiro, fighting its own private battle against the French amongst the trees – and naturally winning. Unsurprisingly, they were far more scathing about the way the victory had later been thrown away by the unworthy truce at Cintra. The British had got Napoleon's men out of Portugal, but not in a way that pleased the soldiers. The French had gone home in British ships, taking with them their arms and plunder. But that was old news. Now the army was indeed quartered at Lisbon, as Blunt had suspected, but it appeared that Wellesley had been sent home to be replaced by Sir John Moore.

While he regretted the shabby treatment of Wellesley, called home to answer with his superiors for Cintra, Blunt and his men were all thoroughly delighted to hear that Moore was now in command of the army. Not only was he a good general, it was Moore who had played the greatest part in the bringing into being and the training of the new light infantry, including the 43rd, and had even commanded Blunt's own 52nd. The soldiers were even happier at the notion of rejoining with Moore in command and they marched away from Vimeiro in great heart.

By now the only cloud on Blunt's horizon was that they were fast running out of rations and he had precious little money to buy more. He was well enough used to being short of cash on his own account, but he was not accustomed to having to act as paymaster and quartermaster with no coin to hand. The original plan had been for *Amethyst* to land the soldiers at Lisbon, where Blunt would promptly hand them over. He had not expected to be leading a march down the Atlantic seaboard.

They pressed on.

Blunt realised he would have to get to Lisbon as quickly as possible. It was absolutely against the infantryman's instinct to imitate the French and effectively steal food, but he doubted whether the locals would accept a promissory note. Taking the winding road through the wooded slopes of the Serra de Cintra, sure enough the rations ran out. Blunt had just enough money to buy them bread and meat in a little hill village and magically, more navy rum appeared from haversacks and water bottles. They pushed on. The men were cheerful enough. They had all been on short rations often enough. Captain Blunt would sort out their victuals, they reasoned, or if not they would sort something out for themselves. They thought it unlikely they would starve at harvest-time. Blunt himself knew he would not willingly allow men in his care go short, but he was at a loss to know how he might make sure that didn't happen.

Finally they came to Cintra itself, the old summer retreat of the kings of Portugal. It was late in the afternoon. The town looked magnificent, sitting on the slopes of the Serra, with the palace before them and the old Moorish castle above it. The soldiers marched into the town – tired and hungry. At the first inn they came to they saw people sitting at tables enjoying the last of the sunshine. An elegant carriage was standing outside. A man stood and took off his hat to salute the approaching file. It was William Truelove.

'My dear fellow, it was the least I could do.'

'It was?' Once again Blunt looked with relief – relief nonetheless tainted by something very like shame, at the table populated by his tired and contented soldiers. The table was, however, no longer populated by the small banquet Truelove had ordered for them. Everything had gone. Most of the men were now asleep where they sat, with one or two contentedly smoking a pipe or gamely trying to hold drunken conversations, but themselves not far from sleep. The men had behaved well on the march and deserved their feast. Blunt only wished that he had been able to provide adequately for them himself, rather than relying on William Truelove's generosity.

'Well it seemed only fair, Robert, as it was my intervention onboard ship that led to you being separated from your rations.'

'I suppose so,' Blunt said. He was too exhausted to worry about it any more. Widowson moved quietly behind him, filling his officer's wine tumbler and doing the same for Truelove.

'Of course it was.'

'How did you know we'd come this way?'

William smiled, 'You're on my territory now, my friend.'

'Your territory?'

'My wine lodge in Oporto is north of here and I often travel to do business in Lisbon, so I know the area well. It was likely that you'd pass this way if you kept to the coast.'

Blunt wasn't sure he was comfortable being so easily second-guessed by a civilian, but he was grateful for Truelove's kindness. 'Well, however you got here, William, I'm obliged to you for your true instinct. I was down to my last farthing and the rations were long gone. Army pay is neither generous nor regular. The paymaster marches slower than most.'

'Well, you can content yourself that you are close enough to the bosom of the army now. You will find General Moore's camp is near the old royal palace at Queluz, a day or so's march from here.'

'Not in Lisbon?'

'Not in the capital itself. No, the city is the same distance again beyond Queluz. So I fear that you may not enjoy the delights of Lisbon town just yet. But I hope you may one day have the chance to see it. It is a fine city.'

'Are you going back there?'

'No, I am taking your road back northwards, to Oporto. I had business in Lisbon, as I told you on the ship, and Captain Flemyng was kind enough to undertake to drop me there – although, for a time, I suspected that he might choose to reconsider. He was most out of countenance with me. He clearly suspected that I was in some way complicit in your escapade with Kingman. I was in mortal fear of being seized to a grating or keel-hauled or some such thing. I think he took rather a dim view of you puncturing his first lieutenant and putting him in the sick berth.'

'Is Kingman alright?'

'Oh yes, but he's not exactly in the best of spirits and he won't be properly fit for duty for a few days yet. I must say, it all caused something of a stir onboard ship. As I say, the good captain was less than pleased with the notion of his premier being shot in an affair of honour. I fear that Flemyng has possibly even been unsportsmanlike enough to enter into communication with the Lisbon military authorities about your part in Kingman's discomfiture.'

Blunt took a drink from his wine, affecting unconcern at the news. 'I'm glad I didn't kill him at any rate.'

'But you're glad you shot him?' William gave him a keen look.

Blunt thought about it for barely a second, 'Yes.'

Truelove sighed, 'Oh well, I only hope it don't get you in hot water.'

'It wouldn't be the first time.'

William smiled, unsurprised. 'I'm sure. And I'm also quite sure you're adept at extracting yourself. In any case, just at present I doubt that General Moore will wish to be deprived of a fighting officer who brings him twenty good soldiers. I dare say you'll do well enough when you pitch up in camp. Now, as to your accommodations here, I have taken the liberty of bespeaking the fine commodious barn behind this establishment as a sort of billet for your men. The people here will put up two day's rations for your march, which will see you comfortably established at Queluz. You yourself are to have a modest room in the inn itself.'

'But – '

William held up his hand. 'You have no money to pay for it? Of course; but I assure you that it is not a problem.'

Blunt looked horribly uncomfortable, 'I won't – '

William knew what was coming and finished it for him, 'Allow me the honour of giving or lending you money? Of course not, my dear sir. No, I would expect nothing but such fine feelings in a gentleman if not, however – may I say with a certain small resentment – in my particular friend and, how do they say it, shipmate? But by happy chance Robert, I can tell you that the issue quite simply does not arise. I was fortunate enough to mention your predicament in having to march a part of your sea voyage to my military acquaintance in Lisbon. So here,' and he placed a small purse on the table, 'Is, I think, eighty dollars – something like twenty pound sterling – drawn against the 43rd. That should, I trust, reimburse you for your personal expenditure and see the poor, weary soldiers here fed and watered until you deliver them safe to their companions.'

Blunt, surprised, stunned even, nonetheless felt a precious wave of relief. His eternal struggle with money would be allowed to abate, for a while, at least. 'You are very good, William.'

Truelove made a dismissive gesture. 'Nonsense; 'twas I who marooned you, after all, so I should see you safe to your destination. And, what's more, I assure you that I act entirely selfishly, for I look to you personally to go and keep those troublesome French fellows north of the Ebro. I tell you in all seriousness, Robert, I positively dread to think of those terrible old moustaches tramping through my sherry vines, doing the same pagan damage they have done on the Douro. No, I flatter myself that assisting you and your fellows' return to the army is my own small contribution to winning the fight. I know you are positively aching to get to work knocking Frenchmen on the head and the sooner you are about it the better.'

Blunt smiled. 'It was good of you,' he repeated. He was moved by his friend's kindness.

'Nonsense. I was able, so I did. You must say no more about it. Now, reluctant as I am to part from you without at least giving myself the questionable honour of being soundly defeated on the chess board once again, I really must press on to Oporto. I need to find out what damage Bonaparte's vandals have done to my company's port lodge and I am also committed to meet my sister there on the last of the month.'

William stood up and signalled to his driver. 'Now, you have my addresses?'

'I have them.'

They shook hands.

'Then I will do no more than wish you God speed now, Robert, and go look to my wine.'

Chapter Three

Rico scuffed at the sand with his boot, a dejected, troubled look on his face. 'Brace up,' Tom said, himself looking perfectly cheerful as they stood in the shade of the curved wall, waiting for the other party to announce themselves ready. 'At least we had our dinner.'

Rico scowled back at him, looking less than pleased with his new friend. 'Tom, forgive me, I have only known you for a very short time, while it has been my misfortune to have been acquainted with that serpent Duarte for considerably longer. He is a man of low cunning, you must realise, full of malice and vindictiveness, hardly a man at all, but he has worked this situation absolutely to his liking. You should have no part in this – no, you should not have involved yourself. It is plain he wants nothing more than to damage me through you and, in this young Valdano, he has the perfect weapon to achieve his unsavoury aim. It is little short of tragic. No, I am sorry, my friend, forgive me but you should not have allowed yourself to be made to challenge him. I have heard all about this one, this Valdano. I have no notion at all of what kind of soldier he may be, but I do know he has been out many times for one so young and has a reputation as a killer.'

Tom continued to look unworried, nonchalant even. He seemed perfectly content, waiting for the potentially lethal duel as if he was readying himself for his turn in a friendly game of bowls. It even crossed the Spaniard's mind that he might be enjoying himself. 'It is your life!' Rico said sharply, plainly exasperated by the Englishman's seeming lack of concern. He gestured about the old bullring. 'Tom, I beg of you, look where you have come. Look around you! This is no refined English pleasure ground. This is a place of blood, a place for dying, nothing more than that!'

It dawned on Tom at last that Rico was badly afraid for him and that he plainly felt that he had been the cause of the Englishman being there, in that "place of blood"; he also realised that he would be wise to do just as he was bidden and take the business more seriously. In a fight there had to be a loser as well as a winner, he could be either. It would indeed be ridiculous to come to Spain to fight Napoleon only to be run through by one of those supposed to be his allies. If this Valdano was indeed a killer with the blade, then Tom must concentrate – and concentrate hard. Yet he knew what Rico and the Spaniards of Duarte's party did not – that he too had every right to consider himself a passably accomplished and experienced swordsman. He also had had his fair share of meetings. In England he had killed a man, had cut others. He was content that he could take care of himself against all but the most skilful opponents, but against that he knew that over-confidence had killed quite as many duellists as fine swordplay.

He nodded in acknowledgement of the Spaniard's concern, tried to offer a look that might reassure him. 'You are right, of course, Rico. Forgive me, I should be more attentive to my, ah, *situation*. Yes, you are right to scold me. I will be on my guard then, I thank you.'

They stood quiet for a while.

Tom flicked a piece of peeling whitewash from the wall. This waiting was annoying; he wanted the thing done. He realised that he was now in danger of drifting from being too relaxed to becoming nervous. He looked at Rico, who was staring moodily across at Duarte's people. 'You didn't tell me that you had fought at Bailen,' he said, needing something to take his mind from his own forthcoming fight for a moment.

Rico snorted derisively. 'No Tom, I didn't fight. I was there true enough, with General Castaños' staff, just as I said, as representative of the Galician Junta. And also it was just as I told Duarte; like everyone else of that party, I sat for several days seeing nothing, doing nothing, while the two armies blundered about down on the Guadalquivir. It was a joke. The French were no more than conscripts and Swiss mercenaries. The tyrant has such contempt for Spanish arms that he didn't trouble to send a real army. And yet, even then, if the Frenchman Dupont had not been such a clown, Castanos' indecision would have cost us dear and the French would even now be at the gates of Cadiz.'

They looked across the shimmering bullring, deserted but for Duarte's party of officers and women, who had somehow found a basket of food and wine and were now contentedly setting out a picnic meal under their parasols on the spectator's benches. They had the air of a holiday outing, looking forward to their entertainment. Duarte, who had eagerly, predictably, volunteered to be Valdano's second, was talking and laughing with his man as they stood in the shade and waited for a pair of matched swords to arrive.

'Tom,' Rico said, taking him by the arm and speaking softly, but urgently, 'Listen to me. I know you are a man of honour, that your bravery is clearly beyond doubt, but I beg you to consider that it is not to late to withdraw. There is nothing to be gained in this fight. There is simply no good reason for you and this puppy to risk your lives here. The disagreement was a simple misunderstanding of language.'

Tom gave him a gentle smile, 'I understood the lieutenant perfectly well, Rico.'

The Spaniard looked at him intently, 'You are quite sure?'

'Yes.'

'Very well then,' Rico nodded. There was no more to be said. He was miserable that it could have come to such a situation, but he knew it must now run its course. He would just have to trust that the Englishman knew what he was about – either that, or that he was lucky, very lucky. He certainly seemed composed enough – Rico just hoped that it was not simply a young man's bravado and that Herryck did at least have some chance of surviving. And yet, the more he thought about the unfortunate business, he realised with an unpleasant shock that – much as he wished his new friend well – he was just as fearful of Duarte gaining satisfaction as of the Englishman suffering hurt. He brushed the thought away, like an offensive insect.

They both watched as an officer of dragoons at last came through the gate and walked importantly to Duarte and presented him with a sword box. Having shown the weapons at length to Valdano, Duarte looked over to Rico, who nodded and walked to meet him in the centre of the ring. Ignoring the smiling Duarte's gaze, Rico reached out each blade, tested its weight and balance and returned them to the box. He was satisfied that the weapons, at least, were equal. Neither he nor Duarte said a word. Each second summoned his man. Tom, as challenger, offered his opponent the choice of the weapons, fine Toledo steel, and watched as Valdano took his blade and proceeded to make a series of quick elegant shadow passes in front of him. Tom simply stood, passing his own sword from one hand to the other, as if he was absently juggling a cricket ball, waiting to bowl on a village green in England.

'To the first blood drawn?' Rico asked.

'To an apology,' Duarte answered curtly.

'So be it.'

The two seconds stepped away.

'Gentlemen? En garde, then.'

Tom, who was still passing the sword from hand to hand, now let the handle settle in his palm, holding the grip lightly but firmly, so he had absolute control of the blade. He saluted Valdano, then he stretched comfortably into position. Left leg forward, knees bent, his right arm back and bent at a right angle – he was ready.

'Ah, a la izquierda,' said Valdano, looking a little surprised, as he himself saluted and took position.

Tom didn't need to know Spanish to guess that the young man had observed that he was left-handed. He knew from long practice that right-handers generally preferred to fight like with like, could be unsettled by the unfamiliar attack of the south-paw, but he wasn't really thinking or listening to anything now, he was concentrating on the fight. He knew that Rico was right, that Duarte had manoeuvred him into the challenge simply to score off the Galician, would have Valdano wound or kill him out of base spite, and that made Tom angry. He became a different being when he was angry – cold and menacing, murderous even. So he would fight – and win.

The two of them briefly touched blades then stepped apart, moving slowly in a wary circle, each pair of eyes fixed on the other. Valdano was the first to attack, moving in quickly with a feint to Tom's left then a lunge at the right of his guard, which Tom saw coming and flicked away. The Spaniard came straight back with another attack, this time feinting the other way, but once more Tom anticipated it and defended comfortably. Again they circled, eyes locked on one another. Tom was concentrating with every ounce of his being. The young Spaniard was quick of hand and feet, clearly a dangerous and experienced opponent, almost feline in the grace of his movements. He was smiling, confident. Tom watched him warily, his mind wonderfully alive, waiting for the cat to pounce. Valdano came on again – parry, engage, break. Distance, Tom, concentrate, no flourishes, keep your feet moving. Above all, watch the eyes.

It was difficult for a left and right-handed combination of fencers to transact business, as the sword arms protected the body more completely than when two right-handers faced each other with their chests more open, but Valdano was frighteningly quick on his feet and again he tried to dart in around Tom's guard with a combination of feints and lightening-fast thrusts. Still Tom fended him off, the clash of the blades ringing out in the empty amphitheatre, Tom skilfully using his feet as well as his sword-arm to keep his opponent at bay. Again Valdano attacked and again Tom defended with a classic parry. They parted and warily circled. Tom's shirt was soaked with sweat and he wiped his brow with his cuff to keep the perspiration from running into his eyes. His tall leather boots were not ideal for a fencing bout, particularly on the sand of the bull-ring, but there was little he could do about that. The young Spaniard was also looking less composed now and his expression was set, the look of smiling anticipation long gone. Neither of them took their eyes from the other's for a second. Again Valdano came on, this time relying on the sheer speed of his combination to penetrate Tom's defence, but once again the Englishman matched him stroke for stroke, the clashes echoing around the empty plaza.

Both men were breathing hard now. Looking on, a helpless but fascinated spectator, Rico was wonderfully surprised at how well the Englishman fought. He had obviously been well taught, if not entirely in the classical manner. Young Valdano was looking angry now. Rico doubted that he had ever been involved in a fight like this before. Duarte's young cockerel was getting frustrated! Once again he came on with a flurry of strokes and once again Tom matched him, but this time the exchange ended with a straightening of the blade. Tom stepped back, Valdano stood his ground, a perplexed look on his handsome young face, now clutching both hands to his belly. His sword had fallen to the sand. Then he, in turn, fell slowly to his knees, the red spreading like an unfolding rose on his white shirt.

Rico was immediately at Tom's side, his jacket, hat and sword bundled under his arm.

'Come, we must leave.'

Tom looked down at Valdano, who was staring at the blood oozing between his fingers, a childlike voice sobbing a forlorn plea to the Mother of God.

'You have killed him!' Duarte snarled, not even bending to his man but glaring venomously at the Englishman.

'For that I'm sorry.' Tom let the duelling sword drop to the ground.

'Come, Tom.' Rico was pulling him away.

Duarte called after them, his voice harsh with fury, 'You will pay for this, Englishman. Your insult will be dealt with. I make a holy oath of that! And you, Federico, what is between us remains!'

But Rico was not listening. He was bustling Tom out through the gate as quickly as he could, back towards the inn, where he had ordered that their horses be kept saddled and ready. They would need to get out of Jerez, and fast. He was glad that they had brought his cousin's fine riding horses. Yes, good quick animals to get them away from there! He found that he was grimly pleased – and not a little surprised – that both of the saddles would be filled after all.

'So, Captain Blunt, what have you to say for yourself?'

He stood stiffly to attention, somewhat apprehensive, directly in front of the Commander-in-Chief of the British forces in the Peninsula. His careworn uniform was as spotless as Widowson's art could make it and his metalwork and leather shone with a rare brilliance. He had waited all morning at army headquarters, which was situated some way away from the sprawling camp of the main army, near the deserted palace of the Prince of Brazil, to find himself being presented as the last item of the meeting's very long agenda. Clearly Major General Sir John Moore had found a lot of business to conduct with his harassed staff and general officers, and now at the end of that mammoth session here was Blunt to be dealt with:

'I am reported for duty, sir.'

'Duty, by God!' This was General Stewart – the Honourable Charles William Stewart, the brother of Lord Castlereagh, a cavalry commander unlikely to sympathise with any shortcoming in a lowly captain of infantry. Deaf, short-sighted and impetuous, he was not Moore's first pick – but that influence with Castlereagh couldn't be lightly ignored. 'Does your duty now include trying to kill naval officers, sir?'

Blunt looked straight ahead, over the heads of the officers. 'If I am correct in thinking you refer to Lieutenant Kingman, General, with respect I didn't try to kill the gentleman.'

'Eh?'

'Didnt try to kill him, sir!' Blunt half-shouted.

Stewart snorted derisively. 'Well, if that be the case, you damned barely succeeded in achieving your intention. Bad business – by all accounts, fellow bled like a stuck pig. It was touch and go, so his captain said.'

'What was the nature of your disagreement, Blunt?' General Moore asked, his voice Scots, but far softer in tone than Stewart's braying. Moore was in his mid-forties, young for command, and he had a kind, open face, his hair prematurely white from long years of active service on several continents.

'The lieutenant wished to flog one of my soldiers, sir.'

'For what reason?'

'Stealing grease, sir.'

'Grease?'

'Stealing is stealing,' said Stewart in a rigid tone. 'This fellow Kingman was quite right to wish to keep discipline.'

'With flogging, Stewart? When I lately had command of the Light Brigade at Shorncliffe I found there was seldom call for flogging,' said Sir John, a smile playing on his face.

'Discipline is paramount,' Stewart replied stiffly. He glared malevolently at Blunt.

'Well, gentlemen,' said Sir John, turning to include the other officers, many of whom looked frankly uninterested in the business of disciplining a captain of infantry. 'As we have discussed, there is much to be done. You may care to be about your business.'

The room cleared rapidly, Stewart being the last through the door, giving Blunt a dark glare as he left.

'So then, Blunt,' the general eased back in his chair, looking evenly at the infantryman.

Blunt remained standing to attention, eyes front. 'Sir John.'

'As usual I find you have been having your adventures. You were ever one for getting into scrapes. But I'm pleased to see you here. My position is not so blithe I can turn my nose up at experienced men. Did you really have to go out against the sailor?'

'I believe so, sir. Lieutenant Kingman was neither just nor compassionate in his handling of the business. I believed what Private Widowson told me. The soldier made a misjudgement, but had intended no crime.'

Moore nodded. 'Well, I will not denounce an officer for looking to his men and it would be false for me to cry out about duelling. If I recall, I had my first wee sword fight when I was eleven years old – and have the scar to prove it.' He gave a little laugh at the memory. 'No, I have few enough able officers about me to worry overlong about a winged sailor.'

'Thank you, sir.'

Moore picked up a piece of paper. 'So, let us concern ourselves with more important matters. You are to join General Beresford's staff?'

'He was kind enough to ask for me, sir.'

'Very well; he's a fine soldier and I'm sure you'll serve him well, Captain Blunt, and staff duty will do your longer-term prospects no harm. But I must tell you that it is my wish that William Beresford will have to wait a while longer for your services. I have work of my own for you first.'

'Yes, sir,' Blunt said, continuing to look straight in front of him, wondering what was coming. Whatever the work Moore had in mind, it was unlikely to be dull. Blunt had known the general for too long to have any doubts on that score. Sir John was an enterprising and thorough commander, himself known to be fond of what he had just described as "adventures". He had been wounded in battle several times and was fond of setting about his own lone reconnaissance missions in dangerous locations. He was the kind of general who led from the front and who commanded by example. Those around him, usually devoted to him, generally had a lively time of it in their turn.

The Scotsman smiled, as if guessing what the other was thinking. 'Sit down, Blunt. It's not often I have the chance to talk with real fighting soldiers just now. My days are spent more in clerking than campaigning. But let me tell you a little of our situation here – or at least some of what poor knowledge I have. But first, tell me, when did we last see action together?'

Blunt took one of the chairs lately vacated by Moore's officers. 'Aboukir Bay, sir; then Alexandria, in the year one.'

He nodded, 'The Egyptian adventure? I mind it well enough, Blunt. We had quite a hot time of it, eh?' Moore's thoughts went back to the perilous landing at Aboukir Bay - the boats coming in steadily against French cannon, which sent out a hail of ball and grape, then the brave charge up the sand hill, waving his hat to urge the men on; and later the vicious hand to hand fight in the old Roman Fort at Alexandria. It had been hard soldiering, many casualties, but the army won a precious victory and it had made his own reputation. 'The men behaved well, fought bravely, though I regret we suffered the same old tale of good soldiers being given poor instructions and inadequate support.' Moore involuntarily touched his left leg, where he had been wounded during that difficult campaign. 'Well, you'll discover that little has altered in our present undertaking. We have been given a mighty task to achieve, without being given the proper means to accomplish it. Tell me, have you had the opportunity to look at our camp here?'

'Briefly, sir.'

'What d'you think?'

'Sir?'

'Come now,' the general offered him a smile of encouragement. 'Please oblige me by being candid, if you will, Blunt. You see, I have not long been here in Portugal myself. Those gentlemen who just left us constitute my staff for this business. Solid fellows I am sure, but precious few of them has served a meaningful campaign. So, I would be truly grateful for the wisdom of an experienced eye.'

'Candid?'

'Yes.'

This would not be easy. His "experienced eye" had been shocked by what it had seen of the army's establishment near Lisbon. The camp was little short of shambolic. He knew that Moore was passionate about the welfare and discipline of his men but, as he had said, the general had only just taken over command and it was weeks since Wellesley had been recalled. A deep breath: 'Well then, I will do as you ask, Sir John. I have only just arrived here, as you know sir, but I confess that the main camp at Queluz does not look at all the thing to me. Certainly the quality of the troops themselves appears to be mixed, which is no great surprise – plenty of johnny raws, of course, but a lot of old hands as well. But soldiers are soldiers. The men have been gorging unchecked on the fruit harvest and, worse, drinking young wine, which naturally leads to diarrhoea.' He knew he was not giving Moore good news, but felt it his duty to continue. 'But even the basic care and health of the men is not at all as you have always demanded it should be, General. The camp is badly laid out; there is dysentery and the latrines themselves are far too close to the hospital. The slaughter men are not even burying the remains from the ration cattle and the stench is unholy. Put plain, if the army stays in that camp for more than a few weeks longer – well, I doubt that you'll have much of an army left to lead, Sir John.'

The general looked back at him, digesting this bleak analysis, then nodded slowly. 'My own view entirely, Blunt. We must most certainly move. And thankfully my orders from London are indeed to shift ourselves, to do what we can to support the Spanish stand to the north on the Ebro. But, more regrettably, that is as far as the orders go. No, I am not informed where or to what extent to succour the Spanish and nor do I have any contact with their new government in Madrid. Any information I receive from the Spanish goes first to London and is filtered back to me in whatever form our own government sees fit. As for the Spanish armies themselves, they have no Commander-in-Chief and I have as yet had no word from any of their generals in the field.'

'Not good, sir.'

'No, not ideal, but I regret it is what we have to deal with. And, as you have seen all too plainly for yourself, Blunt, we most certainly cannot stay here. So what to do? What I propose for the present is to get the men on the march, cross the border into Spain and concentrate on Salamanca. There we will be well placed for a move either north to the Ebro or back south on Madrid, and at Salamanca we might hope for word at last from the Spanish. Even accomplishing that modest ambition will be difficult enough, I dare say. There are no recent maps of Portugal or Spain to be found. We are perilously short of transport and supplies and the French stripped Lisbon of everything of the remotest use before they left. My commissariat, which is zealous but inexperienced, has been reduced to buying up cabs and private carriages for transport. The roads themselves will be difficult enough in any case because the rainy season will presently be upon us. Worst of all, I have precious little gold to buy anything.'

'As the General says, not ideal.'

'No.' Moore said crisply.

Blunt couldn't restrain a small smile. 'But you will march, sir?'

Moore looked back at him, steel glinting in those dark eyes. 'Yes I will Blunt, I will most certainly march – and you, what's more, will come with me.'

Once decided upon, the British march to support the Spanish was likely to offer a testing challenge. Less than three quarters of Sir John Moore's army was assembled there in Lisbon. Around 10,000 men under Sir David Baird were due to land at Corunna in the far north and would tackle the arduous march across the mountains to meet the main army at Salamanca. Nor would the route for the main force be straightforward. Because the road from Lisbon was said by the local Portuguese to be unsuitable for heavy artillery, that vital part of Moore's force had to travel the long way round, east to Badajoz and via the main Madrid road to get to the rendezvous at Salamanca. Thus the British army was in three parts – and, to further complicate matters, its commander had no clear idea just where the French were placed or even where his allies, the Spanish, had their armies. With no reliable maps, Moore could not send such supplies as he had on ahead of the army, so he decided to do his forward scouting for himself – and Captain Robert Blunt went with him.

General Moore travelled fast and light. He rode accompanied only by his aides and by a small cavalry escort. This way he was able to make rapid progress and send back vital intelligence to the main army lumbering its way out of Lisbon. As he had feared, the weather had broken and the rain harried them as they drove north, then east through the pretty wooded slopes of the Serra de Estrela towards Spain. At Almeida, the strong border fortress on the Portuguese side, the general waited for the first of his troops to catch up. But he was impatient to be moving and he was soon on the road again, leading his little scouting party on into Spain. Still he had no reliable intelligence of the Spanish armies or of any French movement. But neither the poor weather nor the lack of any firm news could dampen Moore's fierce determination to gather his army in a position ready to deal with whatever challenge he might be destined to be set by the master of Europe.

The general's scouting party made good ground. Blunt spent as much of the time as possible keeping out of the way. He felt ill at ease in the company of Moore's aristocratic young ADCs and was happier tagging along behind the dragoon rearguard, with the taciturn Widowson and the pack animals for company. Being an unconsidered part of the baggage suited Robert Blunt perfectly well, until the chance for real action came. No great horseman, he was content enough plodding along, enjoying the spectacular countryside, despite the grim weather. But from time to time Moore would call him up and ask him his opinion on the lie of the ground or the potential for local billeting and provisioning. Not only had Blunt campaigned with the general before, he also spoke Spanish with reasonable fluency. He found himself talking to the locals – bargaining with farmers for provisions, asking peasants about mule tracks and river crossings, checking on local flour mills and bake houses, even pleading for hospitality for Moore's party from local nobles. He didn't mind the work; he was glad enough to be kept busy and he was impressed, as ever, by Moore's thoroughness.

When they reached Ciudad Rodrigo, beyond the border on the Spanish side, they were cheered into the city, the fortress guns firing an enthusiastic salute. That was better. Moore was comforted to find that he would at least have a strong, well-provisioned fortress to fall back on if matters did not go well further into Spain. And it became more and more plain to them that the move into Spain was going to be fraught with danger, with or without a sure path back. The general was concerned that his army, marching a number of different routes, was making slow progress, but he had little option now but to press on. The news from France was that as many as 75,000 men were to cross the Pyrenees before the snows, ready to reinforce whatever forces Napoleon already had up there on the Ebro. And yet the local talk in Ciudad Rodrigo was naturally less of what Bonaparte might have in mind, than of the glorious prospects of all of the magnificent Spanish armies which stood ready to face the French. In Rodrigo they were certainly pleased to welcome their British allies, but they were also confident that Castaños, Blake, Palafox and the other Spanish generals had the task well in hand. The talk was all of another victory like Bailen, this time in the north on the Ebro, of pushing the French back over the Pyrenees. And yet, incredibly, still all General Moore had to go on was talk, because he had received no word at all from either generals or Junta.

On to Salamanca...

'This isn't the road we came in on,' Tom said in a small, tired voice. He hadn't spoken at all since they had left the bullring, allowing Rico to lead him quickly through the streets of Jerez to the inn and then placidly following his instructions to ride hard, away from the town. He had felt in no mood to question the Galician's commands, feeling drained by the sword fight, both physically and emotionally. So he had simply done as he was told and he had ridden, following the Gallego's lead. Soon the white walls of the sherry town were out of sight behind them, the beautiful Andalucian horses going at a steady canter. But the oddly mixed feelings of anger, elation and remorse were beginning to fade now for Tom and he was becoming more interested in his surroundings and, in particular, the position of the dropping sun.

'We're going north.'

'Yes.'

'But Cadiz is south,' Tom said lethargically. He was still struggling to focus his mind. He had killed a man before, even in a duel, but it certainly gave him no pleasure either then or now. His earlier cockiness was long gone. He had known all along that with his skill and experience he had a good chance of killing the young Spaniard, had been offered provocation and was fighting for his life, but the fault had been back at the inn, where he had shown no restraint and had allowed the man Duarte to manoeuvre him into the fight. He had been over-proud, naïve and, worse, had been careless with another man's life. That he was good with a sword did not make him any kind of superior being. But he realised that it couldn't now be undone and that he was at least the one who was left alive. Now he must make an effort get a grip on himself and discover Rico's intentions.

'You can't go to Cadiz.' The Spaniard told him.

'Why not?'

'Because you will be killed.'

'By Duarte?'

'Of course.'

Tom was doubtful. 'You think he will challenge me?'

Rico looked over at him, an almost pitying look registering Tom's simplicity. 'I think it unlikely. Don Julian Rodrigo Duarte Vasquez seldom dirties his own hands with such matters, but he is rich and influential enough to find plenty who will do the work for him. You have fought with honour, Lieutenant Herryck, but you have also made an unpleasant enemy. I assure you that Cadiz is now a death-trap for you. Go there and, by another challenge or by assassination, you will be dead in hours. Duarte is vindictive and vengeful. He is also, by the way, capable of being vulgar enough to set the law on you. That too would doubtless see you dead.'

'But I have to get back to Gibraltar,' Tom protested. He had only been given leave of absence for three days.

'Not from Cadiz, nor from any port on this coast.'

'But – '

'Tom, I beg you will listen,' Rico reached over to take the bridle of Tom's horse, bringing them both to a halt. 'Listen to me now. I have your attention? This is not some kind of game. You are a very long way from home and you must realise that you are in bad trouble, very bad. You have killed a Spanish army officer, but worse than that, you have made Duarte look foolish. For that he will kill you – if he can.'

'But it was a perfectly fair fight.'

Rico nodded for them to ride on. 'You are right, for what little that is worth. It was a fair fight and you were, may I say, very impressive. Valdano was quick and dangerous, but you kept him at bay with ease. It was well done. It shows a good military mind that can think to wear an opponent down with defence, then strike so quickly. Maybe it is the mind of the left-handed, who knows? But however good your sword arm, my friend, you must, I beg of you, listen to what I say and accept that your life is forfeit if you show your face in Cadiz. So, we must make a different arrangement. You will have to disappear.'

'Disappear?'

'Yes. We must hide you. Come on,' he kicked his horse into a steady canter. 'Duarte will almost certainly have sent riders out. When they don't find us on the Cadiz road, they will come searching.'

Tom was still doubtful. 'It all sounds a bit dramatic,' he grumbled.

'Welcome to Spain.'

They rode through country heavily planted with vines, fig and olive trees, the rough, chalky soil working hard for the many farms. Tom's mood slowly improved as he thought things over, realised that Rico was right, that he had got himself into an awkward situation and should trust that his friend must know what he was doing in getting him out of it. It was certainly true that he was a long way from England, had no idea of the customs of the country and was in the hands of a man he had met only the day before. But if he was to get to the army in one piece, he acknowledged that he would likely need to be patient. He became intrigued to know what Rico intended. The Galician, however, having successfully convinced Tom of his perilous situation, looked glum and said little. They rode on, the horses tiring now and capable of little above a walk. Tom guessed that they had already come some ten or twelve miles from Jerez. They were deep into the farm country, the land baking in the late afternoon heat. At last Rico reined in his horse and pointed.

'The Casa Rosa.'

'What is that?'

'It means the pink house.'

Sure enough Tom could see a solid building, something less than half a mile distant. It was two storeys high with a red tiled roof and a tall tower to one side. The windows looked as if they were protected by ornate iron grilles.

'Many of the owners keep a house in their vineyards. They use it in summer and for the harvest. In winter they stay in town, because the threat of kidnap for ransom is too great.'

'Is this house occupied? This is surely the summer,' Tom said, feeling the oppressive heat of late afternoon, still something close to a hundred degrees.

'The owner is away, but he is my kinsman. You will be welcome here.'

They rode on to the house.

'Wait here,' Rico said, dismounting and walking briskly the hundred yards or so to another, smaller house. He soon returned accompanied by a middle-aged woman who looked as if she had been interrupted in the process of preparing the evening meal.

'Buenas tardes, senor,' she greeted Tom pleasantly enough and proceeded to open up the house with a large bunch of keys.

'This is Senora Munoz. Her husband is the estate manager. He is still working. Gracias, Senora,' Rico nodded, taking the keys from the woman, who nodded in turn and went off back towards her own house. He gestured for Tom to go inside. They walked through an open, tiled hallway to a cool, shuttered kitchen at the back of the house. Rico examined the keys, then showed Tom which one opened the back door. He placed the heavy keys in the Englishman's hands. 'You will be brought food later at this door, once it is dark. Lock the front door when I leave and don't show any lights. You must stay here until I come back or send someone for you. As you value your life, Tom, you must do exactly as I say. It is essential you are not seen. You understand?'

Tom sighed, feeling tired suddenly and not a little put out at the ridiculousness of the situation. 'Yes, I fully understand your instructions Rico, and I am truly grateful for your concern for me. But I still don't see how an affair of honour, however unfortunate, should create the need for such a brouhaha?'

Rico looked deadly serious, angry even. 'The brouhaha, as you call it, may just save your life. Look, how can I make you appreciate the seriousness of this? You need to realise that you were not involved in an affair of honour, you were part of an unpleasant design by Julian Duarte Vasquez. You frustrated that design and now he will most certainly kill you if he can. If you doubt me, or doubt Duarte's capacity for lethal mischief, I can do little about that. All I can beg of you is simply that you will trust me, on pain of death – your own death.'

Tom nodded, ashamed that he should seem so callow to Rico, again convinced that he had no other option but to do as he asked and to trust him. 'Very well, then. I can't say that I like it. I feel utterly foolish getting into such a scrape, but I doubt that my superiors will be impressed if I end up with my throat cut in an alley in Cadiz. I promise I will do as you say, Rico – and thank you once again, for your care of me.'

The Galician offered a tired smile, 'It was I who got you into this, my friend, so I must try to get you out of it. We must look after one another, eh? Now, I must take those poor tired beasts back to Cadiz and arrange your next move. Look for my return at dusk tomorrow. And remember, no lights and do not for a moment think of stirring beyond these four walls.'

Blunt was in his customary position at the rear of the little column, with the grooms, bat horses and baggage. He was passing time talking to an ancient pig-farmer who, returning from market, was walking alongside the Englishman's horse as they discussed the weather and the melancholy but likely prospects of a hard winter. Widowson, riding alongside his officer, keeping his sharp eyes on the road ahead, simply said the word 'Thickie' and Blunt looked up to see a rider coming back down the line towards them. He was one of Moore's ADCs, a raw young cornet of cavalry, no more than eighteen years old. He was dressed in the fashionable busby, pelisse and frogged jacket of the 15th Hussars. He brought his charger to an immaculate halt and turned to take step alongside Blunt. Widowson had dropped back, but the farmer continued to walk alongside the Englishman, looking with interest at the hussar officer.

'Blunt, the general would speak with you.'

'Very good, Cornet Thicknesse.'

Blunt turned to explain to the farmer that he must break off their conversation.

'Now, man! He's waiting for you,' the hussar snapped impatiently.

'Muchas gracias por su compania, senor,' Blunt said to the farmer, ignoring Thicknesse. 'Y buena suerte con el tiempo en el invierno que viene.'

The old man nodded and, with a warm, toothless grin, wished the Englishman luck in return for the coming winter. Blunt turned to look at Thicknesse, a cold appraising stare.

'Well?' The young aide blustered, not enjoying the infantryman's steady look.

'Well, you call me sir, for a start.'

'What?'

Blunt spoke slowly, quietly so that only the young cavalryman could hear him. 'You heard. And now you can listen to this: I may not have had six or seven years at Eton, boy, nor have I got bits of fur and ribbon on my uniform, but I've had twenty years in this army. I rank as captain and you rank as nothing at all. So, you call me sir in the presence of the men, else I swear I'll have the tripes out of you. Understand, Cornet?'

'Yes, sir,' the hussar said, pale with humiliation and not a little fear of the tough infantry captain. He had heard about this Blunt, knew something of his reputation. However galling it might be, it wasn't the time or place to be falling out with the man – as he said, his senior officer. He gave a little nod of the head, acknowledging the rebuke. 'And now, the general, Captain? He, I believe, has also been in the army a long while – sir.'

Blunt smiled to himself. At least the puppy had some guts.

'Come on then, let's go and see what he wants.'

Up ahead, the column had stopped to rest the horses. They found General Moore easing his stiff muscles by walking with Colonel Graham, his chief ADC, in a grove of cork oaks. He was chewing on a leg of chicken, time for meals on the road being scarce.

'Ah, Blunt. Good. Come and walk with me, if you will. A wee stretch will do you good. This damp weather finds out all of the old wounds, eh?'

'Yes, sir.' Blunt dropped into step alongside the general, on the other side from Graham. Thicknesse, not dismissed, trailed along behind.

'Have you eaten?' Moore waved the leg at him.

'I had breakfast, sir. That will do me until we make camp.' Breakfast had been an apology towards porridge and a piece of fried salt beef, all that Widowson could provide from the ration. But he had eaten worse. There was promise of rabbit stew for supper.

'Tough one, this Blunt,' Moore smiled at Colonel Graham.

'Zeal for king and country keeps you nourished, I dare say, Blunt?'

'Yes, Colonel, sir.' He had time for Graham, another Scot who had spent a huge sum of his personal fortune to raise a regiment years before and who was devoted to his great friend Moore, thirteen years his junior.

'Well, I fear that we're going to need a deal more than patriotic zeal before this business is done, gentlemen,' Moore said, sending the leg bone flying into the undergrowth. 'Our business here is precious little clearer to me. We still have no word from the Spanish and consequently no firm idea of the French dispositions.'

'There is sure to be news at Salamanca,' Graham said.

'I hope so, for there I will have to decide how to proceed – whether to try and hit the French or fall back on Rodrigo, or even back to Portugal itself and with it the possibility of the Royal Navy.'

'That would be a pity,' Graham said, knowing how badly Moore wanted to match himself against Napoleon.

'It would that.'

'I hope we may have the opportunity of a dash at the French, even if we must eventually fall back.'

'So do I, Graham, but only if we have at least a reasonable chance of success – of survival, even. For that we need the army to be whole. General Baird is, I hope, well on the road down from Corunna by now and Sir John Hope is somewhere to the south of us with the artillery column. I can do little about Baird's progress, but it is imperative that I know when Hope will join. Without the guns we are no army at all. And that,' he turned to Blunt, 'Is where you come in, Captain.'

'Sir?'

'Yes Blunt, I need solid, of-the-moment intelligence for once. So, I want you to ride south, down into Extremadura to find General Hope and get his best estimate of his date for joining the main force. You will report back to me at Salamanca. I suspect that it will prove a difficult stretch cross-country if you are to find him from here, so your Spanish will be essential. Speed is of the essence, Blunt. I need to know how we are placed for the rendezvous before I can plan my next move. You understand?'

'Yes, sir.'

'Well, you'd better get on then. Oh, and Blunt? Be so good as to take Cornet Thicknesse with you as escort.' He smiled at the young hussar, 'A bit of experience of rough-slogging in these parts will do no harm for a promising cavalry officer. Will it, eh, young man?'

'No, sir,' said Thicknesse, looking as if rough-slogging with Blunt was about as appealing as bathing in a slurry-pit.

Tom was left alone in the house – a dark and empty Spanish house belonging to he knew not who, miles from anywhere he had heard of, stuck in the middle of a sea of vineyards and not much else. It was a situation that would be ridiculous if it were not also so serious. He was quite happy now to believe Rico's earnest and repeated assertion that his life was in danger, that all of this was in fact necessary, but that was scant consolation. He was furious with himself for his folly. He marvelled at how he could have got himself into such a predicament, being in the middle of nowhere when he was supposed to be part – and, as a trained Royal Engineers officer, a potentially scarce and useful part – of a British army prosecuting the war against Bonaparte's masses. Ridiculous, or worse...

He took a look around the building, if for no other reason than to keep boredom at bay. The rooms were all shuttered, but a little of the fading light seeped in, so Tom could understand why Rico had cautioned against burning lamps once night had fallen. The house was sparsely furnished, but was well enough appointed, with heavy and expensive-looking pieces in each room. His boots echoed on the tiled floors. What must be the dining room looked as if twenty could easily be entertained around its long table and another room held a small but impressive library, in both English and Spanish. He felt impertinent looking around like this, but convinced himself that he was there through no wish of his own and that he at least needed to know the lie of the land. He continued to explore. The wide staircase, to one side of the hall, led up to a number of bedrooms and then on again up into what proved to be the tower he had noticed. Taking care to stay low and out of sight, he found himself looking at a tiled gallery with arched open windows, presumably pleasantly cool in its shade, with views in each direction. A further, smaller stair led up again onto the roof gallery above, which was also covered against the sun and had even better views of the surrounding countryside. It was getting dark now, so he risked a quick look around, peering over the parapet like a truant schoolboy. Tom could see the glow of light from the overseer's house, but from what he could see the rest of the country around the buildings seemed utterly quiet and peaceful, as if nothing extraordinary could ever happen in this pleasant, productive landscape.

Then, with a sudden start, he heard a brisk knocking coming from somewhere below him and he crouched low, remembering with annoyance that he had left his sword on the kitchen table down below. There was nothing for it but to go down and find out what was afoot. Halfway down the stairs he heard the knocking again, realising it was the door at the back of the house. He crept across the kitchen floor as silently as he could. Again the knocking and a gruff, whispered voice, 'Senor, soy Munoz. Abre usted la puerta, por favor.'

The only word he picked up was Munoz – the name Rico had given the overseer – and Tom remembered that he had the man's keys to the house. He picked up the keys from the table – and his sword for good measure – and unlocked the door.

The man stood holding a tray of food. He was dark-skinned with a heavy black moustache, wearing well-worn working clothes. 'Senor?'

'Come in.' Tom said in English, beckoning him inside.

He nodded and did as he was asked.

'Habla espanol?' The man asked, placing the tray on the table. He went to shut the door, handing the keys back to Tom, 'No?' He looked curiously at Tom's coat, which was across a chair. 'No es frances?'

Tom shook his head.

The man looked pleased to hear it. 'Good. I speak a little English. Please, you sit and eat.'

Tom was happy to do as he was told. It had been a long time since their midday meal and a lot had happened since then. The generous serving of lamb and vegetables and the pitcher of wine looked too tempting to ignore. Tom waited to see if the overseer would join him. There was a lot of food.

'Please,' Munoz gestured, 'I will take my meal later. I am used to the hour. But if you are an Englishman you will be hungry now, so you must eat. You are like el Jefe, my master.'

Tom dipped his spoon into the stew, then looked at Munoz. 'Like your master, you say? Please will you sit for a moment, senor, take a cup of wine, perhaps?'

The man looked doubtful, as if it might be improper to sit down in his employer's house, but then, possibly as curious about the stranger as Tom was himself curious about his surroundings, he collected two tumblers from the dresser and sat. He poured the wine into the cups.

'So,' Tom said, 'Your master?'

'My master is English, or part English. His mother, she is a Spanish lady.'

'And he owns these fields, these vineyards?' Tom set about the food. It was rich and delicious. The wine was naturally the same.

'With much else besides; the family business is to send wine to England. And you, senor?'

'Well, I'm certainly English.'

Munoz nodded at Tom's blue coat. 'But not a trader, I think.'

Tom smiled at the thought, 'No, I'm not clever enough for that. I am a soldier.'

'And a friend of Don Federico?'

'Yes.'

He nodded, 'Then that is well enough. Don Federico is of the family. You are welcome here, senor.'

Tom nodded in turn and continued to eat.

'The food is good?'

'Very good, I thank you. It has been a very long day, senor. This is most welcome. Please thank your wife.'

Munoz shrugged, 'A man must keep his strength.'

'Of body and wits alike,' said Tom, still ruefully reflecting that he had shown insufficient quantity of the latter in the day's business.

Munoz took another mouthful of wine, regarding this tall, fair guest. The young man was a long way from his friends. He wondered what mischance had brought him there to Casa Rosa. But that was not his business. Don Federico had said he must be looked after, and that was enough. He wiped his moustache, then stood. 'I must return to my own house.'

Tom scraped back his chair. 'Thank you for the meal.'

'My wife says that you are here because you are in danger and must stay hidden here until Don Federico returns.'

'Yes.' Tom was glad the lady was so well informed.

'Then, senor, you must burn a small light only in this room, where it will not be seen and keep the door barred. I will leave bread, cheese and milk by the door before dawn, then you must stay out of sight. If there is no sign from Don Federico, I will return tomorrow after dark. There is a blanket in that cupboard and I will bring you a jar of water. But of all things, senor, it is most important that you stay hidden.'

It went against the grain, this doing nothing, but Tom was content enough to do as he was told, just as long as Rico was back as he had promised the following evening. He enjoyed his food, surprising himself by finishing the entire bowl, and then he had found and borrowed a calf-bound English edition of the first part of Gibbon's "History of the Decline and Fall of The Roman Empire". He felt that would be adequate to see him nicely off to sleep by the light of his modest candle, so he followed the instructions he had received and lay curled in his blanket, like the family lurcher in the corner of the kitchen. With the doors bolted and locked and all of the windows shuttered the house was utterly silent. Having spent much of the time during recent months in crowded barracks or onboard ship, it seemed a long time since Tom had experienced true silence. He wasn't sure whether or not he quite liked it.

Yet Gibbon had done his work perfectly well, the book resting in his lap unread for a couple of hours, as he dosed fitfully – eccentric dreams full of skewed images of bull rings, drinking dens and beautiful dark-eyed women drifting through his mind, but Tom came instantly awake as he heard what was almost certainly the clink of a spur or horse's bit. He scrambled to his feet, his eyes struggling to adjust to the pitch black, as the candle had burned down. Again there was a metallic, clinking sound. He stood stock still and listened. He regretted the absence of his pistols, which were sitting where he had left them on his bed at the inn in Cadiz, but there was nothing he could do about that and for the moment he simply waited, leaving his sword where it was, as moving it could only make a noise. There was movement outside the back of the house now, soft and deliberate, so that he wondered if he heard it or merely sensed it, but he knew that someone was there. He heard the latch being tried on the back door. He was ready to go for the sword. Again the latch was tried, not budging the locked door, then nothing. He could hear his own breathing loud in his head. Still he dare not move, then he felt himself jump involuntarily as he heard a shout from the direction of Munoz's house and the bark of a dog; and then there was the welcome, quite distinct sound of horses galloping away.

He hadn't managed to get back to sleep again, but his reading had witnessed a fair degree of decay in the greatest empire the world had ever seen and he had even found himself musing just how quickly or not the present imperial tyrant might be induced towards his own decline. It was an interesting question, he thought, and one with no satisfactory answer. If he was honest, Tom had a sneaking admiration for Napoleon Bonaparte – a wholly conditional admiration for the man as military genius and social reformer rather than as empire-building megalomaniac; yet his disturbing conversations with Rico about Spain's almost chronic unsuitability to fulfil the role of France's nemesis in western Europe made him less than confident that this latest empire might decline and fall any time soon.

Light from the galleries filtering down the staircase finally told him of the coming of that day's dawn and shortly afterwards a knock at the door told him of the arrival of sustenance. By the time he had the door open Munoz was halfway back to his house, but Tom saw him give him a little nod, and a gesture back towards Casa Rosa, as if to remind him of his duty. He smiled to himself, half-amused that his duty had been reduced to nothing more than hiding in a deserted pink villa. He took his food inside and locked the door again.

Later, crouching in the gallery, he used his pocket glass to spy the country. He found it a perfectly pleasant pastime, even regretted that he had no sketchbook to run off some drawings, having completely filled his journal with plans, notes, maps and doodles of Cadiz and Jerez. The Casa Rosa was at the highest point for miles around and he had a magnificent view in every direction. It seemed to him that there was an unusual amount of horsemen on the dusty tracks for so rural a setting, but that might be a symptom of his own nervousness. And then, about noon, two of these riders came right up to the house – unpleasant-looking types with wide-brimmed hats and muskets slung over their shoulders. When Senora Munoz appeared with the dog, they called out to her and Tom picked out the word "Ingles" spoken in guttural, unpleasant tones. Whatever the overseer's wife told them it was enough to see them trotting their horses away to the next place, evidently content for the moment that Casa Rosa held no such Ingles. Tom relaxed his grip on the sword handle.

It was a long day.

Rico had promised he would return by dusk. Tom had no reason to doubt him. But by the time the perfect blue sky had bruised and turned towards night there was still no sign of the Galician. All had been peaceful around the house since the noontime visit of the horsemen. He had seen Munoz' wife a couple of times, feeding the hens or watering her little garden, but he had seen no sign of the overseer, who was doubtless at work somewhere in the endless vine fields. He had spotted another pair of riders in the far distance, but they had not come near Casa Rosa.

It was quite relaxing, he found, sitting up there in the pleasant shade under the roof, as night gathered over the fields beyond. He was beginning to think that Rico had perhaps exaggerated his plight after all and that there was sure to be an innocent, rational explanation for armed riders being abroad in the wine country. Just how badly could the Duarte man want his skin? He was even considering letting himself out and going to the overseer's house to find out about borrowing a horse or mule to ride down to Jerez, when he picked out what looked like yet another pair of horsemen – or thought he did – in the dying light. It could have been two, or more; certainly there had been something moving on the road he and Rico had used. He tried his glass, but it didn't really help; whoever it was had vanished behind a fold in the land.

He was about to quit the gallery as being of no use, with only a sliver of moon to illuminate the landscape, when a rider clearly appeared not two hundred yards away, too slim and tall in the saddle to be Munoz. There was also something odd about how the horseman handled his mount, but Tom had no time now to consider riding techniques, nor even to watch their approach. He slid to the stairs and made his way quickly to the hall, collecting his unsheathed sword as he went.

He could hear the horse come to a halt at the front of the house, the creak of the rider dismounting. He waited. The expected knock came on the door. He didn't know who it was, but he knew for certain it wasn't Rico. Tom did nothing, content that the door was locked, that its trusty oak was stout enough to resist blows or even musket fire. But then, with an unwelcome frisson of surprise, he heard what sounded distinctly like the grating of a key. He was horrified to see the handle slowly turn and the big wooden door begin to open towards him. This wasn't in the plan. What was happening? It was too late to think of hiding now; he had no idea what he was in for, but he crouched and prepared to spring, speed his only chance if they had firearms. He held his sword forward, ready to cut, thrust or simply hammer.

The rider, indistinct against the gloomy evening light, stood on the threshold watching him.

'Oh, gracious! I beg you sir, do please put up your blade, else I fear you'll quite likely ruin my best riding habit.'

'Good God,' said Tom, his mouth dropping open.

Chapter Four

'Good God, an Englishwoman.'

At least, he thought in his confusion, she had most certainly sounded English.

She had taken a step forward and now stood in the doorway. He saw a good-looking woman in her early thirties, with fine dark eyes and high cheekbones. From what he could see in the half-light, her complexion was nearer to the warm honey-colour of the local beauties he had seen in Cadiz and Jerez than he would expect in one of his own nationals, but she was certainly striking. There was a lock of dark brown hair showing under a wide-brimmed hat. Her jacket and skirt, though dusty, were of expensive-looking cloth. She wore an amused, slightly questioning expression.

'Well now, I hope that I might be forgiven for nurturing the expectation that a gentleman – and I am sure you are such, Lieutenant Herryck – that a *gentleman* would be kind enough to describe me as a lady. But I am told I often expect too much in life.'

Tom straightened from his crouch, feeling faintly ridiculous. He still held his sword, unsure what exactly was going on.

'I beg your pardon,' he blustered. 'I meant no offence, ma'am. I believed, that is, I was expecting – well, not you.'

'What exactly were you expecting? And by the by, would you be so kind as to sheathe your sword, sir? I am sure it is a comfort to you but it is, alas, doomed to be quite useless for defence. The man behind you might have cut your throat at any time this last minute.'

Tom immediately turned around to come face to face with a tall black man dressed in a turban and a long dark robe. His eyes stared fixedly and intently into Tom's own. He made no move, but held Tom's eyes in his steady, impassive gaze. He also held a wickedly curved knife inches from the Englishman's neck. Beyond the man Tom could see the back door gaping open.

'How – '

'Sword please,' the woman repeated behind him.

Tom had little choice. He kept his eyes on the man and passed the sword carefully around his back towards her.

'Oh heavens, I don't want the ridiculous thing,' she said, a note of impatience in her voice, 'just put it down. You are quite safe, I assure you –

for the time being, at least. Omar, would you go and deal with the animals and see if Senora Munoz has food and drink for now and for the journey.' The black man instantly slipped the knife into his sash and bowed to her. Tom, relieved to see the knife disappear, turned back to his visitor, who remained standing on the threshold, half-hidden in the gloom of gathering night. 'Now, Lieutenant Herryck, may I be allowed to come in?' she said. 'After all, I do live here.'

They had left Casa Rosa well before dawn and were already several miles to the north by the time the sun was fully in the sky and the land was taking on its bleached daily form. There had been very little talking. It had been made plain to Tom that putting miles between themselves and the house was their prime and only concern.

'Where are we going?' Tom asked now, becoming impatient and tiring of the endless silence.

It had all moved very quickly the night before – too quickly to allow for questions, it seemed, or at least for answers. The woman, whose name apparently was Isobel Truelove de Chambertain, did at least confirm that she had indeed been sent to him by Rico. She had even proved this by giving him a note from the Galician, simply telling Tom that he regretted that he was unable to take him away in person, but that the bearer would escort him to safety and that he must completely and unreservedly obey her instructions. He had not seen the Galician's handwriting before, but the tone sounded about right. The woman and her servant went about their work in a businesslike manner. They had brought a horse for Tom and a pack mule, which he was surprised to find, proved to be carrying his portmanteaux from his Cadiz room, as well as other supplies. The servant Omar had also produced for Tom a civilian riding outfit which might make him blend more easily with the landscape than his blue jacket and cocked hat, which were now neatly wrapped up and packed onto the mule. Omar said not a word and the woman talked only to give him instructions. She was cool, briskly efficient, apparently disinclined to do any more than was necessary to command their readiness for departure. Tom, who was as a rule interested in women, was certainly intrigued by this one. She obviously knew the layout of the house perfectly well and was clearly well-known and respected by Munoz and his wife. So perhaps she did live there, as she had said; the wife of the English landowner? Tom, more confused at every turn, felt that it would be easiest to stop thinking about it and simply to do as he was told. They took a quick meal at the kitchen table, locked the house and were gone.

They had set off at a good pace, the woman plainly familiar with the roads, even in the wintry moonlight and then the half-light of dawn. They had soon left his refuge long behind. Now they were riding side by side, picking their way along a dusty, rutted wagon track, the Moor following behind with the pack animal. Tom Herryck, feeling rather like a young schoolboy too callow and insignificant to be told the whole truth of what was happening, found himself wondering if the mule might be better informed than he. He was confused and not a little angry now. If proving to be a fascinating experience, being in Spain was also turning out to be perplexing, surprising and disturbing. He didn't like being so consistently out of control of matters, his fate seemingly in the hands of complete strangers. He looked across at the woman, who had not answered his question about their destination. She also had changed her clothes at Casa Rosa, swapping a practical, less noticeable outfit for the fashionable riding costume she had arrived in. She rode well, straight-backed, with her eyes fixed on the road ahead of them.

'So, where?' he prompted her.

She continued to look ahead. She was wearing a wide-brimmed hat against the sun, but he still saw glimpses of those strikingly high cheekbones. From their short businesslike exchanges at the Casa, he knew her to have fine, intelligent eyes and a provocative way of conversing. If annoyingly reticent, she was certainly a looker, Tom thought. Yes, definitely intriguing, this one. She must know something of the goings on at Jerez from Rico, clearly had the Galician's trust, and yet from her expression she appeared to find the situation part tiresome, part amusing. 'Do you mean where are we going at this present time or as a final destination?' she said at last.

'Both.'

'Both? Very well, let me see. We will presently turn east towards Arcos – Arcos de la Frontera, that is – then north again. But we will avoid Seville, I am afraid, a very large city where your fame will already have travelled. It is a somewhat whimsical route, you may imagine, but we will find our road well enough. So, a wide berth for Seville, then we will cross the Sierra Morena and on into Extremadura.'

Tom was horrified, his modest knowledge of Spanish geography good enough to tell him that they were travelling in exactly the opposite direction to that which would take him where he should be. 'The Sierra Morena? But that is a huge distance from Cadiz.'

She looked amused at his surprise. 'Why, of course it is. Ours would be a very strange route to choose to take us to Cadiz. But then, Lieutenant, we are not going to Cadiz.'

'But I have to get back to Gibraltar,' he protested.

'That is not wise.'

'Well, wise or not – '

'I assure you, Lieutenant, we are doing just what you want and will presently be returning you to your army.' She looked across at him. 'That *is* what you want, is it not?'

Tom, quite befuddled by her calm authority, could hardly argue with her. That was exactly what he wanted. 'Well, yes. I must report for duty, of course, will be most grateful if you are so kind as to take me there, to the army. But where, if not Gibraltar?'

She gave him a look which suggested she couldn't credit that he could ask such a question. 'Why, in Portugal, of course. Where else? That assuredly is where the British army is at present.'

'Portugal?'

'Oporto in particular.'

Tom shook his head at the ridiculousness of it, saying sarcastically, 'Oporto, naturally! Why didn't I think of it myself? Even farther from here, further north even than Lisbon.'

'Yes, Oporto would most certainly be the sensible option, as that is the area where General Wellesley is likely to be found with your comrades. Down in Lisbon, I fear that nasty Monsieur Junot was still in residence with twenty thousand Frenchmen when last we heard.' She turned to him with a smile. 'Besides, I expect to find my brother in Oporto, so it suits both of our purposes equally well. Do you not agree, Lieutenant?'

'Oh, equally well,' Tom said, as he took in this latest news, trying to see a way he wasn't heading straight for a court martial for desertion, or worse.

But Isobel Truelove de Chambertain just smiled and looked back to the road ahead. It was rather a sweet smile he thought, despite himself, trying to find at least some small consolation in his increasingly ridiculous situation. On the positive side, she had at least got him safely away from Casa Rosa and its mysterious visitors. But to what purpose? Once again he wondered if he should not be considering having no more to do with it and turning back to take his chances on getting through to Gibraltar.

It was as if she read his thoughts. She was all seriousness now: 'Remain calm I beg you, Lieutenant. Rico told me about your dealings with Duarte, you know. He also told me that he doubted that you truly realise the danger you are in, that you appear to treat it as some kind of joke. But I promise you, there is nothing amusing about Julian Duarte, nothing at all. He really is the most foul creature and will certainly have you killed if he is able. What Rico told you was the truth, I promise you, and the coast is no place for you. However unpalatable it may seem, however tiresome and provoking, this is by far your best course.' She looked across at him and smiled. 'After all, it is only a matter of a hundred leagues from Jerez to Oporto.'

'More like two hundred,' Tom mumbled, grim at the prospect.

'No, one hundred. But you will find that a Spanish league measures four and one quarter miles by land, while in England – '

'A league is only two and a quarter miles,' Tom said, privately reflecting that the sum added up to a distance of over four hundred miles by the leagues of any nation – and across rugged country with roads barely meriting the description. It would be a huge journey, quite possibly taking them as long as a month. But it seemed that it was a journey about which he had little choice in taking if he was to get to Wellesley's army.

'So you see,' she said brightly. 'We agree after all. And now we know what must be done to achieve a happy outcome. After all, I'm sure you are a very able and valuable officer, a vital part of your army, but you will be of little value to anyone if you are not alive, will you? Now, I think it high time that we stop wasting time in pointless discussion and concentrate the best of our energies on accomplishing some of those leagues. Do you not agree, Lieutenant Herryck?'

They had ridden for three hours more in almost total silence. If not quite sulking, Tom Herryck was brooding unhappily on the strange turn of events that was so successfully keeping him from his duty. It was no small matter to him. He had waited patiently for his chance of real action. His only field service had been at Copenhagen, when they took the city and with it the important Danish naval fleet. But he was desperate to test himself against the French, the ultimate military challenge. A month was such a long time. He dreaded the thought of missing important action. He had skills and training and he wanted to put them to use. But here he was, stranded out in the middle of nowhere without a clue how Wellesley might be getting on over in Portugal. This was such a huge country! Much as he would like to drum up an alternative, he found he had to accept that the woman's plan was now his best chance of getting safely back to the army.

The road, if road wasn't too flattering a name, had been difficult and the heat was hammering at them all of the time. At last they had come in sight of a thin grove of what looked to Tom like half-formed oak trees near the brow of a hill. Isobel Truelove de Chambertain had declared in that way of hers that this was the place for to halt, as it was time to rest the horses and eat. So they took their midday break. Again everything was accomplished in a businesslike fashion; the grave, silent Moor looked after the animals while the woman produced food and drink from the packs. Tom, with no role in this, stretched his legs in the welcome shade, pausing to look here and there through his pocket glass. They were in a good position to see the land for miles around – not that there was much to see beyond an arid landscape with not a single soul in view.

'Come and eat,' she said. 'It is unlikely that Duarte's men will be this far yet. Casual bandits are more a danger. But we are safe enough for the moment. Omar will keep guard.'

Tom did as he was told and sat on the ground alongside the blanket she had laid out with their meal. There was a round country loaf, cheese, olives, ham and fruit, a small flask of wine and a water bottle.

'No glassware or cutlery I fear. I take it you have your clasp knife?'

Tom was delighted to see the food. 'Certainly. What about your servant?'

'He will take his food alone. Pork and alcohol are not to the Mahometan's taste. Omar will be perfectly content. Please eat, Lieutenant.'

Tom did as he was told and gratefully began the meal. 'Is it usual to have a Moorish servant?' he asked after the first few mouthfuls. 'I had thought all of the Moors and Jews had been expelled from these parts at the time Ferdinand and Isabella were sending their man Columbus to the Americas?'

She smiled. 'Create a new world and damn an old one? You are partly right, I suppose. But no, there are still Moors to be found in Spain. Omar himself was slave to a Christian merchant – a cruel, unpleasant man. He removed his tongue, among other kindnesses. My father rescued him.'

Looking in the direction of the Moor, Tom could see that Omar was preparing to pray, having laid down his mat. 'He seems to be a valuable servant, whatever his history.'

Isobel shrugged, as if it were barely worthy of discussion. 'He has pledged himself to our family. In truth, he has really become a part of it. He has saved the life of more than one of us. He is strong, intelligent, discreet and loyal. So he has value, great value, yes.'

'You talk of your family – '

'Do I?' The dark eyes flashed.

Tom inclined his head. 'I beg your pardon. You *mention* your family. At the pink house, when you first appeared at the door, I remember that you said it, the house that is, belonged to you.'

'No. I believe I said that I lived there, which is true – some of the time.'

Tom was no better informed. 'So then, who does it belong to? Rico said it was his kinsman. And Munoz said that his master was English.'

She smiled, as if to say that she would indulge his curiosity, for the moment. 'That is quite true. My brother William owns the house. Federico is a cousin at a certain remove and was also the husband of our sister.'

'Was?'

'She died.'

Tom thought of the Galician's often mournful expression, his almost invariable reserve. Now something of that made sense. 'I am sorry, for both of you. He didn't tell me.'

She nodded. 'That is no great surprise. Nor indeed does it reflect poorly on his regard for you, Lieutenant. Rico simply doesn't care to talk about himself. And what happened to Maria was desperately sad, because they were happy, so completely happy, and they had so little time. My sister was very beautiful, but she was fragile. I'm not sure the cold winter of the north was right for her, but she was determined to be with her husband in his own country. She took a fever and wasn't strong enough to survive it. It was a great loss for all of us, but sadly we learn that such things happen under God.'

'Does Rico believe that, do you think, that it was nobody's fault?'

She gave him a sharp look, as if weighing whether or not he asked the question out of fondness for Federico, then concentrated on peeling an orange. 'I am very fond of my cousin. But I don't claim a facility to read his personality, not at all. I certainly hope that he doesn't hold himself responsible for Maria's loss, but it wouldn't be surprising. The northerners are different, you know, prone to be inward looking and low-spirited – probably because their land is constantly beaten by the cruel Atlantic. But Rico is a fine, decent man. For me, he is rather more like a brother. We trust one another, I suppose. He certainly trusts me enough to have me look after his valuable new English friend. He said I was to take care of you and endeavour to get you where you need to be. He liked you, I think, and Rico does not easily take to people.' She looked at him appraisingly, 'He said there was something in you, that you were a man of possibilities.'

A compliment?

'Where is he?' Tom asked, fascinated by all that Isobel had told him, certainly intrigued by the woman herself, yet also wondering if Rico too had been put in danger by the business with Duarte.

Isobel offered him a segment of orange on the point of her knife. 'Oh, he is well enough. He has also gone north, specifically to Aranjuez, the old royal summer palace near Madrid. The politicians are meeting again. More shouting and arguing, I imagine. It's the old nonsense; they are to try again to form a central government.'

Tom was surprised, 'But I thought Rico said that he had despaired of all that business?'

'Quite likely he did. He had tired of the juntas and their absurdities long before he set out from Galicia. But he promised his father, who is very ill, that he would at least try. Whatever else he is, Rico is a man of his word.'

'Will they succeed this time?'

Isobel looked sceptical. 'Whether they make an agreement or not, I doubt there will be any real or lasting unity, nor any clear thinking. The grandees who represent the ordinary people in these matters are usually of the old ways, jealous of change and of losing their grasp on local power. No, they will almost certainly go on snarling at one another and rehearsing old grievances until it is too late. And what is worse, if nothing is done, the French will likely be all over this land well before the next grape harvest.'

'And your name?' Tom said at length, deciding to change direction after digesting this gloomy, if convincing prophecy. 'What about your name?'

'My name?'

'Yes. It sounds partly English, which you have explained, and partly, well, French.'

She sighed. Then a little nod: 'It is. Chambertain is French. There is precious little mystery to why that should be. My family, my English family, deals in wine. We export from Jerez through Cadiz and we ship port wine from the Douro in Portugal. We have also long had connections with growers in Bordeaux, which is how I met my husband. The wine trade is strong on family alliances. The house of Truelove is not particularly long-established or of the nobility, but our family has become what some consider to be wealthy and that offers attractions to men of distinguished lineage but with empty pockets. So a match was made and sure enough I married my Frenchman. It was a happy arrangement that suited all parties well enough, including myself. But the Truelove girls are not destined to stay wed, it seems. My husband was a good man, a friend to his people and a patriot, but he was a patriot of the unfashionable kind. He was of the French royalist persuasion. His allegiance to the Bourbons cost him his life and I returned here.'

'Again, I'm sorry for your loss,' Tom told her, unable to think of anything else to say. His own family life in Nottinghamshire seemed so very ordinary and uneventful compared to the trials of these people.

But she gave a little shake of the head, 'Oh Lieutenant, I am sorry as well. You will think me glum and Spain a very melancholy place. It is not, I promise you. All of this talk of deaths and wars and bad government shouldn't blind you to the fact that this is a remarkable country, with a spirited and tenacious people. There is much to be admired about Spain, you know, for those with a will to see, listen and breathe in its senses. This is a land of light, poetry, chivalry and great natural beauty – as well, it is true, of blood, poverty and deep religious gloom. But that is the way the place is! You will find it is not a country, Spain, but an enigma – one that I, for one, hold as dear as life itself. And do you know,' she looked at him, fixing him with those disturbingly direct eyes, 'I even dare to hope, Lieutenant, that you yourself might even one day come to love it a little and perhaps feel able to make use of your talents on its behalf.'

'Talents?'

'Oh, I'm sure you have them,' she smiled.

Tom returned her smile, grateful at least that she had opened up and spoken so frankly to him. 'Well, Senora Truelove de Chambertain, if by any chance we find that I do have talents of any nature, here I have been sent with my redcoat brothers to place them at your country's disposal. And you make such a convincing advocate for Spain I hardly dare not try to love it, just as you suggest. Indeed, I can assure you that I have found so much of what I have seen in these few days perfectly fascinating – certainly exotic to my staid English eyes. And one thing is for dead certain, ma'am, it most definitely ain't a place that's dull!'

That night they slept in a deserted farmhouse, the following under the stars, Tom huddled in his boat cloak, the others in their horse blankets, close to the animals for warmth as the heat of the day gave way to a sharp drop in temperature at the fading of the light. But Isobel, however cold the night, wouldn't hear of them searching out a hospitable farmhouse or village inn. Even mule-drivers and farmers working in the fields were avoided where possible, lest they spread news of the riders' passing. She insisted that they must make their way as secretly as possible, thoroughly convinced that the vengeful Duarte would yet be looking for them.

They eventually travelled across the Guadalquivir river well to the east of Seville and then passed on up into to the hills of the Sierra Morena, its sides clad in oak and pine woods, offering welcome shelter from the heat of the day and the chill of the night. The rough mountain tracks seemed to wind on forever. Tom had his compass and a rudimentary map of southern Spain, but he could make no detailed guess as to their whereabouts and could only trust that they were still following Isobel's original plan. Both she and Omar seemed perfectly content as the journey went on, up there on the dusty mule tracks, day after day. The woman, high-bred and outwardly delicate of form, surprised Tom by how easily she took the rigours of the hard road. He had little choice but to follow her example and make the best of it and enjoy the unexpected chance to take in the odd, very un-English countryside.

Isobel had shown him flamingos, eagles – once Omar had pointed to what Isobel confidently told him was a lynx, prowling up in the rocks in search of prey. When he allowed himself to forget the time it was taking to progress, Tom was charmed. He was, after all, a countryman and, even though this rugged, dusty terrain was unlike anything he had seen in the English midlands, he was appreciative of the chance to see such sights. Spain was beginning to captivate him, just as she had warned him it might. But eventually they came down from the sierra and onto the plains of Extremadura, very different country indeed, and they began to go more or less directly north.

'Do you know, I think we might easily risk visiting a town?' Isobel told him after they had crossed the Guadiana river and found their way back to the main northern road. Still the country was poor and sparsely populated – pigs rooting in cork groves, the odd windmill, distant green mountains. Few people: 'We need supplies and these horses are all but finished. Also it would be useful to find out the latest news.'

They had been on the road for almost two weeks now and all of them, humans and animals, were looking the worse for wear from insufficient rest and constant vigilance – with the exception of Omar, the silent Moor, who just seemed to Tom to ride on calm and alert, as if nothing could ruffle his quiet dignity.

'Do you imagine we are safe from pursuit now?' he asked. Long since resigned to seeing the adventure through, he was now far more interested in pressing on than looking backward.

Isobel considered it. 'I imagine it depends just how determined Julian Duarte is to have you killed. The wretch is apt to be something fickle in his unpleasant whims. He is perfectly capable of having found some other pique to engage his spite, but he is equally likely to have formed an obsession, an unpleasant obsession, and devote all of his considerable resources to gaining his revenge.'

'That's a comfort,' he said, not quite liking the idea of being the subject of an obsession.

She smiled, as if to suggest that matters might be worse. 'The real comfort is that, even if his scoundrels are still searching for you, they will have somehow to have found our scent and that will have taken time, luck even, and a great deal of effort. For the present I am more concerned by local bandits or even stray parties of Frenchmen.' She gave him another little smile, 'I too am far from home now, you see, a long way from salt air. And running away is a trying business, is it not?'

'A town would certainly make a refreshing change, ma'am,' Tom said. And a bath and a hot meal would refresh him more than anything, he thought. 'Where do you have in mind?'

'I am sure that you will find that Caceres is a quiet town, a relaxed and pleasing place,' she had said, as they dismounted at the Arco de la Estrella, the low-arched gateway which gave in to the old town from the main plaza, 'It has not the lively charms of London or Lisbon, nor even of Cadiz, but it has everything we need including, I hope, news. So Lieutenant, leave your horse with Omar and come with me. We will meet him at the inn, but first we really must find out what is happening in the world.'

They made an odd couple – handsome undoubtedly, but neither of them at their best in old riding clothes, with the dust of many days upon them, there amongst the elegant buildings of Caceres. A quiet town possibly, Tom acknowledged, but certainly interesting to a northern eye. He even wondered if he might be able to snatch the opportunity to do some sketching. Despite finding paper for him back at Casa Rosa, Isobel had flatly refused his requests to let him draw her, though he suspected that by now he was capable of a decent effort from memory. He had, after all, been in her company day and night for a fortnight, as they had travelled a not inconsiderable piece of Spain. It would at least be something of a consolation if he had some record of his odyssey set down on paper.

This Caceres looked promising. Neither Lisbon nor London it may be, nonetheless it appeared to Tom to be a well set-up, prosperous place, its building old and long-established, apparently untouched by war or the usual local feuding. Isobel had told him that in Caceres' high days, in medieval times, an order of around three hundred knights had each demonstrated his individual power by having a private, fortified mansion built within the walls; but those times were long gone and now it was simply a quiet merchants' town, as likely as anywhere to have reasonable tidings of how matters stood in the world. But, with the complexity Tom was coming to expect from all of his dealings with Spain, Isobel explained that they would need to find exactly the right place to get their information. Isobel spoke the language, of course, but was a woman. Tom might be readily expected to ask for tidings of the great happenings of the day, having clearly been long on the road, but he couldn't speak a word of Spanish. They settled eventually on a ferreteria, or an ironmonger's shop, where Tom could look haughty, disdainfully picking up the odd blade or set of bellows, and Isobel could do the woman's work of bargaining and gossiping.

For the price of a cooking pot, a cheap pair of spurs and a good firewood-axe, Isobel spent the best part of an hour being offered the wisdom of a series of apparently well-informed shop customers. She had no need of a Madrid newspaper with this enthusiastic commentary: she discovered that the long-awaited Central Junta had finally come into existence at Aranjuez, so Spain now at last boasted some kind of national government. Whether or not it would prove to wield any useful power waited to be seen, but there was general satisfaction that the regional leaders were at least talking to one another. The Spanish army, or armies, were now expected to march north on the Ebro and clear away the impertinent French. As ever, the name of Bailen came up again and again. The victory, as Rico had warned Tom, had continued to have its worth blown into something much more than one battle won. The people in Caceres clearly believed Napoleon and the Grande Armée no threat at all. So, the war was more or less over. Isobel merely nodded, asking the odd question, storing up the information to pass on to Tom later, when they could speak in English.

She also received the welcome news that Wellesley's army in Portugal had fought a couple of battles against the French, winning and forcing the enemy to surrender, but having the victory undermined by seeing the capable Wellesley superseded by a new general. Worse, the French had been offered ridiculously generous terms and were now expected to be taken home with all of their arms, possessions and doubtless their plunder by the Royal Navy!

All of this Isobel told him later, once they had found Omar at the inn.

Tom was well enough pleased with what he heard. 'So, General Wellesley has given the French a bloody nose, even if they have been let off the hook. No matter, at least they'll clear off from Portugal. That was the first part of the job we were sent here to do. Perhaps the famous Spanish armies can have their wish and have a dash at them in the north now. And, as to ourselves, ma'am, the way is clear, is it not?'

Isobel didn't look so sure. 'Possibly – although I should not care to say it for certain; even if a truce has been made as people say, Junot was still loitering around Lisbon the last anyone here heard, so it may not quite be all over. We should remain cautious, particularly where the French are concerned. It is only gossip, remember.'

'Well, at least it sounds promising. But you are right; I would hate to come this far, only to present myself to the French to be taken off to Verdun or some other dismal dungeon.'

'That isn't the plan,' she smiled.

The pair of them were at dinner. They had both had the opportunity to wash and change. Tom had seen no good reason to prevent him from putting on his uniform in this allied town and Isobel had changed into her original riding habit from Casa Rosa, which was cleaner and more obviously feminine. Her dark brown hair was elegantly styled in the Spanish fashion, pulled back from her face, which showed off to good effect her dark eyes and angled cheekbones. She looked cool and relaxed, cheered by the news of events across the border. Omar, who didn't appear to need rest, was somewhere dealing with the practical business of finding fresh horses and getting their other clothes clean for morning.

The inn was perfectly respectable, with a formal dining room, and the food was very good. Tom was unsurprised to see several of the men giving Isobel appreciative glances. One or two of them also looked curiously at his uniform and fair hair. But he could put up with curious glances, was content that they were now on the home stretch back to where he belonged, in the bosom of the army. Even the threat of the troublesome Duarte seemed far away now. They ate heartily, each leaving a thoroughly stripped bone to what had once been a tasty leg of kid. Over a plate of thin-sliced cheese they discussed their next move.

As ever, it was Senora Truelove de Chambertain who had assumed command:

'So then, here is our situation. We are well on with delivering you to Wellesley and so far we have eluded Julian Duarte's attentions. If we continue north from here we will come to the city of Salamanca,' she told him, refilling his wine glass, 'where we can again rest and find provisions. East from Salamanca are the border fortress towns of Ciudad Rodrigo and, on the Portuguese side, Almeida. From what we have been told here Ciudad Rodrigo should still be in Spanish hands, but whoever occupies the fortress cities they are likely to be dangerous places at present and we will need to know for sure who has possession of them. We should still be cautious. I'm not sure how much I believe of what we were told about the war back there in the ferreteria, because history has often proved that the Spanish people can be wildly over-optimistic about their army's prowess, so we must certainly remain vigilant. But Salamanca is familiar territory for me and should be safe enough for our next stop.'

'Surely the further north we go, the more likely we are to run into the French?' Tom reasoned.

She offered him a provocative smile, 'I thought that was why you were here, Lieutenant Herryck, to meet the French?'

Tom broke a piece of cheese and smiled back at her, perfectly willing to be teased. 'I look forward with great eagerness to making their acquaintance in the field, ma'am, but not necessarily on my own.'

'No, that would not be wise. In any case, it certainly appears that your General Wellesley's army has beaten them in Portugal. No, I don't have any doubt about that part of the news. My brother knows Arthur Wellesley quite well and he says he is a reliable and capable man. William felt that he was a good choice to send here to the Peninsula to deal with the French and it sounds as if he has done just that. So, Lieutenant Herryck, you are likely to join your friends at last and find that you have no work to do.'

Tom shook his head, knowing he had little chance of a quiet life once he rejoined the colours. 'If what we heard is true, and Wellesley certainly is regarded as a decent commander – indeed I even served in the same campaign as him at Copenhagen – if he has beat Junot, he has so far dealt with but one small army. Regrettably there are several other small French armies in Spain and Portugal and Bonaparte himself has been busy putting together a very large one in the north – and that gentleman moves damnably quick when he chooses! No, the fact is that Wellesley, or whoever has taken over from him, has just one British army and he will have to be very careful with it. The French won't be leaving the Peninsula after one or two defeats by either English or Spanish armies.'

'You believe so?' There was surprise and disappointment in her voice.

'I'd wager a great deal on it. I'm afraid that if Spain wants to be ruled by the Spanish, it will have to fight long and hard. You see, Napoleon Bonaparte is a man with a tidy mind. He sees France's natural borders as being the same as those of the old Roman Empire. The French believe it is their destiny, their right even, to govern all Europe and so will take whatever steps are necessary to achieve that aim. And I fear the unsavoury truth is that they're making a damnedly good job of it! Every other power except England is either occupied or held at bay by treaty. They are most certainly here in the Peninsula to stay, if they possibly can. There is a long and very likely bitterly unpleasant war to be fought if Spain and her allies are to get them out.'

Isobel furrowed her brow, looking suitably gloomy at Tom's analysis. 'Well, naturally I bow to your military instinct, Lieutenant. Perhaps the Spaniard in me is guilty of that national foible of over-optimism. But I forgive myself the lapse, for I believe that no sane person wants war, especially on his own soil. But then that makes it all the more important that we get you to where you can be of use to your army. So, I repeat, let us get ourselves as far as Salamanca and consider the position once we are there. It is a very beautiful old university city and, who can say, you may even have the chance to do some of your drawings? But more to the point, we will certainly find more recent and reliable information, so that we are sure how matters lie. I have good friends there and we will be well looked after.'

Tom sat back and looked at her. 'If the way on is now so straightforward, why do you yourself not consider returning south to Cadiz? I am sure I can find my way along now and I have no doubt you will be quite safe with Omar beside you.'

She shook her head, 'No, I will certainly continue on with you to Oporto, Lieutenant. I gave my word to Rico that I would see you safely to your destination, which I will do, and I really do hope to find my brother there. No, I am afraid that you will have to endure my company a little further along the road.'

'Well in that case,' Tom said, making a poor job of looking or sounding disappointed, 'may I suggest we take the air for half an hour? Having been in the saddle for what seems like an eternity, I confess I would be pleased to see something of this pleasant town – on foot.'

It was dark as they left the inn, but the streets of Caceres were reasonably well lit, by lanterns and by a near-full moon. Isobel linked her arm through Tom's as they walked, a natural and almost sisterly gesture. They both felt more positively human now, due to a combination of being properly fed and knowing more clearly how the world stood. The town itself seemed to share their mood, calm and peaceful. There were plenty of local people out enjoying the traditional Spanish evening stroll, or paseo, in the evening air.

They walked leisurely across the Santa Maria square and past some fine, ornamented mansions and merchants' houses and followed the gentle flow of people around the old town, taking their time in their own paseo and eventually making a circuit that took them back to where they had started at the main gate at the Arco de Estrella. Tom, having succeeded in putting the war to the back of his mind – for the time being at least – was feeling wonderfully relaxed. He felt thoroughly at ease, possibly even something more than that, in Isobel's company. He realised that he simply enjoyed being with her, having been obliged to become so used to her company on the flight from Jerez. Yet he had become so comfortably familiar, so fully at ease with her that he had almost contrived to forget that she was not only a capable guide but a strikingly beautiful woman. He realised that it was probably rather daring of them to be walking out alone, that the locals possibly even took them for a married couple, but he felt that any hint of impropriety was somehow negated by the fact of Isobel being a widow and also some few years his senior. For her part, from what he had learned from their fractured conversations, she just didn't appear to be the sort of woman to be concerned with – and certainly not cowed by – convention and propriety. If she was older than him, what did that matter? Whatever that she was a few years his senior, he had seldom met a more singular looking woman and never one so spirited and acute. He could barely have wished for a more perfect saviour. As they walked under the arch, Tom reflected contentedly that, in his modest experience, life could certainly be a lot worse for a soldier on active service. Yes, it was good to be in the game and have possibilities, to be aware that anything might happen.

That moment, naturally, was when they struck.

They had picked their spot well. They came suddenly out of the shadows of the watchtower, relying on speed and surprise, uncaring whether or not they were seen by the local people through the arch into the old town or down in the square behind them. None of the evening strollers was likely to be armed with anything more than a gentleman's hanger and the attackers were determined and quick – very quick.

Tom, his mind abruptly wrenched into crystalline alertness, thought there were three, each of them cloaked with their heads covered by scarves wrapped to reveal only the eyes. They were lightening fast. Already one had roughly pulled Isobel away and held her while another was busy binding a gag around her mouth to stop her calling out. They obviously knew precisely what, or who, they were after. But now Tom had no time to guess at what they would do with Isobel, for he saw all too vividly from the glint of steel that the third man was coming straight for him, his lethal intention perfectly plain. With no chance of drawing his sword, Tom just had time to bend and pull out his boot dagger as the man came on. Instinctively he stepped back a couple of paces, keeping the wall of the old watchtower to his left-hand side, his eyes locked on those of the man with the knife. Down in the square they had seen that something was happening at the top of the steps. People were shouting now, calling for the watch, but the dark-eyed assassin menacing the Englishman had his work to do – and he would do it quickly.

Tom watched those eyes and he sensed the attack was coming a fraction before the man moved in for him. Again he stepped back alongside the wall, but this time he swept off his leather bicorn hat with his right hand and, almost in a parody of sweeping bow, brought it down to deflect the darting knife-thrust. The man grunted in surprise, as he felt his momentum force him onto Tom's dagger, which drove in deep under his ribs. His knife fell to the ground with a clatter. A woman screamed. Tom left the man on his knees, the dagger pulled messily from him. He picked up the long-bladed stiletto the assassin had dropped and looked for the others. They were gone. His fight had taken just seconds and he knew they hadn't got Isobel past him, so he reasoned they had gone back through the gate, back into the middle of the old town somewhere. The dagger back in his boot, he tucked the other knife into his sash and ran under the arch back into the church plaza, searching the shadows for a sight of them, but could see nothing. Every second that passed took her away from him, but he wasn't going to give up. He knew they might have gone through the town and out of another gate, but he sensed not. But he wasn't likely to find her on his own: he turned and ran for the inn.

Omar was in the stable, sitting alone on a bench, patiently using a cloth to work a shine on the fancy leatherwork of Isobel's saddle. Tom thanked his stars that the man, though unable to speak, understood English perfectly well. He explained, briefly and urgently, what had happened.

'It has to be Duarte,' he said to the Moor. 'They must be his men. But I don't think they've left. Now think, Omar – Duarte, has he any connection with anyone in this town?'

Omar gave no response, but went to his pack and collected his long-handled pistol and nodded for him to follow.

That was fine by Tom. He didn't care who was in charge, as long as Omar knew what he was doing. He followed the tall man as he strode quickly back to the Arco de Estrella. The Moor continued on, walking fast, Tom following, eyes darting right and left. He led him through the streets of the old town until they came to a row of tall, dark houses, three and four storeys in height. Omar stopped in front of one of the houses, glanced at its stout, wooden door and then simply turned and looked at Tom, fixing him with that dark, impassive stare. This was the place, then. And it seemed that it was time now for the Englishman to take charge.

It was not going to be easy. There was a bell alongside the door, but Tom had little intention of using that. If this did prove to be where they had taken her he would be ill-advised to give those dangerous men warning of his presence there. He looked up at the high windows, all of them protected by heavy iron grilles. There were no windows at all on the ground floor. It was a fortress. But it was Tom's trade to reckon with fortresses.

He could hear shouts from streets away, where he imagined people were belatedly beginning to search for those involved in the incident by the gate. How long had it been – minutes? The man he had stabbed would likely be dead by now. He had no time to worry about that. He was wholly concerned at how to get into this house as quickly as possible and get Isobel out of there, before Duarte's men could harm her or spirit her away from the town. He looked up and down the street. Three or four houses further on the last building was smaller, with the same number of storeys, but not as tall as the others. That was where to start. He turned to Omar.

'Now, as you value your mistress's life, I beg you will do as I say. Go quickly back to the inn and get our things together. Have the horses saddled and ready. I will be a few minutes.'

Omar looked back at him, weighing him with his dark eyes.

Tom nodded to the solid door. 'You must trust me and play your part. It is our only chance to get your mistress safe.'

The man studied Tom for a moment longer, then nodded.

'But first, if you please – your head-dress, your turban?'

*

It took three or four attempts, making a horrible noise, which he feared might alert those inside or even the constables who must now be searching the streets, but at last he got the improvised grapnel to take, as his sword caught in the grilles of the first floor window. His "rope" was made of Omar's turban and his own sash knotted together. It wasn't ideal, but it was all he had. He tested it with a hearty pull, then literally took his courage in his hands and hauled himself up the wall. It was about fifteen feet to climb. He clambered up to squat awkwardly clinging to the ironwork of the first floor window. The shutters of the house inside the bars were firm shut and he hoped that nobody was home to be curious about any odd noises they might hear. He slung the sword again, it held first time and again he hauled himself up. It was tough going, but he managed, grunting as he hung on to the metalwork, catching his breath. A patrol of soldiers hurried along the street below him and he froze, but it was hardly surprising that nobody looked up to the man clinging on in the shadows high above their heads.

Then it was quiet again.

He heard a half-hearted warning cry as someone emptied a chamber pot out of a window further down the street; then more silence. He realised that his heart was thumping and tried to calm it. He went on. The next throw was even more difficult, as he hurled the sword high up onto the pantiled roof itself and hoped the blade would hook over the ridge tiles or the parapet of a roof terrace. He tensed his "rope" and once again it seemed to hold. He dare not look down, the stone cobbles were far below now and would give him an unpleasant landing. He pulled and climbed, breathing hard. He only hoped he was being quick enough. He had no idea what they had in mind for Isobel, he only knew that he wasn't going to let it happen. He climbed on.

But at last he was there, on the very peak of the roof, straddling it like a horse. He could see most of the town from up there, the roofs dark against the night sky. It was a fine sight, but he only had eyes for the next roof and then on to the one over Isobel's captors' heads. His hands were bleeding and he had probably lost a couple of nails, but he didn't have time to worry about that and carried on, scrabbling along the roofs like an inelegant cat. He dislodged a tile, which slid into the gutter. He kept going.

Then at last he was there, at the very house, right on top of them. But now he had to tackle the challenge of getting down into the courtyard below. But he found that he was in luck. The top window had no grille, and better, had its shutters half-open. He tied his rope to a bar across the chimney opening, holding on with his bloodied hands, grasping his sword between his teeth. He smiled briefly as he allowed himself a momentary image of Morgan or

Blackbeard in the old buccaneering days, then he concentrated, took a deep breath and was over the side. For a second he feared that the honest cloth might at last fail him, but he swung, holding on grimly, until his momentum allowed him to kick in through the window. He was there. He was inside.

Tom steadied himself and took a moment to get his breath back, to allow himself to think. What now?

It was unlit inside this part of the house at least, but the moonlight flooded in now through the open shutters. He saw that he was in a small servant's room – there was a bed, but it didn't look as if it had been used recently. Sword in hand, he carefully opened the door and found his way to the staircase. Still it was all in darkness, but now he could hear voices, men's voices, somewhere below. The stairs were stone, fortunately, and he was able to move without making too much noise. Down another level and he could see light spilling from a doorway off the hall on the ground-floor below him. He listened carefully. Still the sound of voices, deep Spanish voices, laughter now. But just two, he thought, possibly the two men who had taken her. Two to one, then; that seemed fair enough. With surprise on his side, he would take those odds. On he went, with no time now for any kind of planning. If Isobel wasn't in the house, he was going to look very foolish indeed, but he had to believe that she was – that Duarte's men held her right there in that room. He was at the bottom of the stairs now. Light filtered out of the room with the voices, the doors slightly ajar. There was no scheming to be done now. It had to be straight at them, hoping that it was just the two and that Isobel was there with them. He had his sword in one hand and the assassin's thin knife in the other. It was time:

No dramatic war cry or throwing the doors wide, he simply eased the left-hand door open with his boot, and moved quietly into the room, making as much ground as quickly as could before they knew he was amongst them. Yes, she was there, he registered with a combination of satisfaction and relief. She was the first to see him, her eyes widening in surprise above a scarf tied to gag her. Tom came on. Three, not two men – the first already making a kind of gurgling protest, eyes popping, with the stiletto stuck deep in his throat, blood spurting. The second, a fat man, probably the steward of the house, was too slow off his chair and Tom stepped forward and lunged with his sword, the point taking him in the guts and finishing him. For the sake of saving a vital second, he left the weapon sticking out of the fat man, quickly reaching down for his boot knife.

Two down, done in a moment, but he had not been quite fast enough. He heard the horribly familiar sound of the cocking of a pistol and knew that now he had no chance – that he had certainly tried his best, had almost beaten the odds, but that for all his desperate effort he had now lost and that it would be pointless even to try to fall or dive out of the way. Then the shot exploded, shocking and terrifyingly loud in the confined space.

'What?' Isobel clearly thought the question ridiculous: 'Why on earth would they feel the need to tie my feet, when there were three of the great brutes and they had little me, muffled and hands tied, sitting there as nicely as you like, right there in their nasty spider's parlour?'

Tom ignored her levity, still counting his blessings that she, that both of them, were somehow free and unharmed. 'Well, at any rate, whatever they were thinking, I'm heartily pleased that they underestimated you. Your intervention was most timely. If you hadn't kicked that unpleasant-looking fellow so hard, I would surely have been finished. As it was, I swear I nearly died of fright just at the sound of the pistol going off into the air.'

She gave him a mocking, disbelieving look, plainly unconvinced by this show of timidity. 'I don't think so, Lieutenant Herryck. I don't believe you were put off for a moment. Even once I'd distracted him, he was still dangerous, that last one, and yet you showed the presence of mind to deal with him promptly enough.'

Tom tried not to think about "dealing with" the three thugs. He was still recovering from the shock of his own single-minded brutality. There had been so much blood! Whoever found them in that room would be in for anything but a pretty sight. But it was done – and at least he had got Isobel away from there. Now they were once again on the road – that was what was important. He would have to try to forget Caceres now, forget the men he had "dealt with" and consider the business a matter of duty, like killing enemy soldiers. The man Duarte was, after all, his declared foe.

It was still early morning, the air cool and pleasant. The three of them were well to the north now, long since clear of Caceres, out in the flat farming country, making steady progress towards Salamanca. A kite hovered in the air off to the side of them, his eyes on some morsel on the ground, but no other moving thing was in view. Omar was bringing up the rear, constantly looking back to check for any signs of pursuit. The three riders went steadily on. None of them had had any sleep, but they would keep going until the sun became too hot to continue riding. Tom wondered when they might finally consider themselves safe.

More running away; first from Jerez, now from Caceres.

'And you said it was a quiet town...'

'It was until you arrived, Lieutenant.'

Tom glanced across at her, still quite amazed at how unruffled she appeared to be after her ordeal, how coolly she had dealt with getting them away from Caceres. Half-English or not, Isobel Truelove de Chambertain was very different to any of the ladies he had encountered in the assembly rooms at home. Then he looked back to Omar, who had produced a new turban and who also appeared to be as imperturbable as ever. The Moor gave him the slightest of nods. They were certainly cool customers, these two.

He turned back to Isobel. 'And you still believe absolutely they were Duarte's men?'

'Without a doubt; that house belongs to his father.'

Tom couldn't believe it: 'His father? Why on earth take ourselves to Caceres, then?'

She shrugged: 'There are not many towns in the south country where the Duarte family does not wield influence. Also I heard them talking, those men. They were very confident of their position, you see, quite unguarded in their conversation. They believed that their friend would have dealt with you at the gate and gone into hiding. Even if you had survived, you yourself would have had to run from the authorities or risk facing charges. Their planning was quite comprehensive. They were supposed to wait there at the house, just until the hubbub had died down and then take me back to Cadiz, to Duarte's palace there.'

But that scheme had been thwarted. He was alive, the woman was free. And now they were running again, probably in more danger than before, Tom reflected. Running... that seemed to have been all he had done since he had set foot in Spain! But he certainly hadn't run back there at Caceres, and he was glad. It had been a nasty affair, but he had been left no choice. It seemed to Tom that he and Julian Duarte were beginning to pile up business that would best be sorted out in person. When that business would be concluded he had no idea, but he knew he would be ready when the time did come. He gave Isobel a rueful grin. 'Well, I'm pleased that we got you away from those fellows. They were unpleasant looking brutes.'

She made a dismissive gesture. 'They were certainly an unsavoury group, hadn't washed in days, but I dare say I wasn't truly in peril of my life.'

Tom remembered the dangerous man who tried very hard to kill him at the gate and the others who would doubtless have done the same, given half a chance. 'I admire your confidence in their good nature.'

She offered him a complacent look. 'Oh, they would certainly have cut *your* throat with the greatest of pleasure, that was certainly the core of their mission, but I suspect it was most likely my part to be a poor innocent saved from a fate worse than death at the hands of a rapacious foreigner.'

'Me?' Tom said, shocked.

She smiled at him, 'Who else? Consider it: Don Julian does not appear to be an admirer of yours, does he, Lieutenant? Consider the position: there he is, a pillar of Andalucian society, and here you are, a successor to *El Draco*. He has doubtless widely portrayed you as the worst sort of murderer and the pitiless abductor of a helpless Spanish widow-woman.'

'But – '

She made another dismissive gesture with her free hand, 'It's best not to honour Julian Duarte by speculating on his notions, which are almost always entirely loathsome. We dignify him more than he warrants merely by discussing him. Suffice it to say he is sworn to do you harm, just as he despises my family, and will do almost anything to discomfort us.'

'And yet you say you believed you were in no danger?'

'He would not harm me, no. But he is not above using me as a way of getting at others. Certainly we know now that he is not beyond having you removed by any means, purely as a dart at Rico, whom he hates with a passion. One day I believe Julian's hatred will finally consume him. But now, as I suggest, we are wasting time talking about him.'

Tom was surprised, amused even, that she could dismiss the threat so lightly, but he was happy enough to agree to forget about Duarte, for the moment, at least. 'Very well, no more of the troublesome Don Julian. But since it has come to affect me, this mysterious history you mention, would you at least now tell me something of your own family?'

She shot him a look, 'What could you want to know?'

Tom shrugged, 'Well, simply list its members, if you will. I mean no impertinent curiosity, I promise you, yet I feel I should be better informed: during my stay in Spain I have somehow contrived to become perpetually associated with the clan Truelove. You've mentioned your brother the wine shipper and, sadly, your late sister, Rico's wife.'

'Then you know almost the whole tale. There's not a lot more to my family than that. My brother William, whom I hope to meet in Oporto, is the oldest. Our father founded a company called Truelove and Dunn – Mister Dunn, also sadly departed like my father, being the London end of the business. William took over the running of the company ten years ago, when my father died. Not long after, he bought out the Dunn half of the company and now has an agent in London managing the English operation for us. My sister Maria you know about. She was a year younger than me. Then we have a much younger brother Edward, who is fifteen years old.'

'Is William married?'

Isobel smiled, as if the opposite was an impossibility. 'Oh yes. The Truelove dynasty is in safe hands there. William is very much the family man. His wife Mercedes, who is quite lovely, is the daughter of one of the old Jerez wine trading families. It is a useful connection. But it is a thorough match, so much more than an alliance of business houses. Mercedes is perfect for him. And brother William is in turn devoted to her. They already have two sons and a delightful little girl and will very likely produce more offspring. I certainly hope so. They are a charming family.'

Tom wondered if it was best to leave it there, the tone of wistful longing in the last words was clear in Isobel's voice as she described her brother's young family. But he felt that he knew her well enough now to realise that she was a tough character and would, in any case, refuse him an answer if she in any way resented the question, so he glanced across at her and asked gently, 'And will you choose to tell me something more of your own marriage?'

She glanced across at him, an unreadable expression on her face. Then she looked ahead and simply said, 'It was happy, but it was too short.'

'Yes,' Tom said uncomfortably.

'Really, that is the whole case. He was a good man and I miss him. It's as simple as that.'

'Of course.' He had gone far enough.

She gave him a pinched smile. 'Don't let me make you uneasy. There's no need, I assure you. I am not quite the grief-wracked creature you think me. No, I will perhaps tell you the full story another time, Lieutenant. Not that there's much more to it. And besides, you must allow a lady some little mystery, you know, or she will lose any poor shred of interest whatsoever. And, what's more, young sir, now that you have so thoroughly interrogated me, as a gentleman you must yourself play fair. What of your own family? In all of our time together I don't believe I've heard you mention them once. If you have a terrible tale to tell, I assure you I will not be shocked. So, might you let me know something of your life in England?'

Tom laughed, 'In my case, ma'am, there really is not a great deal to tell; certainly no drama. As I told Rico, my background really is most delightfully mundane. My family lives a comfortable life in Nottinghamshire, in the English countryside. My father occasionally stirs himself to go up to London to see his man of business. We are not an old family, you realise, but he did well in East India bonds and we have a little land. My mother, bless her, spends much of her own time on various worthy committees. I have two brothers, both rather older than myself, both launched successfully on their life's voyages and both, dare I say in confidence, quite unbearably tedious.'

'Tedious?'

'Well, fine enough fellows in their way, but one is a clergyman and t'other waits his turn to take over from my father. Both have made good marriages and I am blessed with a growing tribe of nephews and nieces.'

'It sounds charmingly settled in England.'

'Yes.'

'And?'

He recognized that she was probing but, as she had said, fair was fair. He smiled at her acuity, 'Well, possibly life at Lowthorpe is a trifle too charming and too settled for me.'

'You have no sisters?'

'No, but I do have another brother, a half-brother. Now he is a bird of a very different colour.'

'One of your parents has re-married?'

Tom gave a wry smile. 'Rather more a case, I fear, of my father omitting to marry when he was a much younger man.'

'Oh.'

Tom shook his head, a little grin on his face. 'I am not uncomfortable, ma'am, and I trust I don't make you so. But I do confess I do find it hard to credit it in my father.'

'Perhaps we shouldn't judge too easily. I imagine he was very young, very likely ill-experienced in the ways of the world.'

'Oh yes, and I didn't mean to appear to castigate him or come it the moralist. No, it is just that my father as I know him, he is – how to put it? – he is so dry, so very conservative and prudent a person, full of solid virtue and probity. But clearly as a youth – well, I won't trouble a lady with the details. Suffice it to say he was as likely to fall prey to the charms of a pretty chambermaid as any. But if he wished for a place in society, no marriage to such a person was possible. So, he was unexpectedly a father before he was twenty, with the child's mother paid off and away to make a fresh start somewhere far distant from Nottinghamshire. My father, an eligible catch set to become a wealthy landowner and something of a figure in society, found that he had an inconvenient offspring to deal with. Anyway, as I suggested, he is at heart a good man and the boy was sent off to the Welsh borders to live with my father's cousin, a country parson.'

'And the mother?'

'I have no idea. She has never since been mentioned.'

'So how do you know this?'

'Why, mostly from my brother himself – my half-brother, Rob. When he was a boy he used to visit us at Lowthorpe each year during the summer, though that was before I was even born. He was called our cousin. He used to lead my other two brothers a merry dance, I think. When I came along, I loved it when Rob was there. He taught me to box, to play cricket. We shot rabbit and fished trout together. He was a breath of fresh air in our solid, unsurprising little world. He was so much more alive than my other brothers. But he hated the rules set out for country life, or certainly the socially accepted parts of it. He positively detested the parsonage on the other side of the Midlands where he lived, found it constraining and stuffy. He was never likely to follow the clergyman's calling set out for him. When he was fifteen, he ran away to join the army. He was dragged back, luckily for him, and made to stew for another year or so. But my father had heard about it and, thinking perhaps to fulfil his obligation by setting Rob off on his chosen path, bought him a commission as an ensign in a foot regiment.'

'So have you seen any more of him?'

'Oh yes. That was all long since, the best part of twenty years ago, when I was a small boy. Rob still used to come to us when he had leave or, on a couple of occasions, when he was recovering from wounds. He was a real tonic to me; my other brothers were so distant and serious-minded. Rob was by contrast adventurous, full of life. He was the reason I wanted to be a soldier.'

She looked at Tom appraisingly. 'Did he teach you to fight?'

'A fencing master taught me the fine points of the art of the sword, but yes, it was Rob who taught me how to fight.'

'He did a good job.' Isobel said, obviously not having forgotten the abrupt charnel house mayhem of the room in Caceres.

Tom nodded, unselfconsciously acknowledging the truth of it. 'Rob always said that there are many rules of war, but the first one is simply not to get killed. Everything else follows from that.'

'If war has been his profession for twenty years, and he remains to tell the tale, then he is probably right. Where is he now, your soldier brother?'

'Rob? That I'd truly like to know; the last I heard from him, which was a good few weeks ago now, he was in Kent, at Shornecliffe barracks. He'd come back from service in South America and was waiting posting. We were able to meet a few times, as a matter of fact. But my own orders came suddenly and I left England myself before I found out where he was bound. But wherever he is, you can be quite sure of one thing with Rob – he'll surely be close to trouble.'

Around that time, one thing Captain Robert Blunt himself would dearly like to know was just exactly where he was, or even better what or who he was close to. And he certainly suspected trouble...

It was an odd, unsettling kind of soldiering, he thought glumly, spending days picking his way through this wild, extraordinary country, optimistically searching for a tiny British force while he nursemaided a schoolboy cavalryman. By rights Blunt himself shouldn't even be under Moore's direct orders, but should be with General Beresford, who was presently marching in the opposite direction, far to the north. No, Blunt didn't care for it. He didn't care for any of it: the weather was bitingly cold up so high, he didn't like being on a horse, didn't like the dangerous mountain tracks. To cap it all, he wasn't even certain they were heading in the right direction to find Hope's column. Without a map, his only choice was to trust to the sun, his compass and good old-fashioned guesswork.

There were, of course, compensations – there usually were if you were open to them – for this truly was remarkable territory, rich in the kind of wildlife Blunt was unlikely to encounter in his native Shropshire or anywhere else he had been on his not-inconsiderable travels. He was well used to goats and sheep in the English countryside, of course, but he had never seen ibex before and the many different species of birds of prey wheeling high, commanding the sky above them, were a constant delight. Earlier in their journey they had passed through out of season almond, chestnut and olive groves, but now the going was tougher up in the heights of the sierra. Blunt was country-bred and was used to hardship, had grown up sleeping out in woods and joining the poachers on their nocturnal adventures, but this was different. This was Spain – a huge, dangerous country to be confronted and, hopefully, in time understood. Up there in the mountains the landscape remained strikingly beautiful in a bleak kind of way, challenging and uplifting, but he would be far happier when the job was done and he was safely back with Sir John Moore's infantry, ready to get on with the real business of fighting a campaign against the French.

The odd aside to the taciturn Widowson apart, there was little conversation. Blunt didn't mind that. Most of soldiering was boredom. And it was his life, all he had known in his adult years. His commission, signed by the King's own hand, was his only possession of any true worth. His half-brother wore a sword from Jermyn Street, a uniform coat cut by a Piccadilly tailor and boots from Old Bond Street – Blunt had none of those luxuries, but that was just how his life had turned out. He felt neither resentment nor loss. He was a soldier, a good one, and that was his value to the world. Yet he realised that his professional life was unlikely to see him rise beyond his current rank. He had once even had to go as far as to sell his precious commission to avoid a debtor's cell, only to have it bought back for him. The Army's long-established system of purchase meant that young Thicknesse, with his evident connections and financial muscle, would almost certainly rise to lieutenant or even higher before the present campaign was over – however good or bad a cavalryman he proved to be. But that was the way of it. Blunt had long ago stopped worrying at the inequity of a system that rewarded means above merit.

Cornet Thicknesse also chose to keep to himself, beyond the necessities of communicating on military business. Blunt couldn't blame him. The young hussar officer hadn't asked for this duty, would doubtless prefer to be prancing about under the eye of the general, rather than being here in the middle of nowhere under Blunt's orders. But Thicknesse too was stuck with it. There was understandably little he felt he could have in common with the cross-grained infantryman under whose command he had been placed, so he contented himself passing any leisure time of his own with reading one of his little novels or books of poetry – that only when he wasn't endlessly instructing his servants in every detail of the care of his horses.

So by more or less ignoring each other they got along tolerably well and the little party of horsemen made its way slowly forward. They glimpsed a goatherd in the distance every so often and once met an itinerant priest, who crossed himself at the mere sight of them and went on his way muttering an urgent prayer; but otherwise they remained alone for days on end, passing the odd shrine or a farmhouse in the distance, struggling silently across the mountains.

They did their job, pushing south, looking for General Hope and his guns.

Chapter Five

Salamanca proved to be everything that Isobel had promised. Tom, all too keen to put the unwelcome drama and rigours of their journey behind him, was utterly captivated by the place. After weeks on the road, broken only by their short and eventful break in Caceres, its infinitely civilised comforts came as a welcome relief to the travellers. Built of warm, honey-coloured stone, the city was crammed with an amazing collection of wonderful old buildings. There were palaces, churches and not one but two cathedrals. The many venerable university buildings were, to Tom's delight, built in an eccentric combination of very un-English styles from Gothic to Moorish and the Renaissance. Salamanca, a kind of living Spanish history and architecture lesson, was a revelation to the young Englishman. And not the least of its many charms was that Isobel's "friend" proved to be an elderly gentleman well into his sixties called Tio Enrique, who welcomed them to his home – the so-called Casa Delgado, one of the finest palaces in the city.

Tio Enrique, as Isobel called the dignified old gentleman, who was a kind of uncle to her, was in fact the Conde de Castillo Nuevo and the impressive Casa Delgado was the ancient town house of his family, which had long owned large slices of the rich wheat-lands of Old Castile.

Tom discovered that the Conde had for many years been a close friend of Isobel's father. The first William Truelove had been an energetic businessman and his travels had on occasion brought him to Castile, as he was searching out new markets for his southern wine. The Conde, a cultured and discerning man, had immediately appreciated the genuine quality of Truelove's product and he had also quickly come to value the qualities in the man himself. They became firm friends and the Castillo Nuevo patronage had in time won Truelove many important new clients in Castile and Leon, as well as supplying him with vital introductions to growers across the border in Portugal, where Truelove and Dunn soon successfully established themselves in the lucrative port trade with Britain.

Later, William Truelove the younger had been educated in part at Salamanca and also Isobel and her sister Maria had often come to visit Tio Enrique. The ties between the two families were close; now Isobel had appeared on the Conde's doorstep once again. The Casa Delgado, a magnificent town palace called "the thin house" in mocking reference to its grand dimensions, was as fine a place to stay as could be found in the city. It had certainly been a welcome sight to the weary travellers. The Conde had expressed his candid pleasure at having an English officer, a gallant ally, under his roof. A model of civility, he had insisted that the travellers should be allowed to rest and refresh themselves before he extracted the story of their journey from Isobel over a private, if wonderfully lavish dinner held that evening in their honour.

So, Lieutenant Tom Herryck of the Royal Engineers found himself not using his skills to help prepare for a winter campaign in Portugal, but sitting down as an honoured guest to dine in the magnificent hall of a refined Spanish grandee. It was certainly not the kind of occasion Tom had expected to be enjoying when he set off from England, but he knew it would be quite an experience. Tom was used to dining with the country squires of Nottinghamshire and Leicestershire, but was less experienced in sitting down to dinner with the aristocracy. Like the quality anywhere in Europe, the Conde spoke French perfectly well, but he struggled with English, so Isobel acted as translator for Tom, who struggled with any language other than his own.

Having between them offered the Conde an edited telling of their adventures, which even in short form sounded like something from Dumas or even Cervantes, Tom was at last able to press his host for other news. The Conde was remarkably well informed about the war, being fiercely anti-Bonaparte and, just like Carlos Federico Rivero y Castro, utterly scathing of the prospects of his own country's new central government, recently established at Aranjuez. The old gentleman was both astute and unsentimental in setting out how ill he felt matters lay for Spain. Grimly warming to his subject, he stated quite clearly that there could be no easy future for a country which boasted neither a strong national leader nor a commander-in-chief for its armies. There must be a clear plan, he said, if Napoleon was to be stopped. But Tom's main concern, however interesting it was to listen to the old gentleman's shrewd reading of the Spanish position, was naturally more in how his own countrymen did across the border.

'Ah, our gallant allies! Well, young man, matters in Portugal are being hastened along, it appears, although they remain somewhat confused. It seems that the capable General Wellesley has been recalled to London, along with the other British generals who gave the French such generous treaty terms at the peace of Cintra. That was an unfortunate stroke, however pragmatic a move it may have seemed at the time. But the French have at least sailed away from Portugal, it is said, and a new man, your General Moore, now commands in Lisbon. They say he has twenty or thirty thousand soldiers gathered there.'

Isobel smiled as she told this to Tom, knowing that his heart's desire was to join that command.

'That is truly excellent news, sir,' Tom said with satisfaction, once Isobel had translated everything the Conde had said. 'I know of Sir John Moore and he is a first rate commander. He is the perfect choice – energetic, a good organiser and the men love him. Of course, it is a pity General Wellesley has been removed, particularly after getting us a precious victory or two, but Moore is the ideal replacement. He is at Lisbon, you say? Well, I'm sure the army is in safe hands then.'

The Conde nodded politely when Isobel relayed this to him. 'I am pleased to hear that you approve of him, Lieutenant. If the gentleman is active, that is sure to be good for my country. Yes, good indeed,' the old gentleman said, with a little smile. 'I only wish I could say the same of some of our own Spanish commanders, who have been active only in putting their armies foolishly at risk. However, as to this General Moore of yours, they say he is ordered to cross the border so that he might support those very Spanish armies which are even now gathering to face Bonaparte north of here along the Ebro.'

Tom frowned. 'I must tell you that will be difficult for my countrymen to achieve, sir. If, as your sources tell you, Sir John has indeed mustered thirty thousand redcoats at Lisbon, that is about as large an army as England can put in the field. Small beer for Napoleon perhaps, but a lot of men for us. And getting that army into any kind of a position to damage the French on the Ebro at this time of year won't be at all easy. Supplying it for a winter campaign so far inland will cause headaches, not least because our armies are usually provided for by the Royal Navy.'

The Conde listened carefully to what his guest had to say, clearly pleased that the British did not plan simply to take whatever they needed from the local population, as was the French habit. 'Naturally I cannot speculate with any confidence on the details, Lieutenant, and I'm sure your understanding of General Moore's difficulties is precise, but I do know that we will be grateful for any assistance he may offer us in the fight against the ogre. Spain has arrived at its true crisis: Bonaparte will command in person this time and he most certainly means to make our country bend to his will.'

Tom smiled at Isobel as she relayed this, then turned back to his host. 'Well, in that case, sir, it is clearly England's solemn duty to stand with you. If the fight is to be in the north, then so be it. I'm sure Sir John will know what he's about and I imagine he will like nothing better that to lock horns with Napoleon.'

'I prey that he gets his opportunity,' said the Conde, offering Tom a civil nod, before looking wistfully around the elegant dining room, a picture of peaceful, elegant civilisation. 'Yes, let us trust with all our hearts that our two armies can come together and deal satisfactorily with the enemy in the north – lest we find that the Frenchman is come here, knocking on our doors.'

Roca spoke no English, far preferred his native Gallego to the little Castilian Spanish he knew, but the big man generally had a way of getting his point across. Sometimes he used one of his several knives or pistols to make his message clear, sometimes his massive, ham-like fists; but on this occasion his master had furnished him with a clearly-written note of introduction and he had no difficulty in being admitted into the Casa Delgado. How Don Federico knew that Herryck would be found at the Conde's home was a mystery, but it was not Roca's job to fathom his master's instructions, merely to carry them out. He found the Englishman alone in the Conde's library, studying the big old map books there in the good morning light. Again words were unnecessary for Roca, he simply passed over the letter Rico had entrusted to him.

If Tom was surprised to be disturbed from his work by the appearance of the tough-looking Galician, he was even more surprised when he broke the seal, recognised the hand and read the contents of Rico's letter:

My Friend,

I pray that you forgive the unusual method of communication, but the times do not allow for all of the courtesies one could wish.

In brief, I am at present in the country some way to the north of you. For reasons I will explain later, I need you to join me here. In case this poor note should fall into the wrong hands I can for the moment be no more candid, but rest assured that your presence here is of the first importance.

I regret that I can tell you no more at present, I simply beg that you will trust to our friendship, trust my love of our cause, and allow the man who has delivered this word to bring you to me.

Your servant,

Carlos Federico Rivero y Castro

He read the letter again, he found it so extraordinary.

At last he looked up at the big man who had delivered it to him. He was a nasty-looking brute, probably quite useful in a set-to. 'How did you know where to find me?'

Roca shrugged.

'You understand me?'

Another shrug.

Tom looked once more at the paper. Was Rico really expecting him to turn away from his duty yet again – go north when he clearly must go south and west – for some mysterious purpose he wouldn't vouchsafe? It was crazy. Surely Rico must know he could spend no more time chasing around the country now Sir John Moore's army was on the march.

Tom crossed to the writing table. He took up a pen. Across the bottom of the page he simply wrote:

I am sorry, Rico, I may not.
Your friend,
Tom

He rose and crossed to the big man, handing over the paper. At that moment the library doors opened and Isobel entered.

'Oh, I beg your pardon. I didn't realise you had company, Lieutenant Herryck. Why, it's Roca, isn't it?'

'Doña Isobel,' The Gallego took off his hat and offered a gap-toothed smile.

She gave him a shrewd look, 'Esta bien?'

He gave a shrug and a little shake of the head. 'Pregunta al extranjero. No creo que vaya.'

For a moment Isobel's face took on a look of dismay, annoyance even.

'You know this fellow?' Tom asked.

Isobel was thoughtful.

'Madam?'

She turned back to Tom. 'Why, yes. He is Rico's man. He has often been to Cadiz and Oporto and is well known to our family. So, have you concluded your business?'

'Yes.' Tom had the feeling that once again there was something here he wasn't picking up.

But her breezy air of efficiency returned. 'Then I will take Roca down to the servant's hall to make sure he is properly fed. But first you should know that Tio – that the Conde, has bespoken horses for you and he has engaged a reliable man to take you over the border, for Lisbon, as you requested. They will attend you first thing tomorrow.'

'The Conde is very good.' Tom looked across at Roca, who stared back at him impassively.

'He is. But I only hope his kindness will help you to do the right thing.'

Tom smiled. 'My duty to King George is the right thing. It isn't always easy to put first, but that is the way it must be.'

'Yes, I'm sure it is,' she said coolly, before turning and leading the Galician from the room, leaving Tom alone with his maps and his thoughts of the duty that may be asked of him, when he at last reported back to Sir John Moore's army.

Tom was sitting on the old Roman bridge which crossed the river to the south of Salamanca. The evening light was magnificent. He had a superb view of the city, which he suspected might later serve to form a suitable background for finishing off one or two of the numerous sketches he was running off – splendid sketches of Isobel, who sat just along the parapet from him. Tom couldn't be happier; it was a portrait artist's delight. It was pleasantly warm still and Isobel had her hair loose over a simple rustic cotton blouse. He had hoped to get something of the romantic country girl from her, but those fine patrician cheek bones and dark intelligent eyes could not be easily ignored in the search for artifice. She really was a most striking woman, he thought – if at times infuriatingly contrary. But he was pleased enough to have at last persuaded her to allow him to draw her, after all of those weeks of flat refusals.

Tom himself felt more nearly human now after a couple of nights of the Conde's warm hospitality. He had bought new linen, new shirts and had a new coat – blue naturally, but of the local cut and style – which rested on the bridge alongside him. He had also found a fresh supply of good quality artist's paper. Salamanca, a city which he realised with a pang of regret he must presently leave, was fine by Tom. He found it difficult to imagine a more perfect situation for sketching. The morning would see him bound for Lisbon, but for the moment the war seemed a very long way off.

'Can I talk?'

'How could I stop you? Just try to sit still.'

'I promise I will do my best. These stones are no softer for being ancient. But I'm pleased you consent for me to speak.'

'Don't frown.'

'I frown?'

'Yes.'

'So, put me at me ease, then.'

'How may I accomplish that?'

'Will you consent to come with me, on to Oporto?'

'No.' He said calmly, concentrating on his drawing.

'No?'

'Of course not.'

'You are certain?'

His eyes flicked up to hers once again, 'You know I may not now go to Oporto, or anywhere else in the north.' He wondered for a moment if she had learned of Rico's summons. 'No, I have to get through to the army. It appears General Moore is in Lisbon. I must make my best efforts to get to him and rejoin.'

She gave a little laugh, 'From what Tio Enrique says, it sounds as if they are most likely coming along the way to meet you.'

'Possibly, but if that is so, it won't be anywhere near Oporto. I should go to Ciudad Rodrigo and then on to Lisbon. Indeed, strictly speaking I should already have packed my bags and left this place. I convince myself that a couple of days recovering from our journey is warranted but tomorrow, thanks to the Conde's kindness, I must be on my way west to Portugal. I imagine there is something of a pressing need for trained officers among my brother soldiers at the moment, most certainly if they are preparing the kind of a campaign the Conde describes.'

'You must really go?'

He sighed, wishing she wouldn't make matters so difficult. He asked himself once again if there might after all be a spark of something between them, despite all of her teasing. But he realised with regret that it was too late for that now, too late for thinking of such diversions. 'Yes, madam, I most certainly must go. Indeed, I think I might have a fair bit of explaining to do to avoid the gallows as it is. The Army takes rather a dim view of its officers not being where they are supposed to be. And to make matters worse, I'm not sure my masters will think it terribly impressive that I've slaughtered four or five Spaniards when I'm supposed to be busy removing Frenchmen. But I dare say that I will be able to explain myself, as long as I come it the humble penitent. No, duty most definitely calls, I fear ma'am, and I've soldiering to do.'

Isobel sighed, 'We all have duties, I suppose.'

'And might I remind you that yours is presently to sit still.'

'Yes Lieutenant, sir.'

He continued to draw, his mind now almost wholly back on the task.

But he did have half an eye to the rest of the world. They were at the far end of the long bridge, looking back to the city, almost pink in the early evening light. There was steady traffic across the bridge, the main route in from the south, as the people came to and from the city from the surrounding countryside on foot, with mules and in wagons. There were soldiers arriving too, mostly well-mounted Spanish officers, who Tom imagined might easily be quartermasters or billeting officers, as General Cuesta was rumoured to be bringing his army up from Extremadura, ready to anchor the left of the Spanish line against the French. The soldiers looked very smart and well turned-out. Seldom did they fail to give Isobel an admiring glance or wish her good day. Tom could hardly blame them for that, as she looked utterly charming in her gypsy pose, although it did have the effect of making him feel unfairly proprietorial. But he knew he should no longer be concerned with his companion of recent weeks, nor even with the Spanish army and its roving, goggle-eyed officers. His thoughts should be entirely on Lisbon and Sir John Moore's Englishmen.

He kept drawing.

Still the busy traffic crossed the bridge around them.

The latest coach to emerge from the city gate, a rather shabby affair drawn by four undignified nags, failed to excite his artist's eye, which he kept on Isobel. The vehicle rumbled slowly towards them and finally passed the artist and his model. Tom kept drawing. The light was so good, the setting perfect. And his subject...she really did have an unusual beauty – not quite classical, but utterly striking, a happy coming together of the two nations that had formed her. And her eyes, those dark, mischievous eyes, so elusive to capture, were at once intelligent, playful and provocative. Indeed, quite the last thing he remembered were those fine dark eyes widening first in surprise, then in alarm, but then for Tom there was just blackness.

Tom was uncertain how long he had been unconscious. It took him a few seconds to realise that he was even awake, as he discovered that his eyes were blindfolded, his mouth gagged and his feet and hands bound. He had no idea what was happening to him or, more importantly, *why* it was happening. The back of his head thumped rhythmically where he had been hit, but that would pass. He was much more concerned now to work out where he was and what on earth was going on. He was in a vehicle of some kind, a vehicle with indifferent springs or no springs at all, moving on a bad road, and he was, he thought, trussed up on the floor. He tried to wriggle into a better position and got a kick for his trouble. 'Tranquilo, hombre,' a gruff voice warned him. The instruction had little need of translation. A prisoner, then. He saw no point in arguing and stayed put, trying to gather his thoughts. Then he heard another man speak in what he was fairly certain was Spanish, in one of its versions, and the first one replied with a grunt of assent. They were very close to him. He could smell tobacco, sweat and stale wine. Why had he been taken like this – by whom? He tried to settle down, tried to ignore the cramping muscles and the painful jolting of what he now strongly suspected was the old coach that had passed him and Isobel on the bridge, moments before he had been hit. Isobel! Was she alright? Had they taken her as well? He managed to get out a kind of low growl through the gag, in an attempt to get the men's attention. His reward was another kick. It was infuriating. Even if the gag and blindfold had been removed, how would he communicate? He was literally in the dark. He gave up. He was going to have to be patient. If they had wanted to kill him, it would already have been done. He must bide his time, wait to find out what the next twist might be. The coach continued to bump along the bad road.

Somehow he had managed to get to sleep again. It had seemed the only thing worth doing, as there was no prospect of getting away and the horrible, pitching coach seemed to go on and on. At one stage, one of the men had roughly removed the gag and given him some water and a few mouthfuls of bread. Then he was muffled again. Later the carriage had stopped and they had hauled him out, still blindfolded, and freed his hands so that he could piss, but he had soon been tied again and shoved back inside. This pattern was repeated several times. He had no idea whether it was day or night now. On they went, the coach bumping along the cruel, uneven road. He hadn't the faintest idea where he was being taken, by whom, or for what purpose. It could be Duarte, of course, the most likely culprit; or could it even conceivably be the French, or their creatures, snatching a lone British officer? The coach just seemed to keep going, so he dozed on, his mind playing with the possibilities – none of them good.

But now he was most certainly awake, for they had stopped again. Tom wondered what would happen next. He hoped that they had reached wherever was their destination. He heard the men talking, definitely Spanish not French, one of them opening the door and jumping out.

'Momento, hombre,' the other man said, then Tom felt the rope around his feet being sliced free. He was able to try to move his feet at last. With a delicious pain he felt the blood beginning to circulate properly. He stamped his boots down gingerly against the carriage floor. But he was not going to be given time to relax. He was roughly hauled into a sitting position, then he felt the man pushing him from behind with his boot, shoving him firmly out of the door. He felt his own boots touch the ground, then he stumbled and fell. He was hauled to his feet and, with one of them on either side of him, he was marched staggering away from the coach, still gagged and blindfolded.

'Escalera,' the voice warned gruffly and Tom found himself climbing awkwardly up steps, still with the men guiding him. Then they were on a wooden floor, their steps creaking and echoing, and at last they stopped.

'Tenga, Jefe. El ingles.'

'Bueno,' said a voice Tom felt he somehow recognized, 'los lazos, y con ciudado, eh, cabron!'

The bond on Tom's wrist was cut, then the gag and blindfold were removed. He flexed his numb fingers and blinked in the murky yellow candlelight.

'Lieutenant Herryck, I rejoice to see you.'

'What?'

'You are not unwell, I hope?'

'Rico!' Tom tried to take a step forward but stumbled and was caught by his two captors, then helped to a chair.

'Gently, now.'

Tom, blinking furiously, didn't want to sit. 'What's happening – why have I been brought here?'

'Here, my friend, wine. Take a moment to recover yourself. No, let me,' Rico waved away Tom's clumsy attempt to take the proffered cup and instead helped him to drink. 'Good,' the Spaniard said gently, 'now a little more.'

'Thank you,' Tom said after Rico had refilled his cup. His eyesight better now, he looked around him. They were in what looked like it had been an old mill building or maybe even a brew house, but which was now derelict. 'Where, or what, is this place?' He felt groggy, partly from the long uncomfortable journey and partly from the wine beginning to do its job, but he had a lot of questions for Don Carlos Federico Rivero y Castro, and that seemed like a good enough place to start. Where? Why would most certainly be next.

'This? Why this is just an old corn mill, deserted long ago. It is of no significance, just a rendezvous for my men. We are some miles from the town of Zamora and tomorrow, at first light, we ride for Astorga and beyond.'

'Ride?'

'Certainly.'

Tom's brain felt as numb as his hands and feet 'Astorga? Why Astorga?'

'Because Castaños is there with the main army of Spain.'

Tom, despairing, tired beyond fury, tried to make sense of this. 'The Spanish – the Spanish, you say? But Rico, good God, man – don't you see that I need to be with the British army? This is all crazy. Astorga is far to the north and Lisbon is west. I don't understand any of this. Why have I been brought here?' He took more wine, shaking his head, slopping the drink. 'I don't see what you're playing at, Rico, not at all. Why in God's name did you make the effort to get me all the way from Cadiz if I'm not to return to my army?'

Rico held up his hand. 'I beg you be calm, my friend. You are to return to your army, I promise you, but not quite yet.'

Tom felt in no mood to be calm. 'But – and what about Isobel? What has happened to her? Where is she?'

'Relax, *tranquilo*, my friend, she is perfectly well. She is either still in Salamanca or more likely she will have gone on to Oporto, as she planned. She is quite well, I swear to you. I would imagine my cousin's only concern was the necessary bang on your head. And, clearly, your head is strong. So, come – wine, food. You must be half-starved after that cruel journey. You eat, you sleep and tomorrow I will tell you all about it, I promise, and I will answer all of your questions – as we ride for Astorga.'

They camped the next night out in the open, on the north bank of the Esla river. Tom, wearily accepting this latest turn, knew only that they were somewhere up in the north-west of Spain now, a very long way from Lisbon. Rico was accompanied by four men – Roca and the others who brought him from Salamanca in the coach. That conveyance had been abandoned back at the mill and Tom had been given a sturdy riding pony – nothing like the fine mounts Rico had provided in Cadiz, but better suited to the tough northern terrain. They had avoided stopping in towns and villages, carrying their own supplies on a spare horse. There had been little talk, though Rico had, as he had promised, answered some of Tom's questions:

Isobel, it seemed, had been in some way a party to the plan to – Rico had not liked the word kidnap – to *escort* Tom away from Salamanca if he were to refuse the Galician's summons. That at least explained why she had at last consented to let Tom draw her – and, in suggesting the old Roman bridge, at a place where it was easy for Roca and the others to take him away. Tom could easily see now how it had all been worked out. He felt he had been made to look a fool, once again out-manoeuvred by this odd Spanish family. He believed he would be having words with Senora Truelove de Chambertain when, if ever, he saw her again.

'You had to have me knocked over the head?' Tom grumbled after Rico had finished, offering the Galician a resentful look, as they sat around the soft light offered by the glowing remains of their small camp fire. Two of Rico's men stood picket, the other two were asleep. Tom rubbed the back of his head, which was still sore.

Rico nodded at the bigger of the guards. 'It was Roca over there who hit you. You should be grateful; he tells me he was especially gentle.'

'Gentle?'

'Claro.'

Tom looked again at the huge, intimidating Gallego, who grinned insolently back at him. 'Well, I'm sure I'd hate to be in your Roca's way if he wanted to be severe, the animal. But I repeat, you felt it quite necessary to have me kidnapped?'

An apologetic look: 'I did try asking you.'

'You did,' Tom conceded.

'And you said?'

'No.'

'Naturally you did. Your duty, I expect?'

'Of course. Don't you think I would be glad to oblige you if I was not so-bound? But you would not accept my refusal, must impose your will, even instructed your ape there to bring me away by force.'

The Galician looked penitent. 'I am sorry.'

'I should hope you are!'

'You left me no choice, Tom.'

'No?' the Englishman snapped angrily.

'I repeat, I apologise to you. And I regret that you were roughly handled, Tom, but it was necessary. Look,' he offered a mischievous grin, 'I assure you quite candidly that I have no wish to be your enemy. Ha, I have seen you with a sword, remember? In Cadiz, you know, they make ballads about you – "El Zurdo", the left-handed one. Your deeds in Jerez and Caceres make you famous. No, you are certainly not a man to pick fights with.'

Tom frowned, suspecting Rico was teasing him, but appalled that this might in part be true. 'That's not the kind of fame I wish for, not at all.'

The Galician simply shrugged.

'I still don't understand why you want me here,' Tom said.

'Not here, further north.'

An impatient sigh: 'Further north then; Astorga, you tell me. Fine, Astorga – it may as well be the moon for all the say I have in the matter. But for the life of me, Rico, I just don't see why you want to drag me away from my own army, especially when you went to the great trouble of keeping me out of Julian Duarte's clutches. Why, eh? I remember Isobel talked some nonsense about you saying I could be useful. That is very kind I'm sure, but I fail to see how I can be useful heaven knows how far from my country's army!'

'But you will see.'

'So you keep telling me. And it's damned vexing, if you don't mind me saying so. Anyway, what about you? Aren't you supposed to be in, where is it, Aran, Aran – '

Rico coaxed a little more life from the embers with a stick. 'I think you mean Aranjuez. A place many leagues from here, where the so-called Supreme Junta presently has its home. No, my friend, that is not where I should be, nor any other true patriot. Yet I do confess that I did go there, as I promised I would, to observe the working of this fine government and it took no more than a day for me to see that it was as rotten as a corpse. The same old arguments are being rehearsed, the same old jealousies, and still they cannot even decide who is to lead the army! No, the Junta will not serve Spain at a time of true crisis such as this. Others will have to do that.'

'So, is that then why we are heading towards General Castaños? I remember that you told me you knew him, that you had been with him at Bailen. Is Castaños the leader you want?'

Rico scowled, 'We are going to see his army, yes. But I don't think Castaños is the man to beat the French, certainly not without help. And you know well enough by now what I think about Bailen, Tom Herryck. Why, Castaños himself didn't even want to be there! And I for one do not blame him. He is not the best fighting commander, it's true, but he is not entirely stupid like some of the others and he plans well enough. He even had the good sense to propose falling back on Cadiz, safe behind its walls. But the fools of the southern Junta didn't listen to him. Luckily for Castaños' army, the French general at Bailen was himself a fool.'

'There are not many of those.'

'Exactly! That is what our people do not realise. To be lucky once does not entitle you to expect to be lucky the whole time. Men like Soult, Junot and

Ney are nothing like fools and the foul Corsican himself, God rot his soul, is certainly anything but foolish.'

'You really think he will come to take personal command?' The thought of Napoleon himself in charge of the Grande Armée there in Spain was both exciting and terrifying to Tom. It almost made him forget he was supposed to be sulking.

'Of course he will come. Wouldn't you come if you were he, if you had been checked for the first time in years, had men to spare, and had the rest of Europe safe under your boot?'

'Thankfully I am not he.'

'He will come. You'll see soon enough.'

Tom became more intrigued by what Rico was telling him. 'So how will you – how will *we,* the allies – stop him?'

'We will stop him.'

'Yes, but how, Rico? You seem to have little enough faith in your own army and, I regret to say it, compared to the numbers Napoleon can command, General Moore can only have a small force with him – and that is still in Portugal.'

The Galician shrugged. 'Spain is a big country, Tom. Small armies can get lost, but big armies they – what is a good English word? – yes, they *shrink.*'

Tom found the word amusing. 'Shrink? You think the French army will shrink? Good God, Rico, it's been doing nothing but grow these twenty years past.'

'It will shrink.'

'I'd love to know how.'

Rico smiled his funeral smile and nodded. 'You should sleep, Tom. You will find out what I mean when the time comes. It will not be long now, I promise. For the present you should rest your fine mind for a while. You will soon need your wits about you, so I urge you to sleep while you can. We ride north at dawn.' He kicked dust over the fire and again it was dark.

Blunt was lagging behind.

Together with Widowson, just as uncomfortable on horseback as his master, he had dismounted and was leading his mount, giving a little ease both to the animal and to his own, sore backside. He had let the cavalrymen press on some hundred yards ahead. Even picking slowly along the hazardous mountain trails of the Sierra de Gredos, the nags they had been given could not compare with Thicknesse's fine chargers. At least they were making progress and Blunt was bored to death with the young hussar's moaning about the road, the weather, the country...

So the two redcoats marched, making their way steadily along at the tired horses' pace, content that they were at least less likely to be thrown off a cliff's edge and spared for a while from the pitying, condescending looks of the cavalrymen.

Then they heard the shot.

'Pistol,' said Blunt automatically.

'Just round yonder bend,' Widowson nodded, immediately reaching for their rifles and powder horns from the pack mule. 'Must be Thickie.'

'Come on,' Blunt said, dropping the reins to his horse without waiting for Widowson to unwrap and charge the weapons. He reached out a pistol from the saddle holster and went forward.

He rounded the big outcrop of rock that had hidden the others from him and he came upon Thicknesse's two men, dismounted with their carbines drawn and ready. Cornet Thicknesse, who had indeed discharged his pistol, stood some way further on, aiming another at a man standing not two feet from him. The Spaniard was wrapped in an old cloak, with a curious conical leather cap atop his lined, oddly flat face. He had short bandy legs and he held a long whip in one hand, his other tucked in his wide cloth waistband. He looked more curious than fearful to see a pistol's muzzle pointing at his snub nose. A clue to his trade came from the line of pack mules which stood waiting patiently for their master to give the word to move on.

'What's this, Cornet?' Blunt snapped.

'Fellow wouldn't stop when I told him. Put a shot around his ears.'

'You did what?'

'Teach him his place, eh?' Thicknesse smiled, but kept his eye on the mule captain, who continued to chew his tobacco, politely waiting for the foreigners to finish their conversation and get out of his way.

'It is his road, you know,' Blunt said.

'What, a damned mule johnny?'

'Mr Thicknesse, if you'll just – '

'Watch out, he's going for his piece!'

Blunt's hand shot out and knocked the cavalryman's pistol down before he could fire.

The muleteer, seemingly unconcerned by Thicknesse's antics, had produced a flask which he silently offered to Blunt.

'Muchas gracias.' He glared at Thicknesse, then accepted the flask and took a pull, was pleasantly surprised. It was not the rough aguardiente he expected, but something far finer. 'Ah, bueno. Es coñac?'

'Si, senor.'

'De su pais?'

The man shook his head. 'Es coñac de la Mancha.'

'Es muy fuerte, gracias.' Blunt offered the flask to Thicknesse, who looked as if an adder was being waved under his nose. Blunt took another taste, then gave it back. The driver himself took a gulp, before returning the flask to his sash.

'Widowson?'

'Sir?' The soldier had come up with the animals.

'Rouse out a bottle of rum.'

'For yon dago?'

'For the devil himself, if I say so.'

'Aye, Captain.' The soldier sighed and reluctantly went back to the pack mule to fetch the precious liquor. Widowson didn't drink, but he knew the value of spirits and other supplies in so remote a location.

'Have we the time for this?' Thicknesse complained.

Blunt ignored him and turned back to the mule driver.

'Cuales nuevos, hombre?' He asked what the news was. The mule trains took all manner of supplies from one remote town or village to another and they were the prime source of gossip in those parts. The Spaniard, particularly once presented with a bottle of fine navy rum, was a positive font of knowledge. Blunt learned from the muleteer, among other things, that the price of wax candles had risen, that the cargo of olive oil he carried was some of the finest he had ever tasted, that the mayor of Jarandilla's wife had run off with a toreador half her age and that the priest of Villareal had been visited by demons and turned into a goat, which had refused to repent and had been obliged to be slaughtered. And down in Caceres, the most peaceful of places, there had been a treble murder in the townhouse of a distinguished Andalucian nobleman. The slaughter had evidently been prodigious, blood everywhere, it was said. Incredibly, the assassin was rumoured to be an Englishman. And in Madrid the Josefinos – and here he spat at mention of the Spaniards who supported the return of Napoleon's brother as king – those miscreants were getting excited as they expected the French to march south any day now. This clearly disgusted the mule driver. Blunt was given a short lecture on the particular vices and abnormalities of the average Frenchman. And then, after profering various other pieces of news from far and wide, the driver offhandedly told him the location of Sir John Hope's artillery column to the nearest mile.

Calahorra, Navarre, late November 1808

'Have you seen enough now, Tom? You comprehend?'

It was a hard question to answer. The Englishman was, in fact, struggling to make any sense whatsoever of the scene he was examining.

'Yes?'

Tom looked back at Rico, an expression of pained confusion on his face. 'But I don't understand.'

'What don't you understand?'

'You told me this was the Army of the Centre, the famous General Castaños' army – the army that won at Bailen. General Blake should be to the west with your Galicians and Palafox has the right wing. That is what you told me. But these are truly Castaños' men? This then is supposed to be the centre of the Spanish line.'

'Very good, Tom. You are correct in every particular.'

'But Rico, you did say this really is the Army of the Centre?'

'I did and it is.'

Tom looked down again from their vantage point high on a wooded hill on to what they could see of the camp. Finding Castaños had not been as straightforward as Rico had suggested. His army had pressed on from Astorga. The Spanish were on the move all across the north. Castaños was positioning himself to confront the inevitable French advance and Tom and Rico had followed him. They had ridden for more than a week, trailing Castaños' army, which had marched east to take up position on the Ebro at Calahorra. Now they had found them at last. Once again Tom worked the glass over what he could see, before snapping it shut.

He was still confused, half-hoping that, whatever Rico said, this wasn't really the famous army he had heard so much about. Certainly they looked nothing like the Spanish troops he had seen in the late summer down in Cadiz. These were no soldiers: some had no musket and hardly any of the men he saw here even had greatcoats against the cold, many simply wearing ponchos over light summer shirts.

'Forgive me, Rico, I wish no offence, but those fellows surely aren't soldiers,' Tom said, the concern plain in his voice. 'I'm sure they are brave men, patriots, but they have the look of farm workers who have simply been given a musket. There are no uniforms, there is no drill. They don't even look as well organised as you would see in our English country yeomanry.'

Rico nodded gravely, looking unsurprised by what Tom had said. 'I know nothing of your yeomanry, but these men are mostly of the local militias. The soldiers you saw in Andalucia, those commanded by Castaños at Bailen, were regular troops. These are not. They are volunteers; they consent to give their time, possibly their lives, for Spain. You are right, they probably are brave enough, but they are certainly not soldiers and most of them would prefer to be at home tending their fields or animals.'

'Good God. Does General Moore know this?'

Rico gave a very Spanish shrug.

Tom continued to gaze down on the army. If Castaños' men were nervous of facing Napoleon's hordes they didn't show it. He saw a few officers moving about, haughty and arrogant, in the manner of the proud specimens he had seen in Cadiz, but in general the camp seemed to be relaxed and at ease, with cooking fires burning and clothes drying on lines, some of the men involved in games of one sort or another – a scene more in the image of a holiday fair than a military encampment. Tom was deeply troubled, not just for the prospects of these men if they came up against Napoleon's teak-tough veterans, but also for Sir John Moore's army, if it should be tempted to support them. 'Very well. Now I see it – and I thank you, Rico. I understand now why you brought me here. Do you mind if I take down a note in my pocket book?'

'That is precisely why I brought you here. You write your notes, my friend. But hurry, we must go on.'

'Go on,' Tom said, a note of suspicion in his voice, 'not go back?'

'We can't go back yet, my artist friend. How could we, when you have seen only half of the picture?'

Tom was to discover that the second half of the picture was going to be rather more difficult to view than the first. Looking in on the gentle chaos of General Castaños' Spanish army was one thing, but doing as Rico wanted them to do now, going off to examine the French forces which were apparently flooding in across the Pyrenees, was an altogether different undertaking. But, if he had misgivings about this latest errand, Tom was getting used to the idea that it was pointless using reason as a negotiating tool with his Galician friend. That simply didn't work with Rico. He suspected that the quickest way of getting to Portugal was going to be by gritting his teeth and putting up with doing as he was told, hoping that he would soon be allowed to be on his way.

The party of horsemen had gone north-west towards the French. Then they had left Rico's men with the horses and the two of them had crossed the Ebro at night – neither safe nor easy. They were both dressed in dark clothes. Rico had even blackened their faces and had tied a black bandana around Tom's head to cover that distinctive – and dangerous – blond hair. They worked their way with difficulty along the rocky, tree-lined bank, several times hearing patrols moving above them. At last Rico, who surprisingly seemed to have some idea where he was in the pitch black, somehow took them up and out into the open country. They moved silently, like a pair of wraiths. Tom hadn't an idea where they were heading, but he blindly stuck to Rico, having no wish to be stopped and taken up for a spy. Once there was a "Qui vive?' and a shot, but there was no follow-up. The French sentries would not leave their post in the dark of night in a fiercely hostile foreign land – not alone, certainly.

'Where are we?' Tom whispered, feeling quite done in, as they took a break at last, well hidden in the roots of a big tree. They even enjoyed some shelter from the rain, which was falling heavily now.

'The nearest place you may have heard of is the city of Vitoria. We are in the country of the Basques.'

'Not your own Galicia?'

'That lies many leagues to the west. Here we are closer to the Pyrenees, closer to the French border.'

'Are we, by God? You do like to show me the world, Don Federico. So tell me, just why are we here?'

'You will see,' Rico picked up his haversack and water bottle. 'But only if we move. It will soon be dawn. If we are in the open they will kill us.'

They were not in the open at dawn, they made sure of that. Spanish territory or not, this was presently enemy country. Tom in particular, a soldier dressed in civilian clothes, was in the greatest danger of being shot as a spy. Yet first light found them safe enough, crouched together high in the bell tower of a deserted church – or at least Tom hoped that it was deserted. There was a little roof over the bell itself, so they enjoyed some shelter from the persistent rain. They were breakfasting on some cheese and a loaf Rico had produced from his haversack. The Spaniard had crushed some garlic on his bread, but Tom preferred to take his crust dry.

'You've been here before, haven't you?' Tom said softly, taking a pull from the wineskin Rico offered. He was just about able to make out Rico's face now, despite the blacking they had both put on.

'Yes, a week ago. It is a good place to watch the world pass by. Below us is the main road to Madrid from San Sebastian, the royal road.'

'Which the French are presently using?'

'Naturally; it is a good road, with the correct surface for moving heavy vehicles. It is the very route used by both the Romans and the Moors for conquest and then for retreat. Now the Frenchmen tread it. They are able to bring in their cannon and their supply train. They find they can advance quickly and in large numbers. But Bonaparte does not know Spain. I only hope he imagines all of our roads are like this one. His other armies may get an unpleasant surprise.'

'So you think he is heading straight for Madrid?'

'Of course. The Corsican is the evil of the world, the very devil himself, but he certainly believes in action and moves lightning fast once he chooses to strike. He will not have been amused by having his brother thrown out of our capital city. So, yes, he will go for Madrid. He will believe that if he cuts off the head, he kills the beast. But he will be wrong. Spain is not like that, not at all. Madrid is solely a geographical capital, not like Paris or your London. He will find that merely taking Madrid will not win him his war here, not by a long shot. Now Tom, if you feel it is light enough, you might look down on the road. See for yourself, eh? Just be sure you don't make any noise and don't let anyone see you, or they might interrupt my breakfast.'

Tom shook his head at the audacity of the Galician. He found it difficult not to smile, as he fully took in the extraordinary position his breakfast partner had chosen for them. It would have been difficult to have found a more dangerous place to shelter from the rain or a more perfect place to watch the road. The church tower was separate, though attached to the main building and had its own staircase. Tom now strongly suspected that there had after all been soldiers billeted below them overnight. Even if the church was empty, the sight of camp fires all around them had suggested that they were tucked away in the very heart of a large army on the move. But just how big was that army and was it indeed moving on Madrid as Rico believed?

They would find out soon enough. They had long since heard the trumpets and drums of reveille, seeming to echo all around them. There was smoke from those fires which could be made to light to cook a little breakfast. They could hear horses, many horses, being made ready to ride or to be harnessed to guns and supply wagons. He could hear mules, oxen...

Soon had come the sound of marching men, as the first of the army got on the move. Now Tom simply did as he was told and looked down on the scene below him. What he saw down there on the great royal road brought both a chill and, in spite of himself, something of a thrill to his heart.

'You may as well relax and enjoy the show,' Rico said, slicing more cheese. 'We two won't be going anywhere during daylight, unless you wish to meet them in person.' He gave a little laugh.

Tom, utterly fascinated, ignored him and concentrated on what he was seeing. He realised now that he was most certainly looking at the unparalleled fighting machine that was the Grande Armée. These were not just reserves and conscripts coming to support the armies already encamped in Spain; many of these were experienced, seasoned troops on the long road down from the French mustering point of Bayonne, where Napoleon himself was rumoured to have been in command, gathering his best regiments from all over Europe. Could this display of might mean that the ogre was now himself come to lead his Eagles against the Spanish and English? Tom glanced at Rico. As if he read his thoughts the Spaniard simply said, 'The Corsican? Oh yes, he's here. Or more likely he's down the road there, at the very front of that lot.' He gestured idly to the road with his knife. 'I saw him just the other day.'

'You saw him? You saw Napoleon! My God, Rico – but why didn't you tell me?'

Rico shrugged. 'Don't get too excited. He's just a man, nothing more. He looks even shorter than me, would you credit it, the foul Corsican devil.'

Tom wasn't convinced that the Emperor could be so easily dismissed. 'You don't measure genius in height.'

Rico raised an eyebrow. 'Oh, he's a genius is he? And what marks the stamp of a genius, Lieutenant Herryck, do you think? A so-called republican who nonetheless had himself crowned Emperor by the Pope and who gives his brothers countries to make them kings? A general who deserted his defeated army in Africa and left them to rot – God grant that he will do it again in this land; a monster hungry for other men's countries, whose ambition has seen hundreds of thousands killed in battle or by plague and starvation. Is this your genius?'

Tom had heard it all before. 'He's all of those things, I grant you. Of course he is proud and ambitious, possibly even half-mad in his greed. Yes, he is surely the very ogre of the world, just as you say. But you must at least concede he is rather a clever and efficient ogre, eh?'

'Huh,' said Rico, folding his knife and putting it away, clearly unwilling to pay his devil any due whatsoever. 'Watch your soldiers. Go on, watch. There are a lot of them to see.'

'You don't need to watch?'

'I've seen them before. I need to sleep.'

Just as Rico had said, they had no chance whatsoever of getting away from the church until nightfall, so Tom spent most of the day watching the army marching past. It was part of his training to observe, to accumulate potentially useful intelligence, so he was content enough. He had not yet been in action against the French but even so, very few Englishmen had enjoyed the opportunity to see the Grande Armée on the march. Tom was determined to take full advantage of the opportunity. It was as if a spectacular pageant was being staged for his sole benefit down there on the Spanish highway. This was a frighteningly big and powerful army. There below him rode breast-plated cuirassiers on their heavy mounts, dragoons and lancers, chasseurs and hussars of the light cavalry. The regiments of line infantry seemed endless, though Tom was relieved to see that some of them, at least, appeared to be newly created units, or raw foreign conscripts. But, to his dismay, most looked like seasoned troops, veterans of campaigns across Europe. And, of course, there was Napoleon's beloved artillery – trundling past in companies of eight guns each, with fifteen men to each gun. On and on the parade went by. It was a breathtaking sight.

The regimental bands were playing jaunty marching music. From time to time there was a rousing cry of "Vive l'Empereur", which generally brought a snort from Rico, asleep or awake. But otherwise the army just got on with it, soldiers drawn from France, Holland, Germany, Poland, Switzerland, Italy – marching remorselessly on to undertake whatever task their master had in mind for them. Tom watched them, curiosity turning into fascination and amazement and then into something much more like black, fearful apprehension. The day wore on and still they came.

Later, as Tom dozed for a while, Rico took a turn to watch, noting down as best he could the different regiments or at least the particular type of soldiers passing along the royal road.

'Why did you want me to see this?' Tom asked later, weary now from his long vigil, but still in shock at the massive scale of this French invasion. The daylight was beginning to go at last.

'So that you can report what you have seen, both here and with Castaños' force in Navarre.'

Tom found this odd, 'To whom – to General Moore? That's a fine notion, Rico, and I surely would if it were practicable, but I don't even know where he is. He was supposed to have marched out of Lisbon, but he could have sailed home for all I know. In any case, surely your General Castaños will have sent reports to our army?'

Rico shook his head. 'Moore has not gone home. Last I heard he was heading for Salamanca. And you are over-optimistic about my countrymen, my friend. Our military machine is not quite so formidable as the one you have watched passing before you. I doubt whether Castaños has a clue what is on the road right here, just these few leagues from his own position. He is probably not even in touch with the other Spanish armies to the right and left of him, never mind new foreign allies he barely trusts. But he is no coward. If the French appear, he will doubtless fight them.'

'With that rabb – with the army we saw across the river?' Tom asked, understandably appalled at the prospect of a fight between a small force of ill-equipped volunteers and this huge army of healthy, well-disciplined veterans. 'Napoleon will surely brush them aside and press on to Madrid.'

'Yes, he is most likely to do just that and then may the Lord almighty protect anyone else who falls in his path.'

'You mean Moore?'

Rico continued to watch the endless stream of soldiery, marching there under their bronze eagles, dull in the Spanish rain. 'Yes, of course. You see how it is now, Tom? If your general doesn't know how perilously weak our Spanish armies are here and how formidable is the French strength, he might be so unfortunate as to make the discovery in the most costly way.'

Tom looked worried, seeing all too clearly the very real potential for disaster, possibly terminal disaster, for British arms. 'There aren't enough redcoats in all four corners of the world to fight this size of army on anything like even terms. And commanded by Boney himself! It isn't a comfortable notion at all, Rico, for either of our armies. Napoleon has regularly thrashed huge forces of Russians, Austrians and Prussians – often combined. No, it doesn't bear thinking about.' Then, brightening a little, 'But still, you know, Moore is by all accounts a canny operator. You said there were other French armies – you never know, perhaps he could somehow manage to manoeuvre one of those into a more even fight.'

Rico did not look convinced. 'Perhaps – but he is certainly in a bad situation at present. Maybe he could have a chance against a Soult or a Ney, so long as he can keep clear of the Corsican himself. Possibly then we will get the opportunity to see how good your Moore really is. That would be interesting, eh?' Rico smiled, glancing down at the enemy once again, his eyes narrowing, as he stared more purposefully at the scene below them. 'Now what's this? Ah, mierda! I worried that this might happen. Here Tom, softly now,' Rico nodded for Tom to get up alongside him and look carefully over the parapet. 'There, those two on horseback.'

It was gloomy now, still raining, and night was coming on. But there was light enough to show their present danger. Rico had pointed out two mounted officers, who in their turn were pointing up to the belfry itself. Then they were clearly arguing about something, with more pointing up and down the road, still busy with sodden, marching soldiery. Then they looked up at the bell tower once again. One of the men dismounted.

Rico shook his head. 'Fools will have lost their regiment or some such thing. And now that one has had a clever idea. He will come up here to look up and down the road.'

Tom looked about for somewhere they could hide but there was nowhere in the cramped space and, as if to confirm Rico's theory, they could already hear boots on the ladder.

'Here!' Rico hissed and they moved over as silently as they could to crouch behind the trap door.

It seemed like an age until finally the old wooden door swung ponderously up and over to slam at their feet. First a red-cockaded bearskin hat appeared then a man planted his hands on the floor to lever himself up. It was his own momentum that allowed Rico to grasp him by the shoulders and heave him clear off his feet. Tom ignored the astonished look on the soldier's face and punched him hard in the midriff, doubling him up, then Rico hit him on the head with his pistol butt, knocking him senseless.

'Quick, his clothes.'

'His clothes?'

'You must put them on.'

'Me?' Tom protested.

Rico was already untying the clasp of the man's cloak. 'Get on with it, man. He is more your size and it is the easiest way to get away. He has even brought you a horse. Make haste now; the other one down there won't stay patient for long, sitting in the rain.'

'But – '

'Christ's bones, we have no time! Get the uniform on, I tell you. Please Tom, hurry now, it is your only chance.' Rico himself pulled on the cloak for a moment and gathered up the French officer's hat. He appeared head and shoulders above the parapet and gave a wave, desperately hoping the other waiting below would take it as a sign of success in spotting whatever they were looking for and buy a little time for Tom and himself. He darted back, frantically started stripping off the unconscious man's pelisse, coat and boots. 'Come on. You must go down there, get straight on the horse and go like the devil himself. Stop for nothing. Head the way the army is going, then cut away south-east when you are able. You will have to get over the river how you can. But you must do it! You must find your General Moore and tell him what you have seen here and with Castanos on the Ebro.'

With difficulty Tom got into the jacket, but the Frenchman's tasselled boots were too small and his breeches the same. He left his own on. He tied on the Frenchman's sash and took his despatch case and sword. He unknotted the bandana from his head and wiped off the worst of the blacking.

'The hat,' Rico smiled, pushing it at him. 'The hat makes all of the difference.'

Tom jammed on the fur hat. 'But what about you?'

Rico cocked an ear, then looked over the side, cursing once again. 'Two empty horses. Wait. The other one must be coming up.' He pushed the unconscious Frenchman behind the trap door, then quietly closed the door itself, keeping his hand on the ring-handle. They waited, breathlessly listening to the steps on the ladder, then at last the door began to lift. Rico actually helped it to open, then pushed down with all his might, cracking the man a fearful blow on the head and sending him tumbling unconscious or lifeless down the ladder.

'Come on, you know what to do! It will be difficult for you, but you must get through. Moore must know what he faces!'

Rico was shoving him onto the top of the ladder.

'Quick, now.'

Tom looked up into his face, streaked with black, the eyes alive with excitement. 'But what about you, Rico? How will you get away? Will you take the other horse?'

'No, you take both of them. It will look as if you are a despatch rider or something of the kind and you will be less likely to be stopped. The green uniform will help, I think. These two are from the chasseurs, Bonaparte's favourites. Change your hat for the other fellow's – he has the white cockade of an officer.'

'But I can't even speak French.'

'Then don't stop to talk to anyone.'

Tom looked at his friend, then he shook his head at the impossibility of the man. 'And you?'

'I will be fine.'

'But how will you get away?'

Rico smiled, his teeth and eyes white in the gloom. 'Don't worry about me, my friend. I will be well enough. Just please concentrate on your own work and forget about me. Trust me, I know how to disappear.'

"It will be difficult for you," Rico had said. On countless occasions during that long night Tom had had cause to reflect on the Galician's evident mastery of understatement.

At first, against all the odds, the hastily conceived plan had worked well enough, as the chasseur officer with his spare horse galloped importantly along the dark road. The soldiers were now stopped for the night and had moved away from the road to set up their bivouacs, struggling to light their cooking fires in the rain. He got the odd call of encouragement or, knowing soldiers, possibly of genial abuse, but nobody tried to stop him. Tom was amazed, if delighted, at how far he had got from the church. It was a madcap scheme, hardly a plan at all, but it was working. But then at last, with the horses tiring, he decided it was time for him to get away from the road and to try and find the river. He hadn't the faintest idea where he was, or where he might find boat or bridge, but he at least knew that he must certainly cross the river if he were to get through to the Spanish lines and then, hopefully, south to Moore's army.

So he nudged the horse off the road and into the darkness. Now it was really going to become tricky, Tom thought.

If he had left the main French army behind, he had not escaped the voltigeurs, the light infantry troops who so efficiently screened the army's front and flanks. They seemed to be everywhere. He had got away with a couple of challenges in the dark with a "Vive l'Empereur!", but once he had been shot at and a second time his spare horse was hit and he had to leave the animal as he rode for his life on the remaining mount. He wasn't on roads now and it was pitch black. He knew the poor horse must surely be exhausted and he was likely to misplace a step and founder at any moment. Tom was worn out himself, the cold biting into him, but he knew he needed to get under cover, hidden somewhere until he could see how matters stood in the light of morning. He had no idea where he was, so he simply tied the animal to a tree and removed the saddle. He left it on the ground but took with him the chasseur's document satchel and the pistols. Then he warily pressed on into the night until, by good luck, he found a stone sheepcote where he was at least able to pull his cloak about him and settle for a couple of hours' sleep in the straw and animal droppings.

He was woken soon after daybreak by the sound of men calling to one another. They were Frenchmen – and they were nearby.

He peered out cautiously through the doorway. More voltigeurs, perhaps a dozen of them, moving steadily across the fields – confident, skilful killers. But even then, it seemed he might just get away with it. The Frenchmen walked on. None of them seemed interested in his little stone sanctuary. They were looking for enemy skirmishers, not a lone Englishman in chasseur's green. Then he heard the first gunfire, far in the distance. The French must have found Castanos' army at last. He didn't give much for the Spaniard's chances, but he had no time to worry about that. If the battle was underway, that might just work in his favour, as it might help him to slip away in the confusion which would surely ensue. The French uniform might help, but it would likely cause him a problem at some stage, but he could worry about that once he was on the far side of the river.

The last of the voltigeurs disappeared and Tom had the chance to make his move. He could only vaguely remember the direction he had come the previous night and he hoped that, so early in the morning, the horse might still be where he had left it. It was all guesswork, a gamble. He could hear the sounds of the battle quite distinctly now, cannon somewhere distant and the odd pop of small arms nearer at hand.

It had seemed he had come a long way in the dark, but he found that he had left the animal only a couple of hundred yards away. With a wave of relief he saw that the big black horse was still there, the saddle at its feet, calmly cropping the grass. Possibly no soldiers had been this way and the local peasants who might otherwise have seen the fine horse as a temptation too hard to resist, would be making themselves scarce with a battle in progress not far away. He patted the animal's flank and wished him good morning. He bent down to pick up the saddle.

'Arrêtez vous la. Ne bougez pas!'

He dropped the saddle and turned to find himself facing two bayoneted muskets levelled at him, the soldiers just a few feet away. A third man, a voltigeur officer, was walking towards him, a smile on his face.

'Le Capitain a dormi bien?'

'Er, bonjour.'

'Vous avez trouvé le cheval, je comprends. C'est un animal très robust, n'est pas?'

'Bonjour?'

The Frenchman smiled again and held out his hand held out for Tom's pistols.

Tom was miserable, thoroughly furious with himself for getting caught so tamely after having come so far. It was a stupid mistake. He should never have gone back for the horse, he realised now, should have kept going on foot.

By virtue of being made a prisoner, he had at least succeeded in getting south of the Ebro, he reflected darkly. But that was poor consolation when he knew he must get his information through to Moore's army. Time would be vital to the British commander and Tom was letting it slip by. Following his capture, he had been marched a few hundred yards to where a transport wagon waited. He was bundled into this and, along with his captors, he took a rocky ride seven or eight miles to a village on the far side of the river which was dominated by a large monastery, obviously serving for the present as a French field hospital. The monks themselves were huddled in a group in the courtyard, standing forlornly in the rain. There seemed to be few casualties coming in as yet, but from the sound of the gunfire, much heavier now, there could soon be business enough for the aproned medical men and their orderlies, who waited to do their gruesome work. But Tom was not a medical case and he realised with grim certainty that he had less chance of being alive that evening than most of the injured who were likely to appear at the improvised hospital. He had been taken in French uniform and, once interrogated, he knew that he would almost certainly be shot.

He was taken to a room just off the cloister, pushed into a chair and his hands roughly tied to it. One of the men who had brought him in casually dropped the despatch satchel and Tom's other possessions onto the table in front of him. Then the soldiers went out, locking the stout wooden door behind them. There was a little light from a high window, but otherwise the room was gloomy enough to fit Tom's mood. How could he have been stupid enough to go back for the horse? He realised that it would probably have taken a miracle to avoid capture in the middle of an enemy army, but he felt annoyed with himself, nonetheless. At least he might have had a chance. Not the least of his frustration lay in the fact that his crucial intelligence would lose value with each passing hour. Irritably, he tried to loosen the fastenings on his wrists, but it was no good. He gave up and tried to think of some kind of story he might be able to spin to his captors, but he knew it would take a great feat of imagination to find a convincing reason why an Englishman was in French uniform on the edge of a battlefield. A Scot or an Irishman, perhaps? They certainly existed in Napoleon's army, but probably not in the chasseurs and certainly not if they couldn't speak the language. For the first time Tom began to confront the unappealing likelihood that there might simply be no way out of the dilemma he was in.

Then he remembered the boot knife. Yes, the voltigeurs had missed the little blade! That, at least, was one card he might play.

He waited. He waited with something more like hope now. He had to believe that he had a chance – and when it arrived he must be ready to take it. So he waited.

At last they came. He had heard the indistinct sounds of the continuing battle, but nobody had been near him for hours. Then the door opened and a soldier with a bayoneted musket stepped inside, then another. They were followed by a tall, finely-moustachioed officer, who to judge by his cloak and mud-spattered boots had been specially sent for to conduct the prisoner's interrogation. He took the seat opposite Tom. He said nothing, just looked at Tom with a cool gaze from his dark eyes, as if weighing up his fair-haired prisoner; then he reached across the table and took the despatch satchel, broke its seal and took out the papers inside. Tom hadn't even bothered looking inside the case, reasoning that his lack of serviceable French rendered it pointless. He was interested in the French officer's reaction. There were a couple of sealed documents which he looked at, eyes widening in surprise, left unopened and returned to the table. He unfolded a large map, studying it for some time. Then he looked up at Tom.

'English?'

So, it was to begin:

'On my father's side; I believe my mother has some Scots in her line.'

The officer, a full colonel of the Imperial staff by the look of him – grey busby, blue tunic trimmed with gold lace, cloak trimmed with astrakhan – was unimpressed. 'Yes, yes. The drole Englishman, eh? Yes, this is the way we start; you must have your little joke, yes I understand. But you are going to be killed as a spy, you see, so it is not really so funny, eh?'

'I've been happier, that's for sure.'

'And you are a soldier?'

Tom said nothing.

The colonel continued to stare at him. He tapped the satchel with his forefinger. 'My name is Faucon and it is my job to find out what you were doing with this, far from your own people, dressed as a courier of the Chasseurs. I assure you that I will acquire that information, monsieur, and it will be in your interest not to put me out of countenance. So, the men say you have no French.'

Tom again said nothing. Whatever the fellow's threats, he didn't want to make it too easy for them. In fact, a very good teacher had spent months cramming enough French into Tom's reluctant mind to allow him to pass out of Woolwich Military Academy. A terrible student of languages, he had promptly forgotten most of it. Let them guess whether he understood or not. The officer sat back. He stroked his luxuriant moustache thoughtfully, 'We have defeated the Spanish today, you know?'

'Congratulations.'

'They are running back to Madrid. But we will catch them and thrash them again. Then they will run for Seville. We will catch them there also. Then we will drive them into the sea.'

'It must be a comfort to have your future planned so thoroughly.'

The Frenchman looked at him, then sighed expansively, as if to say that it was Tom's choice if he wished to make light of his very likely fatal predicament. Then he tried again, 'Where did you get this?' he gestured to the satchel and the papers on the table.

'I found it.'

'You killed the man?'

Tom shrugged. 'Actually, no. He was asleep when I left him.'

The colonel nodded. 'You will still be shot.'

'That is regrettable.'

Tom's personal effects were also laid out on the table. Faucon picked up his pocket watch and examined it. 'Very fine, very fine piece indeed. Of course, I also recognize its manufacture. This is a Leroy, French-made. You stole it?'

'Certainly not; it was a coming-of-age gift from my father.'

'No inscription?'

'We are not a showy family.'

'It is French, you stole it.'

'Those are my own effects.'

'Stolen.'

Tom sighed, 'My glass there is a good English Dolland, my sword from Prosser, my pocket knife Sheffield steel. My boots, bless them, are by Gilbert of Old Bond Street.'

'And the documents?'

Tom had no ready answer to that.

'So, you will be shot.'

'And I will still be unhappy to be shot.'

The dark-skinned officer puffed out his cheeks, looked thoughtfully around the room, then looked back, directly into Tom's eyes. 'Or possibly you don't have to be shot.'

'No?'

'No. Possibly you can talk to me.'

Tom looked politely interested. 'Talk? What shall we talk about? Fox-hunting, or the latest gentlemen's fashions? This horrible weather, possibly? No, it won't do, I'm afraid. I confess I can't abide small talk.'

The French colonel raised an unamused eyebrow.

'Well,' Tom said, 'did you have a topic in mind?'

Faucon fixed him with a dark stare. 'About the English.'

Tom smiled agreeably. 'Ah, well I'm your man then. Let me see. We're a proud nation state. Lots of interesting history, you know – kings and queens and so forth. Our poets are generally well thought-of. We don't make good wine, I fear, and prefer our cheese on the firm side, but we do like to sail, take pleasure in music and theatre and enjoy all manner of healthy sport and country pursuits.'

His audience was distinctly unimpressed. 'The English army. You can talk about that.'

'What about it?'

'About where it is, about who is in command; about the numbers and discipline of the men; about the quality of the, how do you say, the commissary; about guns; about which regiments you know to be here.'

'Ah,'

Faucon nodded, 'Yes, you choose to tell us that, my amusing Englishman, you tell us whatever you know, then you go to Verdun or Bitche, not to stand against the wall to be shot.'

Tom sighed, 'That kind of talk.'

'Well?'

Tom thought for a moment, considered his other option, which wasn't much of an option at all, then he looked at Faucon and said, 'Very well. As I seem to have little choice, I will tell you what I know. I am not sure how useful such old news will be to you, or how astute is my grasp of affairs, but I will share what I know. But first, Colonel, I must tell you that I need to be given some food and drink. It is a little complicated, you know, what you are asking, and I have not eaten in a very long time.'

The officer looked at him, clearly asking himself whether this Englishman was genuinely intending to cooperate, whether he would be better putting him immediately to more direct persuasion, then he barked the order over his shoulder. One of the sentries went off to find Tom's refreshment.

'So?' Faucon turned back to him, his eyes hard now, clearly alert for the ring of truth or falseness in what Tom might tell him.

'Well, where to begin? Let me see, your map – is it of Spain?'

'Spain and Portugal.' The Frenchman turned the map so that it was the right way around for his prisoner.

'That will do admirably.' Tom sat forward, as if to study the map, but was prevented from doing so by being tied to the chair. 'Please, my hands?'

Faucon looked at him coolly. He produced a small pistol, cocked it and lay it on the table before him. 'Alors,' he barked to the remaining sentry, 'ses mains.'

The guard propped his musket by the door and came to untie the ropes. The officer picked up the pistol and held it idly in his hand, its threat obvious at a range of four feet. The guard finally pulled the rope away. He stood back and Tom flexed his hands bringing the blood slowly back to his fingers. He smiled at the officer then he jerked himself violently backwards and tipped the table over, sending the colonel flying backwards off his chair. The guard had just turned to resume his post and, as he swung back around, his reward was a knife slash across his neck, a jet of dark blood gushing out, announcing his death. Faucon was surprisingly quick to recover, but not quick enough to stop Tom reaching his pistol. Neither of them could know whether the priming had held, whether the gun would fire, but Tom still held the bloody dagger. The French colonel stood perfectly still. He gave Tom a look of cold appraisal, trying to judge his man, but he knew he was likely to be as dead as the guard if he moved. Tom didn't think Faucon would do anything rash. He looked like the sort of man who would realise he wouldn't be able to do anything to stop the Englishman with a bullet lodged in his own guts. He stood in the middle of the room watching as the Tom went to turn the key in the door, all the time keeping him covered with the pistol.

Tom walked back towards him, a smile on his face. 'Now Colonel Faucon, your coat and cloak if you please.'

The man didn't question him, began to remove the clothes.

'I believe I will have that fine busby as well,' Tom said. 'As quickly as you please, sir, if you value your life. I have certain business to attend to. You should congratulate me, you know. It appears that I've been promoted.'

He was back in the game again.

Tom found it instructive, how having acquired the uniform of a higher rank had helped his cause. All he had to do was march purposefully along with an angry scowl fixed to his face under the colonel's big plumed shako with its eagle crest and he was able to move past any number of French soldiers without hindrance. It was night once again as he had walked away from the monastery and marched on through the village. There were troops coming the other way now, wounded men being brought in from the battlefield. But the soldiers were in good heart, clearly members of the winning side. "Colonel" Herryck ignored them and pressed on, in all appearances determined to get to the scene of the battle.

The key he had used to lock the bound and gagged Faucon inside the room at the monastery had long since been tossed into a well. But the key wasn't the only thing he had taken away. At the edge of the village he had made the further transformation from a French staff colonel to a humble monk, putting on the habit he had taken, which miraculously was almost long enough for him. He had no idea whether you could be shot for impersonating a monk – and he had no intention of finding out. He just knew that once again he had a chance – a very slender chance, for sure, but a chance nonetheless – of getting back to the army.

Chapter Six

Robert Blunt wasn't a man to whom contentment came easily – he hadn't had the kind of life which bred such a tranquil and luxurious emotion and he was, in any case, by nature cautious and pragmatic – but he generally found at least a kind of satisfaction in doing his work, the job of soldiering, efficiently and well. So he might surely have been forgiven for feeling just a little pleased with himself that cold November evening...

He flattered himself that he had followed Sir John Moore's instructions to the letter. He had made the difficult journey across the Sierra de Gredos mountains and, by a combination of intelligent guesswork and latterly by information gained from the talkative mule-driver, he had found Sir John Hope's artillery column as it moved ponderously towards its connection with Moore's main army. Blunt had been informed that progress for the guns, if frustratingly slow, was going along steadily enough and that the column was well-placed to reach Valladolid, beyond Salamanca, by the beginning of December. That was the information Sir John Moore needed in order to plan the next step in his campaign and Blunt immediately set off on the return journey to deliver it to him. He had felt content for a while. He believed that getting back to Moore should be far less complicated than finding Hope's column. His quickest route to Salamanca was now back up through the pinewoods of the Sierra de Gredos to Avila and then on to his goal along the good Madrid road.

The two infantrymen, neither of them natural or comfortable riders, were mounted on borrowed nags, ordinary march-horses, while Thicknesse's party rode his three beautifully conditioned chargers. Wherever possible, as they moved now on well-travelled roads, Thicknesse demanded that the horses be stabled overnight. Early starts seemed to be an impossibility, as the horses were prepared with inordinate care, surpassed only by the attention given to the cavalrymen's uniform. Blunt was the senior, of course, but it wasn't as simple as that: he and Thicknesse were in more or less constant conflict as to the distance they should cover each day – the cavalryman concerned with his duty to his precious mounts, which he endlessly told the infantryman took up to three years of painstaking labour to train and prepare, while Blunt was concerned solely with his duty to Sir John Moore. But he knew that part of that duty was to bring the young hussar officer back safe and sound. Moore had made it privately clear to Blunt that, as the son of a landed member of Parliament, Thicknesse was a valuable commodity to a general not universally loved by the ministry in London and should at all costs be preserved, meaning Blunt's overwhelming instinct to press on and leave the cavalrymen to their brushes and polish had somehow to be resisted.

But they had managed to make progress, put in some good hours on the road, and had at length reached the impressive walled city of Avila, some two days from Salamanca. Again they stopped. Even if the impatient Blunt had been able to persuade Thicknesse that their duty was to continue, he recognized that the bitter cold of coming night would make such a course of action foolhardy. Reluctantly he accepted that they would be better feeding and resting themselves and the animals and making an early start next day. But even then, the two officer's ideas of "feeding and resting" were to prove very different: Thicknesse insisted that they seek out the best inn and the best stabling available; Blunt, constrained by having to subsist on his basic travelling allowance, agreed to stay there, solely so that he knew where Thicknesse was and could turf him out early in the morning. Thicknesse booked a room, Blunt was happy enough to join Widowson and the groom bedding down in the stable.

But first they needed to eat. The hussar felt his priority was to look first to his "cattle", then to his toilet and grooming before sitting down to dine; Blunt's priority was to look straight away to his stomach. He and his servant found a table in the corner of the main dining room and he ordered food for the pair of them, together with wine for himself and milk for Widowson. Soon they were contentedly tucking into a bowl of the local stew – certainly not to Widowson's conservative taste, which ran to very little "foreign" – but nourishing and warming, as well as being reasonably inexpensive.

Once they had taken the edge off their hunger and ordered another bowl, Blunt had the opportunity to look around him and observe their fellow diners. It was a mixed bunch – one or two men dining alone, possibly travelling merchants; several families, a young couple and, noisiest of all, a party of officers, Spanish by their look, but all loudly conversing in French, as if there was nobody else in the big dining room. They were welcome to it, as far as Blunt was concerned, as long as he got fed.

At last Thicknesse made his appearance. He had changed into his full-dress regimentals.

'Is 'e set on goin' out dancin' then, our youth?' Widowson asked in an undertone.

Blunt just grunted, carrying on eating.

Thicknesse stood looking at his two comrades, as if deciding whether or not to join them. But to his evident relief he was rescued from his dilemma. One of the Spanish officers, noticing the gorgeously dressed hussar, stood and invited him to join their party. The Spaniard was himself splendidly attired in a spectacular white and gold uniform. They might have been made for one another, Blunt thought. Having established that Thicknesse, like any well-bred European gentleman, could speak good French, the Spanish officer introduced the young Englishman to the members of his party with much bowing and expressions of enchantment. Blunt and his servant might have been invisible.

'Young Thickie there looks like a pig in shit, don't 'e, Gaffer, doin' 'is parlez-vous an' the like wi't the dons,' Widowson said, disapproval etched on his face.

But Blunt had been watching the group of Spaniards more closely, intrigued now, trying to work out what such a set might be doing in Avila. 'At least it keeps him from under our feet, I suppose,' he said, deciding again that it was not his business.

Widowson watched more wine and a vast dish of meat arrive at the Spaniards' table. He spooned up the last of his stew. 'If you say so, sir. An' who can tell, eh? 'Appen they'll like 'im so much they'll mebbe keep 'old of the wet-nosed little bugger.'

Blunt grunted a laugh, 'Nice thought, soldier, but I promised Sir John I'd give him back to him in one piece. No, let him enjoy himself. He hasn't had a chance for any prithee sirrah and 'pon my soul for a few days. Let him get it out of his system while he can. We'll be back on the road again soon enough. You finished?'

Widowson drained the last of his milk. 'Yes, Captain, sir.'

Blunt left some coins on the table and stood up. 'Let's go and get some sleep. If we get a decent start tomorrow, we might even persuade our young beau over there to push on and get the job done by nightfall.'

'Tha'll be lucky,' Widowson muttered to himself as his officer walked across to the Spaniards' table.

'Buenas tardes, senores,' he greeted the company. 'Mr Thicknesse, we leave at first light and I expect you to be ready to ride. Enjoy your meal, but make sure you get some sleep.'

The young cavalryman – irritated at being interrupted from a fascinating, enlightening discussion of the better kind of horseflesh with a captain of the

Cazadores a Caballo in his splendid green uniform – gave Blunt a quick glance, then turned back to his new friend.

'Cornet?'

Another irritated glance: 'Yes, mother,' Thicknesse said.

Several of the Spanish, who obviously understood some English, laughed delightedly at this.

Blunt looked at Thicknesse for a moment, then simply repeated, 'First light.' As he turned to go he heard one of the Spaniards loudly saying something about 'Quel type vulgaire et mal élevé…'

He decided he didn't understand any French and kept walking.

It was bitterly cold and there were flakes of snow in the air as the Englishmen rode out from the magnificent walls of Avila, but first light it was, and they were all present and correct. Satisfied as he was with their prompt start, Blunt could still almost have wished that Thicknesse had stayed in bed. The young man had not only risen as fresh and bright as if it was a fine May morning at a civilised hour, but he insisted on talking – and talking. And he had but one topic of "conversation". He was full of the quite wonderful time he had passed with his new Spanish friends, full of their courtesy and civility, full of their generosity in insisting on paying for his food and wine. They had been such cultivated hosts, so completely modest about their own business, but much concerned to praise their gallant English allies and full of curiosity about Sir John Moore and how his fine army might proceed in the coming campaign.

'And what did you tell them?' Blunt asked, only half-listening, squinting to look ahead as the wind blew eddies of snow in front of him. They were alone on the road, making their way down the hill away from the city. Blunt was restless, more than just dyspeptic after the rich food. He knew now all too well that he had made a mistake, that he should not have left the boy with the Spaniards, yet their early start had given him some small hope that they might perhaps get away with it. But he was beginning to get more and more of a bad feeling, smelling trouble on the freezing wind.

'Tell them about what?' The boy asked.

'About Sir John and our army?'

'Why, what a curious thing to ask, Blunt. I answered their questions, of course. Why should I not? As a member of Sir John's staff, I might be expected to know more than most. The Spaniards were simply interested in how we might prosecute our campaign. I was pleased to be of service to them. They are our allies, you know.'

'Are they?'

'Of course; they are Spanish officers.'

Blunt gave him a pitying look. 'Yes. And you are a British officer, of a sort. And did they ask you what you were doing in Avila?'

Thicknesse, clearly not caring for Blunt's tone, but unable to gainsay his superior officer, simply answered the question. 'Naturally they did. It was only polite interest.'

'And you told them…'

'The truth, of course; why should I not? I repeat, they are our allies, Blunt. They were merely being polite. I doubt they gave a fig about any of it. After all, what possible interest could they have in Sir John wishing to know about General Hope's progress?'

'What indeed,' Blunt said dryly, holding up his arm for them to halt. The five horses came to a stop. Then, without turning, he said to Widowson, who had been riding just behind him, 'Get the rifles off the pack mule.'

The little private didn't hesitate, but scrambled awkwardly down from his horse and set about the fastenings on the pack.

'What - '

'And you, Mr Thicknesse, prime your pistols and have your men do the same with their carbines.'

'Pistols?'

'That's what I said.'

'You can't possibly believe – '

'I believe that,' Blunt said gruffly and pointed to the road ahead. The young cornet squinted to peer through the snow flurries. A man, a man he recognized as one of the Spanish officers from the night before, had come round the bend was standing in the middle of the road, a hundred yards ahead. He had drawn his sword and held it casually at his side, nonchalantly tapping his boot.

'What on earth? Why is he here?"

'Cornet,' Blunt sighed, 'shut up.'

'But – '

'Weapons, men,' Blunt said crisply, ignoring the cavalryman and climbing down from his horse. 'Widowson keep an eye on our backsides. You, Cornet Thicknesse, make yourself useful and be so good as to go and use your perfect French to find out what he wants.'

The cavalryman, looking pale, glanced at Blunt but said nothing, instead turning and spurring his charger to trot down the road towards the Spaniard. He was greeted with a flamboyant bow from the smiling officer. The cavalryman dismounted and made his own bow. The rest waited for several minutes while Thicknesse spoke at length to the Spanish officer. At last he remounted and cantered back to them.

Thicknesse looked utterly confused, shocked even. 'I don't believe it.'

Blunt stood checking his pistol's priming, eyes fixed on the Spaniard, whose white and gold uniform was visible under his cloak. 'You are having difficulty believing anything this morning, Mr Thicknesse. What does the fellow say?'

'I'm sure it must be some kind of misunderstanding.'

'What does he say?' He shoved the pistol carefully into his sash, glanced down to check for his boot-knife, and then checked a couple of times that his sword would run free from its scabbard.

'He says he wants us to surrender ourselves to his protection.'

'And?' Blunt said, sounding unsurprised.

'And his party will escort us.'

'His party?'

'He says he has men all around us.'

Blunt nodded, his face set in grim concentration. 'I'll bet he does. How many servants did you reckon the dons had, Widowson?'

'Half a dozen, sir.' The private passed Blunt his rifle, primed and ready to fire.

Blunt subconsciously welcomed the touch of the familiar walnut stock in his hands. 'And there were, what, six at table last night? A round dozen, then. So how will they have played it do you think, Cornet Thicknesse? They'll have crept out ahead of us on foot to wish us good morning here. If they'd taken their horses Widowson and I would have seen them. So they'll have waited for us to get out of the way, then they'll be bringing the horses on in our wake. But that will take a while and would need at least three of them. So, it's likely five against nine.'

'Good God, you don't mean to fight?'

Blunt looked up at the young cavalryman. He gave a little shake of the head. 'Do you know what an afrancesado is, Mr Thicknesse?'

'Is it Spanish?'

'Yes. It's not generally an expression used as a compliment. It roughly means a lover of the French, or at least of French ways. Afrancesados themselves, you see, are generally quite pleased with the notion of Boney or one of his relatives running Spain. The French will more than likely be back in Madrid soon enough and there will be some Spanish, some afrancesados, who see which way the wind is blowing and will be more than happy to cosy up with the crapauds. Those fine gentlemen you dined with last night are most certainly afrancesados.'

'What,' Thicknesse said, his voice full of scorn for the suggestion. 'Simply because they choose to speak French? That's a preposterous notion, Blunt. Anyone with a pretension to be a gentleman speaks French. Sir John speaks French, General Wellesley speaks French – '

'And you speak French. Yes, of course you do, Mr Thicknesse, of course you do. Perish the thought of an English gentleman not spending his waking life talking another man's language. All part of good breeding, I suppose. Oddly enough, I don't myself have much French – but I do speak a bit of Spanish and that's what your friends' servants speak. It's interesting what you can pick up in a mean old stable when folks think they can talk freely in front of ignorant foreigners. It seems that your fine Spanish gentlemen are on a little mission of their own – in fact, they're on their way to meet no lesser personage than the Emperor of the French. They plan to offer him Andalucia.'

'But that's – '

'Ain't it just?'

The young man looked appalled. 'No Blunt, you must be mistaken.'

'And it follows that, if these afrancesado gents get their wish, if Boney is to have the south given him on a plate, then he most certainly won't want Sir John Moore's army, guns and all, to his rear.'

'So you believe they mean to stop us delivering Sir John Hope's letter?'

'Looks that way.'

'Hell.'

Blunt hadn't taken his eyes from the man in the road. 'Ah, and now I believe your particular friend in the white coat seems to have lost patience.'

The Spaniard had contemptuously sheathed his sword, had saluted them with his feathered hat and had turned and was walking away, out of sight around the bend in the road.

'Time to choose partners for the dance, I believe. How many behind, Widowson?' Blunt asked, keeping his own eyes front.

'Two as I've seen. One o't buggers each side.'

'Fair enough. You go left I'll go right. Once you've fixed your man, go forward and we'll flush the ambush.'

'Ambush?' Thicknesse said, still hardly able to credit what he was hearing. 'Are you sure about this, Blunt?'

Blunt nodded to their front, 'Just around that bend, I should think. But don't worry, and trust me, you'll like this part, Cornet,' he turned to look the hussar in the eye. 'Now listen carefully, boy, these are your orders. You'll hear two shots. Wait. When you hear further shooting, and only then, you pin your ears back and go like the hounds of hell down that road and then you keep going. You understand? You don't stop for anything, anything at all. You can take your two fellows with you, but you don't stop, not until you get to Salamanca. You understand?'

'Yes, sir,' the boy said unhappily.

Blunt allowed his expression to soften, 'Come on, now. Couldn't be simpler, could it, eh? I told you that you'd like it. Think of it, you're off the leash, away on your own, but with nothing to worry about because you act under my direct orders. Why, you even get to lead your very own cavalry charge!'

'But if there really is an ambush, even if we do get through – '

'There is and you will. These fellows are no sharpshooters and they will be on foot, while you are on your precious bloodstock. Keep going, get to Salamanca and give this to Sir John.' He handed up the despatch they had been given by General Hope.

Thicknesse dutifully pressed the despatch into his sabretache. 'What about you?'

'Take all of the horses. We'll see you in Salamanca.'

'You're sure?' The cavalryman looked thoroughly unhappy.

Blunt gave him a half-grin. He was a fool, but he was young enough to learn. 'You'll be fine, Mr Thicknesse. Just be patient for a few minutes, wait for your moment, then go like hell.'

'Yes, sir.'

'Good lad. Crack on, then, and just do your duty. Now, let's us all get busy about our work. These people are our enemies, the army's enemies, and they must be dealt with. Widowson?'

Salamanca, late November, 1808

Sir John Moore waited for news.

It seemed to him that it had been an uncommonly long and frustrating wait. Ideally, of course, he would like good tidings – which for Sir John at that particular moment would be represented by useful, positive intelligence which might help him to plot his next move against Napoleon – but reliable news of any kind would be better than the scraps of dubious information he was being fed by those supposed to be his friends and allies. He was amazed, infuriated even, that he had still had no word from either the Spanish government in Madrid or Aranjuez or even from any of their army commanders in the field. He had brought his own precious army to stand alongside the Spanish, was ready to do his duty by his allies, yet he didn't know with any certainty where they were. Even his own masters in London kept him criminally starved of decent intelligence or clear instructions. Worse, they lavished gold seemingly indiscriminately on indifferent agents and on the various fractious regional juntas, but they failed to send any coin in the direction of Moore's army.

The only shred of decent news he had received in several days had been that Sir John Hope's column was at least safe down to the south of him and making progress towards its union with the main army. But even that good word had been tainted by young Thicknesse's report that Robert Blunt was very likely dead or taken prisoner by a renegade Spanish force. Moore knew that he could ill-afford to lose experienced officers like Blunt of the 52nd even before he faced the French on the battlefield. And that was the sum total of his news! Otherwise all that he heard was next to useless – unreliable rumour about the movements of the French or unlikely tales of Spanish success in the north.

And yet, if he was starved of the accurate information he craved, in the short term at least, he had some grounds for satisfaction. He had chosen an excellent base for his campaign. The people of Salamanca had been generous and welcoming. Food was found for the troops and horses. The local nuns had even given him a precious gift of five thousand pounds for his empty war chest and had allowed a large portion of the army to billet in an abandoned convent. The fact that Bonaparte was no admirer of the Catholic church and had in his time mistreated and imprisoned two popes won him few friends among the devout and made the good Catholics of Salamanca unusually trusting of the heretic English.

Moreover, a local grandee, the Marques de Cerralbo, had gone further and had made his magnificent palace of San Boal available to Moore, who now had his headquarters there. Maps had been found – maps by Senor Lopez, whose plotting of Portugal was largely a work of his own imagination, but whose maps of his native Spain were at least passably accurate – and Sir John and his staff spent hours pondering how they might react to different circumstances, different tactical challenges; but by necessity it was still all guesswork. They simply had no idea how many men the French had, nor where they were. They didn't even know where their Spanish allies were or who was in overall control of their armies. The November days became shorter and still the British commander had no clear notion how he should act once his army was finally united.

One evening Sir John was walking alone in the walled courtyard of the palacio, impervious to the cold, his troubled mind more than ever full of the endless ifs and buts of his next, vital move. At last there had been some movement from the Spanish. He had finally heard from the Central Junta, which had requested most urgently that he immediately move to take up a position to defend Madrid. Again he was put in a difficult situation. His instinct was against this suggestion, as it would make his army vulnerable to a concerted French attack, but he felt that honour demanded that the British army at least make some kind of stand against the French on behalf of their beleaguered allies; yet he dare not risk cutting off the army from its escape route to the west. Had he delayed in Salamanca too long? As he continued to pace, weighing his options and trying to find the ideal compromise, a door from the main house opened quietly and his host the Marques presented himself.

'I apologise most sincerely for this intrusion, sir.'

'Your Grace cannot intrude in his own home.' Sir John said, his tiredness overcome by the uplifting presence of this dignified and hospitable gentleman.

The two men walked a few paces together. 'I know you have much to consider, General, and it is with reluctance that I disturb you. But I beg your forgiveness solely because I do myself the honour of presenting a gift to you.'

'A gift?' Sir John immediately felt uncomfortable; the man had already been so wonderfully generous. He felt embarrassed that these kind Spanish people should offer such stolid support when his own government almost seemed to have forgotten his army.

'I believe it to be a gift you will find yourself able to accept.' The Marques smiled, clapping his hands as he did so. Immediately the doors from the house were opened once again and two of Cerralbo's servants came out into the courtyard. Between them, walking unsteadily, supported by the men either side of him, came a hooded monk.

'My gift, Sir John.'

Moore looked curiously at the monk. 'A man of God?'

'Possibly,' the Marques said dryly. 'But I think probably not a man of the cloth. They seldom wear English boots.'

Tom Herryck was almost asleep. He was slumped forward, his arms on the table before him just about keeping him sitting up. He had several days' growth of beard and his fair hair was filthy and matted. He had been taken directly to the general's quarters and he still wore the faithful monk's habit. But Sir John Moore, fundamentally a kind man, knew he dare not let the engineer rest, not yet. There was far too much at stake. As Tom stared dreamily about him, the general was pacing the room, his face dark with thought. Senior staff officers sat around the table, which was covered with maps. Major Colborne, Sir John's military secretary, was bent over the captured despatch Tom had brought, his expression betraying his amazement at what he had read, not once but several times.

'This really is quite astonishing,' Colborne said at last, that astonishment plain in his shocked voice. 'If this document is to be believed – and I am convinced that it is genuine, signed by no less a hand than Bonaparte's chief of staff Berthier – if it tells true, then the total French strength in Spain is presently something over 300,000 men, with up to 7,000 of them cavalry. An incredible figure, quite astonishing! By God, even once our own army is united, they still outnumber us by almost ten to one!'

For a moment there was silence, then there were a couple of low whistles and a general murmuring of shock and astonishment among the officers. To a man, their faces were glum and concerned, several of them looking downright terrified at the thought. It was truly staggering information. The British command had simply had no idea that Napoleon himself was in Spain, or that he had assembled such a vast force about him.

'And you say that they have already broken through the Spanish centre, Herryck?' Sir John asked. His voice was gentle, but the urgency of his tone was unmistakable. He was not awed by Bonaparte's presence, but he needed to be absolutely certain of what he was facing. He knew he must press the young man hard.

'Yes, sir. I saw General Castaños' men retreating east as fast as they could. The French cavalry had nothing between them and Valladolid.'

'Where General Hope is presently heading with our artillery train,' Colborne said, as if his chief needed reminding.

Moore ignored this, wanting as many pieces of this jigsaw as possible. He continued his interrogation of his young officer. 'And of the Spanish army, this is of the first importance, you are quite sure you do not exaggerate its lack of quality, Herryck?'

Tom raised his tired eyes to look at the general. 'Quite sure; it's a militia at best, sir – though I think, to be fair, it might be better described as a kind of peasants' uprising. I saw General Castaños' army there with my own eyes. I've also seen something of the Spanish army he was involved with down in Andalucia, which was in every way superior. The bulk of the men I saw in the north were simply not trained soldiers and could never be expected to stand in open battle against a determined French army.'

'Andalucia,' Sir John said thoughtfully, now fully conscious of how perilous was the position of his army. 'You know, if we'd the slightest inkling of the true strength of the French and Spanish at the beginning of this, we'd have been far better placed landing at Cadiz rather than Lisbon and Corunna.'

But, whatever his regrets, the army wasn't in Andalucia, it was there in Old Castile, menaced by the Grande Armée under Napoleon himself.

'What do you intend, sir?' Sir Thomas Graham asked after a brief silence. All of the officers present knew now that the British were in a near impossible situation, still divided, facing a vastly superior force, hundreds of miles from the safety of their ships.

Sir John looked uncomfortable. 'I'm not sure, Graham. It's a pretty piece of work, true enough. We have at last heard from the Spanish government and they now beseech us to go south to the defence of Madrid. From what Herryck tells us, there is precious little in Bonaparte's path otherwise.'

'That would risk the destruction of the army.'

'Yes.'

'And Boney is in all probability coming for us even now,' said another of the generals, voicing what they were all thinking.

'We might easily fall back on Ciudad Rodrigo,' Colonel Graham pointed to the map. 'Then back into Portugal if necessary, with the comfort of our ships being in Lisbon harbour.'

'We are here to fight.' General Stewart said gruffly.

'But not to lose Britain's only army.'

'Thank you, gentlemen,' Moore said firmly. It was not the time for his officers to be falling out with one another.

'Sir,' Tom's voice came out as a dry, uncertain croak. Not only was he exhausted, he was by far the most junior officer present.

'Lieutenant Herryck?'

'May I speak, Sir John?'

The general smiled, 'Mr Herryck, with the priceless information you have delivered this night, you have every right to be heard. Go on, man.'

Tom took a deep breath, 'Well, sir. It is simply this. If you have had no clear information about Napoleon's strength and whereabouts, does it not follow that he might be equally ignorant of our own location here? Forgive me for such presumption, but it seems a fair guess. The Spanish irregulars have badly disrupted his communications. He may even still believe you in Lisbon. It seems to me that, if he is indeed intent on taking Madrid, he will simply head straight down the road in his old way. He may not know that we are but a short distance to the west of him.'

'By God, so we could get in behind him?' Graham said.

'And do our duty to the Spanish,' Sir John nodded thoughtfully, clearly balancing the possibility of some kind of morale-boosting strike against the French with the far safer option of a rapid march to the coast. 'Very well, very well indeed. At least we now have a few scraps of fact to chew on. There is plainly much to consider. Gentlemen, we must talk more on this. Mr Herryck,' he turned to the young Royal Engineer officer, looking so thoroughly out of place in his shabby disguise amongst so much scarlet and gold. 'You, sir, have done your duty, and damned well. For that you have my thanks and those of the army. Now, I suggest you leave me to turn over these matters with my colleagues here, while you go and restore yourself. Get some rest, young man, for I believe I may well have further use for you in the coming days.'

Oporto, late November 1808

'Bom dia, Senhor da Costa.'

The Portuguese looked up from his ledger to see a handsome, dark-haired woman standing in the doorway of his office. He smiled with delight, as he stood to greet her. 'Why, Senhora Isobel, what a charming surprise.'

'I trust you are well?'

The manager of Truelove and Dunn's port lodge gave a resigned shrug, 'I am as well as anybody in our trade can hope to be at present.'

'Are things that bad?'

He gave her a mournful look. 'You will see for yourself, senhora. You have come to see the *chefe*?'

'If my brother is here, yes.'

'He is here. Might I give myself the honour of taking you to him?'

'Of course,' Isobel smiled. She and da Costa were very old friends.

The lodge of Truelove and Dunn was situated in the Vila Nova de Gaia area of Oporto, right on the River Douro. It was the area of the city where many of the famous British port shipping companies, known collectively as the British Factory, had their lodges, where the wine was stored and blended. It was a busy, prosperous neighbourhood, almost a little piece of England – but unluckily for the wine traders it was a piece of England that the French had recently succeeded in occupying, however briefly.

Isobel followed Senhor da Costa, who had been with the company since her father first set up in Oporto, as he led the way through the gloomy lodge. There were no cellars, but the arched galleries were only sparsely lit by small barred windows. It was dark, sepulchral. There were interesting breeds of fungi growing on the walls and, as they got further in, large, dense cobwebs spread up into the arches. Isobel knew this place well, had visited the lodge many times, but she could see that, as the Portuguese had hinted, all was not as it should be. Looking around, she was shocked at how few pipes, or port casks, were in the racks. The French had been busy. They continued on, deeper into the dark, cavernous place. At last, at the very back of the lodge, they finally came upon the owner, deep in conversation with a tall, elderly man called Ferreira, who was the wine taster. The two men made no sign that they had heard or seen Isobel and Senhor da Costa approaching, so intent were they on their work. Isobel stopped and watched with interest as first Ferreira, then her brother shook wine around the oddly shaped little saucer, looking with intense concentration, then sniffing and finally tasting the wine.

'Will it be fit to drink?'

William looked up. 'Izzy!' His expression instantly transformed from troubled, concerned concentration to one of simple delight.

They kissed and stood back to look at one another. The two Portuguese stood by smiling. They had both known the Trueloves since they were very small children.

'You look well,' he said.

'I have been out riding,' she said archly, describing her lively journey from Cadiz. 'But you yourself look tired, brother.'

'Do I? Well, you can blame the damned French for that, Izzy, if you'll forgive the saltiness of my language. They have done a pretty job here.'

'Is it so very bad?'

'In truth, no; certainly not as bad as I feared. They were in the city for half a year and a Frenchman will account for a powerful amount of wine in that time, but we had got the more important vintages away to England and our friends here,' he indicated the two Portuguese, 'made certain the animals took away only the less valuable, unblended wines. They were gone from the city before this year's vintage came in, so thanks to Arthur Wellesley we are still in business, just about.'

Isobel nodded, 'I am pleased to hear it. The French are unruly guests. I only hope they can somehow be prevented from returning to cause more damage. For such a cultivated nation, their soldiers can behave quite barbarously at times. But come Will, let us not spoil our reunion by being gloomy. Why not finish your work here with Senhor Ferreira, then we can go back to the house and exchange tales of our adventures. Will that not be agreeable? I long to hear the latest news from London and I can tell you something of my journey here and, more important than anything, of course, how your family does at home in Andalucia.'

William Truelove and his sister had always been firm friends. They shared a comfortable familiarity born of liking, respect and love for one another. In Oporto, the family had for many years kept a small house, the Casa Cidade, not far from the company's lodge. It was there that brother and sister enjoyed a reunion supper. Both William and Isobel had been born in Andalucia, each knew Oporto well, and the two of them thoroughly enjoyed the full range of Portuguese as well as Spanish cuisine. But Senhora Leite, the cook-housekeeper at the Casa Cidade, had a firm idea of her duty and took it as a challenge to her honour to provide traditional English cooking for her "foreign" employers when they dined at the house. So it was that evening that they had boldly, doggedly worked their way through boiled beef (over which the kind-hearted cook had failed to resist the urge to sprinkle some very un-English spices) with something that had once been potatoes and a pudding that had the name of spotted dick, but apparently none of its ingredients. The good local Monte cheese and, naturally, a decanter of port came as a welcome relief. But neither William nor Isobel was at present concerned with their bellies, they were far too taken up with each other's stories.

Naturally they had started with the family. William had been away from his home in Cadiz for many weeks, pursuing Truelove and Dunn's interests in London, Lisbon and now Oporto. Fiercely devoted as he was to his wine and the continuing success of the company, William was first and foremost a family man. Isobel had reassured her brother that his wife and children were all perfectly well when she herself was last in Cadiz. In turn, William could tell her that their young brother Ned was doing well enough at his school in England. Then they swapped tales of their respective journeys.

Having been confident that it would be difficult to trump the shocking notion of duelling servicemen, William was astonished by his sister's story. His glass of fine tawny had remained untouched for half an hour. 'What a tale you tell, sister! I can barely credit that you have been involved in such goings-on. And you say the last you saw of your dangerous Englishman was of him being smuggled away to do our cousin's bidding?'

'I am sure Rico had his reasons, but yes, that was the plan and that was what happened.'

'I must say that it seems a little extreme, Izzy. What did Rico want with this Herryck?' He took a sip of his wine at last.

'I don't know.'

William frowned. He liked his cousin well enough, trusted him and valued his many qualities, but despite his affection for him, he was never quite comfortable with the dark intensity and brooding nature of the Galician. Rico was family twice over, but William had always found him difficult, impossible even, to fathom. And he knew that Isobel esteemed their Galician cousin almost as another brother. He sighed, 'Well, whatever his need for the fellow, I hope he looked after him. If he is a Royal Engineer, your Herryck, they are something of a scarce commodity in the British army.'

Isobel took a small taste from her glass. 'You're right, of course, Will. Rico will certainly have had his reasons. He simply said that it was important Lieutenant Herryck joined him and that was good enough for me. He arranged for him to be taken off from Salamanca in that fashion purely because he didn't believe the Englishman would agree to go to him of his own free will.'

'And clearly Herryck did not agree. But who could blame him, if he felt that his duty was to be with his countrymen? Moore's army is likely to be hard-pressed, you know. He is plainly a man of spirit. The poor fellow obviously wants to play his part.'

Isobel nodded; a little smile. 'Ah, there is no doubt of that. He's in thrall to his duty, young Mr Herryck. But possibly our cousin already has a part written for him.'

William frowned, then gave a rueful smile. There was nothing they could do about it now. 'You are probably right. I'm sure cousin Rico knows what he's about. He's a serious-minded fellow, but he usually knows his business.'

'Yes – and now, what of your own Englishman, Will? He sounds like he might be another serious one. Was Cintra the last you heard of him?'

William smiled again, thinking of the proud, stubborn Robert Blunt. 'Yes, we parted there. He went down to join Sir John Moore's army at Queluz and I came on here. I know nothing more about him, I'm afraid, but I pray he is doing well enough. And you're quite right, Izzy – I mean about Blunt's nature. He is another solemn one, rather like Rico, but just as worthy, I think. I certainly liked him.'

'I am pleased. And I liked my own Englishman.'

'Yes?' William cocked a brotherly eyebrow.

'Not in that way, Will,' she rebuked him, wagging a finger. 'Too young and too uncomplicated for me; but he was entertaining, my lieutenant of Royal Engineers. That is one gentleman who is never likely to be described as "solemn", I'm quite sure of that!'

He nodded. 'Good. I wish him well in whatever mischief Rico has schemed him into. And I hope also that he may keep his good countenance. Heaven knows, there's more than enough to be solemn about at present.'

Isobel, content with her glass, pushed the decanter to her brother. 'So, Will, shall you tell me what are your plans now?'

'My plans? Good question, sister. Well, I suppose I've done as much as I can here for the time being. Our people at the lodge are so wonderfully capable that they have made the best of the French occupation and we are able to carry on, in a fashion. My instinct is that now I need to get back to Cadiz and look to the sherry side of the business.'

'Shall we sail down together? The *Esperanca* is here?'

Truelove smiled as he thought happily of the *Esperanca* – the family's weatherly little cutter, his pride and joy, and as fast a vessel as any to run them quickly down to Cadiz. 'Yes, she is tied up by the quay, sure enough. That will be our quickest and probably safest route at present, however the sea winds should behave. But do you know, Izzy, I might first take a leaf out of your own book and go and pay a brief visit to Salamanca. I've a mind to look in and see how Tio Enrique does.'

She was surprised. 'Salamanca? Is it a good time to go just at the moment? The whole of the British army is likely to be there, you realise, in all of its glory.'

'Yes, I know.'

Isobel gave him a shrewd look. 'So, come then – what do you have in mind? I know you, William Truelove. You seldom do things without a purpose.'

He picked up his glass, 'Let us just say I would like to see if it might be possible to do a little something to help our friends in the British army. Heaven knows, I have precious little faith in the Spanish military, or the Portuguese, come to that. But I don't like what the French have done here and I don't want them back – either in Oporto or in Spain.'

She was intrigued, 'And how do you propose to do that, to help General Moore and his army?'

He toasted her with his port glass and offered her a glittering smile. 'Why, sister, however else but by offering up my best talent.'

Chapter Seven

When Tom Herryck had finally been released from his long, long session with the general and his staff, he was fed and put to bed in one of the rooms there at the Palacio San Boal. He slept without moving for ten hours and then, kitted out in borrowed uniform, he was interviewed again, as they tried to squeeze from him everything he had seen of the French and Spanish armies and all that he had been told by Carlos Federico Rivero y Castro. The next day followed the same pattern. While this was going on, more and more information was coming in to Moore's headquarters from other sources, as the news of the Spanish defeats followed Tom into Salamanca, with Blake, Castaños, Cuesta and Palafox all beaten in succession by Napoleon's marshals. The Spanish government (now rather precipitately fled to Talavera, well to the south-east of the capital) in their turn bombarded the British with further demands to halt the remorseless French advance. Little seemed to be going right for the allies – there was even a rumour at headquarters that Sir John had already ordered Baird and Hope to turn their columns around and retreat.

When Tom had at last told his tale to the satisfaction of even the most pedantic of the staff officers, he was instructed that on General Moore's own orders he was to go and rest again until his new duties were assigned to him. However useful he had proved to be as an unwitting intelligence agent, with the army sure to march soon – in one direction or another – Tom believed that his future value was much more likely to be in using the skills he had been trained in as a Royal Engineer.

It was thinking of his need to revert at last to his proper place in the army that reminded the temporarily red-coated Tom of where he had left his blue RE uniform, what seemed a very long time ago. Feeling weary, despite his sleep and having been well fed, he found his way across town in the late afternoon to the Casa Delgado. The steward who opened the great front door not only recognized him, but seemed unsurprised to find Tom there on the doorstep after several weeks' absence. He invited him into the entrance hall and left him to wait there. Tom hoped and expected that the Conde de Castillo Nuevo, whom he had greatly liked, might himself make an appearance, but instead he found himself looking at the tall, dignified figure of Omar walking towards him. Tom felt his stomach lurch, because he guessed that where the Moor was, his mistress would not be far away. He wasn't sure that he was in the right frame of mind for a confrontation with Isobel Truelove. He was still smarting from her part in Rico's scheme to spirit him away from there and wasn't utterly confident that he would behave in a gentlemanlike fashion... Omar stopped and bowed civilly to Tom, then he inclined his turbaned head to the left, indicating the door that led to one of the reception rooms. Tom, thoroughly fed up with weeks of running and hiding, decided he had better go and face whoever awaited him.

But inside the elegant, high-ceilinged room, Tom was surprised to find that he was met by neither the Conde nor Isobel. Instead he found himself facing a good looking, dark-haired man in his late thirties who had been sitting reading in a chair by the fire. He rose to greet Tom with a smile and an outstretched hand.

'Lieutenant Herryck? Your servant, sir. My name is William Truelove. I'm very pleased to meet you.'

Tom took his hand, quickly working out who this must be. He was dressed in a well-cut coat and wore superb leather top-boots. He had an intelligent, open face, but the bright, darkly mischievous eyes were unmistakable, a clear family likeness. 'Delighted, Mr Truelove, sir; I believe that I've heard something of you from your sister.'

'My naughty little sister?' William smiled again, obviously knowing all about what had happened when Tom was last in Salamanca. 'Yes, I regret that she and Federico led you something of a dance. Indeed you could be forgiven for harbouring some resentment of her actions when you were lately in this city, sir, but I beg you not to think unkindly of Isobel for her part in my cousin's manoeuvring. She is a wilful, capricious creature, my sister, but she had the very best of motives on that occasion, I do assure you.'

'Events would appear to have proved that,' Tom said a little stiffly, thinking back to his exhaustive sessions with the British command, passing on what he had learned in the north. 'I suppose I must accept that she and Rico acted with the best of intentions.'

'You are very generous, Lieutenant. You clearly recognize the greater good and are prepared to accommodate yourself to its needs. A lesser man, I think, might have felt a sense of wounded pride or some other unworthy emotion.'

Tom shrugged, as if to suggest that his recent experiences had rendered pride a petty luxury at a time when the future of Europe itself was in the balance.

And there was little point in admitting that his vanity had indeed felt itself quite thoroughly wounded.

William, as if sensing Tom's acceptance that the matter might now be closed – or at least set aside, gestured to a comfortable-looking chair by the fire. 'Please, sit down. Can I offer you some refreshment?'

Tom was grateful to take the weight off his still sore feet. 'A glass of wine would be most acceptable, sir. I know that fine gentleman the Conde keeps an excellent cellar. But, if I may ask, what does so renowned a sherry and port wine expert as yourself recommend here in Salamanca?'

William examined the Conde's selection, then he chose a decanter from the sideboard, taking out the stopper and sniffing approvingly. 'I find it generally wise to try the local product whenever possible. Take a glass of this good red wine, if you will. I suspect the Conde has a taste for the fierce little grapes they cultivate north of here in the Duero valley.' He held the glass to the light, 'Yes. See how black the wine is, how very robust! There, drink deep now, Lieutenant. I believe you have had a trying journey and this will be the very thing.'

Tom did as he was told. 'That is really very good, I thank you. I find I have been missing my wine these past few weeks.'

'Then please allow me to refill your glass, sir,' William took his own glass and sat down in the high-backed chair opposite Tom. 'Your health, Lieutenant; I give you joy of your recent adventure.'

Tom gave him a rueful smile, wondering just how much the man knew, above what must have slipped out of Sir John's headquarters. But the sentiment seemed a genuine one: 'Thank you, Mr Truelove; that is kind in you. Although, if I am frank, I should confess that my life would certainly have been far less adventurous and likely a sight more tedious during these past weeks but for the stewardship of my person by members of your family.'

William gave a little chuckle. 'All's well that ends well, though? The intelligence you gained in the north should be of advantage to Sir John Moore, I imagine. And now, at least you're safe back with your friends and you can all get yourselves ready to make life uncomfortable for Bonaparte.'

Tom happily toasted the thought, thrilled to the heart at such a prospect. 'That is ardently to be hoped for, sir. I am sure Sir John himself would share your kind sentiment.'

William's face took on a more serious expression. 'And that is why, Lieutenant Herryck, I have given myself the honour of speaking with you here. To be candid, I have a request to make of you. In the light of what you have just said about cousin Rico and Isobel making your life, ah, *interesting*, I almost hesitate to continue. And yet I find duty dictates that I must persevere. So, might I ask you if you would be so good as to consider acting under the instructions of a member of my family on one more occasion?'

Tom narrowed his eyes, 'In what manner of business, Mr Truelove?'

'Quite simply in the bringing of a proposal of that family member – in fact, myself – to the attention of Sir John Moore.'

A proposal? Tom was confused. 'But how do you think I can help, sir?'

'For two reasons: firstly, Sir John quite understandably esteems you as a diligent officer and a most reliable source of important information and secondly because my own poor attempts to seek an interview with him have been rebuffed. No rudeness is intended, I am sure, but the military quite naturally find themselves too caught up with events at present to be bothered with a mere civilian.'

Tom could see that would be the case. Sir John Moore was the most polite of men, but he was under intense pressure. The Palacio San Boal had become an ant's nest of activity as the army made its preparations to march. 'I apprehend your difficulty, sir. May I be so bold as to ask the nature of your business with Sir John?'

'Oh, of course, Lieutenant, of course; it is quite simple. I want to give him ten thousand pounds.'

'Ten thousand pounds?' Tom couldn't help himself. It was an enormous sum.

William gave a waft of his hand, as if the amount was unimportant. 'A trifle over, if the truth be told – the total doesn't quite merit that elegant term of guineas, but it amounts to around ten thousand, two hundred of sterling in silver coin; something of that order.'

'And this is for Sir John?' Tom was well aware how desperately short of ready money the army stood. If this offer was genuine, it was amazing news. 'That is an extremely generous gesture, Mr Truelove.'

'You believe so?'

'Of course.'

'It seems a perfectly reasonable sum to me. You see, like many other Britishers in Spain and Portugal, I make a handsome living from the wine trade. If the French come, that trade will likely cease, certainly for the British. I flatter myself that I know my business. I am sure that Sir John is equally gifted in his own line – I simply want to play some small part in helping his current enterprise to prosper. We of the trade are patriots too, you know. So, to be vulgar, you might say that your excellent general presently finds that he lacks the tin to do the job at hand and I'm in a position to put some his way. After all, Lieutenant, business is business.'

And now, the morning after that surprising, if ultimately satisfying conversation with the estimable businessman Mr Truelove, at long last Tom Herryck was getting back to thinking of his own line of business.

It felt good to be back in uniform – at least to be dressed in his proper Royal Engineers' uniform of blue jacket and black cocked hat, with a new crimson sash to replace the one lost in the adventure at Caceres. Once again the guest of the Conde, he had found that his things had been cleaned and laid out in his room at the Casa Delgado and Tom had been able to present himself to Sir John Moore feeling that at least he was correctly dressed to perform his latest duty. He had been accompanied to the Palacio San Boal by six of the Conde's brawniest servants, who carried a small fortune in Maria Theresa silver dollars, the most acceptable currency in all of the Peninsula. William Truelove's gift – in fact, the gift of several of the great port houses of the British Factory in Oporto – could hardly have been better timed for the cash-strapped British and meant that Sir John was very much back in business again. The general was surprised and delighted. He had previously calculated that his army had funds enough only to see them through to the end of the month and that would soon be upon them. Now, to Moore's relief, the army could pay its way for a while longer. Had he been a more ambitious man, Tom Herryck might have been disappointed not to get a brevet majority or at least a medal, the general was so overcome by Truelove's timely offering. But the Royal Engineer was happy enough simply to have done his duty, to have contributed to the possible success of the campaign.

Once again Tom had been dismissed from the Palacio San Boal with the commander's thanks ringing in his ears and once again he had been told to rest, relax and prepare himself for the call to duty. Major Richard Fletcher, the Royal Engineers' commanding officer, would soon be needing his few available officers on whatever road Sir John should choose to send them. But just for the moment, Tom was at leisure. He returned to the Casa Delgado. Yet he was loath to enjoy the Conde's hospitality to too great a degree, simply because he reluctantly admitted to himself that he still did not wish to encounter Isobel Truelove de Chambertain. She had tricked him, played him for a fool, and he had no wish to risk further mockery. He had put it behind him, but had no wish to be reminded just yet of the part she had played in his recent past. So, under the general's direct order to relax, he hastily collected his sketch book and headed back out into the city, determined to use the time to run off some decent drawings of the place, while he still had the leisure and opportunity.

It should have been a pleasure, an honestly deserved pleasure, to be busy with his sketchbook once again. But he found to his annoyance that his mind just wasn't on his work and, however hard he tried, he couldn't get enthusiastic about the city folk and the hordes of redcoats who were now milling about all over Salamanca. He just wasn't in the mood. Even the beautiful buildings of the majestic old city could not work their magic on him. The lively times of the past few weeks had got him out of the habit of relaxation. He felt listless, morose even – not feelings which came at all naturally to Tom Herryck. He wandered the streets, aimless and unmoored, hoping the call from Major Fletcher wouldn't be long in coming.

Eventually he found himself drawn back to the Puente Romano, the long bridge over the Tormes where he had been sketching Isobel when Rico's men had stolen him away. He didn't draw, wasn't in the mood, but at least he found it was more interesting here, watching the traffic coming and going – certainly more so than in the coffee houses and taverns of the city, full of noisy soldiery. There was a guard of infantry on the city end of the bridge, redcoats this time, and occasionally a cavalry patrol would clatter across one way or the other, but otherwise it was mostly the local people about their everyday business. Tom thought it instructive that the last time he had been there the soldiers had been not British but Spanish. Now who could tell just how long it would be before it was the French who came marching across the old bridge?

He didn't want to waste time on that depressing thought. He liked Salamanca, liked what he had seen of its people. He despised the notion of Napoleon's soldiers looting its treasures as they had done so often before in cities all over Europe. He turned his eyes away from the wonderful view of the elegant roofs, towers and spires and looked out instead into the open countryside. Down in the meadows on the far side of the river there were a few cows cropping the tired winter grass. In the distance he thought he could see two, possibly three, soldiers stepping wearily towards the city along the river bank.

'Lieutenant Herryck?'

He turned to find himself facing a young hussar officer.

'Your servant, sir.'

'I am Cornet Thicknesse, sir, 15ᵗʰ Hussars. You are commanded to attend on Sir John.'

'Very well.' So the call to duty had come quickly, as he had hoped. He wondered what was in store for him. Tom turned back to look at the soldiers down by the river. Three, definitely three; two were in faded red coats and one appeared to be dressed in something that might have once been white.

'Sir?'

'One moment, Mr Thicknesse,' Tom kept his eyes fixed on the approaching men. He thought of taking out his pocket glass to examine them, but then he realised that there was no need.

'Lieutenant Herryck, sir?'

'Mmm?'

There was a note of petulant impatience in the young ADC's voice now, 'The general, sir – '

'Please tell Sir John I will attend him shortly.'

Tom got up and began to walk across the bridge. By the time he had reached the far side, the soldiers were themselves climbing wearily up the bank to the road. He found that Thicknesse, probably fearful of returning to headquarters without the officer he had been sent to deliver, had followed him and was standing at his side.

'Lieutenant, sir, this is insupportable. You must come with me to the Palacio immediately. The general specifically said – Good God!'

Thicknesse stood with his mouth hanging open, while Tom continued on to where the three men now stood catching their breath. He looked at them, nodding his head, smiling. He saw that the man in the dirty white uniform – a Spaniard by the look of him, his head bowed down with long, dirty hair hanging loose over his face - had his hands tied in front of him. The English officer had his left arm across his chest, held in a sling. The private soldier had a bandage around his head, his shako jammed on over it.

Tom smiled a greeting, 'Hello, Rob. Where have you popped up from?'

Blunt, who was filthy from head to foot and clearly worn out – and who looked as if he had in fact marched all of the way to Salamanca from the barracks in Kent, still managed to grin at his half-brother. 'How do, Tom, handsome in you to come out to welcome us. You always was a civil sort of fellow. You look very fine and well-turned out in that blue coat of yours. But tell me, will you, is there somewhere for a soul to get a wet and a bite in this billet? Me and Widowson's fair clemmed.'

Tom took his brother's good hand. 'Of course there is, Rob, of course. Why, you've arrived at the horn of plenty and fiddler's green rolled into one. Are you badly hurt?'

Blunt shook his head wearily. 'I'm well enough. Someone stuck a blade in my arm. Nothing I haven't had before. It's clean and will heal, I reckon. Poor Widowson here fared worse – he had the top of his ear removed by an unlucky shot.' He looked affectionately at the soldier. 'He's a tough old coot, though. He'll mend. Good day, Cornet Thicknesse. I see you got here safe and sound. I trust your horseys are well?'

Thicknesse, still shocked at Blunt's arrival and unable to find anything to say, simply offered an all purpose nod.

Amazed and delighted as he was to have Blunt turn up there, as coolly as if he were on one of his visits to the Herryck house at homely Lowthorpe in Nottinghamshire, something else had caught Tom's attention in the travel-worn trio. Something he didn't quite like: Tom looked intently at the Spanish officer, his head bent on his chest, dark hair straggling down. No, he quickly changed his mind. He found that he did like it. Having Blunt here was wonderful, great news – but this was a real bonus. He stepped forward and put his fingers to the man's half-bearded chin, jerking his head up to look at his face. He was rewarded by a stare of pure, unambiguous hatred. Tom stepped back, his eyes still on the Spaniard. 'And this gentleman you have with you, Rob – is he quite well also?'

Blunt considered his prisoner, who was now looking fixedly ahead of him, affecting to ignore the Englishmen.

'Him? Oh, I imagine he's well enough, more's the pity, the wretch. Just suffering a case of damaged pride, I'd hazard. We had ourselves a bit of a country shoot back there, you see; spent a few days at it, in fact. He thought he and his friends were doing the stalking, but it turned out that it was Pedro here who ended up in the bag. Poor loser, I reckon. If there's anything more to it than that he certainly ain't told us. He won't dignify my Spanish with a civil reply and doesn't speak any English.'

'Really?'

'Not that the bugger lets on. He likes his French – don't he though, eh Cornet Thicknesse?'

The cavalryman, thoroughly embarrassed, said nothing.

'You're wrong about the English though, Rob.'

'Yes?'

Tom smiled. 'Quite wrong, in fact. You'll find he probably speaks it rather better than you do. He's very much the man of parts, this one, all of them unpleasant. Have you not introduced yourself to the captain then, Don Julian Rodrigo Duarte Vasquez?'

The Spaniard simply looked back at the smiling Herryck with a cold expression of loathing.

Blunt looked surprised. 'You know him? You amaze me, Tom. How did you come to meet this character, then?'

'Oh, he tried to kill me.'

Blunt grinned and clapped his good hand around Tom's shoulder. 'What a coincidence, brother, he tried to do the very same to me. None too efficient, is he?'

Tom, a soldier who was by nature keen on doing his duty, convinced himself that he had obeyed Sir John's summons with reasonable haste, in the circumstances. But that reasonable haste had perforce included a brief pause at a wine shop, with Thicknesse sworn on peril of unspecified damage to his person to say, if asked, how difficult it had been to find Lieutenant Herryck in the crowded city. Tom himself believed that it would have been inhuman, if not plain foolhardy, to deny Blunt and Widowson some sort of refreshment after several days' hardship in the wet and cold of Castile's tough, barren countryside. Besides, Tom was desperate to know at least something of how they had come to have Julian Duarte – a man who had gone to considerable lengths to do Tom harm – as a prisoner and what mischief the Spaniard might have been planning. It was a good tale. And yet what Blunt told him about Duarte came as something of a surprise. From boasting about the power of Spanish arms back in the south, at their fateful meeting in Jerez, he was now apparently trying to back the French horse. He would put nothing past Duarte, of course, treason included.

Widowson didn't drink alcohol, Thicknesse wouldn't and Duarte wasn't offered any. The story, quickly told, took only two or three bottles.

However, when the little party finally, rather sheepishly, presented itself at the Palacio San Boal, Sir John Moore was so surprised and delighted to have Blunt returned to him, in addition to hearing of an afrancesado plot thwarted, there was no thought of quibbling about timekeeping. That was not to say that time wasn't at the very forefront of the general's thoughts just then – it had become paramount, as the army frantically prepared itself to march. But with his customary desire to know as much about the wider picture as possible, he did find a few moments to listen to Blunt's brief – and vastly understated – tale of his running engagement, over several days, with

Duarte's renegades, as the two riflemen gradually whittled away their enemy's numbers, finally capturing Duarte himself in a nasty little fight in the harsh country north of Avila. So Duarte's hopes of contacting the French with information about the British dispositions and an offer of Spanish complicity in Andalucia had come to nothing. The duplicitous Spaniard himself was not far away as Blunt made his report, held in one of the side rooms being questioned at length about the intentions of the afrancesados by Moore's intelligence officers. Sir John – already faced with problems enough – was mightily pleased that the planned offer had not been made to Bonaparte and he thanked Blunt for his part in it.

'And you, Herryck – I find you have a connection with my old comrade-in-arms here, Captain Blunt?'

'We are related, General.'

'Indeed?'

'I am his half-brother, sir.'

'I should have guessed. You plainly have the same facility for finding adventures – and, leaving Captain Blunt's tale aside and returning to the business at hand, that is why, Lieutenant Herryck, I have summoned you.'

'Yes, sir?'

'I have work for you – damned important work, if I may say. Come over here to the table and look at this map. You too, Blunt.' Moore laid his finger on Madrid, sitting squarely in the centre of Spain and of the Peninsula itself. 'Gentlemen, we find ourselves in a scrape. See here, this is Bonaparte's first target. He aims at the Spanish capital. Whether our friend Duarte and his like have their way and welcome him or whether the Spanish fight, the French will surely get their prize, and soon. I am indebted to you Herryck for the true picture you gave me of Castanos' army. I have heard only today that he has been beat again at Tudela, north east of here. So, Madrid will surely fall to Bonaparte. That is now a near certainty. But what then – what do you think our Corsican friend will do then, Blunt?'

Blunt looked at the map, sizing up the options for the French with Madrid safely in their possession. 'I doubt he will sit on his hands, General. With the numbers he appears to have at his disposal he can do pretty much what he wants. He will likely press on south and deal with Andalucia, whose army is still unbeaten. Either that or he may head for Lisbon, meaning to deal with you, sir.'

Moore nodded, clearly satisfied with Blunt's assessment, looking again at the map and pointing west to Ciudad Rodrigo. 'Very good; so the logical move for me is to move our army back to the border in readiness to fall back on Lisbon or the northern ports, where the Navy can succour us as needs be.'

'Yes, sir,' Blunt said unenthusiastically, not much caring for the notion of such a tame, if sensible, retreat.

'That is the logical step, for sure. Indeed my first instinct was to retreat. But my orders are to aid the Spanish, if at all possible. And I plan to carry out those orders. Now, look to the north. I have lately heard from General Baird, marching down from Corunna with ten thousand of our best men. He tells me that Marshal Soult, the Duke of Dalmatia, is at Burgos with his 2nd Army Corps. He holds a force of a similar size to Baird's, there to guard the French lines of supply down from the Pyrenees. Now, if we can unite our whole army, something approaching 40,000 men, and find Soult and beat him – then Bonaparte must surely quit Madrid and come north to reckon with us. If the Spanish people rise and join us, he will be in for a difficult time. Equally, if the Spanish want nothing of it, our way is still clear to fall back north-west through the Galician passes, which are better suited to British infantry than French heavy cavalry and artillery. Once we reach Vigo or Corunna, it will be perfectly possible to take ship – perhaps for Cadiz, so we might consider joining with the Andalucians for the fight in the south.'

The two men nodded, seeing the logic and daring of what their commander proposed. It was an ambitious plan, but had much to recommend it. The British could help their allies without throwing away their own army on a doomed defence of Madrid.

Moore looked up from the map, obviously delighted at last to be in a position to do something positive to progress the fight against the French.

'And, if you please, you said you had work for me, Sir John?' Tom prompted, as politely as he might.

'Why yes, Herryck – a good deal of work, if fact.' He pointed back to the map, running his finger in a circle around the top north-west corner of Spain, 'This area could be key to our fate, especially if we are obliged to fall back on the Atlantic. Now there is a Spanish army there somewhere, probably the best the Spaniards have. Their new general, the Marquis of La Romana, has sent word that he would, in principal, be prepared to act with us in a coordinated northern campaign. General La Romana is a seasoned, intelligent commander and his Galicians are held to be steady enough. They were even chosen by Bonaparte himself to be used as a garrison in Denmark when France and Spain were allies. But by a piece of excellent good sense Sir Arthur Wellesley caused the Spanish general to learn what was happening here and the Royal Navy spirited the Spaniards away from Denmark. They formed the Army of the Left under Joaquin Blake, which was badly beaten in the summer. But General La Romana now commands and the Galicians have rallied to him. I have every confidence in them as a fighting force. What I need now is General Romana's absolute assurance that he will stand with me in Galicia if the army is forced in that direction.'

'Yes, sir,' Tom said. He realized that he was going to be leaving the army on another "adventure". The nature of the task was in essence straightforward enough – however he saw all too clearly that actually finding La Romana in the wilds of Galicia would certainly be "a good deal of work".

But General Moore clearly had no misgivings about Tom's suitability for the task. 'You are my man, Herryck. As one of my precious engineers you have the right kind of eye for this work. You will doubtless be able to gather priceless information about the suitability of the terrain as you go. But, aware as I am of your many accomplishments, I do not believe that speaking the Spanish tongue is among them?'

'No, sir.'

'Well, that would make life devilish uncomfortable for you in the north there, but by happy chance I have lately been delivered of an officer who does speak the language. Should you care for his company?'

'Very much, sir,' Tom said, glancing at his brother, then positively smiling at the general.

'And you, Blunt?'

'I will do whatever you command, Sir John, but I would certainly be honoured to serve with Lieutenant Herryck.'

Moore looked at the two officers and nodded. 'Then gentlemen, there is no more to be said. I wish you both good luck about your business and look forward to receiving your report.'

Captain Blunt and Lieutenant Herryck were to leave the following day. Their mission agreed, Sir John had personally made sure that his staff would arrange for them to be suitably provisioned and equipped for their arduous and important journey into the wintry north. It was not likely to be a routine task, seeing the Englishmen penetrating deep into enemy-held territory. The general had every confidence in the two brothers, but he wanted to make sure that they had the best possible chance of getting through to La Romana. He had even had his French valet Francois take a reluctant Blunt's measurements for a new uniform coat to replace the faded object he habitually wore. It seemed that nothing was too much trouble, not if it was in the interests of the two officers whose mission might prove to be of the highest importance in determining the fate of Sir John's awkwardly placed army.

Tom had taken Blunt back with him to the Casa Delgado, where the Conde had immediately insisted that the travel-weary soldier should also be his guest. Moreover he had arranged for a dinner to take place that evening, in honour of his British visitors. Tom privately wondered whether his half-brother, not by nature a social animal, was up to it, either from lack of willingness or simple lack of energy, following his long march from Avila. But once Blunt discovered that happy coincidence that his friend and former travelling companion William Truelove was also staying at the Casa and would be of the party, any desire for much-needed sleep or reluctance to join in such august company was promptly overcome. Blunt was delighted; he privately wondered if he might even have the opportunity for a game of chess with his shipboard opponent...

The meal was a splendid affair in every way. The Conde, customarily a modest and charming man, was nonetheless used to doing things in the grand manner when he entertained at the Palacio. He was unlikely to stint himself in offering hospitality to his long-time friends the Trueloves and his esteemed officer guests. The Conde would do things in style. The room was lit by several hundred candles. His long dining table positively glittered with silver and cut glass. The company too looked suitably splendid. Tom Herryck had finally been reunited with the baggage trunks which he had left in Gibraltar and consequently could now wear his full-dress uniform. Robert Blunt had been supplied not only with a fine new scarlet campaign jacket, but also a full set of regimentals, courtesy of the Commander-in-Chief, and he was decked out in rare splendour, feeling very uncomfortable indeed. A new jacket cost five guineas and a pair of epaulettes ran to two pounds four shillings, so he was grateful to Sir John, but he was thoroughly ill at ease turned out in such finery. It didn't help that his wounded arm, healing well, was heavily bound still, making it awkward for him to eat with any great grace.

The civilians had also taken great pains to look at their best. The Conde and William Truelove each wore elegant Spanish evening wear. But all of these fine gentlemen, so handsomely turned out, were naturally outshone by Isobel Truelove de Chambertain, who looked quite stunning in a ruby-coloured gown, cut daringly low, her dark hair elegantly turned under a mantilla, her bright eyes flicking this way and that.

The meal, probably the last decent one the two soldiers would enjoy for some weeks, was a great success. The chef at the Casa Delgado was renowned all across Castile for his skill and accomplishment: the courses kept coming, each surpassing the last. They had eaten stuffed pigeons, soup with crayfish and lamb, chicken in almond sauce – and now the Conde presided over the undoubted highlight of the meal.

He gestured at the huge wooden platter which had been placed before him. 'As I am sure you can see my friends, this merry pink fellow is what William's father long ago told me is named suckling pig in England. Here we call him *cochinillo* and he is the very king of our Castilian cuisine. There are, of course, many fiercely held beliefs about the method of cooking the animal to achieve the perfect texture and flavour. It is a subject of passionate and frequent debate amongst our people. However, in this house we hold that the pork is at its best if it is simply roasted slow and long over a holm oak fire. He cooks beautifully, but retains his juice and flavour. We shall see if he is fit to be eaten, eh?' The Conde surprised the Englishmen by picking up an ordinary china dinner plate, using its edge to slice portions from the meat, passing them in turn to his guests. The pork proved to be as juicily tender and flavoursome as the Conde had promised. There were approving noises around the table, along with the serious business of eating.

'The pig has been important in this land for many centuries,' the Conde explained, in time presiding over a second round of servings, 'not only as food, you realise, but as a political symbol. In their time the Romans bred swine for food here, but when the Musulman held sway, pork was outlawed as unclean. But after 1492, the year of the Catholic Kings' triumph, when both Mahometan and Jew were exiled from Spain, only those of either faith who were converts to Christianity might remain in this country. The Inquisition has unflinchingly used the willingness – or more importantly, the lack of willingness – to taste pork as a telling test of the depth of those conversions, unkindly making the poor, worthy animal a tool of division and misunderstanding.'

'Whilst I try to respect the faith of any man, Conde,' Tom said, when Blunt had translated for him, 'I do feel a certain sympathy for both Moor and Jew in missing the joys of this delicious meat. So, will you please allow me the honour of toasting your very own king of Castile, the estimable Senor Cochinillo.'

Tom caught Isobel's eye and smiled as he toasted her in turn. He had not previously seen her in formal evening wear and she looked handsome indeed. She returned the compliment and smiled back at him. All was well between them now. With the prospect of action, real soldier's action, assured at last and, even better, finding himself alongside his much-revered brother, Tom was relaxed, euphoric even. As the party had assembled for dinner, any prospect of uncomfortable looks between him and Isobel had been quickly dispelled by a well-judged joke by William about Tom's recent "holiday" in the north and the dinner itself had gone along charmingly. For her part, Isobel was glad that any bad feeling was gone about her role in Rico's necessary subterfuge. She liked Tom Herryck and he didn't seem at all the kind of man that was suited to brooding. He was like her brother, she guessed, always likely to see the best side and move forward without wasting time worrying about what couldn't be redone. It was a good trick, she thought, if you could do it.

Her eye moved on to Herryck's own brother, Robert Blunt, the quiet soldier. Now here was a fellow of another stamp entirely, the mingling of half-blood contriving to make him very different from the younger man. She watched him for a moment as he sat labouring over his meat. He was plainly uncomfortable – certainly literally so in his bright new uniform, with his arm damaged – but also ill at ease in the company and the circumstances. He had been openly delighted to find William at the Casa Delgado and the two of them had obviously formed a lasting friendship during their sea crossing, to judge from their easy companionship the moment they met again. But he clearly felt out of place at Tio Enrique's table, struggling through the ordeal for the sake of his brother and his friend. She was intrigued by him. He was not at all good-looking, certainly not in contrast to the other gentlemen present, all of them handsome in their way, but he nonetheless had an interesting face, with a sad, distant look to those odd eyes. He took part in the conversation when invited to and was civil and polite, but he showed no enthusiasm for the occasion. Only once or twice when William or his own brother had said something that caught his imagination did his face come to life, and that brought about a truly startling transformation, duckling to swan. But generally he stayed quiet, and glum, tight as a shell. She suspected that he would be happier in a mean hovel somewhere, eating ration beef and looking forward to facing the French on the morrow. This then, was a man of action, plain and simple.

'A glass of wine with you, Captain Blunt.'

He gave a stiff little bow. 'Me gustaria mucho, Doña Isobel.'

'Ah, I forgot, you are a linguist.'

'You flatter me, ma'am. At a press I can speak a little Welsh.'

She laughed, 'Then you are surely even more of a linguist than I believed, Captain. And yet your gift has certainly not passed to Lieutenant Herryck, I find.' Isobel looked at Tom, who obviously heard and again toasted her ironically, then went back to his talk of wine with William and the Conde.

'He has gifts of his own, I'm sure, ma'am,' Blunt said, looking affectionately at the younger man. 'Though I freely confess I'm just not always quite sure what they are.' This time Tom pretended that he hadn't heard them, ignoring their teasing and concentrating instead on what his host was telling him.

'But, in all seriousness, Captain Blunt, it is rare indeed to find an English soldier who speaks decent Spanish.'

Blunt shrugged, his face once again blank and serious. It seemed for a few moments that he might leave her remark without comment, but then he stirred himself and told her, 'It was taught to me, in South America. I was very fortunate to have a good teacher.' He dropped his eyes and his face looked even sadder for a moment, possibly reflecting on a story – some fascinating tale he would almost certainly not tell her, not now, at any rate. This redcoat wasn't the sort for storytelling, it seemed. Perhaps not so plain and simple after all, she wondered? But then he mastered himself and brightened, with some little effort, 'But still, I suppose that you are right that I can manage some poor attempt at speaking a little Castilian, senora. And I certainly hope now to have the chance to hammer a portion of the local language into brother Tom's noddle.'

'You are to serve together, I collect?'

'On a particular errand, yes.'

'Who will look after whom?'

Blunt offered a little smile and shrugged, 'We can likely both look after ourselves.' He nodded at Tom and said in Spanish, 'But I reckon he will certainly do a deal of the thinking. He is bright and he has a good, quick mind. That is no doubt why Sir John picked him for this chore.'

'And why did he pick you?' Isobel asked, 'apart from your excellent Spanish, of course?'

Blunt looked at her, not quite comfortable being quizzed so frankly by this beautiful woman. 'Who can say? It's not for the likes of me to fathom General Moore's mind. Probably because he knows me from the old days; he commanded my regiment for a time and we have shared service together on campaign. Also a lot of his people here are little more than johnny newcomes – inexperienced, that is.'

'So he trusts you?'

'We are both professional soldiers, the general and me. So is Tom there, even if he's still a tad green.'

Isobel looked over at the blue-coated engineer, who was smiling delightedly at something William had said. He did seem very young compared to the other men around the table. Then she remembered the room in Avila, when Tom Herryck had dealt so finally with three dangerous killers more or less entirely on his own. She turned back to Blunt. 'I hope you will indeed look after one another, Captain. It will be a comfort to you both, to have a brother at his side. Will you return to Salamanca do you think when your, your errand, is complete?'

'Only if the army returns here.'

'And is that likely?'

Blunt raised his eyebrows in a "who knows" fashion. 'That, I would say ma'am, rather depends on how Sir John and that argumentative Corsican gentleman choose to arrange matters between themselves.'

Early the next morning Herryck and Blunt, with Widowson in tow, made their way across the courtyard of the Casa Delgado, fully dressed for their mission. Both of the officers felt the effects of their wonderful dinner and, for his part, Widowson had been looked after hardly less splendidly in the servants' hall. They made a silent trio. It was not yet dawn, and bitterly cold. Blunt had reverted to his faded old campaign jacket, once again artfully patched and mended, and Tom Herryck wore his familiar blue jacket and red sash under his boatcloak, while the other two wore their greatcoats. The two soldiers had their Baker rifles, while Tom carried a light cavalry carbine. Each of them had a light pack, suitable for either riding or marching. Omar was there with the porter to open the gate for them, the rest of the household being still asleep. The Moor nodded to the men as they passed out into the street, a silent blessing for their journey.

Outside they found a number of dismounted dragoons, stamping their feet and rubbing their hands against the cold, their horses standing patiently by, their breath fogging in front of them. The cavalrymen looked with interest at the two infantrymen and the engineer they were detailed to escort. Their officer, however, was of General Moore's staff.

'Good morning, gentlemen.'

'Good morning, Mr Thicknesse,' Blunt said, his voice early-morning rough. 'Couldn't you sleep?'

'I am commanded to escort you as far as Astorga, sir. I have Sir John's despatch for General Baird. There is also a note addressed to both of you gentlemen. I suggest you read it immediately. It is in the general's own hand.'

Tom took the paper, struggling to stop yawning, and broke the seal. He read the brief note by the light of the lanterns burning on the palace walls. He gave a grunt of disgust and passed it over to his brother.

'What does it say?' Blunt asked, himself failing to suppress a yawn.

'Duarte is gone.'

'Run?'

'It would appear so.'

'That's a turn up. What, escaped from General Moore's own headquarters – that over-dressed macaroon? I wouldn't have thought the weasel had it in him.' Blunt looked at the note with interest.

Tom took the news more seriously. 'I wouldn't underestimate him, not for a moment, Rob, for he's proved himself a thoroughly nasty piece of work. He's likely to be a threat to anyone who gets in his way, a threat to his own country even. But it seems he was allowed to get away for a purpose. He carries the false information to our enemies that Sir John intends to run for Lisbon.'

Blunt looked up, nodding as he saw what the general had done. 'Ah, a bit of a ruse, eh? Makes sense, I suppose. Confusion to the enemy and all that – pity it had to be him, though. After he'd done his damnedest to see us off at Avila and we'd brought him all the way here, I wouldn't have minded seeing that bugger handed over to the patriots, to see whether he could talk himself out of a richly deserved garrotting, or worse. Well, there's nothing we can do about that, I suppose. Your friend is probably halfway to Madrid or wherever he might find Bonaparte's camp by now.' He slung his rifle onto his back, making ready to get underway. 'I dare say one of the pair of us will cross his path some time or other in the future, Tom. We'd best forget him for now and be about our own business. Now Cornet Thicknesse, I see you have some of your nice horseys for us. They're not good ones I hope?'

The teenager did his best to look down his thin nose. 'They are mounts suitable for infantry riding, sir.'

Blunt winked at his brother. 'Oh good, my favourite kind. I'm sure my comrades and I will be more than comfortable on your knackered old carthorses, Cornet, just so long as they step true and get us where we're bound. So, shall we then, gentlemen?'

'Sir.'

Cornet Thicknesse turned to his dragoons.

'So Tom,' Blunt said softly, looking fondly at the younger man, 'Off we go together.'

'Bit like the old days,' Tom smiled, 'going rabbiting in Borders Wood.'

'Perhaps; difference is,' Blunt said, shifting his pack ready to mount up, 'these French coneys are likely to shoot back.'

The party of horsemen was riding the bleak country north for Astorga, where General Baird had established his base. The difficult hundred mile journey could take anything up to a week or more, but their orders were for them to press on as quickly as was possible. They were to give Baird his instructions in order that the army might join together as soon as possible, ready to strike at the unsuspecting Marshal Soult, who presently guarded the northern road from San Sebastian to Madrid with a force much smaller than Moore's British army. Then, the first part of the mission completed, the two brothers would push on to try and find General La Romana.

It was a hazardous and demanding challenge, but both Blunt and Herryck were content that they had useful work to do for the army and they were especially pleased to be together on their mission. It was no exaggeration to say that Tom had more or less hero-worshipped his half-brother and, for his part, Blunt had always been fond of the youngest Herryck boy and was glad to spend time once again now with the young man. It was hard going for them travelling bad roads in the wintry conditions, but they were in good spirits and made fair progress, getting across the Duero river at Zamora inside a couple of days. Cornet Thicknesse, under Blunt's command as senior officer and under direct instruction from Sir John Moore this time, made no attempt to hold back their rapid advance. Men and horses were driven hard. The winter weather was unyielding – cold, grey and wet, but they went forward at a pace.

They were making their way in tough, dangerous country now, pressing north into the rugged hills of Leon. As well as the possibility of running into a French patrol, there were known to be bands of local bandits and groups of disaffected soldiers from the broken Spanish armies haunting the land. Their best chance of remaining unmolested was to keep moving, as fast as possible. The escort was made up of a half-troop from a light dragoon regiment, in their distinctive busby helmets, dark blue dolman jackets and fur pelisses. Tom felt quite comfortable with them, if for no other reason than for once not being made game of for the colour of his coat.

Blunt too was happy enough with their escort. This was the cavalry's version of light infantry, intended precisely for chores such as this. The troopers were young and had seen little meaningful action, but their corporal, an Irishman called McIlroy, had the mark of a seasoned campaigner and kept the men under a tight leash. Cornet Thicknesse, his precious despatch from General Moore safely pressed to his bosom, sensibly left command of the mission to Blunt and the management of the cavalrymen to McIlroy. So, they continued on, pushing forward as fast as they dare on the rain-sodden, rutted tracks.

With dusk approaching on the third night, it was time for them to look for some kind of shelter, unless they were to make a miserable bivouac in the open in the still pouring rain. They had covered a lot of ground that day, constantly on the alert, and now they were all tired and hungry. Every last man longed to get out of the weather and at least get a fire going for tea and to dry some of their sodden clothes. Thicknesse, impatiently riding on ahead with no cover man alongside him, clearly believed he might have spotted the very thing, pointing excitedly through the hanging gloom to a set of dilapidated grey buildings a hundred yards or so off the road. The riders looked optimistically at the farm, which certainly had the appearance of being deserted. A lot of the timberwork was broken, rotted or hanging loose, but most of the slate roofs looked as if they might be more or less intact. The cornet obviously believed it would do and gestured them on. They began to wheel off the road.

Corporal McIlroy, looking around cautiously, signalled for a dragoon to drop wide of each flank as they approached the farm. But Cornet Thicknesse wasted no time in trotting straight into the farmyard.

'Wait, man!' Blunt shouted, from fifty yards behind him. He was loath to interfere in the cavalrymen's business, had been plodding along at the rear with Tom and Widowson, but he was the only one who had seen the wisp of smoke rising into the mist from the farmhouse chimney.

Down in the yard Thicknesse jerked his mount to a halt, all at once taking in the row of horses in the open barn and the astonished look on the face of the man pissing against the farmhouse wall. His jacket was undone, but it was unmistakably the green coat of a French dragoon. Thicknesse reacted first, pulling out his carbine and taking aim at the man who, realising his danger, had turned to run for the farmhouse door. The Englishman jerked at the trigger, the hammer fell uselessly on damp priming and the Frenchman let out an urgent cry of 'Aux armes!' as he darted out of sight.

'Shit,' Blunt muttered, still back on the road. Thicknesse was spurring his horse out to the rest of them, mud flying from his charger's hooves. Now Frenchmen in varying states of undress were pouring out of the farmhouse.

'Come on,' Blunt turned his mount and signalled for the others to run. The horses were tired, but he had no idea how many French there were and any chance of surprise was long gone. If it was a full squadron of Frenchmen, a thin half-troop of raw dragoons on tired mounts would be easy game in a straight fight. McIlroy was shouting orders, harrying men and animals into action. The young cavalrymen wheeled around. They headed back for the road, the horses struggling on the sodden earth.

There were shots. But the English dragoons were getting away. Then McIlroy shouted that Thicknesse was down. Blunt yanked his long-suffering mount to a halt and turned around to see that Thicknesse's horse was indeed lying still but that the man was slowly getting to his feet.

'Swords,' he said simply and they turned, making ready to charge. The Frenchmen were dismounted, had mostly fired their carbines and only one or two had swords. Seeing the Englishmen coming on, swords drawn, they scattered for the cover of any building that was close. McIlroy skilfully got Thicknesse up behind him and they turned their weary mounts for the road again. That was when the single shot rang out.

They had made a sort of blanket-tent to keep the worst of the rain off while Widowson worked under its cover. It wasn't much, but it was the best they could do. Neither of the men under the crude shelter noticed the weather, as the old soldier did what he could with the flame-disinfected blade. Blunt had been hit in the back of the left shoulder. It was not anything like a fatal wound – unless infection took a grip. But it was bad enough. The bullet had missed bone, but had driven deep into the muscle. He had lost a lot of blood and he clenched his teeth against the pain, as his servant probed as gently as he could in the sticky gristle to make quite certain he had removed all traces of cloth, as well as the troublesome bullet.

'Rum,' Widowson said. Tom passed the flask, half-expecting the soldier to take a swig, before he remembered that Widowson was that rare animal, a military abstainer. The wound rinsed, the soldier commenced to stitch it, working in neat careful moves with his needle. Blunt was awake, still sweating despite the bitter cold. Content that Widowson had done the best he could, Tom looked away, outside to where the others stood nervously on guard. They should be safe enough for a while yet. He thought it unlikely the

French would follow: there hadn't looked to be more than a couple of dozen and they hadn't even been shrewd enough to post sentries in hostile country. That spoke of inexperienced troops, new to this part of the world. He doubted that they would want a battle with British regulars – they would be happier getting back to their main force with a report of a surprising contact with the enemy. He saw Thicknesse standing on his own, his head bowed, looking thoroughly abashed by his foolishness. The young cavalryman knew exactly whose fault it was that Blunt was lying wounded. He looked wretched, fully conscious of his folly. But at that moment Tom was in no mood to give him any word of comfort.

'Done, Mr 'Erryck,' said Widowson, bobbing out of the tent, his expression giving away as little as ever.

Tom pushed back under the blanket canopy. Blunt was sitting awkwardly, bandages pinning his arm stiff against him. His face was the unhealthy colour of uncooked pastry.

'How are you, Rob?'

A scathing brotherly look questioned the cleverness of the enquiry.

Tom ignored him, seeing Blunt's irascibility as a good sign. 'Well?'

'Bloody angry, that's how I am. I ought to knock that little bugger's head off for him.'

'He's young.'

'He's a fool.' He grimaced as he struggled into a more comfortable position. 'My own fault, I suppose, for imagining he knew what he was about. I dare say I'll live to get worse knocks than this, but what matters is that he's put our mission at risk with his capers. And, what's more, the mewling pup – he's got my arm in a sling again when the damned thing was almost healed from the last time!'

Herryck gave him a consoling smile. 'I'm sure our gallant hussar didn't do it on purpose. Eton doesn't teach you everything, you know, Rob. You went to a much tougher school.'

Blunt looked anything but consoled: 'I'd like to school him with my boot, the young dolt.'

As a matter of fact, Tom felt much the same, was furious with the boy's rash behaviour and its consequences to his brother, but he knew it would do little good to either of them to dwell upon it. 'Yes. Well, we'll know to keep a closer eye on him now, eh?'

' 'Old thy 'osses! There'll be no we abaht it, sir,' Widowson said sternly, just outside the tent.

Tom looked out at the private and then at his brother.

'The good doctor here tells me I'll bleed to death before Astorga,' Blunt said. He would doubtless have shrugged, were he able.

Tom looked again at the little Derbyshire man.

Widowson nodded. 'So 'e will, Mr 'Erryck. Ah've patched 'im up proper, but 'e's shed a fair drop o' claret. Captain should bide here a while. A day's rest, then gently does it back to't surgeon at Salamanca.'

This was bad news in any number of ways for Tom Herryck, putting him in an unenviable position, but he knew better than to argue with the trusty Widowson if Blunt himself had accepted the old soldier's opinion. If he must rest then that was that. Yet even a day's delay could be crucial for the whole of Sir John Moore's army and Tom knew all too well that Blunt would not countenance them stopping there for a moment longer on his account.

As if to confirm what his brother was thinking, Blunt gave a weary nod and said, 'You know you must press on, Tom. There isn't a choice, we've got our orders and that's that. You have to go as fast as ever you can and get the job done. Thicknesse must deliver General Baird's orders to him then you yourself must get on and find La Romana.'

However reluctant he was to accept it, Tom knew that he was right, knew that their vital work was still to be done and that he dare not trust the hapless Thicknesse to lead the mission on. 'And you?' he asked miserably.

Blunt offered him a wan smile, his face still pastry-pale. He eyed his blanket shelter, which at least kept him dry. 'Oh, I'll be well enough. A bit of sleep, maybe a brew of tea, I'll be good as new, I'm sure. Widowson here will get me back to Salamanca, if that is what must be done.'

Tom didn't like it at all. 'You're certain – '

Blunt cut him short: 'Yes I am, Tom, never more so. I'm a soldier, remember, and I'll do what has to be done. And you too are King George's man, first and foremost, and will also have to do what has to be done – Lieutenant Herryck. Even sappers are soldiers, eh? You're in charge now, duty in hand, so you'd best look to getting your men ready. You've a hell of a long ride ahead of you still, to get to Baird and then on to La Romana. Remember, Sir John is relying on you, Tom – and so am I.'

Three days later, having pushed his command as hard as tired mounts and bad roads would allow, Tom Herryck's bedraggled little party of weary horsemen at last found General Baird. Following Moore's earlier, more cautious order his men were dutifully retreating along the road to the coast just beyond Astorga. Thicknesse was able to hand over his all-important despatch. Baird would turn his men around once again and Sir John Moore's audacious plan to isolate and surprise Marshal Soult could now be put into action. Cornet Thicknesse's part of the work was done and he could briefly rest his men, then take McIlroy and the dragoons back to the main force, mission accomplished.

And to his surprise, right there at Astorga, Tom thought for a while that he might even have found the subject of his own mission, the Spanish General La Romana. He was mistaken in this hope, but he had certainly found a fair portion of his army. He could have wished that it were otherwise. Astorga, the crucial fortified supply base, a key part of Moore's contingency plans, was in turmoil. It didn't take Tom long to decide that he had arrived at the scene of a disordered, shambolic mess.

General Baird, once he had landed his men from the ships at Corunna, some weeks before, had been in far better shape than his commanding officer in far distant Lisbon and now at Salamanca. He commanded some of the best, most disciplined men in the British army. He had marched across the mountains in good order, amply supplied with both cash and provisions and had set about establishing a base camp here at the well-fortified town of Astorga. His thinking was sound enough, reasoning that the town could supply an onward strike into Spain or could provision the main army if it retreated to the Atlantic ports. His planning chimed neatly with the strategy Moore's despatch now outlined to him and Astorga looked as if it was ready to play a key role in the British campaign. But General Baird hadn't reckoned with the exhausted and hungry near-rabble that was what remained of General La Romana's much-vaunted Spanish Army of the Left, many of them presently availing themselves of those same British stores.

Chapter Eight

'Where am I?'

Even his voice didn't sound like his own – more an old man's tired and brittle croak. His throat felt dry, choked, as if it had swelled in on itself. He lay still. He didn't even know if he could move, had the sensation that his body was bound – a shroud maybe? He lay flat, looking up at the ceiling, all fine plaster and dark crossed beams. He could smell a fire burning. There was something else, a scent, crisp and pleasant – rose water maybe?

'You are in the Casa Delgado,' said a soft voice. He remembered that voice. The Casa Delgado – he remembered that, too. Or he thought he did. He tried to turn to the direction the voice had come from.

'Lie still.' A cool hand touched his forehead, resting there for a moment. It was a pleasant sensation. 'Sleep,' the voice commanded. 'Sleep now.'

Later, or maybe even another day, he woke again. He turned his head, still stiff and painful, but a little easier now, and saw her sitting alongside his bed, a book in her lap.

'How do you feel?'

It was a good question. He wanted to say that he felt as if he had been driven over by a troop of horse artillery, or possibly enthusiastically tortured on one of the Inquisition's famous racks, but instead said simply, 'Alive.'

'That is quite achievement enough, Captain Blunt. You have been very ill indeed, you know. We thought we might lose you. Here, drink this.'

He managed to take the tumbler with his good hand and did as he was told, his throat still feeling swollen and parched.

'Widowson?' He said, beginning to remember parts of it. Yes, the fight at the farm, a bullet in the shoulder.

'He is perfectly well. I believe he is presently playing at chequers with Omar in the kitchens. He is quite a resourceful man, your servant, is he not? How he got you to Salamanca when you were in a raging fever and had about a cupful of blood left is something of a mystery, but he did.'

That, at least, didn't surprise Robert Blunt. 'He is a good soldier, Widowson. How long have I been here?'

'Several days,' Isobel told him. 'Tio Enrique – the Conde – had his own physician treat you. Evidently your wound was quite clean. The doctor complimented your man's needlework. But the fever had taken quite a grip of you. He seemed to think you were principally in God's hands.'

Blunt grunted what might have been a snort of laughter.

'Not a religious man?'

He managed to give his head a gentle shake. 'Not any more. No, I'm sorry, ma'am, I simply found it droll to think of the Almighty giving his attention to someone like me.'

She frowned, 'Surely God has time for all of us?'

'Of course you're right,' said Blunt, realising he was in difficult territory, was probably straying close to offending the woman, a woman who had shown him kindness and care. He needed to get a grip on himself. Whatever his own views, he should realise he was a guest in a Catholic household. A rapid change of tone was called for. He cleared his throat, 'And you ma'am, you are still here in Salamanca, I find. Will it not be safer for you and your brother to go south to your home?'

'William has gone back to Oporto to look in on the work they are doing putting our lodge back into decent order. Then I imagine that he will sail down to Cadiz.'

'But what about you? The French – '

She laughed, a pleasant, warm sound. 'I will be perfectly safe here if the French come, Captain, I do assure you. I was married to a Frenchman, speak the language, and know perfectly well how to deal with those gallic gentlemen. No, I think it is rather more pressing for us to do what we can to get you fit and well, so that you can get yourself away from here before they come. General Moore's army has been long since cheered on its way and only a few invalids such as yourself remain of the British in Salamanca now.'

'Then you are right. I must go.' Blunt felt weak as a kitten.

'But not yet, I think.'

'I've no wish to be a prisoner.' He grimaced at the thought, realising that unpleasant outcome was all too possible.

She gave him a reassuring smile. 'And nor will you be, Captain. I am sure you are far too valuable to General Moore to be allowed to fall into the hands of the French. So we shall not allow that to happen. But at present it is quite plain that you haven't the strength to walk to the door, never mind thinking about a day's march. So, you must rest. It is hard for you heroes to be patient, I know, but unless you rest and recruit your strength you will not leave Salamanca at all, either as a prisoner or at liberty. So then, sleep if you can. I will come and see you later.'

'Yes, rest.' Blunt said, realising that she was right – and also that he was sleepy once more. Sleep was the thing. But he did also find that he hoped that she would indeed come and see him again. It was a fine thing he thought, drifting away, to have the attention of a nurse, of so very kind and beautiful a nurse...

If finding elements of the Army of the Left had been easy enough for Tom Herryck, finding General La Romana himself had proved to be less straightforward. The Spaniards had been through a tough time and were plainly delighted that their allies were so well-provisioned. Many of these men were almost in rags, without boots and basic equipment, but despite their present lack of discipline, Tom saw that they at least had more of an air of being true soldiers than the untrained levies he had had seen the previous month, when he and Rico had found General Castaños' doomed army at Calahorra. But at present the men were ill-disciplined and out of control, glorying in the opportunity to enjoy supplies which had been shipped hundreds of miles from the ports of Great Britain for Moore's hard-pressed army, while their own government in Madrid had kept them starved. It had taken Tom no time at all to see that this was nothing like the tightly disciplined force that Rico had told him about or that Sir John Moore had hoped for. But however disappointed he was by the chaos of Astorga, Tom had a job to do. With no Spanish of his own and seemingly no-one in command of the local men, it took Tom some time to discover that General La Romana himself had his headquarters at Mansilla, a day's ride away.

With the first part of their mission at least accomplished, Tom had left Cornet Thicknesse to get on his way with General Baird's acknowledgement of Sir John's instructions. The boy would doubtless enjoy being in command of the half-troop of dragoons, though Tom had given him strict orders to do nothing without consulting his experienced corporal. It was important that Sir John learned as soon as possible that his instructions had been successfully delivered to Baird so that the army would concentrate as he planned. The next morning he himself set off for Mansilla, in order to tackle the other part of their mission, eventually reaching the Spanish camp after dark on that short, wintry day.

Once in the presence of General Pedro Caro y Sureda, the Marquis of La Romana, Tom was relieved to find a man of considerable presence and a composed, experienced soldier. The Spanish troops at Mansilla were almost as ragged as their comrades at Astorga, but they were clearly under discipline and gave Tom some hope that their commander could in time pull the rest of his army back together and put them in the way of the French as Sir John had asked. La Romana took Moore's handwritten letter and tried to make sense of it but, despite speaking and reading English perfectly well, it was no good as he couldn't make out the Scotsman's handwriting.

'Might I enquire of you if you are aware of Sir John's intentions, Lieutenant? If not, I must ask you if you would perhaps be so kind as to read this letter for me, or I fear your journey might be for nothing.'

'I will gladly read the letter for you, but I believe I know the main heads of what Sir John asks of you, sir. He sends his best compliments, of course, and he fervently hopes for the cooperation of the Army of the Left, as he attempts to confound the French. We have but one army, as I am sure you are aware, but Sir John intends a bold stroke. He plans to attack Marshal Soult's army, threatening the French line of communication, in an attempt to draw Napoleon away from Madrid.'

The general nodded, clearly considering the ramifications of such a move. 'It is a reasonable strategy General Moore proposes, a bold one even. But if he succeeds, he may wish an unpleasant future for himself. My information is that Bonaparte has a most formidable army at his back.'

'Yes, sir; of course, you are in the right of it. If Napoleon comes, we could not face his whole army with any hope of success. In those circumstances Sir John would have no choice but to fall back.'

'For where, for Galicia?'

Tom was relieved that La Romana had such a clear grasp of the tactical situation. 'Yes, sir – Vigo or Corunna. The Royal Navy might take the army off from either of those harbours, should Sir John be obliged to retreat. Yet to do that he will have to make for Astorga and the mountain passes. I believe one important purpose of his letter is to ask you to keep the Army of the Left clear of those mountain passes so that our army might march without hindrance. Most crucially, he asks if you and your men will consent to stand here, sir?'

'To cover a British retreat?'

'If it comes to that,' Tom saw no point in equivocating.

'Such a retreat would not be popular with our people.' Romana frowned.

'Nor would it delight our own soldiers.' Tom said, knowing it to be perfectly true.

'Nevertheless.'

Tom pressed on, 'I fully understand your Grace's concerns. But I beg you to consider sir, if Napoleon is drawn away from Madrid, that has to be in Spain's best interests, for at least such an outcome will have given your southern army time to ready itself.'

'And that is Sir John's first intention, you say?'

'He is firmly committed, sir.'

Romana nodded thoughtfully. 'Very well; what you say is true. Seeing a British army destroyed serves no purpose for Spain, who has lost armies enough of her own.'

'Then you will stand, sir?'

'Lieutenant Herryck, I have some 20,000 men at my command. Most of them require reclothing from head to foot and we suffer a pressing need of everything from muskets to cartridge-boxes and haversacks. Nonetheless, you may tell Sir John that I wish him good fortune in his strike against the Duke of Dalmatia and that I will hold here at Mansilla, awaiting his word. I trust that a retreat for the British will not be necessary, but if it is, then the Galicians of the Army of the Left will most certainly stand.'

'Now where in damnation did they spring from?' Tom Herryck said softly to himself, pulling up his horse. It had to be to himself for, as he turned and looked back over his shoulder, he could see his ragged Spanish escort riding as fast as they could back down the treacherous mountain road towards their friends at Mansilla. General La Romana had kindly given him the escort, in the charge of an officer who could manage a few words of English, and they had spent two days blundering about the bad roads trying to find the British army. But the cavalrymen, tired and unhappy at their unglamorous mission, plainly felt that now their duty was done. As he looked again to his front, Tom realised – far from finding Sir John Moore's army – that what he had in fact found here in this lonely, misty spot was as nasty a pack of bandits as he had yet seen, calmly straddling the road and hillside ahead of him. There were probably thirty of them and, as he looked up the hillside to his left he was unsurprised to see a couple of musket-men covering him with their pieces. He screwed his eyes up against the icy rain and looked again at the men in his path. He saw that one or two of them wore the vestiges of uniform, but none of them was properly clothed for these freezing conditions – indeed several of the men were barefoot on the frozen ground, yet all of them were heavily armed.

'Ah well, faint heart and all that,' he muttered to himself, urging his horse forward. He made his ground slowly towards the men, wondering if by some miracle they might just step aside and allow him to pass. But that optimistic notion disappeared as one of the band, taller and broader than the others, stepped forward and took hold of the horse's reins. Tom realised with a start that he knew the man. He was called Roca. He nodded to Tom and said simply, 'Venga conmigo.'

Tom had little choice but to go where he was led. Here we go again, he thought. He found that he was strangely complacent about being be taken along by a man who, back in Castile, had knocked him unconscious and carried him a hundred miles trussed like a chicken in a fetid, bone-rattling coach.

The Spaniard said nothing more. He led the horse on for fifty yards, then turned off the road and walked the animal, with Tom still aboard, certainly more curious than fearful now, up into a stand of trees. Tom could see from the smoke that a campfire was burning.

'Desmonta,' the man told him to get down, then pointed to a figure sitting by the fire, languidly stirring a cooking pot. 'Mira, es El Espectro. Vaya.'

As his guard turned to walk the horse away, Tom guessed he had been told to approach the man by the fire. He wondered what "El Espectro" meant, but it didn't really matter, for he knew the cook rather better by the name of Carlos Federico Rivero y Castro.

He sighed and walked towards the fire, feeling it all rather familiar.

'Is it this cold in England, Tom?'

'Not often.'

'You had better have some stew.'

'Thank you.' He sat on the ground, quite pleased to be out of the saddle, so thoroughly soaked as to not bother about the damp earth. He was too weary even to feel any great indignation at being ambushed once again by Rivero's men. At least Rico generally knew his business and would know where they were in that Godforsaken corner, possibly even where Moore's army might be found. Life was generally interesting when the Galician was around. For a moment his mind pictured the civilised meal he had shared with this man in the late summer heat of Andalucia, not many weeks before. Now he was being given stew by a bandit captain in the freezing cold in the middle of nowhere.

'There you are,' Rico said. 'We call this *caldo*. Go on, you will enjoy it. It is potatoes and green winter things with a little ham and paprika to warm you. Here, I will pour you some cider.'

He was right, the food and drink were just what he needed. 'It's very good.' Tom spooned the stew down eagerly. He had been living for days on dried sausage and stale bread.

He ate.

'Is this the northern banquet you promised me, then?'

Rico barked a little laugh, 'No Tom, we are not in my own country here. Your feast awaits another day.'

Rico was unshaven, even his neat little pencil moustache growing thick and unruly, but otherwise looked the same. He stared at Tom for a moment, then nodded. 'I am pleased to see you, my friend.'

Tom gave a tired smile. 'And I you, Don Federico; although your men did seem to unnerve General Romana's cavalrymen.'

'Not much of a surprise, eh? It takes little to inconvenience horsemen if the country is not to their liking. That is why we fight on foot.'

'You fight?'

'Of course.'

Tom, abandoning any show of good manners in the company of a friend, put his bowl out for more. 'So, does that mean that you've given up the political line, all of that trying to get your leaders and your armies together?'

Rico, having passed Tom his stew, was lighting a little paper-wrapped cigar. He sat back, as if he were seated in the drawing room of a fine house. He gestured with the cigar, 'The time for talking has gone, if ever there was any point in it. And armies no longer matter for us. The war of armies is lost for Spain, Tom, even if the generals do not know it. You saw the French coming across the mountains, saw the power they can muster. We cannot compete with Bonaparte in open battle, so the big war is over. But now the guerrilla, the small war, will be fought by true patriots. The Corsican will find soon enough that there is more to conquering Spain than marching over the Pyrenees and down to Madrid. He will discover now that if he wants so much as a copy of *le Moniteur* bringing from Paris, he will need a regiment to escort it – the guerrilleros will see to that, I promise you. These men I have here, this little band, some are my own people from my home and others are soldiers who have come from beaten armies. But they all want to fight, to kill Frenchmen and damn Bonaparte. And it will be the same all over Spain. He will be harried and attacked wherever he sends his armies – no battles for the French with the guerrilla bands, just a constant cutting and draining of their life's blood.'

Thinking of the band of killers he had just seen Tom could easily believe that Rico was making no idle boast. 'Well, I'm sure I'm pleased to hear it and I'm certainly charmed to meet an old friend here – '

'But why have I stopped you when you have important information for General Moore?'

Tom was surprised again, wondering just how Rico knew that, but he simply said, 'Yes.'

'Because, my friend, you have other even more important information to pass on to your commander.'

'I have?'

'Yes.'

Tom laughed, 'I'd be heartily pleased to be told of it.'

'Do you know where Moore is?'

'No.' He said simply. He went back to his stew.

'He is close to here, as a matter of fact, at a place called Sahagun. Your English cavalry found some French horse there and fought a small battle. Your side won, won handsomely, but at a price more expensive than a few dead dragoons, I would say, for now Soult knows your army is here. The surprise has gone. But your General Moore is ready to fight him, perhaps in two or three days, Christmas Day possibly.'

'But surely that is good?'

Rico shook his head, that solemn look fixed on his face. 'No, Tom. It is not good, not good at all for you British. Not anything like good, indeed, with Bonaparte himself now close at Moore's back.'

The spoon stopped in mid-air on its way to Tom's open mouth. 'Napoleon himself? He has left Madrid?'

'With at least fifty thousand men. He is already across the Guadarrama mountains headed for Valladolid. And he is moving fast. He wants Moore finished. By now he is maybe three day's march from here.'

Tom was horrified. 'But with Soult to the other side of us and Napoleon coming up from the south, we would be trapped in between them, hammer and anvil. My God, we could have no chance against two such armies.'

Rico drew on his cigar and nodded. 'You are the one in uniform Tom, you are the proper soldier, so you are probably right. Finish your stew, my friend. Then I fear you must get back on your poor nag and go and tell Sir John Moore that it is time for him to run.'

Blunt tried to keep warm. It wasn't easy. It was Christmas Eve and the weather was seasonally sharp in Salamanca. He wore his full uniform, including his greatcoat and shako, but still the cold got to him. He wondered whether he was getting soft, just old, maybe – or whether the effects of the wound and fever were still biting. He had convinced himself that he was fit, had reported himself so to the town major, the officer who was in charge of the hundreds of invalid soldiers still in the city. He would soon get orders to march, doubtless once again taking whatever men were fit back to their regiments. It was likely to be a far more arduous task than when he had brought the men of the 43rd from Kent to Lisbon, but he was happy enough at the notion that he would be able to play his part by getting useful fighting men back to Sir John. If they were at last going into battle against the French, Moore would be grateful for every last one. It would be up to Robert Blunt to get those men through to him. But time was pressing. He knew that after all of the long weeks of waiting, of tedious preparation for action, the game was likely to move fast now, played out by Moore and Bonaparte somewhere in the northern mountains. So the Salamanca contingent would need to move fast. They must try to catch up with the army quickly before he lost any chance of guessing their whereabouts. He hoped that he was up to the job.

He had offered to walk with Isobel and the Conde's household party as they went to church for mass. It was no hardship for him to join them. In the past few days he had found that he had almost become a part of that household himself. Everyone at the Palacio had been kind to the English soldier. Once up and about, his recuperation had leapt on, although he was initially allowed little opportunity of serious exercise beyond walking the courtyard or the odd short visit to the city. He had been scandalously well looked-after. They had fed him like a prized feast-animal. He and the Conde had enjoyed some lively contests on the chessboard and he had taken up his host's kind offer to make free use of his well-stocked library. He had also made sure to spend time with Widowson, smoking and drinking tea in the huge kitchens as they checked over their kit and weapons, jawing pleasantly over past campaigns and old comrades.

But most of all, as he made his way slowly back to full health, there at the Casa Delgado, he found himself confronted by the fact that he had taken the greatest pleasure from his comfortable, informal fireside talks with Isobel Truelove – a simple and genuine, if dangerous, pleasure that he had not enjoyed with a woman for a long time. The credit for the ease he felt in her company naturally fell to Isobel herself. However reticent he had been at first – and Robert Blunt was a mighty champion of reticence – she had slowly won his confidence and made him keenly anticipate their increasingly relaxed, companionable talks. He found that he was ineluctably drawn to her company, not just because she was both beautiful and intelligent, but because she had the rare grace and cultivation to know just when she had reached the point, the difficult and dangerous point, where a woman's natural desire to find out what lay behind another human being's social defences might possibly stray into causing pain. Blunt's defences were sturdier than most, had been built up by bad luck and cruel disappointment, but he had felt them shuddering under Isobel's gentle probings. He was sensible of her kindness, sacrifice even, in spending time with him, an ill-looking stranger of no position in the world, but only a man completely immune to the charms of woman could fail to be in some way entranced by such attention. He had come to prize the time he spent with her, pitifully grateful for her kindness. But Robert Blunt, unlucky in love and scarred by tragedy, nonetheless remained a man: he smelled danger. He knew deep down that he was drifting into something that he couldn't control, dare not even hope for, and that it was high time for him to run away and go back to his own world.

But that evening he had walked with Isobel and the others to church, convincing himself that he was doing it not for pleasure, but further testing his returning health and fitness. Refusing her mischievous invitation to join them in the cathedral, he had remained in the square outside, huffing and puffing as he walked around and around trying to keep warm in the freezing night air. Yes, he thought, it was high time to leave this place. He disciplined his mind to think about the forthcoming march, how Tom might be getting on in the north – anything but thinking of her – as he waited for the people to come out, a joyous throng on that cold Christmas Eve, *Nochebuena* in Spanish, now almost Christmas Day. He could hear them singing. They sang well, these Spanish, he thought. It was a pleasing, reassuring sound, not utterly dissimilar to the hymns in the Shropshire country church of his youth. He had even played a couple of those hymns, as he taught himself to play the creaking, wheezy old organ in his stepfather's church. He found himself humming. It didn't seem like wartime; Blunt hoped that the people of Salamanca were finding peace and contentment in their worship – while they could.

He stood stamping his feet, hands deep in the pockets of his coat, and waited for them to come out. Was that finally the last song? But instead of the big doors swinging wide, he saw the small wicket gate open and the hooded figure of Isobel came out to him.

'Will you be my escort, Captain?' She looked at him, smiling brightly.

'Is the service not over?' Blunt said, worrying that she was cutting short her observances to stop him catching cold.

She shook her head. 'No, but I have made my peace with God. I confess, the Roman service is still something strange to me. I am only Catholic by marriage, you know. The Truelove family is very firmly of the English church, always has been. In the south our little community even has its own church at Sanlucar.'

'You are sure? I'm happy enough to wait. I wouldn't want to cause trouble between you and the Almighty.'

'No,' she said. 'Let us walk. It's cold and late for an invalid.' She took his good arm.

'No longer an invalid, thanks to you and the Conde.'

'And your estimable Widowson. Where is he, by the way? I haven't seen him at the Palacio today.'

'Scavenging, I dare say.'

'Scavenging?'

'For the march.'

'He is leaving?'

'We're both leaving.'

She stopped abruptly and turned to look up into his face. It was dark in the shadow of the tall buildings, but she could see his eyes, those strange, sad eyes. 'You're going from here? When?'

'When the officer in command of the English hospital tells me the men I am to lead are ready. It could be tomorrow,' he said flatly.

'But that is too soon,'

'Too soon for what?'

'Too soon for me.'

Blunt didn't know what to say.

Isobel looked up at him, as if to try and read what was passing behind those eyes. Then she reached up to kiss him, her gloved hand clamping his good shoulder, pulling him to her. Blunt was taken utterly by surprise. He felt a physical shock as their mouths came together, her lips warm and soft, a spark flying down his breastbone to the pit of his stomach at the warm, velvety touch of her. She clung on to him for seconds, hours. He stood bent over, holding her in the small of her back, hoping that the cold might leave them frozen like that.

At last she drew away and looked at him. 'It's a long time since I did that.'

'Me too,' he said, stupid with surprise and pleasure.

'Tomorrow, you say?'

'Possibly.'

'Come along. You're getting cold – and it's late.'

They walked quickly back to the Casa Delgado.

*

When Tom Herryck at last walked into the British camp at Sahagun, tired and half-frozen, having crossed the last mountain passes on foot, expertly guided by one of Rico's men, he found an army in the highest of good spirits. He was surprised. It was brutally cold, there was snow falling and all around he saw the dead bodies of cavalrymen who had been involved in the skirmish with Soult's outriders, still unburied because the ground was too hard. But the men of Sir John Moore's army, gathered around the sparse camp fires, were in no mood to be downcast by the bitter weather or their losses; they were too full of the cavalry's success and the anticipation of at last getting to grips with Marshal Soult, the "Duke of Damnation", and his French army up at Burgos. Tom knew that just a couple of days before he arrived the light cavalry under Lord Henry Paget had given the French chasseurs and dragoons a bloody nose in chasing them out of Sahagun town, with two colonels captured and scores of French casualties. All of the army was thrilled, it was just the kind of fillip they needed. To a man they expected the order to march on Soult to come with the dawn. Tom, for his part all too aware from what Rico had told him that an advance was the last thing that was likely to happen, took a deep breath and had himself directed to Sir John Moore's headquarters.

Later, as Tom sat quietly on a chest while Sir John gave rapid instructions to his officers about the inevitable retreat, he wondered how the soldiers would take it – badly, for sure. They had marched hard for weeks to reach this grim spot, finally to have the chance to tackle the French, only to have that chance suddenly taken away from them. It would not be a popular decision, certainly not the Christmas present the soldiers had expected from their general. But Tom knew that Moore had no choice. If the British gave Napoleon time to come up in their rear, they would surely be destroyed. Some kind of retreat was the only possibility.

Tom realised he was in danger of falling asleep as he sat there, listening to the low voices unenthusiastically organising the retreat. He tried to think what Robert Blunt would make of it. He too would be bitterly disappointed that there was to be no fight; that they must retreat. But he was a thorough soldier and would see Sir John Moore's dilemma easily enough and reluctantly recognize that the British dare not face Napoleon's masses out in the open. Blunt would know better than any that there are times when you stand and times when you had no choice but to run and wait for better odds. It was the craft of warfare, practiced through the ages. But whatever turn the campaign should take, Tom only hoped that his brother had recovered completely from his wound and was fit and well enough to be worrying about such matters. Blunt would certainly want to be around if the battle did come. Tom gave a little shiver. He would be a lot happier once he had firm news that he was fully recovered. The sight of the dead cavalrymen had been a sobering reminder of the ultimate price of soldiering.

He had also been shocked and saddened to hear that Cornet Thicknesse, the eighteen year-old Etonian, had been quite badly wounded in the fight here between Paget's hussars and the French cavalry. Now, apparently he was down in the chapel by the town bridge, their temporary hospital, his shoulder laid open by a sabre cut. Tom knew such wounds could be awkward to treat properly in the difficult conditions of a field hospital. The boy was impetuous, foolish even, but he was undoubtedly keen and brave. He hoped that someone would not have to write a letter to break a mother's heart. Yet Tom had the dark suspicion that there would be a great many more deaths and letters before this campaign was finished. He made up his mind that he must look in on Thicknesse before the army departed.

'Herryck?'

'Sir John.' Tom came out of his reverie and snapped to attention. He was beckoned over to join them at the map table.

'More work, Lieutenant,' the general said, with a kind look. Moore himself had the appearance of being tired and drawn, the burden of his difficult command weighing heavy. His face was pale under the near-white hair. But he somehow managed to remain energetic and focused on their new predicament, his eyes glinting with quiet determination. 'You are well met, young man. Your surprising intelligence of Bonaparte's whereabouts has come just in the nick of time. The position is all too plain. We have little choice now but to run for it, I fear, and run hard. Come, look at the map here. Now, if you see, we have three places where we could cross the Esla and make for Benavente, then on to Astorga and our way north-west to the safety of the coast. In the north your friend General La Romana is at Mansilla. Whether or not he hangs on to the bridge, his men will have stripped any food or fuel for miles around, so that will not serve. At the village of Valencia there is a ford, but that will likely be difficult for crossing the whole army with any ease just now, as the Esla is in flood. So, for the lack of any alternative, I propose that the main army strikes south to the bridge of Castrogonzalo and crosses there to Benavente and then on up into the Galician passes, where Bonaparte's heavy cavalry will find it impossible to follow.'

'Yes, sir,' Tom said, seeing the logic of the plan. If the French were allowed to bring their guns and cavalry into play the British would stand no chance. It had to be the mountains.

'Your part, Herryck, is to return to General La Romana at Mansilla and to ask that he holds the bridge there for as long as possible and then that he fall back on Leon to the north. That way he leaves the route from Benavente through to Astorga free for our own army to pass. It is of the first importance to us that the way is left clear and that La Romana holds off Soult as long as he is able. Your message delivered, you yourself will make your way down to join us at Castrogonzalo, where there will doubtless be fit work for an engineer.'

In the event, Lieutenant Herryck would have liked nothing better than to busy himself with the work he had been trained for. But Tom knew he must complete this latest mission before he could think of rejoining the army at Castrogonzalo. Yet he discovered to his horror that there was most certainly work for an engineer, right there in Mansilla.

Setting off before daybreak, Tom had somehow found the strength to make the return journey to the Spanish headquarters and he had delivered his important message to General La Romana. Getting back to Mansilla had, in fact, been far easier for him than his tortuous journey to find Moore. He had a decent map now, a firm idea of where he was headed and, best of all, suddenly he possessed a superb mount.

As he had promised himself, he had paid a visit to Cornet Walter Thicknesse before he left Sahagun. The boy was comfortable enough, cheerful even after the cavalry's great success, but he was badly cut up and clearly bound for England, as soon as the wounded could be got away. In a gesture of true kindness the cavalryman had insisted that Tom should have his third horse, Annie – an animal of better condition and purer breeding than many an officer's pride and joy. A token twenty guineas was offered and accepted for the mare, but both men knew that it was more a gesture of faith and of potential future friendship. Tom wished the cornet a safe journey and swift return to the army and Thicknesse, with raised eyebrow that suggested some possible knowledge of Tom's latest mission, wished him the same.

And so, thanks to Annie, his splendid new ally, Tom made good time covering the 20 miles to Mansilla and was duly able to inform General La Romana of Sir John's demands of him. The Spaniard had listened politely to the British request and had agreed to do what Sir John asked. And yet, in the face of this, he had immediately ordered the withdrawal of his main army to Leon and he had detailed what Tom thought to be a woefully insufficient force to remain in Mansilla to defend the town. Worse, quite shocking to Tom, the Spanish had made no preparations whatsoever to destroy the vital bridge over the Esla, a sure route of advance for Soult's French. When Tom had protested to the general as he made ready to leave, even offering to do the work himself if powder was provided, Romana had shrugged and asked him how he imagined the local peasants would get to market if there was no bridge?

His best arguments, largely conducted by an otherwise laughable mime show with the few remaining officers, none of whom had any English, proved equally fruitless. The bridge was not going to be blown. It would be held, the Spaniards told him. Convinced that if Soult's cavalry came they would sweep through the place with little difficulty and soon be in a position to threaten Sir John's march from the flank, Tom resolved that his duty now was to obey the second part of his orders and make for the main army at its crossing place of Castrogonzalo, where he could at least inform Moore of his danger. His cloak pulled tight about him, hat pressed low, he spurred Annie away from Mansilla, once again searching out the British army.

However unhappy he might be with General La Romana's response to the British request, particularly in leaving the vital bridge intact and under-defended, Tom Herryck at least now had the advantage of being on the Allied side of the River Esla and from Mansilla he was able to pick up the relatively good Leon to Benavente road, which would eventually bring him to the bridge at Castrogonzalo. The mare was making short work of it, despite the grisly weather. He reflected ruefully that the same road might easily bring Soult's cavalry just as quickly if Romana didn't do anything to delay them, but he could do nothing about that now. He must press on and make his report. Only as he neared his destination, once again absolutely spent from a tough journey in foul weather, did he realise he had passed both Christmas Day and Boxing Day in the saddle without even knowing it. In Nottinghamshire, he reflected ruefully, he would no doubt have been down to the Jug and Bottle inn to join the local party for the Boxing Day meet. There he would be, among the friends he had grown up with, gleefully flying along on one his father's best animals down at Melton; he would eat like a prince, then doubtless dance the night away at the Lowthorpe Ball. Tom savoured the thought for a few moments. Yet he knew he must somehow resist the pressing temptation to let his thoughts stray too much to England and instead get his mind back on that cold, hard road and concentrate on getting his work done.

Once he had eventually made his disturbing report at British headquarters at Benavente, there on the supposedly "safe" side of the Esla, adding yet more cares to the many that troubled Sir John and his staff, Tom was dismissed to make himself useful as best he could. Outside, among the shivering troops, the mood was as cold as the weather. It was plain that the army was now in full, rapid retreat, the soldiers surly and dejected, with many of them drunk and unruly. The proud spirit of unified purpose he had glimpsed at Sahagun was quite gone. In many cases the mood wasn't far short of mutinous. It was a grim picture; Tom had never seen British soldiers in such a dangerously rebellious frame of mind. Many of them now resembled the ragged Spanish troops he had seen at Astorga. He couldn't find it in himself to blame them for their frustration, having convinced themselves that they were going to fight, but he fervently hoped their officers could bring them to order once the French appeared. It was bad enough that the odds were already stacked against them, without morale collapsing like this. Who could tell how they would behave when Napoleon came? The cavalry, light infantry and elite regiments were holding up well, but looking at the reduced condition of many of the ordinary line regiments, he was glad he wasn't a betting man.

Tom wondered what to do with himself. There was nothing he could do about the retreat, which he at least knew to be plain common sense, but he was in no mood to get back on the road himself. The mare Annie needed feed and rest. The headquarters grooms agreed to look after her and he was free to go and try to find a bed. Yet, despite being dead-tired from days with little or no sleep, he couldn't settle to the idea of rest. More from curiosity than any great sense of purpose he made his way down to the Castrogonzalo bridge. He had to pick his way carefully for he was going against the tide of the march, as the majority of Paget's cavalry reserve were now trotting wearily through to Benavente, having at last crossed the bridge following their running skirmishes with the French.

He could hear gunfire now. He moved forward carefully, but a green-coated rifleman, leaning against a wall enjoying a smoke, told him, 'You're alright for a stretch yet, sir. It's only Froggy cavalry pushin' their luck an' Black Bob has our lads over on the other side to keep 'em honest.'

He knew Black Bob was Robert Crauford, the fire-eating Light Brigade commander he had met on a couple of occasions when he was summoned to Sir John. He suspected that Crauford was probably enjoying himself.

Tom came in sight of the bridge. What he saw at first confused him, as he focused his tired mind on what was happening, then he felt himself becoming angry. He could see that most of Crauford's men were on the far side of the bridge, deployed to keep the enemy at bay. The light troops were spread out, taking cover behind walls, broken wagons and fallen trees, with a thin screen of hussars of the King's German Legion between them and the French cavalry, which was probing forward to get at the bridgehead – all textbook stuff. But Tom wasn't much interested in the fighting men, he was more concerned with those of Crauford's soldiers who were attempting to deal with the task of demolishing the sturdy bridge of Castrogonzalo.

He strode forward to the edge of the bridge, a bullet fizzing past his head from somewhere. Tom didn't even hear it.

'Who's in command here?'

'Flamin' Black Bob, God rot him,' muttered an anonymous voice.

Tom ignored this, 'Who's in command, I say?'

A Rifles' officer, stripped to his shirt, but incongruously still wearing his distinctive "sugar-loaf" hat, called up from the foot of the arch below him, 'Who are you? Are you RE?'

'Yes. Where is your own officer of Engineers?'

'No bluecoat here, my friend; no, not a sapper in sight. Just the poor bloody infantry. We've been trying to sort this beauty's business for her for almost a day now.'

'But you're laying the charges in the wrong place.'

'Eh?'

Tom gestured to the men working doggedly to hack chambers where they might place the charges. 'You're shaping to blow it at either end. It probably won't budge a stone. The powder would do its work far better at those two arches in the centre.'

Forty or fifty weary, dirt-streaked faces looked up at him.

'You want to take over?' The man said hopefully.

'Too bloody right I do.'

Tom would have given a month's wages to have even half a dozen properly trained sappers, but he had to make do with the efforts of the exhausted light infantrymen. There was a pioneer corporal and a couple of his men in their torn, filthy buff aprons, but this was work way beyond what could be expected of them. The Romans, Tom reflected ruefully, knew what they were about when they were building a bridge and they had intended this one to last. But all of the men – hungry, cold and tired, their frayed uniforms soaked – worked on, hacking away to create chambers for the powder, desperate to deny the bridge to Soult's men. From time to time, as he supervised the moving and re-laying of the barrels of powder, Tom looked up as the French tried another attack, watching as the skilled marksmen of the reserve sent them packing again and again. A couple of times Crauford himself came to ask how it went, gruffly telling Tom to get on as quickly as he could, then returning to the command of the rearguard. Halfway through the day, fresh troops came to act as pioneers, allowing their spent colleagues to creep off to get some rest. Tom stuck to his task, determined that this was a crossing place Napoleon would not use, not for a good while. They worked on, packing the centre arches of the bridge with powder, while Crauford's men kept the marauding cavalry at arm's length. It was perishing cold. A storm was blowing and there was the constant roar of the wild river rushing below, but still they worked on.

At dusk, finally content that they were ready, or as ready as they were likely to be, Tom stood down the exhausted soldiers and he sent a runner to Crauford to tell the Scotsman he might begin his withdrawal. The plan was to blow the farthest arch, laying planks across for the last of the covering infantry to make their way to safety, then to destroy the near side, putting the stately old bridge well out of commission.

First the German cavalry clattered over. Then the officers' whistles blew and, under the welcome cover of night, the infantrymen of the Light Brigade trooped across in complete silence – more from extreme exhaustion than any caution. By midnight the last of the British were over.

Crauford rode up and nodded to Tom, 'Now laddie, here's your moment. Let's find out to what purpose you've worked my men half to death.'

Tom, down to his shirt despite the cold, his face covered in grime and his fair hair filthy, managed a nod of his own, 'Very well, sir. I've done the best I can. We've got one arch out of the way, so now we can deal with the rest. I've used just a five-minute fuse. With your permission I'll see if we can't produce a little noise to wake up those French gentlemen over there.'

Crauford grunted and rode off to a safe distance, to wait with the weary, brave men of the rearguard.

Then Tom Herryck, himself quite worn-out but wearing a contented smile on his powder-streaked face, blew up the bridge at Castrogonzalo.

*

Tom woke up suddenly, with no idea where he was, instinctively reaching for his pistols, which were not there. He looked up. A huge Highlander sergeant was standing over him, a grim expression on his face, his bayoneted musket held in his hands like a child's toy. Tom saw a couple of red coated soldiers scurrying away down the corridor.

'What – '

'Ye'll need to be takin' care, Lieutenant. Yon laddies were after makin' yer journey the lighter.' He nodded to the pile of kit, including Tom's sword and pistols, which lay at his feet.

Tom blinked, still stupid with sleep. He realised with a jolt that the sergeant had just saved him from being robbed by men of his own army. He wondered how long he had been asleep. It had been in the small hours of the morning when, along with the other cold and exhausted men of Crauford's rearguard, he had reached Benavente. All of the houses had been shuttered and bolted against the British. The locals wanted nothing to do with their retreating allies, so many of them drunk or just plain violent. For the soldiers, puzzlement at the retreat had turned to resentment and many were behaving badly, as they blamed the locals for the lack of any kind of support. The Spanish army was nowhere to be seen and the people denied their allies food, wine and shelter – so the British soldiers were angry, resentful and dangerous. Tom couldn't blame the Spanish for barring their doors. Once Moore's unstable horde had departed the French would arrive – and they really knew how to strip a place. He had been too exhausted after his long ride and his hours at the bridge to care where he laid his head, as long as it was dry; like many others he had found a place to sleep in a deserted convent and now he had been rudely awakened.

'Dinna think o'er bad o' them. There's none too blithe o'er this runnin' from monsewer. Ye tak care, Lieutenant.'

Tom mumbled his thanks, still appalled that he should have needed the big sergeant's protection amongst his own countrymen.

The Scotsman went to find his fellows.

Tom loosened the boat cloak he had slept in and fetched out his watch from his waistcoat pocket. It was gone nine o'clock, even though it still seemed to be dark outside. He gathered up his kit and made his way to the middle of town. He found the place in uproar. Most of the army was already gone, on the road for Astorga. The reserve was preparing to march now. Luckily, Sir John Moore and his staff were still there and Tom's horse had been kept for him. The town itself was a mass of abandoned equipment and supplies being burned by the commissariat to keep them from the French. Infuriatingly, the enemy himself was literally at the gate, making mock of their hard work the night before. They had forded the Esla further down from the blown bridge, and Paget's hussars were again fighting a magnificent rearguard action to keep them clear of the retreat.

Such Spanish people as he saw looked back at him with open hostility. The British were falling back, abandoning Spain, and nobody liked it. But Tom had no time to worry about local sensibilities now. There was no time to do anything but to run for Moore and his men. It was get out of Benavente right away or give themselves up to the dubious mercies of the Chasseurs of the Imperial Guard. Tom got the horse saddled as quickly as he could. Now Moore and his staff party were riding out and that really did mean that it was time to get away. He got aboard Annie. As he rode past a commissary officer who was doggedly burning a pile of precious supplies, the man simply passed a piece of salt pork up to Tom then went back to his work. Tom gratefully put the meat in his saddle bag, wondering how long it might have to last him.

Captain was a company commander's rank and Robert Blunt had been given a company – of sorts. The likelihood of the French arriving in Salamanca any day now had animated the few hundred British who remained there in the desire to get away. The road to Lisbon was still open for the sick and wounded, but those who were fit enough for active duty were needed by Sir John Moore's army – if it could be found.

Blunt's "company" was made up of seventy one private soldiers from over twenty different regiments. A conventional line company might be expected to contain around one hundred men, officered by a captain, a lieutenant and an ensign, with three sergeants and a couple of corporals. Blunt's temporary command was, by the singularly unconventional nature of its coming into being, different. He even had a couple of artillerymen and three cavalrymen, whose horses were long gone with their regiments. But this raggle-taggle assortment of soldiers were men who had at least expressed the willingness and desire to rejoin the army, so Blunt was happy enough to be leading them to where they could be of use. As well as the rankers, Blunt was relieved to find that he had a lieutenant of the 42nd Highlanders, the famous Black Watch. The 42nd had arrived in Portugal too late for Vimeiro and, to compound that insult with injury, Lieutenant John Anderson had damaged his back on the march to Salamanca. But he was fit now, fighting fit, and keen to get back to his regiment before he missed another battle.

Blunt also had his "regulation" three sergeants. He was delighted to find that one of these last was Sergeant Wheel of the 43rd, who had sailed with him on the *Amethyst* and shared the march down to Lisbon, keeping a firm grip on their little troop. Like so many who had spent any time at the unsanitary camp at Queluz, Wheel had suffered a bout of dysentery, but he too was fit now and Blunt was glad to have for sergeant a man he knew he could rely upon. The other two sergeants were old hands from line regiments who also looked as if they knew what they were about. He sensed that the march was likely to be demanding and eventful, but he was satisfied that with these men they would have a good chance of getting the job done.

Yet even Blunt, seldom surprised, had not expected matters to move so quickly. They had barely got out of sight of the city, when a courier came clattering down the road towards them. He reined in for a moment to give Blunt his news, before riding on into Salamanca.

'Bonaparte himself is after Sir John, Captain. He's got half of France at his back, so you'd best look to your priming if you're going north.'

'What of Sir John?'

'Running for the coast, I imagine – Vigo or Corunna.'

The rider spurred on for the city.

So the ball was in play at last – but it was grim news. If the Emperor himself was after Moore, the British would have little choice but to abandon the promising northern campaign and run for the coast, just as the courier had said.

Blunt called Anderson, the Highlander lieutenant, to him. He produced the good map the Conde had given him.

'Shall we go on?' The Scot asked doubtfully.

'We'll be no use to Sir John in Lisbon.'

'We'll be nae use to him in Verdun prison,' Anderson said, but he was grinning gamely enough.

Blunt ran his finger up the map and pointed. 'The last I heard, the army was around here, but that's on the wrong side of the Esla now. Our army has to head for the coast. There's no merit in hunting for Soult's ten or twelve thousand if Boney is going hell for leather to come at our rear with three or four times that number. And General Moore is too canny to risk taking on the French at odds of two or three to one against us. Sure enough, he'll go for the coast, as the galloper said. So, if we press north we'll probably find the army marching west from one of the Esla crossing places like Benavente or Mansilla. But against that – if we're too late, we'll miss them and find the French instead.'

'What do you propose, sir?'
'How's your map-reading, John?'

Lugo, early January, 1809

Tom tried to look on the bright side; it wasn't easy.

These were dark days for the British, days of shame and misery for honest soldiers, as Sir John Moore tried to keep his tired, dispirited army from destruction. But it was anything but easy for the Scots general. He faced not one, but two enemies: not only was Napoleon hot on his heels, pursuing him with all of the vigour and determination that had won the little Corsican all of continental Europe, but his own soldiers threatened to do the Emperor's work for him with mind-boggling feats of drunkenness, indiscipline and plain stupidity. It was little surprise that the Spanish ran from the path of their "allies", as sections of Moore's disaffected army sank to the grisly depths of theft, murder and rape.

Many, like Tom Herryck, still fondly nurtured the hope that the chance would yet come to fight their pursuers – and with that confrontation would surely come the opportunity for the soldiers to regain their self-respect. He knew what they were going through; the men suffered terribly in the frozen mountains, the army coiling like a snake for miles through the white, treacherous passes. They were tired and hungry. Most of their criminally ill-made shoes had disintegrated and only a proportion had decent greatcoats. The cavalry did little better, the animals suffering from the lack of decent feed and the absence of rest. They resembled an army of scarecrows. With most of the supply wagons broken and abandoned, they lacked for almost everything – yet still what they most wanted was the chance to fight. All of the frustrations and resentment would melt away at the sight of the eagles lined up against them. But for the moment the army was cold, hungry and depressed, as the men doggedly trudged on through the vicious Asturian winter, cursing the weather, the French, the Spanish and, most of all, their own craven generals.

And for much of the time, it fell to Tom Herryck's lot to ride at the very front of that sullen, undignified retreat.

He realised that, for the most part, he was luckier than many in the army. His journey north-west from Benavente – difficult enough in any season, but perilous in the extreme in dead of winter – had been infinitely better than that endured by most of the others now with him at Lugo, some forty miles from their objective at Corunna.

He had received his orders direct from General Moore on the road out of Benavente. Lieutenant Herryck, the engineer who had impressed once again, this time by finally blowing the troublesome bridge of Castrogonzalo, was to move to the head of the army and ride on in advance of the line of march to check that the remaining bridges on the route to Corunna were viable for the passage of the retreating British.

It would be important work: Sir John had already detached some of his finest men, the light troops under Crauford and Alten, to go west by a different route to his main force. They were marching down on the Vigo road to lessen the pressure on the difficult mountain tracks that led to the coast a hundred and fifty miles away. But still they had to keep the remaining twenty thousand men of Moore's main army moving ahead of the remorseless French pursuit. The enemy cavalry had already hacked down exhausted or drunken stragglers in their hundreds. The British marched on. But they dare not risk being held up by a broken bridge or a blocked mountain pass. Tom was given a cavalry escort who would both act as his protectors and, shockingly for the relatively immaculate hussars, form a workforce if work there was to be done. So off they went. At least it was useful employment, Tom reasoned, a real engineer's job for the good of the army.

But nothing was easy or straightforward on the long road to Corunna. Simply getting ahead of the long strung-out army in the first place had proved difficult enough. The narrow roads were choked with a slow moving mass of dumb humanity – men too exhausted, stupid or downright angry to let the cavalry through with any ease on the narrow, hazardous mountain tracks. Tom's important mission was getting nowhere. They had given in and eventually formed the plan of waiting until the long straggling column stopped for the night – but even this proved flawed, as they cleared the forward guard well before daybreak, only to find the road already clogged by women marching their heavily laden mules on ahead, "to get a drop of tay brewin' for the lads" at the next halt. It was hard enough to get the way clear on the perilous mountain path and now the soldier's wives, who had long ago been forbidden even to join the original march out of Lisbon by Moore himself, showed no inclination to stop their dogged progress to let the riders through. Only when Tom threatened to shoot the women's precious mules were they able to get past. The riders were sent on their way with a volley of stones, snowballs and bitter abuse. But finally they did manage to get beyond the lumbering, dishevelled mess that was Sir John Moore's army and they made for Astorga.

What they found there in the little walled town horrified Tom. General Baird was long gone, but the supplies left for Sir John's men were being put to good use – once again by the Spanish Army of the Left! The way was effectively blocked to the British, by men who should be miles away to the north. Everything that had been agreed between the two generals had been ignored: the moment Soult's men had appeared at Mansilla, the feeble Spanish rearguard had fled to La Romana's main force at Leon, leaving the vital bridge intact. In turn Leon had been abandoned and Romana's starveling army had tumbled down on Astorga, in direct contradiction of the agreement made with Moore. Tom found that the town was in even more of an uproar than when he had previously visited and he dreaded to think what would happen when Moore's half-starved, resentful troops reached what they trusted was a haven, only to find it sacked by their own allies.

But Astorga, if a mess, was at least passable for Moore's army, once La Romana's men were cleared out of the way, so Tom knew he should continue with his duty and on he went. They rode through Bembibre and Villafranca, then on towards Lugo. The roads were in poor condition, the weather was appalling, but however imperfect the path, it certainly seemed possible that they would get the army through. Indeed Tom feared most for whoever was going to have to destroy some of the sturdy old bridges, once the rearguard had at last passed over. The bridges were wonderfully constructed and the engineer in him envied the skills of those craftsmen from centuries before. Bridges like the deep-spanned crossing at Nogales or the squat, square-piered bridge at Constantino would probably take days to demolish. But presently his job was simply to assess their viability as crossings for the army, not their strengths or beauty. So Lieutenant Herryck noted the bridges were sound and they pressed ever closer to Corunna.

Arriving at Lugo at last he found the camp of Sir David Baird, whose men had marched all of the way from Corunna to Astorga and beyond to link with Moore's main force, and who had now marched almost all of the way back. But the Scot Baird, an Indian veteran and hero of Seringapatam, was a taut commander and their camp was orderly, the men appearing to be in reasonable spirits, unlike their friends suffering back in the mountain passes. There was feed for Annie and a hot meal for Tom and his escort. Salt beef had never tasted so good.

From Lugo he went on to Corunna itself. This wasn't really Tom's concern, but he felt he should at least get a rough grasp of the situation there so that he could inform Sir John of how things stood. Here, at last, Tom found real grounds for satisfaction. The town was in a state of readiness, it seemed. The fortifications were in reasonable condition and the local people had turned out to help the British in their preparations for the defence of the town and harbour. Here at least the soldiers and the locals were working side by side in their common cause. The only thing that was worrying at Corunna – and this was very worrying indeed – was that the big harbour itself was quite empty of the expected English transports.

Back Tom went towards the army, content that his news was for the most part encouraging. Yet, when he made contact again and moved past the advance guard, he discovered that the word "army" was fast becoming far too glorified a description for what was, in fact, a near-mutinous rabble. Dispirited by retreat and outraged that their Spanish "allies" closed their houses against them and hid their food, more and more of the soldiers had begun taking matters into their own hands. This generally meant breaking open the wine cellars and getting horribly drunk, stealing doors, shutters and furniture for firewood, slaughtering whatever livestock could be found. The army appeared simply to have fallen to pieces. The usual firm discipline which characterised the British army was long gone.

He was horrified by what he saw there at Lugo. Surely this wasn't an army that could expect to mount a fight – a fight against Napoleon himself! The bulk of the infantry was little more than a disgrace. As he made his way down the line, Tom had even seen a battalion that consisted of no more that its commander, two sergeants with the colours and just thirty men marching behind, where there should be hundreds. It was a mess.

Tom heard that at Bembibre, as the rearguard had finally limped into town under the command of Moore himself, his astonished officers believed they had come upon the scene of a massacre. But the "bodies" littering the streets were merely his own men lying dead-drunk and the blood flowing in the gutters was in fact wine. When Sir John led the last of his army out of the town, having spent a precious day trying to get as many of his soldiers as possible on the march again, a thousand men were left there, drunk in cellars or lying frozen on the open ground, too insensible to march – and doomed to be easy meat for the swinging blades of the French dragoons.

And at Villafranca it became worse, as the first troops into the town had looted the supplies meant for the whole army. At last the patience of the decent, kindly Moore had snapped and he had hung a food thief and shot another, obliging the whole army to march past their corpses. This was King George's justice for those of his soldiers who thieved! It was bad for all of them; but they were an army and must, at peril of destruction, stick together. But for many such gestures were too late, for discipline had gone and the only real chance of bringing them to order was for the army to stand and give battle. Even Moore's own generals were whispering against him, questioning the wisdom of his strategy and whether indeed he had ever truly planned to fight.

But at Lugo, just forty miles from Corunna, the stoical Moore at last showed his own colours, as he finally halted his ragamuffin army and made ready to face the enemy.

Looking at the map, Blunt's plan had seemed perfectly sound and sensible – push north west to avoid the French coming up from Madrid and hope to cut the British army's line of march on either Vigo or Corunna. It looked quite straightforward. What the map didn't tell him was that he proposed to cross some of the wildest country in Spain at the worst possible time of year. Some of the paths were little more than sheep-walks and the weather was dreadful up in the snow-capped Sierra Cabrera mountains. It was an enormous challenge for his small command. But Blunt was disinclined to worry about that; he had his orders and they were to get his company to Sir John Moore; so that is what would be done. On they went.

One helpful advantage they did have in their favour was that the remote mountain villages they passed through had not seen the armies of Spain, France or Britain and the soldiers were given shelter and could buy fresh supplies. Also the hills were filled with game for the sharpshooters to bring down. When they bivouacked in the open, nervously listening to the wolf packs and watching out for bear and wildcats, at least they had meat for the pot and could find fuel to burn their fires.

So Blunt took his seventy five soldiers on, keeping them moving as fast as they were able, determined to find Moore's army if it were at all possible. It was hard going, especially for men fresh from the hospital, but they had been rested, were well-equipped and in Blunt they had an officer who was not only tough and determined, but who knew these men would be no use to the army if he pushed them too hard. His Black Watch lieutenant Anderson and the sergeants were good men and the ordinary soldiers, with their different coats and a dozen different accents, were united by their will to get back to the army before the chance was gone to have a go at the French, most especially if the enemy were likely to be under Napoleon's personal command. They would cheerfully put up with the freezing cold, the dangerous mountain tracks and the long forced marches if only they could get to Moore in time to have a crack at old Boney.

So the little company struggled its way over the bleak and unforgiving Sierra Cabrera, hardly realising that their trials along the treacherous, frozen tracks up beyond the trees were nothing to the horrific agonies being suffered by the starving, demoralised soldiers of the main army, slowly retreating along the mountain passes to their north.

And at the very beginning of the march, as he determinedly set out to take these men to do their duty – a march that was sure to be rigorously demanding on all of them, most especially their company commander – Robert Blunt promised himself that the one thing he would not do, dare not do, was to think about Isobel Truelove de Chambertain. But that challenge was even more demanding than his task of finding the army; he could still summon the smell of her perfume, the touch of her skin. So for days, as they struggled through the wild and dangerous country, through the ice-storms and frozen wind, he had found that it was difficult, impossible almost, for him to think of anything else.

Tom Herryck also battled his emotions – a different sort of challenge – as he tried to combat his weariness and disappointment to somehow rally his spirits, but he still felt thoroughly miserable. It was contrary to his nature to let circumstances master his habitual positive outlook, normally finding consolations in any adversity, but now even he felt driven low. The foul weather which had dogged Moore's army since Salamanca still showed no sign of letting up. Tom was well aware that he was better off than most. He had lost a good few pounds, it was true, but his uniform was mostly intact, mercifully free of the lice that afflicted many, his horse keeping going despite a lack of decent feed and constant work, and he had kept healthy. But for once he was unwilling to acknowledge his good fortune. He was cold and hungry, his precious salt pork long gone and his clothing thoroughly soaked under his cloak – but all of that mattered for nothing compared to the depressing, almost unbearable knowledge that he had let the army down.

And yet at Lugo, as he had rejoined after his bridge-scouting mission, it had looked so promising; at last the army had halted and turned to face Soult; at last there was the imminent, so heartily desired, prospect of battle. There had been food and fresh supplies and a chance to get at least a little rest. The mood of the men was completely changed; the destructive spirit of bitterness and resentment was gone at a stroke. There was also time for the commander himself to make a concerted attempt to restore discipline, to focus the attention of the army on its task. Sir John Moore had made it plain that he was disgusted by the behaviour of his command on the long march, officers as well as enlisted men, but that he now expected them to show what the were made of, by dealing with the Duke of Dalmatia's approaching army in a manner that would bring proper credit on Great Britain.

The men, many of them in rags with worn out shoes or no footwear at all, were ready to do just that. It rained all through the night, but they didn't care. Their fondest wish was to fight at last and to avenge all of the ills of their terrible retreat through the mountains. Hundreds of men who had been "lost" on the march slowly trickled into camp to rejoin their fellows ready to take on the enemy at last. They were tired and hungry, but they were ready to fight. Once again they were an army.

And the position at Lugo was a strong one for the British. Tom could easily see why Sir John had chosen this ground: the army was formed along a high ridge, with a river guarding its right wing and impenetrable heights to the left. In front of them was a network of farm walls that made ideal cover for the English and German riflemen to snipe at the French advance.

But the French didn't advance.

At noon on the first day, they saw the Duke of Dalmatia himself arrive in front of his troops. The British had hoped for Napoleon, but Soult would do – and yet the wily marshal seemed content simply to look at the British and wait for more men to come up. The next day the army formed again and, though there were half-hearted feints by the enemy against left and right, cannon fire and skirmishers probing for weaknesses, still the French wouldn't come. Then both armies passed a bitingly cold night warily watching one another's position. There was little sleep for anyone. But again, the following morning, the army was in good spirits, primed to fight and willing the French to come. They stood patiently in their ranks, desperate for the first cannonade, for the tirailleurs to come swarming towards them. Sir John Moore rode amongst his men, impressed that order had once again been restored. He was excited, thrilled by the chance of action. He was more desperate to have his fling at Soult than any Highlander or Rifleman. His enthusiasm passed to the men. But as the day went on and the French refused to budge, their spirits fell and the mutterings began again.

That night, with food stocks running short and the French bringing up more and more men, the British ran once more.

Tom, who during those days of inactivity had taken up a battle position with the artillery, the natural cousins of the engineers, was once again called to the general's staff to receive orders. And he was given the very job he had dreaded! To his shame, for a moment his heart sank when he was told he was to wait with the reserve and assist in the destruction of the formidable sequence of Galician bridges, as the army left each of them behind. Tom had seen those bridges. They would represent a serious challenge in time of peace with a generous supply of ordnance and days to prepare the charges. But with the French breathing down their necks and hardly any trained men available, it would be a near impossibility. Already at Constantino an attempt to blow the bridge had failed miserably and Paget's rearguard had been forced into a messy skirmish with the French cavalry. Tom knew better than anyone that there were more challenging bridges to come. But then he realised that if the army could not rely on its engineers to at least try to make the best of it, nobody else was likely to hold up Soult's remorseless pursuit. They would do their best.

So the army stole away from Lugo. On a coal-black night, with a howling gale blowing, they had built up fires to fool the French that the British remained encamped on their ridge and the disgruntled, cheated soldiers had set off once again for Corunna and the ships.

Tom stayed behind with the cavalry regiment which tended the fires and painstakingly destroyed the precious equipment and supplies that couldn't be carried away. It was cheerless, depressing work. Every so often a shot would ring out as yet another exhausted horse or mule was destroyed. It was heart-rending for Tom to see such waste, yet he agreed utterly with the principal that nothing must be left to comfort the enemy. Finally at dawn the hussars themselves pulled out to trail behind the army. Again, as on so many occasions during the grim march, their last task in leaving Lugo was to drive out the stragglers who loitered drunk or just plain exhausted in the town.

But if Tom was both moved and disgusted by some of the sights he saw along the road – men trying to get on with naked, bloodstained feet, women with children sitting abandoned and dying in the mud, discarded packs and weapons; the dead bodies of men and horses everywhere – he was far more disgusted with himself when they came to make their attempt to blow the bridges. Fine minds and a thorough training in England had not equipped the bluecoats for this. Time and again Tom and his colleagues struggled in the foul weather to set an effective charge on the well-constructed old bridges and time and again they failed to destroy them. It was a thankless, hopeless task; they were always under threat of attack from the French and there were no trained sappers to help the officers, but their worst problem by far was the powder, much of which was soaked and useless. Each time the little demolition party worked frantically on the bridge, finally calling in the hard-worked rearguard, then blowing the charges under the fire of the French. Each time they failed. They could make an explosion, they could do that well enough – but they couldn't make an explosion that would destroy the bridge. So the bridges stayed intact and the French came on, to the shame and frustration of the weary RE officers.

The engineers fell back before the French cavalry as depressed and dispirited as the most miserable foot soldier and in just as much danger of losing their lives. Finally, together with the reserve, they trailed dispiritedly towards Corunna itself, unhappy and ashamed, but at least mildly consoled that they were at last near their destination. The final bridge, just a few miles from the town, crossing the Mero river, still had to be blown. But with fresh powder available from the magazines in Corunna and the rebukes of the long-suffering rearguard ringing in their ears, this time the engineers made no mistake. Despite their repeated warnings, the men of the 28th and 95th stood close to the charged bridge, insolently showing their scepticism at the sappers' efforts. But when the command came and the fuses were lit, the resulting explosion did what the French had failed to do and had the men of the reserve running for their lives! The engineers went into the town a little happier.

Into Corunna – where still there were no transports in the harbour.

Chapter Nine

Lieutenant John Anderson of the 42nd Highlanders concentrated hard, his breath fogging in the near-frozen air, as he held his spyglass on the village. It was long past dawn now and the grey light had reluctantly brightened the scene below them.

Blunt's company, to a man determined to reach Sir John Moore's army, had achieved a remarkable march of a hundred miles in less than a week, crossing difficult, snowbound terrain in a relentless series of long, energy-sapping marches. They had lost two men, for whom the tough slogging had been too much after weeks in hospital, and another had been left with friendly villagers when it was clear he couldn't go on, but the rest were as well as they could be after days in the frozen mountains. They were tired and footsore, but they were well-fed and reasonably fit. And they were soldiers once again; Blunt had made sure of that. He had fallen back on years of experience in training and preparing men for battle and he had moulded them into a compact fighting unit. He had fifteen men from regimental light companies or dedicated rifle regiments and these men formed the advance under the experienced light infantryman Sergeant Wheel. Where possible on the treacherous mountain paths, the main body of men marched together in a unit of fifty or so and in the rear came their little baggage train of mules and any men who were incapable of marching with full pack.

The mis-matched company of former invalids and wounded kept going at an impressive pace, sometimes managing as far as twenty miles a day. Indeed they had made such good ground that Blunt guessed that they were precious few miles from the important town of Ponferrada, where the westward road taken by Moore forked either for Vigo or Corunna. Ponferrada was the key to the success of their attempt, he felt. Once there they would find out soon enough if the army had passed through and, if so, which route it had taken. That was the hoped-for result, but the reverse side of this little equation was that there was also the very real chance of bumping into the Grande Armée at Ponferrada – and that was what presently concerned Blunt and Anderson, as they examined the cluster of houses in the valley below them. It was eerily silent. There should at least be goat-bells, children, dogs barking. Blunt didn't like dogs, but he didn't like silence either.

'What do you make of it?'

'Ours, for sure,' said the Scotsman.

They had come in sight of the village in the valley late the previous evening. It was plain that it was occupied, that there were soldiers there, but in the fading light it had been impossible to tell by which side. Blunt's men were too tired after a long day's march to consider any action. It was frustrating being so close to shelter, but Blunt was taking no chances. They had camped for the night, with no fires, and waited for morning to give them the answer.

'Englishmen, I'd reckon,' Anderson said, adding to his prognosis.

'Oh yes, why?'

'Because they're pished.'

Blunt raised an eyebrow, 'And the Scotch never drink?'

'Seldom, Captain – and then only in moderation.'

The two grinned at one another, then looked back to the village. Borrowing the spyglass, Blunt could see quite plainly now that it was definitely redcoat soldiers who had taken over the place. Only a few were up and about, others would be sleeping it off. There had been anguished screams the night before, as well as the roaring of drunks.

'Sergeant Wheel,'

The man appeared at his shoulder, as if by magic, stooping low to join the officers out of sight of the village. 'Captain?'

'Put your light troops around the village. I know that will take time in these conditions, perhaps an hour, so take it steady, then fire two rapid shots once you're in place. Then we'll go in. You hold your positions, let no-one out of the place, and you keep an eye on that road out on the other side to Ponferrada. I don't want any surprises.'

'Yes, Captain.' The sergeant managed an awkward salute and went to gather his men.

Blunt looked down at the mist-shrouded village. It was raining lightly now and there were still traces of yesterday's snow. There was smoke coming from the chimneys, but he knew that it was anything but an ordinary winter's morning in this remote spot. His men were ready, muskets loaded and bayonets fixed. They waited, cold and impatient to be moving, keen now to find out what had happened here.

Then, once Sergeant Wheel's two shots let them know he had got his men into position, Blunt signalled to Anderson, who had taken a dozen of the fittest men to the very edge of the village. At the Scot's command, they doubled down the single street and formed at the far end, bayoneted muskets held at the ready. Then Blunt himself walked slowly into the village. He knew that this was going to be bad: before he had even got to the buildings he had passed the corpses of two men, Spanish civilians, who looked as if they had been shot trying to get away. He didn't allow himself the luxury of pausing to consider what might have happened. He signalled the rest of his company to follow him in, a sergeant calling the step, until they came into the little plaza. The scene in front of the church looked anything but Godly; another civilian plainly dead and British soldiers asleep on the ground, seemingly uncaring of where they had dropped, one or two possibly even frozen to death. There were broken bottles and jugs and empty wineskins everywhere in the churned snow. The few men who had been awake as Blunt's men marched in looked stupidly at the newcomers. What they wore could hardly be called uniform, but it had certainly once been British. Anderson had come back to join them, leaving his men guarding the way out of the place.

'Good God.'

'Pretty, ain't it?' Blunt said. He wasn't particularly shocked; he knew the British soldier's abiding weakness for drink and he had seen worse than the drunken wretches lying around asleep in the village square. Spanish wine could wreck discipline, just as easily as English ale or West Indian rum. His own men were rounding up those few who had been awake when they marched in, kicking their friends from their slumbers and searching the buildings for others. But Blunt and Anderson knew from instinct and experience where the worst trouble would be. It was always the church.

'Have you got men behind the building, sir?' Anderson asked.

'Yes, Sergeant Cubbin has three men covering the back,' Blunt said. 'Let's go in.' He drew his sword and signalled for the doors to be opened. As they swung inward, the scene that greeted the soldiers did at last make Blunt catch his breath.

The church had been used for a dormitory by around a dozen British soldiers, who were in various conditions of coming to wakefulness as the light streamed in – but before sleep, the church had also been used as kitchen, latrine and worse. The dead body of the priest was suspended from the beam, the chain of his crucifix hanging out from his mouth. There were several local women, half-dressed, looking terrified in a huddle in the corner of the single room. Two others, young girls by the look of them, had either not been so lucky or perhaps fortunate to have the suffering curtailed. Their dead bodies lay naked and unregarded on the stone flags. There was a stink of stale wine, shit and blood. One of the soldiers stretched in an expansive yawn and blearily asked what was going on. His neighbour elbowed him into silence, looking warily at these new arrivals.

'Out,' Blunt said, not trusting himself with more, 'Out!'

His men were none too tender with their bayonets, herding the redcoats out into the square.

'Widowson!'

The little man was already there.

'See what you can do for these women. Sergeant cut that priest down.' He turned and went outside.

Blunt's men had gone through every house now, turfing out the half-awake, confused soldiers. There were about forty in total. He had them lined up.

He looked at the group of men they had taken from the church. 'Who speaks for you?'

Silence: he knew if there was an officer among them, which he doubted, he would certainly not dare declare himself.

Blunt wasn't in the mood to wait, 'Lieutenant Anderson.'

'Company, present!'

Fifty muskets were levelled.

'Prepare to fire.'

'Tobin!' One of the men called out, his voice filled with panic.

'Which is Tobin?'

A corporal stepped forward, or at least a man in a corporal's jacket, shifty eyes over a dark beard. 'I am, yer honour.'

Blunt looked at him. He was one of the men who had been in the church. He had taken the buttons from his coat to make it difficult to identify the regiment, but he still had his stripes. Looking around, Blunt guessed that there were men from half a dozen different line regiments here. His own command was just as disparate, but the difference was that Blunt's men were here to fight the French, not to ravage defenceless Spanish villages. He looked back at the man called Tobin. He was standing unsteadily at attention, but his eyes were on Blunt – ferrety, calculating eyes trying to weigh up the officer.

'You,' Blunt said, pointing at random at another of the men from the church. 'What are you doing here?'

'Sir?'

'Why are you here? Why are you not with the army?'

'We was just havin' a rest, sir.'

Blunt looked at the sorry group, at the devastated village. 'A rest?'

Another man took a step forward, a dozen musket barrels swinging to aim at him. He held his hands up, 'It was Tobin, sir, he said – '

'Shut it, you,' said the man called Tobin. His reward was the butt of Sergeant Cubbin's musket in his guts.

'What did he say?' Blunt snapped at the private.

'He said we was due some leave. We's been on that bloody road for days, beggin' your pardon, sir. Bloody murder it is, short rations an' sloggin' day after day. Tobin reckoned it was only proper we had a breather, like. He said we could mebbe just cut off for a day, have a wet, an' catch up later. Just a day or so, honest, sir; we'd be sure to go back. None of us wants to miss out on doin' the crapauds' business for 'em. Tobin said we'd not be long gone. He said we'd be sure to find somewhere in a couple of hour's tramp an' – '

'And you found this place.' Blunt looked back at the church. The women were coming out, two of them supporting another who could barely walk. They didn't look at the soldiers. Widowson had used some of the deserter's greatcoats to cover the priest and the dead girls.

Blunt called over to the women, trying to keep his voice soft and unthreatening. 'Donde esta el alcalde?' He asked for the mayor.

'Alli.' One of the women gestured with her head to the dead bodies at the edge of the village, a glazed, uncomprehending look on her face. 'Es mi marido.' Her husband.

Blunt looked back at Tobin, who stared back at him defiantly. He struggled to keep his anger in check. 'What have you got to say for yourself?'

The man shrugged. 'We done nothin' wrong. Just a little furlough, like, it was. We'd 've gone back, wouldn't we, eh, boys?'

There was a general rumble of assent. Blunt ignored it.

'And this?' He gestured at the despoiled village.

Tobin spat. 'What of it? They're just dagos, so they are. They wasn't goin' to give us nothin' – no grog, no vittels, no women – nothin'. We're here to fight for their God-rottin' country and they don't give a shit for us. We asked nice enough, but they didn't want nothin' to do with us.'

'So you killed, stole and raped?'

Tobin looked genuinely amazed at the disgust in Blunt's voice. 'They're just dagos, I say! What have they done for us, when we come here to save 'em, eh? Their lousy so-called soldiers run, they give us nothin' a man can live on and they leave us to freeze and starve up there in their poxed mountains. They're not worth the breath you're wastin' on 'em, they're not. The crapauds've got the right idea – take what you need an' stick 'em if they don't like it.'

Blunt looked around the square. He saw a barn, its door hanging off. But its roof beam was in place.

'Sergeant Cubbin. Hang this man now.'

'Captain?'

'You heard me.'

'Yes, sir.'

'You can't do that!' Tobin shrieked, all of his brash confidence suddenly drained. But nobody was listening to him; they had seen the look on the captain's face. Tobin was begging for mercy now, his tone suddenly humble, whining even, repeating that they would have gone back, would always have gone back. His friends made no move for him, didn't even look at him, terrified for their own skins. He looked back at Blunt, but he got no consolation from the glacial, despising stare. He was taken away, screaming for help from his friends. But they knew well enough that they had problems of their own, knew that their own lives were held finely in the balance. They were all watching the tough-looking captain. Blunt went to speak softly to the mayor's wife. There were eleven men left who had been in the church. She pointed at two of them. Blunt gestured to his sergeant for them to be taken away. He had learned that those two men had played no active part in the killing or the assaults on the women. Nine men remained. He bowed to the woman and went back to stand in front of the group of prisoners.

'You nine, you nine *men*, are guilty of the worst crimes a soldier can commit. You have deserted – ' a quickly suppressed cry told Blunt that behind him Corporal Tobin had met his end, the soldiers dragging down on his legs to finish the hanged man as quickly as possible, ' – you have killed and molested innocent people – people you are here to protect. You have stolen, you have run from your duty. There is no question of your guilt. You are a disgrace to the uniform you wear and you will be punished, every one of you, here or elsewhere. So, will you accept my judgement?'

The men looked at one another, trying to digest what he was saying, appalled at the swiftness of this justice, but over Blunt's shoulder they could all see Tobin's body still jerking on its rope and, trusting that this was an English officer, one of their own, each one of them privately hoped for mercy, for himself at least. 'Yes, sir.'

Blunt looked at the nine renegades with barely disguised revulsion. They were trained soldiers and had soiled the reputation of their kind with their craven behaviour. 'Lieutenant Anderson, these men with draw lots. Three will be hung, the other six will be placed under close arrest. You others,' he looked at the group of about thirty men who had not been involved in the worst of the crimes, 'You men will march with us, without your weapons, and you will behave like soldiers, if you can remember how. Your regiments will deal with you when we join the army. But I warn you, and you had better listen, if any one of you steps out of line, he will be shot. Now you will witness punishment, after that you will form a burial party. Then we leave this place. Carry on, Lieutenant.'

Blunt's company, now increased by a half of its original numbers to over one hundred men, stood formed in the little plaza. They were an uncomfortable group. The executed soldiers had been buried as well as could be managed in the frozen earth, with stone cairns over them – well away from the village. The Spanish corpses had been laid out in the church. All of the deserters had been searched for coin and that money had been given to the villagers. Blunt knew they should have done more, but it was time to go. The sergeants were marching vigorously up and down the column, checking the men, ensuring that everyone had all of the equipment he should be carrying, making sure the pack animals were correctly loaded and that the prisoners were well guarded. They all wanted to be gone, couldn't leave the village quickly enough. The men who had marched so hard from Salamanca regarded the deserters, particularly those guilty of the worst crimes, with open contempt. It would be unsurprising if some of these suffered painful "accidents" before they were given up to the provosts to receive the army's justice. The small mountain village had witnessed a disgrace to British arms. For Blunt this had been grim, nothing to do with soldiering and he wanted to be away, to get these men back on the road to the army, where they belonged. He was about to give the longed-for order to march when one of Sergeant Wheel's scouts, a tall German rifleman of the 60th, came doubling into the village and ran breathlessly up to him, his worried expression betraying some new, urgent alarm.

'Crapauds, sir!'

'The French?'

'Oh Got, yes.'

'Where, man?'

The rifleman, still panting after his run, gestured over his shoulder, 'Road, sir. Cavalry – ze're coming on damn quick!'

So quick were the enemy coming, in fact, that Blunt could already hear them. Cavalry riding against unformed infantry; a nightmare.

'Company will form line!'

The first pair of horsemen trotted into the village as the British were frantically unslinging muskets and wheeling themselves into position. The two Frenchmen reined in their mounts with admirable skill. Amazed looks on their faces, stunned to see redcoats forming a line against them, they turned their horses around and galloped back out before anyone could take a shot at them.

Blunt had seen pigtails under the cloth covers that protected their helmets. Dragoons then – but he hadn't got time to worry about the detail of just who these French outriders might be, he had to get his own men in order, prepared to fight. The majority of the soldiers had only just knocked the charges out of their muskets, ready to march. Now training was telling as cartridges were bitten, weapons quickly made ready.

'In two ranks!' The men awkwardly got themselves arranged in two rows, one ready to kneel down, the other standing, the unarmed prisoners huddled untidily behind them. 'Sergeant Crump, six men as rearguard at the back end of the village. Sergeant Cubbin, an eye on our wondering friends here. Shoot any prisoner who makes to step out of line.' He looked to his more reliable soldiers, 'The rest of you men, you hold steady now. At my command, rear rank will present, front rank will fix bayonets and kneel.' Blunt, his eyes front, could do without thirty five prisoners to worry about, but he knew he must keep discipline if they were to survive. His sergeant would mind the deserters and Blunt would deal with the enemy. The French would most certainly come. He hoped that they imagined they were dealing with a band of undisciplined deserters – a ripe crop to be easily harvested with scything sabres. He glanced along his line, the men looking steadily forward, understandably apprehensive, but calm enough. They would hold.

And then a trumpet blast – and the French did come, charging towards Blunt's company, swords drawn, brass helmets with horsehair manes – yes, dragoons, he recognized – galloping bravely down the narrow street towards the bayonets. There were perhaps a dozen of them, still a terrifying sight in that confined space.

But Blunt was in command, was ready; he had done all this before. He waited, waited a long second, another.

'Rear rank, make ready now,'

A second more, the horses huge now, breathing great jets of steam, coming on fast.

'Rear rank, fire!'

The sound of the volley was deafening in the enclosed square. Four horses had gone down and another had lost its rider, shying away from the rows of bayonets in front of it and galloping wildly off to the side. Another horse wheeled in circles, making terrified noises, blood oozing from a wound in its throat, its rider hanging on to its neck, disabled and unable to control it. The other Frenchmen had turned and fled. As he ordered his men to reload,

Blunt heard the pop of rifle fire. That was alright: Wheel's skirmishers were doubtless dealing with any horsemen who might have been trying to work around the village to find their flank or rear. If it was just cavalry, with no infantry support, they could be dealt with. The sergeants with him there in the village dressed the line, busy with their pikes, steadying the men and getting ready for the next attack. The wounded rider had somehow turned his mount around; they let him go. Then the firing beyond the village abruptly stopped. It became eerily quiet, just the noise of a dying horse and the triumphant caw of a distant crow. The soldiers took a breath, one or two spat, and they made ready for whatever came next.

Blunt looked at his men, checked behind, then back to the direction where the French had come from; he cocked his head to one side, listening carefully for any clues there might be on the crisp morning air. But it was quiet, eerily still. He walked forward, picking up a sword from beside the body of the officer who had led the charge. It was a fine weapon, a killer's blade. Anderson came to stand alongside him. 'What do you think?'

Blunt looked to the edge of the village, tapping the sword – yes, a good one, nice balance – against his shoe. 'I don't think they'll come again. It's too quiet; you'd expect to hear officers geeing them up. I doubt there's many of them, probably just a troop foraging or just come down that road out of curiosity to see where it led. But it won't stay quiet for long; they'll most certainly be back with plenty of their friends soon enough, now that we've caught their attention.'

'Trouble, then?'

'Yes, Lieutenant, trouble.'

'So?'

Blunt sighed. He didn't like it, but there was only one choice: 'Back the way we came. If the French are marching on the road up there, it means that we must have missed Sir John. So there's little merit in carrying on that way. We'll work out something else, but first we need to get away from here, and fast. Bugler, call the outposts in. Sergeant, get the men formed for the march, lively as you like.'

The village people who had run for cover when the French appeared now began to drift out again to see the British leave.

Blunt looked around impatiently, waiting for his skirmishers to rejoin, wanting to be away from that unlucky place. Sergeant Wheel was coming in with the rest of his men – but then he saw with a tremor of alarm that none of them had their rifles or muskets. Then others appeared, like wraiths, men walking down through the trees, coming up from the frozen little stream, seemingly hundreds of them, and all of them armed to the teeth.

'You will keep your men under control, Captain?' Blunt spun around to see a short, brown-coated man leaning against the church wall, a thin cigar in his mouth. 'I would truly regret doing harm to those who have come into my country to do God's work of killing Frenchmen.'

'Who the hell are you?'

The man said nothing, content to enjoy his smoke, as his men herded Blunt's company into the village square, like so many sheep.

'All of them.'

'No.'

'They must die. It is justice.'

'No, it is revenge.'

'Is it not just for such men to die?'

'I – the army has promised them fair trial.'

'But still, they will die. Here, now.'

'No,' Blunt said.

'We are wasting time discussing this, Captain. They are all guilty of rape or murder or both. It is simple justice.'

'I have executed four men already.'

'And these others?' He gestured beyond the door, where the remaining thirty six renegade British soldiers stood uneasily under the guns of twice or three times as many guerrilleros. 'They too are guilty.'

'Of what?' Blunt said. They sat in the house of the murdered mayor. His wife, an extraordinarily stoical woman, had silently brought the men wine, then gone off with the other women to the church, where the process of grieving was beginning. The village was in mourning, its tragedy fresh, but justice was already being haggled over.

'They are renegados, deserters, you have said it yourself. They are all guilty,' Carlos Federico Rivero y Castro said again.

Blunt sighed heavily, trying to find some kind of inspiration. It was not very easy. He was struggling hard to reason with this man, this man who spoke frighteningly good English, who he knew only by the name his guerrilleros gave him – "El Espectro", the ghost. He had certainly shown the ghost's facility for appearing from nowhere. It was a clever trick. How they had captured fifteen of Blunt's experienced skirmishers without giving the slightest sign that the British were being surrounded was a mystery to the

210

Englishman. But at present Blunt hadn't the luxury of examining his own shortcomings, he had to worry about saving the lives of thirty six British soldiers. His own command, the men who had marched from Salamanca, had been permitted to keep their weapons, laid on the ground at their feet, but all were under the watchful eyes of El Espectro's numerous band. A fight would be an uneven one. He must try to reason:

'Only a few committed the worst crimes – the others simply stole because they were hungry.'

'And thirsty,' Rico said archly.

'They are soldiers, not choirboys.'

'They are murderers and rapists.'

'Not all of them,' Blunt said doggedly.

'Deserters, still.'

'The army will deal with that.'

Rico granted the point, 'So?'

Blunt sighed again. He found it difficult to fathom this Spaniard, calmly smoking and drinking wine while they weighed the lives of men. He was a cool customer – this ghost – thought Blunt, as he pondered his next move, if he had one. He knew that he was held in check and had little room for manoeuvre. It was a crazy situation. Outside all of his men were paraded, without their weapons readily to hand, under the guns of two hundred angry Spaniards. At any moment the French might return in much greater force. And here they sat over wine, the ghost-fellow smoking his little cigar.

'So, the six,' Blunt conceded at last, realising his only chance of saving his command was for him to sacrifice the men who would likely swing or be flogged to death if ever he got them back to Moore's army.

'You give them freely?'

Now this wasn't fair: Blunt knew he had been offered no real choice, feeling weary and infuriated, hating what he had to do, sacrificing a few ne'er do wells to save other, better men. But he was anything but comfortable about it: 'I give them to you because I have to, because they truly are the guilty ones, because I want to get real soldiers back where they can fight. But I tell you, senor, I tell you man to man, I'm damned if I do it willingly or in good conscience.'

'But you give them?' Said the other, unaffected by the Englishman's passion.

'Yes.'

Rico nodded, flicking away his spent cigar stub. 'Good. So, you will deal with them yourself?'

Blunt, near the edge now, made an unhappy grimace, 'I've enough English blood on my conscience this day.'

'Very well,' Rico merely raised his hand and clicked his fingers. His lieutenant, a huge man who had been standing silently at the door, nodded and left them.

'So, what will you do, Captain – '

'My name is Blunt. I will do what I said, damn you, try my best to get these men to their duty.'

The Galician looked thoughtful. 'Blunt? I know that name.'

The Englishman couldn't care less. 'Not mine, I dare say. It's common enough.'

'Possibly,' Rico smiled to himself as he remembered Tom Herryck's tales of his rugged half-brother, the veteran soldier. This would likely be the man. The thought amused the Galician. 'So, Captain Blunt, if you can't use the road, which will be speaking French for a while, what do you propose to do with your little army here?'

'I'll find another road.'

'Yes?'

Blunt said nothing.

Rico shrugged, 'With difficulty, I fear. You should know that you are not in the middle of London town here, senor. We Spaniards are sparing with the roads we cut through our mountains.'

'Well, we certainly won't give up without trying.'

'Naturally.'

Blunt, angry at everything that had happened that bleak, ill-starred winter's morning, gritted his teeth and asked, 'Do you have any suggestions?'

'Of course.'

Blunt gave him a look to suggest he wasn't in the mood for guessing games.

Rico patted the breast pocket of his coat to see if he had another cigar. 'It is quite simple, Captain. Your General Moore is making his way to La Coruña. I will take you there.'

'Indeed?'

'Assuredly.' He found there was one last cigar. He would save it.

'Through the French?'

'Through the mountains; but if we find any French, Captain Blunt – if we do find the French – then yes, you have my assurance that we will go through them also.'

*

212

Tom had been busy. After all of the long weeks of struggling through the brutal Spanish winter, with its trials of bitter cold and constant hunger, after the shock of actually feeling shame and frustration simply at being a British soldier, after all of the tawdry horrors of that cruel march – it would at last be perfectly possible to say that he was enjoying himself. Having finally made it there, having got to the coast, Corunna was proving itself to be an interesting proposition, certainly a welcome relief for all of them after the ordeal of that terrible, morale-sapping retreat.

The men had cheered long and loud when they came in sight of the ocean. They felt the temperature increase in the almost balmy sea air near the town, began to see greenery and even trees in fruit. It was extraordinary: Tom was as glad as any that the terrible march was over, that the army had finally reached Corunna. He was one of the lucky ones and had been allocated a billet with a Spanish family; he had a little servant's attic room in a merchant's house not far from Sir John Moore's headquarters at Canton Grande. He was well fed and had been given those two great luxuries – hot water for washing and a soft little bed to sleep in. All of the people of the house were amazed at how tall the blond Englishman was, and indeed Tom's feet pooped out of the end of the bed sheets, but he didn't care. He got ten straight hours of sleep and a hot meal. The women had kindly washed and dried his linen. It had been so long! Tom luxuriated in the feeling of a fresh shirt next to his skin, clean white breeches to button. Not since Salamanca, many weeks before, had he encountered such civility: he was restored to feeling something like a human being. He was even able to shave off his odd, gingery beard!

But for all of his enjoyment of this gentle treatment, he realised with a grim resignation born of growing experience that it was likely to be all the rest or relaxation he got for a good while. He didn't mind that now, though, because he was doing his job, the work he was trained for. And there was certainly plenty of work to be done by the sappers there in Corunna, strengthening the ancient defences of the city and citadel ready for the expected French attack. Major Fletcher, the senior Royal Engineers officer, also had them mining the approaches to the city walls – anything to make it harder for the enemy. The local people, quite appalled at the condition of the ragged, emaciated British soldiers entering their city, had nonetheless simply crossed themselves, muttered a prayer – and then got on with helping their allies make the place properly defensible. The men had turned out to help dig trenches and the women had brought ammunition up from the magazines. The redcoat soldiers too were in good spirits. The ships to take them away still weren't there, just a few fishing boats and merchantmen down in the big harbour, but the men had a solid faith that the Royal Navy would be there sooner or later, certainly once the storm that was keeping the fleet out to sea had fully died down. At least there were no more mountains to cross. They also cherished the precious, long-nurtured hope that they might at last have their longed-for throw at the French.

Then Tom had been called to one of Sir John's briefing meetings. Most of the senior officers were there, though men like Crauford were absent, having marched south with the Vigo contingent. But there were still good men – experienced officers such as Baird, Hope, Graham, Hill and Beresford – there to give Moore their counsel. Tom was intrigued; although there was a strong sense of relief that they were at last at the sea, the mood amongst the staff officers was serious. It was clear that none of the generals – least of all Moore himself – thought that the French would let them embark unmolested, so they would have to win the right to make their escape. As poor in condition as it was when it fell into Corunna, Moore's army had stolen a precious couple of day's march on the French. Had the fleet been there, they could have waved goodbye to Soult from the ships: but the Royal Navy was out in the Atlantic still. So they examined their situation. It could certainly have been a great deal worse, with the men properly fed and re-equipped, but fighting a defensive battle in such a place would still throw up its challenges, Tom realised. The town of Corunna was on a peninsula, with hills inland of it – hills which overlooked its walls within easy cannon shot. Sir John would have preferred to set up his defensive line along the outer ring of hills three or four miles from the town, to keep those cannon away; but he no longer had enough fit men to cover that length of front, so his army would establish itself on the lower, inner ridge, called Monte Mero, about 2,500 yards long. The village of Elvina – its network of walled corrals perfect for covering riflemen – might act as a redoubt at the western end of the ridge. Moore would keep Paget's reserve and one other division in front of the town and he would place Baird and Hope's men along the ridge. There they would have to hold.

They would defend Corunna until the ships came.

One significant problem with this plan was that the Spanish held a vast magazine on the hill of Penasquedo, three miles away, well outside the proposed British lines – a hill which the advancing French would presently occupy. It was unthinkable to let the enemy take possession of such a vital resource; clearly the magazine would have to be dealt with. After dutifully consulting Fletcher, Moore had considered the matter and had decided that he would call for Lieutenant Tom Herryck and send off his favourite engineer to try his luck at Penasquedo.

The task facing Tom and the men allocated to him from the artillery was considerable. Blowing any magazine was a tricky business: the magazine at Penasquedo was full. There were 400,000 pounds of powder in hundred pound barrels, as well as 300,000 musket cartridges. It was an enormous amount of powder, four thousand barrels. It was a treasure-trove of ordnance but it couldn't be got away and the French, not far off now, mustn't have it. So the magazine must certainly be destroyed. Blowing up a huge quantity of gunpowder was not easy: to blow the magazine effectively would mean almost certain death for the men who lit the fuses. The blast would be enormous. These were brave men, but none were keen on suicide. It was Tom who first had the notion of blowing the nearby smaller magazine, with a powder trail leading to the other, vastly more dangerous stock of powder. At least that would give them a fighting chance of getting clear before it went up.

As they worked on the charges, bullets pinged off the stonework around them. The French voltigeurs had arrived. Tom's party carried on, working as quickly as they could. If the plan succeeded and the whole magazine blew as it should, Tom had reflected with a smile, it would doubtless blow out every window in Corunna and set the boats in the harbour rocking on their moorings like toys on a boating lake. It was a nice little job, he thought. Yes... he was interested to see what would happen.

Blunt was at the seaside.

He looked carefully at his tattered map. Widowson, who somehow knew these things, had informed him it was the 14th of January. He calculated that they were some twenty or twenty five miles from Corunna now and would be there by the next evening or perhaps early on the following day. Blunt wondered if they would be in time. A local fisherman had told him that the British had made it through to Corunna, but that their ships weren't there, held back by the weather. Blunt knew that would likely mean that Moore would fight. He looked at the little column marching slowly but steadily ahead of him. He allowed himself a grunt of satisfaction. The men were tired, had every right to be, but they were in good heart, so near to their destination. Even the deserters from the village seemed happy enough to be almost there, hopeful that their good behaviour on the march and the severe punishments dealt out to Tobin and the others might possibly keep them from the worst of the army's disfavour, particularly if there really was a chance of battle.

So Blunt was pleased with his redcoats; he had every right to be: he knew that they really had achieved a great deal to get that far. Yet back at the mountain village, when Blunt had stepped out of the mayor's house with the man called El Espectro, to find the six men he had agreed to give up lying at his feet with their throats cut, he had feared the worst for the rest of his command. But, however ruthless his idea of justice, the mysterious Galician warlord had been as good as his word. He had artfully spirited them away from the French cavalry, striking west and eventually marching their ill-assorted column of soldiers, deserters and guerrilleros along lonely hill-tracks, past the pilgrim city of Santiago, on away from the dangerous high road, even to the Atlantic itself. It had been well done, he acknowledged, a decent piece of soldiering. Blunt admitted to himself that his company had been fortunate – that they would never have made it without the help of the Spaniards.

The two leaders were the only ones among more than three hundred men who spoke one another's language with any facility – many of the locals speaking only Gallego, with little Castilian Spanish – but the two groups had contrived to get on. Blunt found that he had developed a grudging admiration for the Galician's easy way of command and his sure touch in getting them safely through that dangerous country. The two men, each of them proudly patriotic but neither of them naturally garrulous, found that they were happy to do business with one another, if in a reserved, rather costive fashion. This mood of necessary cooperation transmitted itself to the soldiers and partisans. Blunt recognized that it was not necessarily a system of march Horse Guards or the Quartermaster General would have approved of, but it had worked. El Espectro's men – some of them ex-soldiers, others simple peasants – had even shared their food with the hungry soldiers; but not with the deserters from the village, who made do on the sparse British rations. They even had the luxury of a couple of dry nights' sleep in village barns. From the few details El Espectro had revealed to Blunt of what he had seen of Moore's army on the march through the mountain passes, his own hundred men would arrive in Corunna in better health and readiness to fight than most of the other British troops. But that was scant consolation; the Englishman found it difficult to credit these tales of soldiers burning houses, looting, killing civilians and stealing everywhere – but then he remembered the village in the hills, not far behind them. Maybe that behaviour was more typical than he had hoped and the hard-pressed Moore was not faring so well, just as the Spaniard suggested in his cool, matter-of-fact manner.

All they could do was continue their march and hope to reach Corunna before the ships took their friends away. Finally, the last of the mountains were left behind and they had reached the coast, within striking distance of their target. Then the Spaniards, at the back of their self-contained, enigmatic leader, had simply melted away back into the hills and left the British to accomplish the last leg of their long march on their own. El Espectro, the mysterious Galician ghost, had disappeared once again.

Now Blunt put the map away and brought his mind back to the present. He stepped out to catch up with the others. The last pull up to Corunna should at least be straightforward, as long as he kept the grey, roaring Atlantic to his left. They were almost there. The day after tomorrow, he decided.

Then they heard it – a great rumbling thunderclap of noise that shuddered the very ground under their feet and stopped the column dead in its tracks, the poor mules braying in fearful protest. It was as if some powerful ancient god had made his petulant displeasure known to the mere mortals down there. The rumbling went on for minutes. Nobody knew what to make of it. They stood and stared open-mouthed as a vast mushroom cloud slowly rose in the sky to the north.

Blunt stood alongside Widowson.

'Hell of a bang, Private.'

'Yes, sir. Better than Guy Fawkes' night, it were.'

'Someone would have to find a fair bit of powder to make a thump like that.'

'If tha says so, Captain. It were a reet good old wallop, sure enough.'

'It was that.'

They stood and watched the odd, distant black cloud as it slowly ascended to the heavens.

'Tom Herryck have anything to do with it, you reckon?'

The old soldier considered the possibility for a moment. 'Dunno. Shouldn't be surprised, though. 'E's a bogger fer knockin' things abart, that Mr 'Erryck.'

Blunt grinned, knowing his brother would have liked nothing better than getting involved in making some kind of massive, showy explosion. If Tom wasn't building things, he was usually knocking them down. It had certainly been quite a bang. He hoped that it was something the British had planned and not some terrible misdemeanour. He started to run through what the explosion might mean, how it might affect any coming battle. Then he realised that the quickest way to find out was simply to press on and get to Corunna, so he hitched his haversack and rifle into place and called, 'Sergeant Wheel, the company has stopped. Another hour before we halt, I believe.'

'Yes, sir. Sorry, sir.'

'Let's get moving, then.'

The weary soldiers had understandably been intrigued by the extraordinary noise to their front.

He walked along the line, as he watched the sergeants chivvying the fatigued band of soldiers into order once again. Then, knowing just how tired these men must be, how much they had put in to this long march, Blunt softened his tone to address the company with carrot rather than stick: 'Come on now, lads. Form up handsomely there. That was a fine big bang over yonder, but we must get on. Look lively, eh? I know you probably feel about done in, but I promise it's precious little further now and it sounds like the party's about to start. It might be that our lads are going to have a right good crack at the crapauds at last. Don't want to miss out on all the fun, do you?'

'No, sir!'

'Then come on, handsomely does it, eh? Let us step out like good 'uns and see if we can't get along and help the boys do for old Boney and his mates.'

They were too tired to raise much of a cheer, but he had judged their mood well enough once again. A penny whistle was already trilling "The British Grenadiers" and they were soon back in step, a company once more, marching fast to Corunna.

Tom was still a little deaf. It was hardly surprising; the magazine had done exactly as he had expected and had erupted massively, shooting flames a mile into the sky. He had been told that in the town the explosion had terrified citizens and soldiers alike. And there had been a more lasting price to pay: several artillerymen who had not heeded warnings to get well clear had been killed outright by the dreadful intensity of the heat blast and others had been felled by falling rocks. But the job had certainly been done and the enemy had been denied the precious powder. The demolition party themselves, uniforms half blown off and hair like madmen, had somehow made it back to the British lines under the furious fire of the French skirmishers.

Now, as the dual preparations for battle and retreat continued, it was serious business for Moore's army in Corunna and other melancholy chores were being fulfilled, as hundreds of horses were being slaughtered right there in the town and down on the beach. It was a horrible necessity. At last the fleet had arrived, Admiral Hood with over a hundred ships, but even then there were not enough cavalry transports. Only the fittest mounts could be taken off. Tom's own loyal Annie, utterly worn down, cruelly lame from the simple lack of nails to re-shoe her, had been taken away by a kindly hussar groom, down to the beach to be destroyed. Tom was heartbroken and hoped that Walter Thicknesse would forgive the loss of the fine animal which had served him so well. The engineer wasn't the only horseman in Corunna to hold back a tear at the sad fate of so many good friends.

But down in the harbour, alive with activity now, the soldiers themselves were finally being evacuated. The wounded were already onboard ship and much of the artillery had been loaded. The cavalry too, with no part to play in the forthcoming battle, was taking its turn to be rowed out to the transports. But the remainder of the army stood to, ready to fight. The men who had staggered to Corunna in their tattered, lice-ridden coats – filthy, bearded and exhausted – were now transformed: they had been fed, many had brand new muskets with fresh powder and – most merciful of all – there had been a supply of desperately needed shoes there in Corunna. This was a mighty relief to men who had marched in broken boots, rags wrapped around their feet, or no proper footwear at all, for a hundred and fifty miles. But, for the time being, hardship was forgotten. 15,000 infantrymen, who had been wistfully looking at the sea before Soult's French arrived, now cheerfully made ready to turn around and fight. But not quite everybody in the rejuvenated British army was ready for battle, it appeared...

Tom could have been forgiven for blaming his temporarily damaged hearing when he picked up a rumour that some of Moore's generals, the very men who had been carping all through the retreat, baying for action, had now approached the Commander-in-Chief to suggest that he ask Soult for terms! It seemed quite incredible to Tom. Apparently these shy gentlemen had firmly believed that the Duke of Dalmatia might have been gracious enough to allow the fleet to sail off unmolested with the British safely onboard, if only the town and its stores and arms was surrendered to him. To the delight and relief of the rank and file, Sir John had firmly declined to put Marshal Soult's grace to the test and had doggedly continued to prepare for battle.

On the morning of the 16th, with the mist slowly clearing to leave the prospect of a bright day for once, the army was drawn up, just as Moore had ordered, occupying the heights two miles to the south of the city. His plan was to draw Soult's main attack onto his own apparently weak right flank in front of the city, which he had protected with his trusted reserve under Edward Paget's command. But the key to the battle was likely to be the village of Elvina, to the right of the British centre. Tom knew this for a certainty, because the general had asked for him to join his staff for the day. Moore was a shrewd enough commander to see that the battle might adopt an unforeseen character and expert knowledge from all departments might be useful. The young engineer had certainly been useful to the general before and perhaps even the talented, experienced Sir John was not averse to surrounding himself with officers he believed were lucky for him. So Tom Herryck would join the staff for the duration of the battle. He had been found a horse, a cavalry mount spared for just a few hours longer. The last act of this great drama was about to be played out and Tom was delighted to be a part of it.

They had established a kind of rendezvous for the generals and staff officers at the crossroads south-west of Elvina, which was marked by a distinctive cluster of large rocks. When the battle finally came, the action was likely to be fast and furious and good communications would be paramount. They were fighting at unfavourable odds against the best army in the world and they needed to know what they were about. It was unlikely that Soult would decline to attack this time, not with his Emperor's orders ringing in his ears and the enemy near to their ships and about to escape him

General Moore and his staff were in position at six in the morning. It was misty, but dry. The British, after the harrowing retreat across the mountains, were rejuvenated and ready to fight. Sir John, as keen and as eager as any of them, had made his plans and now he wanted to put himself wherever the action was at its hottest; this was to be his day. He was full of energy. He had picked out a lively cream and black charger. Tall in the saddle, he rode up and down the line, talking to the soldiers, smiling, and constantly looking over to the French positions, examining Soult's men with his spyglass to see if there was any sign that they would come at last. He wanted to be sure of every detail. He sent Tom Herryck down into Elvina, the fortified village at the centre of the line, to see if anything could be done to further strengthen its defences. Tom had a good look then returned to the crossroads rendezvous to report that its low walls and the rocky terrain surrounding it made it as good a place as any for light infantry to operate and, at the same time, more or less useless to Soult's cavalry. But he had also seen that Elvina was still likely to be an uncomfortable billet for the infantry, as the French had been working through the night to get their artillery set up, well within range of the British positions. Lord William Bentinck's brigade of General Baird's division was drawn up just behind to support the sharpshooters. Bentinck was the son of the Prime Minister, but like the rest of Moore's army he could expect no favours that day. The village and the waiting regiments massed behind it were likely to take a pounding from the French guns less than half a mile away, up on Penasquedo, but there was nothing they could do about that. They dare not surrender Elvina, if the battle was to be won.

As the mist finally cleared and the smoke from the breakfast fires died away, they waited for a sign that the French meant business. They waited so long, as the morning dragged on with no move from Soult, the men began to dread that it would be like the days at Lugo and that they would once more be cheated of their battle. The French had also made the hideous journey over the Galician passes and they had not received the succour of hot food and new equipment, so they too would be in poor shape. It was perfectly possible that they might simply sit down opposite the British and wait for more and more reinforcements to come up. Despairing that Soult would once again disappoint him, Moore even gave the order for Paget to start withdrawing his reserve, ready for embarkation. He went down into Corunna town to see all was done properly and to get something to eat. Tom stayed with Sir Thomas Graham and the others, their glasses sweeping the French positions. But not long before two in the afternoon the first of the tirailleurs could at last be seen advancing towards them and then, banishing the silence and the doubt, the French fired a gun and their artillery began blasting away from the ruins on the heights of Penasquedo, where Tom had lately made his huge explosion.

At this critical moment, Sir John Moore galloped onto the field to join his command. He rode up to his staff officers, pulled his horse to a halt, dirt and pebbles flying, and instantly his glass was out, examining the enemy. He exchanged a smile with the others; this was it! Soult was surely coming this time. Then they waited, keenly watching the French attack, the officer's horses involuntarily shuffling at the sound of the cannon, which were worryingly close. Men flinched in spite of themselves, as they heard the fizz of the 8lb balls flying by, the odd one even pitching amongst their horses' legs. The French cannon were effectively unopposed, as the British had embarked the majority of their artillery and had only a few six pounders to reply to the massed French guns.

Just as Tom had predicted, the men of General Bentinck's brigade above Elvina took a terrible mauling from the guns, limbs shot off and whole rows of men knocked away, but they held firm. These included the men of the 4th Foot, the 50th and the 42nd Highlanders, some of Moore's toughest troops, and they would take a deal of moving. It was a bloody business, but they stood firm against the French round shot, stoically waiting their moment. Everyone knew that Bentinck must hold on there, or the day would surely be lost. So the redcoats stood firm, took the dreadful pounding. It was horrible to watch, Tom thought, but there was simply nothing else to be done. So the cannon thundered on – and the redcoats dropped. But then the French infantry came at last, vast masses of men in solid columns, their drums beating out the ominous thud of the pas de charge. This was it, Tom realised, the real attack. On they came, a great blue killing machine, first forcing the British skirmishers out of Elvina and then pushing on confidently up the slope towards Bentinck's waiting infantry.

'En avant,' they cried, 'En avant, tué, tué!' Forward, kill, kill...

At the crossroads, Tom watched transfixed as the French drove on, a vast blue wave, then he became aware that the general was spurring his charger away. Instinctively he followed. Moore was riding hard, headed for the very heart of the action above Elvina. Tom followed, struggling to keep up with the flying Moore. They arrived amongst the men of the 42nd, The Black Watch, under attack both from the murderous artillery and the masses of approaching infantry. The French fire was intense, bullets fizzing everywhere like deadly wasps, lethal cannon balls crashing like hammer blows through the ranks of soldiers. Almost immediately after they reached the 42nd, a Highlander had his leg torn off by a cannon ball and fell screaming, right at the feet of Sir John's horse, but the general stayed calm, stilling the animal.

'This is nothing, my lads,' Moore called encouragement to the Scots. 'Steady, keep your ranks now. Take that man away.'

'Sir, the enemy is dividing,' Tom said.

A ball landed in front of their horses, sending dirt flying everywhere, causing the animals to rear up, nostrils flaring. Tom held hard to the reins, pressing his horse firmly with his knees to keep control.

Moore quickly steadied his own horse, then looked down at the French infantry column getting ready for its final rush to breach the British centre. If they succeeded, if the enemy got through, Moore knew they were finished. But he also knew that he wasn't going to let that happen! He took it all in and saw it was his moment. He had just the right men to hand, old friends who had fought hard for him before: 'My brave Highlanders, think on Egypt now, remember that day, eh lads? Very well, 42nd, charge!'

With a great roar the Highlanders fired a withering volley and then instantly charged screaming like wild men down the slope to give the French the bayonet, the lethal blades glinting in the sunshine. They chased them all of the way back through Elvina, before being themselves thrust back by the massed French beyond. It had been a magnificent effort, but now they were in trouble. As the French began to advance once again, their sheer force of numbers pushing back the hard pressed Scotsmen, whose muskets were now unloaded, Sir John Moore again rode down amongst them, sword drawn, roaring encouragement:

'My brave 42nd, if you've fired away your ammunition, you still have your bayonets, eh? Come now, my lads, think on Scotland!'

It was a primitive, visceral plea, but it worked. Back went the doughty Highlanders, stirred by the call from their countryman, yelling their ancient battle cries, to tangle with the advancing French once more. Moore, content that the Highlanders would hold, that the Guards were coming up to support them, doffed his hat to them and turned back. Marvelling at his coolness, Tom followed the general back to the crossroads, where they could make some attempt to see the shape of the rest of the battle through the increasing obscurity of the smoke.

For the moment the British were holding, just.

Blunt's company had still been away on the other side of the city when the firing had started, but most of them knew the sound of artillery well enough and they also knew that soon the infantry would be fighting – their fight. By common consent the prisoners had their bonds untied and Blunt's company headed for the battle. They marched past the walls of the city, past the men of Paget's reserve, themselves impatiently waiting their turn, curious to see this odd group of soldiers from so many different regiments, marching on towards the sound of the fiercest fighting. Sword drawn, Blunt led them to the smoke, to the heights above Elvina.

It was a struggle to see through the fog, but it was quite a sight – a battle in full cry.

'Good God,' said Anderson, catching his breath as he looked down on the bloody chaos of the village. 'It's the 42nd, my own 42nd!' The Scot, who had made the long, frozen march from Salamanca in a practical pair of plaid trews had somehow found time to put on the dark green and blue kilt of his regiment and now he looked down on the red-hackled bonnets of his countrymen, as they fought for their lives around the village. Despite the difficulty of looking through the smoke that now wreathed Elvina, it took only a moment to see that the Highlanders were in terrible trouble. The Scots had done magnificently; with another mighty effort, with a quarter of their number gone, they had pushed the French back once again. But now the enemy had reformed in far greater numbers and were ready to sweep the brave Scotsmen from the village for once and all.

'Captain?' Anderson said beseechingly.

But Robert Blunt needed no persuasion. This was what he had waited for, almost what he had been born for. The marching was over, it was time to fight. He turned to his command, a fiery glint in his eye.

'Now's our moment, lads; now we get to show 'em, eh?' He looked at the group of renegades from the mountain village. 'There are plenty of brave men's muskets on the ground. If you men choose to pick them up and join us, it will no doubt go well with you later.' He let his glance hang on those flawed examples of soldiery for a telling moment, then he looked to the others. 'As for the rest of you, my brave Salamanca boys, on my word company shall form line and advance. March steady now, heads up. Let's go and do our job, men; let's go down and find out if we can't finish the Jocks' work for 'em and see the backs of those God-rotting crapauds down there in that village of ours!'

The battle was at its very crisis. At the command post by the crossroads, Moore and his officers stared anxiously through the smoke at the repeated French attacks. They could see that it was touch and go in Elvina, brutal hand-to-hand fighting deciding its fate. Beyond the embattled village, on the British right, the French were pressing hard against Fraser's 3rd Division which defended the town of Corunna itself. But Moore's men were holding. Tom saw the general smile in satisfaction at the bravery of his outnumbered, exhausted army. It was clear that the soldiers had redeemed themselves in Moore's eyes, were fighting as he believed a British army should fight, with courage and determination. All of the doubts and tribulations of the long, long march from Lisbon were gone and Moore's army was acquitting itself admirably. It almost seemed as if an odd kind of justice was being done at the very end of that difficult campaign. Were the war-gods smiling on them at last? Then, to Tom's utter horror, he saw the general suddenly catapult backwards, right off his horse, falling heavily to the ground. Instantly his staff officers were around him. Tom dismounted and joined the press around the general. He lay there motionless, but with his eyes open and a surprisingly calm expression on his face. At first Tom thought that he might not be badly wounded, as he made no sound of pain, but as Colonel Graham bent to examine his old friend, they gently turned him and saw that there was terrible damage, that his whole shoulder had been taken away by a cannon ball. He was still alive, conscious even, but it was a shocking wound and the sad truth was that the general could have no chance of surviving.

But still, lying there with his life's blood draining from him, Sir John Moore was concerned only with his battle, his precious fight to keep the French from Corunna.

'Herryck, how do the Highlanders do?'

Tom, still stunned by what had happened to Moore, made himself listen to what he had been asked. Tearing his eyes away from the stricken commander, he looked squinting through the smoke down into Elvina. He tried to make sense of what was taking place around the village. It was a surprise; miraculously it looked like the Highlanders had rallied yet again. Incredibly, it almost seemed that there were more of them; that they had somehow found reinforcements, but certainly they were holding. He was able to tell the general, who weakly smiled his satisfaction.

A surgeon had arrived to examine the wound.

'You can do me no good,' Moore said.

The surgeon needed only a cursory examination to see that it was true, then he stood. 'I fear it is a quite hopeless case,' he said softly to Graham.

Half a dozen burly Highlanders arrived to carry Sir John back down to Corunna. They lifted him gently into a blanket, as he asked yet again how their fellows were doing below.

Tom Herryck, shocked and saddened by seeing the general so grievously wounded, abandoned his horse and walked alongside as they carried him as quickly as they dare. They took him back to the house that had been his headquarters. Tom, and one or two of the other officers who could be spared, were with him. Still he held on, making no complaint, asking after his aides and wounded friends.

Beyond the town the battle raged on.

Towards dusk the firing could be heard to slacken. Moore sent Tom back out to the battlefield to search for Sir John Hope, who had taken over command, to ask for news. Tom couldn't find General Hope, but he didn't need to. All was quiet, the French had fallen back to their lines. He went back to the house in Corunna town.

'Are the French beaten?' Moore whispered, his face white and contorted with pain.

'There is no doubt of it, General,' Tom said. He had no need to embellish the truth for the dying man. He had seen that the enemy was being pushed back, that Moore had finally got his victory. 'The day is certainly yours, sir.'

Moore managed a little nod of satisfaction. 'That is well, then. You know, I always wanted to die this way. I may only hope the people of England will be satisfied and that my country will do me justice.'

Tom had tears in his eyes, as he watched the life finally drain from the drawn and weary face of the hero of Corunna.

After all they had been through to get to Corunna and the safety of the ships, after all of the misery and ill-discipline of the march, the evacuation of Moore's army went extraordinarily smoothly. The exhausted men slowly began to be withdrawn from the battlefield under cover of dark. The soldiers, proud and satisfied with their victory, but heartbroken at the loss of their general, filed quietly along to their allotted places on the quays and were rowed out to the boats, regiment by regiment. It was a difficult operation and could easily have been jeopardised by drunken, careless behaviour, but the men got on with it as well as they could. It was the least they could do as a mark of respect for their brave commander, to behave as true soldiers at the last.

Moore had said that if he fell in Spain he wished to remain there. Early next morning his officers carried out this wish. It would be a hasty, difficult burial for such a hero. The ground was frozen and the French were already advancing into the abandoned British positions, but they managed somehow to dig a grave by the walls, overlooking the harbour. Dressed in his full uniform, a blanket covering his dead, waxy face, Sir John Moore was lowered into the grave by the sashes of his officers. The Guards' chaplain read a hasty service. It was a poor sort of funeral for a great man. Sir Thomas Graham was there, a tear for his great friend. But only a few others of his staff were present to hear the chaplain's hurried words. Several of Moore's senior officers were themselves badly wounded and the French still had to be watched as the last of the troops were embarked. Already, not much after dawn, the French guns were firing on them.

The hurried service done with, Tom wandered aimlessly back through the town. He felt thoroughly low. He didn't know what to do with himself. Even the pretty dark-eyed girls who smiled sympathetically at the tall blond

Englishman couldn't perk his interest. That part of Tom's being was closed still. He was too taken up in trying to put into any kind of context all that had passed since Salamanca. It was a curious tale: the little British army of Sir John Moore, however badly parts of it had behaved, had lured the great Napoleon away from Madrid, had outrun him, had beaten one of his finest commanders and was now making its inevitable withdrawal in good order. That was no small achievement. It had been a month that felt like a year to Tom. So much had happened and yet he realised that he had not once taken up his pencil to draw since he had been there in Salamanca. He had spent precious sleep-time writing up his journal – his duty after all – but no drawing on that gruelling march. The images of the soldiers in rags, the women dying by the roadside, the drunken, doomed deserters – they were burned into his mind, would possibly inspire him to take up his sketchbook some time in the future, if he could bear to recall it; but for the moment he couldn't bring himself to consider anything so trivial as drawing.

The British had come such a long way only to sail away from Spain in the Royal Navy's ships. It hurt him that they were retreating, not chasing off the beaten French, but he knew there was no other choice. He believed that it had been worth it – indeed that Sir John Moore had done the best he could in disrupting the French strategy so thoroughly, but that they had been given little alternative but to run once Napoleon himself set off after them. He allowed himself a little smile as he thought that Robert Blunt would no doubt say: "Stay alive and wait your chance" … no doubt. Well, Moore himself had failed in the first part, but he had certainly succeeded in giving his valuable army another chance. However badly some had behaved, the fact remained that those soldiers made up Britain's biggest field army. They had covered 150 miles in eleven days in the most appalling conditions. In getting the bulk of the army away in the face of Napoleon's concentrated efforts – ultimately convincing the Emperor himself that he had more pressing and rewarding business in Paris – they had achieved a considerable feat and preserved both Lisbon and Seville but, like everyone else, Tom just felt empty. He remembered what Moore had said about hoping his country would do him justice and wondered how the whole army would be judged in England, once the fleet got them home. How would the good people of Falmouth or Plymouth look on bearded, lice-ridden ragamuffins with no shoes? Then he decided that he simply didn't care, that he and thousands like him had done their duty, many of them paying with their lives. Those who had been safely tucked away in front of the comfortable fireplaces in London could think what they liked. Tom Herryck knew exactly what had happened on the road to Corunna and outside the walls of the city itself; he had been there.

But still he felt utterly unsatisfied, gaining no real joy from the victory. They had fought and won, but there would be no prize for the winners. They would get away safe, but that was it. Tom felt only sadness and frustration. It gnawed at him; there was a sense of incompletion. He realised that what he would really like to do just then, above anything in the world, was to blow something up.

'So there you are at last, Blunt.'

Major General Sir William Carr Beresford was a great bull of a man. Balding with fierce lamb-chop side whiskers, his left eye was useless and discoloured and his odd glare frequently discomforted those who had got on the wrong side of him. But Robert Blunt had no cause to fear the general. They were firm friends, these two, who shared certain similarities of character, and not a little history. Blunt had originally been summoned to Portugal to be on Beresford's staff, even before Sir John Moore had established a more pressing call on the infantryman's services all the way back at Lisbon. Now General Beresford was in command of the last few British troops in Corunna. The Spaniards had gallantly agreed to hold the city until the ships were clear and Beresford's men were now the only British remaining, holding the citadel until the last minute. Blunt's face was still streaked with powder. There was a fresh hole in the sleeve of his jacket, where a ball had winged him without drawing blood. The fighting had been fierce around Elvina, yet the ball had come not from the French but from one of the Brown Bess muskets picked up by the mountain renegades. The man who aimed at Blunt had been shot dead by Widowson. But the rest of the freed prisoners had fought well enough there at Elvina, six others losing their lives. In all, over twenty of Blunt's men were killed, as they joined that desperate and bloody fight to hold the line, savage hand to hand work with cold steel. Many others had been cruelly wounded. One of his sergeants had taken a bayonet thrust to his guts, while Lieutenant John Anderson was under the surgeon's knife and would do well not to lose an arm.

Beresford examined him, 'Well, whatever you've been about, dear fellow, I'm pleased that you could make it through. Were you delayed on the road?'

Blunt's face twitched into a pinched smile. He thought of mentioning being twice wounded, of thwarting a treacherous afrancesado plot, of being nursed by an angel, of being rescued by a ghost – but thought better of it. 'I had a little trouble finding you, sir,' he said simply.

The general grinned, knowing Blunt's taste for understatement. He would hope to tease something of the tale from his captain at a later date. But for the moment Beresford had more pressing matters to concern him: 'Well, I'm damned pleased to have you here, Blunt, however you come, although I trust you haven't joined me just in time for us to become guests of the Duke of Dalmatia.'

Blunt looked out of the window at the French army, now cautiously approaching the city. They had set up a battery at the southern end of the bay and were peppering the ships. The end clearly wasn't far off.

A knock at the door saved him from comment and heralded the entrance of a blue-coated officer.

'General, forgive me, I wondered – Rob, by God, you're here!'

Each was as surprised and delighted as the other. Ignoring the fact that they were in the presence of a general officer, and showing the lack of reserve that always characterised their relationship, the two brothers embraced with a thunderous bear-hug. The last Tom had seen of Blunt he had been leaking blood in a field in Old Castile. Now here he was, his uniform in tatters and his face still black from the battle, but more or less in one piece. Each of them was mightily relieved to find the other alive and well.

Blunt was the first to recollect himself. 'Hello, Tom. Good to see you. You've lost a pound or two on your travels, I see.'

'You look just the same, Rob, damned well, in fact. Widowson must have made a good job of patching you up.'

'Well, perhaps,' Blunt said, feeling slightly uncomfortable. 'So, ahem, very good. Now, hadn't you better finish what it was that you were saying to the general here, Lieutenant Herryck?'

Beresford looked at the engineer indulgently. He knew of Herryck as Moore's favourite who had dealt with the bridge at Castrogonzalo and who had played a part in creating the volcanic eruption of Penasquedo, as well as bringing important intelligence to headquarters. That once elegant blue coat was now almost as badly holed and torn as Blunt's. He had liked the look of the young lieutenant, obviously another fire-eater like Robert Blunt. 'Don't trouble yourself on that score, Captain. I can guess all too well what the rogue was thinking of saying. You want me to let you blow something up, don't you, eh, young fellow?'

Tom was surprised, 'Well, sir...' Tom had indeed got great plans for the citadel and its healthy stock of powder.

Beresford smiled and shook his head. 'Sorry, my boy. It won't do. I'd like to let you have your fun, but I fear we've promised the place to the Galicians under their General Alcedo. Not that I care for the arrangement, you understand, but orders is orders, eh? They won't keep hold of it for five minutes once we've gone, of course, but there it is.'

'No fireworks, Tom,' Blunt muttered.

'Pity.'

'Maybe next time.'

The general had moved to the window and was looking down into the harbour, the occasional plume of water showing where the French gunners were trying to damage the last of the transports. 'No, regrettably the town will fall to the French. To be frank, gentlemen, rather than being concerned about the fate of the town, I'm more worried about getting my men away with so few ships remaining. The French are bound to hit something soon. No matter, I dare say we'll manage well enough – now, who the devil do you suppose that fellow is?' He turned and gestured for Tom to come over and use his glass to examine an elegant little cutter which had just dropped anchor.

'Portuguee, ain't he?' The general asked.

'Yes, sir,' Tom looked down at the trim little craft, then passed the glass to his brother, along with an unreadable look. 'She appears to be called the *Esperanca*, sir.'

Blunt took the glass and kept the vessel in view for a good while. Then he snapped it shut and said stiffly, 'Portuguese flag, yes General. But I believe the lady and gentleman onboard of her to be of British extraction.'

General Beresford looked surprised. 'British? Are they, by God? Must be a mighty spirited family; so what in heaven's name has brought them here at a time like this?'

'Good question,' Tom said softly, looking across at his brother who, as usual, was giving nothing away.

It would be an interesting journey home.

This is a work of historical fiction. While I have tried to remain true to the facts and spirit of the events of the Corunna campaign – all of the major events of the story happened broadly as described – one or two minor liberties necessarily must be taken in order to give my fictional players some meat to their roles!

There are countless books about the Peninsular War and the Napoleonic period in general. It is a gripping subject that rewards continued study. A bibliography and some recommendations are available on the Bicorn website (www.bicorn.co.uk).

I enjoy spending time in museums and libraries – but I would like to single out The Royal Engineers Museum and Library and Nottingham's Angel Row Library for the particular kindness and efficiency of their staff.

All of the research (hence all of the mistakes) for this book is my own; but I would like to thank my select band of skilled volunteer-readers, who made useful suggestions and corrections to my rambling prose. Those kind and bright people are:

Alan Duggan, Peter Hall, Ann-Marie Moreno and Ken Ross.

I am grateful to them and hope that I will be able to recruit them all for our next *Ties of Blood* campaign...

www.bicorn.co.uk

The Colour of Blood
Ties of Blood: 2

Sir John Moore's army has been thrown out of Spain; Napoleon is poised to add the Peninsula to his other European possessions. The Spanish and Portuguese armies are beaten – so who can stop him?

The British send another army, this one under the command of the rising young general Sir Arthur Wellesley. With a tiny force of redcoats he is tasked with facing the massed French veterans of Soult, Ney, Victor...

Lieutenant Tom Herryck, the heroic young engineer who acted so bravely on the retreat to Corunna, is kicking his heels back in England. His half-brother Robert Blunt is training Portuguese soldiers in Lisbon. What part will these two play, as Wellesley sets off on his mission to root the French out?

The Colour of Blood – following the adventures of Herryck and Blunt in the 1809 Talavera campaign.

www.bicorn.co.uk

www.bicorn.co.uk